Brazen Gambit

Eric Small

Brazen Gambit (An Arnie & Zellie Cozy Mystery Series – Book 1)
Eric Small

Eric Small
P.O. Box 840003
St. Augustine, FL 32080
www.ericsmallbooks.com
ericsmallbooks@outlook.com

Disclaimer:
This is purely a work of fiction. Any resemblance of any character or any situation in this book to any person or situation is unintended and purely coincidental. The characters and places, other than nationally known entities which are also used fictionally, are figments of my imagination. Middletown, New Jersey is a real place, as are Monmouth County and the neighboring towns such as Red Bank and Eatontown. Many of the depicted streets actually exist, but the town descriptions are intended to provide general geographical information only, not as completely accurate portrayals.

Permissions:
Cover Design: Rik Feeney / www.RickFeeney.com

Stock Photography:
©Alexey Pushkin |Dreamstime.com, ©Michal Eyal|Dreamstime.com, ©Pichayasri|Dreamstime.com, ©Subarashii21|Dreamstime.com, ©Syda Productions|Dreamstime.com, ©Vanda Grigorovic|Dreamstime.com, ©Zhanna Millionnaya|Dreamstime.com

Author image used by permission from Lifetouch Portrait Studios, Inc.

Dedication

For Denele - my wife, sweetheart, and best friend.

Acknowledgments

This book benefited greatly from my wife Denele's unwavering love, support and encouragement, and her many helpful comments and suggestions during the writing and editing process.

As with all my endeavors in life, I greatly value and benefit daily from the love, support and encouragement I regularly receive from my family – my mother Sally, my brother Steve, and my sister Nancy, as well as from my late father Richard, whose love of books and reading had much to do with my own love of words.

I am also grateful to my editor, Nancy Quatrano, for her outstanding professional advice and assistance in helping polish this manuscript, and to Rik Feeney, for his cover design and essential technical expertise.

I owe a debt of gratitude to Middletown, New Jersey and Monmouth County. It is a beautiful area, and an outstanding place in which to grow up. I received a great education in its fine public school system.

CHAPTER ONE

Our first client was a real doozy. She walked into the Moo Mart, ignored Eddie's 'Can I help you?' and strode right over to where we were sitting. She stood about five-eight with a buxom figure and platinum blonde hair. She wore a white semi-sheer blouse, a blue skirt with the hem just below her knee, and I am not making this up—cowboy boots.

Without so much as an introduction, she said on a breathy exhale, "I want to hire you."

Zellie took a moment to silently appraise her, but I didn't wait. The lady was a little *meshugina*, to be sure, wearing that outfit in a Moo Mart in New Jersey. But she certainly was easy on the eyes.

"Maybe you should sit down and tell us about it," I said.

As it turned out, that was probably a bad move. Did I mention that Zellie is way smarter than I am? But this was our very first client, and I was desperate to get our new business started. Also, I wanted to keep looking at our new client's chest. But that wasn't the main reason, I swear!

She sat down, fairly daintily, I thought, for a woman with her ample figure.

"Why don't you tell us your name, and why you're here?" I prompted.

She took a deep breath, her chest heaving in an apparently practiced way. "My name is Marilyn Beaufort, and my dear Stanley is missing," she said in a voice that could only be characterized as a whisper.

"Is Stanley your husband?" Zellie asked.

"Yes," she replied. "Well actually, my ex-husband. We've been divorced for about a year."

"I hate to be pushy about personal matters, Ms. Beaufort..." I started.

"It's *Mrs.* Beaufort," she interrupted, then softened her tone, "but please call me Marilyn."

"Okay, Marilyn," I continued, "but if you're divorced, presumably you're living separate lives. How can you be sure he's missing?"

"I should explain," she answered slowly. "Look, I know we're divorced. I'm not delusional. But we were together for over twenty years. You learn a lot about someone in that amount of time. We were not completely out of each other's lives. We had a regular breakfast date every Thursday at Audacious Bagel."

Zellie and I exchanged glances. We knew Audacious Bagel, because we had breakfast there at least once a week. Everyone in Middletown did, it seemed. Truthfully, since retirement, we were probably there most days. But I had never seen Marilyn before. And she was someone you'd notice. By Zellie's reaction, she'd never seen her either.

"Just out of curiosity, Marilyn, how did you hear about our agency?"

She paused for a moment.

"Well...I went to every other agency in town, and they quoted me exorbitant fees, none of which I could afford. I hate to say it, but Jack Buckles, over at the Quicksilver Agency, said that if I want it done on the cheap, there's a new agency opened over at the Moo-Mart. I'm afraid he said it rather contemptuously, Mr. Fischer. Also, when I met with him, all he could do was stare at my boobs. Don't get me wrong, I know men do that." She looked at me, and my face reddened.

Zellie softy chuckled at my discomfort.

"But there was something nasty about the way he did it. And when I said I might just do that, he made obscene comments as I left his office. I will say this to you both. Maybe part of coming here was that I thought your rates would be less. But most of it was that I didn't like his attitude, and I always support the underdog. It's just in my nature, coming from where I do."

"And where is that, Marilyn?" Zellie asked.

"I wasn't always part of the Middletown society that Stanley introduced me to. I met Stanley in a bar in Keansburg, where I was a cocktail waitress."

Keansburg is a part of Middletown Township, which is a group of towns that also includes Middletown and Lincroft, New Jersey. It has always had the reputation, probably not really deserved, as the "tougher" part of town. Zellie started to look more interested.

"What bar?" she asked.

"The Stone Parrot," Marilyn replied. "I worked there for five years in the eighties."

Because of Bruce Springsteen's background at the famed Stone Pony in Asbury Park, it seemed that every bar was named Stone-something. Come to think of it, the "Stone Something" actually *is* the name of a bar.

"I worked there for a summer, to help pay the bills," Zellie said. "But it was in the nineties. Was Greasy Sid the manager when you were there, Marilyn?"

"He was," she answered. "And I think he still is."

Zellie turned to me. "I worked there the summer you were in California. Greasy Sid was probably sixty years old at the time, and was the bar's short order cook and manager. He seemed to always have grease spatter on the T-shirt he wore over his huge beer belly. I remember him as a pretty good guy, though."

"He was nice to me, too," Marilyn said. "He was younger when I knew him, of course, but he really was a gentleman then."

"He must be in his eighties, now," Zellie mused aloud. "Let me speak privately with Mr. Fischer for a moment, Marilyn, please."

We huddled together in the cereal aisle. "This office space is a little awkward, isn't it?" I whispered.

"Beggars can't be choosers, Arnie," she said with a laugh.

"What do you think about Marilyn?" I asked. "Should we take the case?"

"Of course, we should take the case. We can't very well turn down our first case, can we? But she's lying to us."

"I know," I said, "but I'm not sure about what. And you were lying, too. I don't ever remember you working at the Stone Parrot."

"That's because I never did," she said sweetly, "but I wanted to see what she'd say. I'll tell you later what I mean."

"Okay," I said. "Let's go talk to her."

"We'll take the case, Marilyn, if you're willing to pay our rates. I think you'll find that our rates are less than Jack Buckles' but our service is much more personal and effective. We charge two-hundred per day plus expenses, but will not exceed two-thousand total without getting your further approval. We will need the first thousand as a retainer up front."

CHAPTER TWO

She was lying, all right. Pretty much about everything. First of all, her last name wasn't Beaufort, it was Bean. The phone number she gave us to reach her was disconnected. And she was never married to someone named Stanley Beaufort. Stanley Beaufort didn't exist, at least in New Jersey. I checked. I have pretty good computer skills, and it didn't take long to access a few databases and determine that.

We also called the Stone Parrot and found out (from Greasy Sid - that part is true, he's a legend, that's how Zellie was able to lie to Marilyn so convincingly) that someone named Marilyn did work there in the eighties, but as a bouncer. She weighed over three-hundred pounds at the time.

What was her motive for hiring us at all? The person we were supposed to find didn't exist, and our client was not who she said she was. All this investigation had taken about two hours, tops.

"What's the protocol for this?" I asked Zellie.

We were sitting at our favorite booth in Audacious Bagel or "AB" as we sometimes called it, sipping our coffee. Audacious Bagel is not a typical deli. They actually employed "bagel baristas" (BBs) to bring you your choice from over a hundred types of bagels. Everything from plain to 'chocolate chip raisin cinnamon deluxe.' Personally, I think of a bagel as not including much of anything, and always order a plain one, although Zellie has been known to get a raisin, which I guess is moderately okay, and Ted almost always gets 'hamburger-infused,' whatever that is.

Maybe it's my Jewish upbringing, but I just can't see a lox and "hamburger-infused" bagel and cream cheese. Last time we were there, my favorite BB, Delilah, personally recommended a pizza bagel. I must admit, it was pretty good. Delilah is great. She went back to school at night to study marketing. She practices her marketing skills on anyone who will listen, and we always do.

When we walked in today, she was wearing yellow pants and an electric-blue shirt with sparkly sequins on it, along with the required Audacious Bagel visor that said in small letters "Audacious Bagel Barista, Changing the Bagel Paradigm," whatever that means.

"I think it means I'm supposed to sell you new and different bagels, Arnie," she said, when I asked her once. "You always get a plain bagel in a place known for pushing the envelope on the definition of bagel. If you want a plain bagel, you can have it, but there's a whole world you haven't explored." She added in a whisper, "If you try something new, you might surprise yourself and like it a lot."

Delilah talked me into a lox and cream cheese-infused bagel, which was good. "I'm working you up to something new and different, Arnie," she said. "I know you'll love everything I have to offer."

Zellie rolled her eyes when Delilah left. "She wants you," she said.

"It must be my animal magnetism," I replied, going back to my bagel.

"Yeah, that's it," she replied with a dry laugh.

"But really," I pressed, "what should we do about Marilyn? We can't find someone who doesn't exist, and we can't just keep her money." I paused. "Can we?"

"Well we can damn well keep two-hundred of it for the two hours we spent wasting our time on her jerking us around," she snapped.

"But don't you wonder what this is all about, Zellie?" I asked.

"Of course, I do," she said. "But I don't have the first idea how to reach her."

"We'll figure it out," I said. "And we should track her down to file our client report."

Zellie laughed. "You're almost evil in your moral code," she said. "We're going to track her down at *her* expense, aren't we?"

"Yes, we are," I replied. "It's the right thing to do. She paid for us to find out what happened to Stanley Beaufort, and she's entitled to a report on our findings."

I finished my bagel, dropped a couple of bucks on the table, and stood up. "Great bagel, Delilah," I called to her. "Thanks."

Delilah smiled brightly. "I wouldn't disappoint you, Arnie. Thanks for coming in."

Zellie took my arm and pulled me over to the cashier to pay.

"You really shouldn't lead her on," Zellie said. "You don't want to give her the wrong idea. Young women are sensitive about these things. I know," she added.

I looked at her in amazement. "She's no kid. She's probably almost thirty. And we're just engaging in a little harmless flirting. Are you jealous of Delilah?"

Zellie arched her chin. "Absolutely not," she said.

I put my arm around her. "I've known you my whole life. You're unbelievably confident. This isn't like you. Something's wrong. What's bothering you?"

"Oh, it's nothing. The whole Marilyn thing must have just upset my Karma."

CHAPTER THREE

"Did you tell Arnie how you felt about his flirting with Delilah?" Zellie's girlfriend Marla asked. They were walking to Mrs. Minniefield's house to meet Arnie and Ted and the dogs.

"Oh, they always do that, it doesn't mean anything. Maybe it does to Delilah, but not to Arnie. I don't think I'm jealous, but I think I'm a little frustrated."

"It's no wonder," Marla replied. "I don't know how or why the two of you do your little dance. You've known each other your whole lives, you're best friends, you love and respect each other, the sex is terrific (Marla knew about that), you spend all your free time together, and now you're even business partners, but you are not in a relationship."

"I think I'm just confused right now. Arnie and I have this agreement..." she trailed off. "This *stupid* agreement," she added. "Oh, I didn't mean that."

"Too late, girl," Marla said. "The cat's out of the bag."

"I guess I know that," Zellie said, "but there is a reason for our reluctance. We've been close friends for so long, we've supported each other through tough times, including my bad marriage to asshole Dan, and Arnie's disaster with Jennifer...."

"You actually spoke her name," Marla said. "I thought you guys only used pronouns when referring to that person." She grinned at Zellie. I wondered if she actually existed."

"Oh, she was real enough, but I don't think Arnie ever really got over her. Maybe that's one of the reasons we both avoid commitment, or we're afraid of losing each other, or whatever. So, we do the little dance, as you call it."

"What are the rules of this agreement?" Marla asked. "Is it in writing, like a contract? Are there specific dos and don'ts? You guys kiss each other, put your arms around each other when you walk, you hold hands often. Is it just no sex? Is it like an open marriage, but without the marriage?"

Zellie sighed. "I know it's weird. None of it makes any sense right now."

"If it ever did," Marla replied. "One thing I know, is if you feel this way, Arnie probably does, too."

"We're almost there," Zellie said, relieved to end the uncomfortable discussion. "That's Mrs. Minniefield's house - the white one on the corner. And there are the guys."

***

"Hey, there they are!" I exclaimed. "Just in time. We can go in together, and you can meet Mrs. Minniefield, Marla. She's really a terrific lady."

"She really is," Ted said, "even if her dog is a little on the odd side."

While Ted knocked on the door, I pulled Zellie aside. "Is everything okay?" I whispered in her ear.

"Everything's fine, Arnie. We can talk later."

If everything was fine, why did we need to talk later?

CHAPTER FOUR

Zellie and I formed the A to Z Agency a few weeks ago. We really didn't know what we were doing when we started it, and some might say we still don't. Our office is in the corner of the Moo Mart - in that little area with the two reclining chairs, the sofa, and the small coffee table.

We didn't want to pay for a real office, and Eddie, the manager of the Middletown Moo Mart, didn't mind that we used the space, if we drank a cup of coffee or two in the process. Zellie has the looks and personality to get clients. I have the real-world experience. Or is it the other way around?

Nah, she's way better looking than I am. With her five foot five-inch frame, shoulder length brownish-blonde hair with soft curls, a perky nose and shapely figure, Zellie can turn heads. She made the Rutgers sweatshirt, jeans, and tennis sneakers she wore look stylish. And her outgoing personality is a natural for sales, and in our case, finding clients. I'm more the reserved, quiet type. I'm about a half inch shy of six feet, with short, dark, slightly-graying hair, and about 180 pounds.

For the moment, I focused on my questionable transportation. Don't get me wrong, I love her. She's got style and class. But, of late, she's become something less than reliable. She coughed pitifully, and then failed to start. And even if I got her running, she would suddenly lose power and stop–at very inconvenient times, like at a stoplight on

Route 35. One of these times I was going to get creamed on that very busy road.

I live in Middletown, New Jersey, a town in central New Jersey, not far from the shore. You may have heard of "the quiet greenery of Monmouth County." Middletown certainly has its quiet and green spots, mostly in the neighborhoods like the one I live in, but it is a sprawling municipality, with no actual town center, and Route 35 is anything but quiet and green.

My name is Arnie Fischer, like fisherman, with an extra "c." At one point in my life, I went to medical school, and fully intended to become a doctor. I left not too long after I started. But it's not as simple as that. While mulling a decision to quit, I ran into "Her." And I knew I had a different path in life. But that's a story for a different day. Right now, I had to get the car started. I had people waiting for me.

With a sudden roar, the ignition caught, and the engine hummed contentedly. I drove to the Moo Mart. I got out of the car, went inside, and promptly tripped over my dog Lazlow, who was in his customary spot in the doorway.

He was lying there innocently enough, but I knew that masked his deep-seated need to persecute me. What is it this time? I wondered. He probably killed a bird and dragged it into the house, or ate something rancid and is going to barf in my shoes when we get home. Again. Sometimes I ask myself why I have a dog at all. They're really gross, you know.

My dog is a four-year-old cocker spaniel, named Lazlow. I love Lazlow, despite his extracurricular activities. Maybe because of them, I don't know. I named him after the guy who gets the girl in "Casablanca." You know - *Ilsa* - Ingrid Bergman. Lazlow gets all the girls. He's a regular chick magnet. Unlike the movie Lazlow, though, my Lazlow is dumb. No, not just not very smart - truly, astonishingly, incredibly dumb.

Anyway, I managed to right myself before I faceplanted on the floor, greeted everyone, and retrieved my dog from Betsy, who had taken him out and walked him for me. After making plans to meet Zellie later, I headed back home with Lazlow.

I've known Zellie Morgan pretty much my whole life. She's absolutely my best friend and I love her to pieces. Her given name is Zelda, but no one calls her that, not even her parents.

Zellie and I have been through a lot together. When I dropped out of medical school, Zellie was the first one to tell me I was a good decent person anyway. She consoled me, gave me good advice (which I ignored much to my detriment) and provided greatly needed support that my parents couldn't or wouldn't give. My folks are good people, but they simply couldn't acknowledge that I quit medical school for many reasons, not just for "Her."

Zellie probably thought it was about "Her," too, but never once tried to lecture me or dismiss my reasons for leaving, which included, among many other difficulties, an aversion to dead bodies.

When Zellie and that jerk Dan broke up, I held her and consoled her, too. He was never good enough for her, but I refrained from saying it, because somehow, I knew Zellie wouldn't have wanted to hear that. Maybe it would have sounded judgmental about her choice of a husband. I don't know. But he was never good enough for her. She deserves a kind, smart, loving, decent man.

I know I should talk to someone about "Her," and probably will one day. But not to Zellie. And certainly, not to Ted, the Barbarian, who doesn't believe in shrinks, and is completely unsentimental. At least Ted is a wholly decent person, unlike Tom Hooten, the owner of the Moo-Mart franchise, who possesses unmatched business acumen, but an almost legendary disregard for his employees, and even the people who frequent his stores.

But I had to admire his vision. He took a narrow-aisled little convenience store that sold milk, cigarettes and a few assorted sundries and transformed it into a chain of beautiful, high-volume coffee shops that also sold groceries, and yes, milk and cigarettes. The stores all had comfortable seating areas, which was good for us.

As for Zellie, I guess I'm a little conflicted. I know I shouldn't be, because with one notable exception, we've never really had any kind of sexual relationship, and I've always told her everything. But she's smart, nice, decent, and vivacious as hell. She's also a wonderful confidant and friend. And maybe that's the point. I'd truly hate to screw up our friendship for any reason. But somehow, talking about my relationship with "Her", to Zellie, bothers me on a level I don't really understand. Maybe I'm in love with Zellie in a different way than I thought. I don't know, and I certainly don't intend to pursue it.

Ted worked for the Federal government for many years. I was never sure of what he did there, but he certainly is an accomplished inventor, with many patents, although none that any of us would recognize. I've known him since junior high school. Even back then, he always had big ideas. He still has big ideas. While I admire his tenacity, I must acknowledge that his big ideas never seem to amount to anything. But that's the beauty of it. He's retired, has a pension, and can pretty much do as he pleases. Lately, he's explored corporations. By that I mean he has formed a dozen or more. I don't really know whether any of them are businesses, or were formed just because he figured out how to do it and it was a new project. I do know that he incorporated his house (Ted's House, Inc.), and himself (Ted, Inc.), but has not incorporated his dog, Larry.

"Dogs should not be messed with," he says.

Larry is a genuine mixed breed something or other - probably a combination of a bulldog and a dachshund and five or six other breeds. He has a long, hot dog-like body, but with big shoulders (do dogs besides Larry have shoulders?), a scrunched-up face and floppy ears. I don't know where the floppy ears come from, but Larry has them. He's a great dog, and he and Lazlow get along famously. He's adorable, reasonably smart (smarter than Lazlow, anyway) but is incredibly hard to keep track of, wandering off and generally making a nuisance of himself in the neighborhood. Ted kept losing him, so he put him on a leash. Of course, the leash goes both ways, and Ted can't seem to get the hang of the fact that he needs to hold onto it. So, Larry walks around the neighborhood dragging a leash behind him. I guess technically that complies with the town leash law ("All dogs must be leashed"), but probably not its spirit.

Anyway, back to Ted. He's sort of an Ichabod Crane-looking fellow. At about six four, and 165 pounds at most, he's skinny as a shoestring potato. It almost looks like his height is too much for the rest of his body. He has reddish, thinning hair, with a touch of grey at the temples. He's honest and smart, and I'm glad to have him as a friend.

CHAPTER FIVE

"I think Zellie is jealous of Delilah," I said to Ted. We were walking over to pick up Lazlow and Larry at Mrs. Minniefield's house on the corner.

"What makes you say that?" Ted asked. "Zellie is pretty self-confident, and Delilah is just a kid."

"Delilah is almost thirty," I protested. "Not that there's anything between us," I quickly added. "And Zellie and I are just best friends and business partners anyway."

"Sure, you are," Ted said. "And the Pope is just another Catholic. Any idiot can see that you two love each other. You guys are tripping over each other to honor that silly agreement not to ruin your lifelong friendship by becoming romantically involved."

"Hey, it was a blood oath we took. You don't mess with a blood oath," I said.

"What is it *really*? Are you two not physically attracted to each other, or something?"

I laughed to myself. The truth was that we were very attracted to each other and incredibly sexually compatible. We explored that as recently as last year, not that either of us was telling Ted about it. We called it off because we both got scared of messing up a good thing.

"Of course, I'm attracted to Zellie. Only a dead man wouldn't be. And I think she believes I'm attractive. It's just more complicated than that," I told Ted.

"No, it isn't, Arnie. You two are just avoiding commitment because of your disastrous past relationships. Both disasters, I might add, could have been avoided if you two didn't have your stupid blood oath. Zellie is smart, beautiful, and a totally decent human being. You are too, except for the beautiful part."

"Ted, I don't expect you to understand, although your track record for extreme lack of commitment makes you something of an expert at relationship avoidance. Zellie and I have known each other since we were born, and have been best friends since we were five. Potentially screwing up a lifelong friendship in exchange for a little nooky doesn't seem worth the cost."

"Well, I think you two are screwing up a lifelong love affair by not hooking up, but what do I know?"

CHAPTER SIX

Mrs. Minniefield lived in a small white house with black shutters, and a big fenced-in back yard that all our dogs loved. Thus, Mrs. M became the *de facto* dog sitter for Lazlow and Larry, who came over to play with her dog, Fideaux. I once asked Mrs. M why she called him Fideaux (pronounced like fit dough without the letter t) instead of Fido, and she looked at me with those perceptive, intelligent eyes.

"Does he look like a *Fido*?"

And she was right. Fideaux just has a snooty look about him. Hard to explain.

Zellie and I have known Mrs. M our entire lives. She's been living on the corner of the street we both grew up on for something like forever. As far as either of us can recall, she has looked the same for the last forty years. She's somewhere between seventy and a hundred, looks like she's about sixty, has a large body with broad shoulders, white hair, and piercing sharp gray eyes that just scream "intelligence." And she is smart, about pretty much everything - book smart, people smart, she's the whole shebang. As a result, we kids all asked her advice about everything. And we've always called her Mrs. Minniefield, or Mrs. M, never, ever, by her first name of Mabel. By the Mrs., we always surmised that she was married at one time, but no one really knows whether she was ever married, or if there once was a Mr. Minniefield. If so, it was a real long time ago.

"Hi everyone," Mrs. Minniefield said. "Nice to see you all. You must be Marla," she observed.

"It's a pleasure meeting you," Marla said. "I've heard a lot about you. All good," she added.

"Please sit down everyone, and tell me what's been going on with all of you."

We sat down in her cozy living room. She had two big overstuffed easy chairs sitting across from a loveseat, and a somewhat dainty, smaller chair in between the two. Mrs. Minniefield sat down on the dainty chair, Ted and Marla grabbed the easy chairs, and Zellie and I commandeered the sofa.

"You two always seem to end up next to each other, don't you?" Mrs. Minniefield asked rhetorically, and with a smile. "And now business partners. Bring me up to date with the latest A to Z Agency news."

Both of us ignored her first comment. "We have our first client," I said.

"She's a complete liar," Zellie offered.

"Well doesn't that seem interesting," Mrs. Minniefield said. "Although I would think having a liar for a client is pretty much the normal course of events in that business."

"Well, this one is lying about pretty much everything," I said. "Even who she is and what she wants us to do. Also, she has completely disappeared, even though she gave us a retainer. We decided to track her down, at her expense of course, to give her a report on our findings."

Mrs. Minniefield laughed. "Well that seems like poetic justice. How are you doing with that?"

Ted stood up. "Marla, why don't we go outside and see the dogs, while these detective types talk shop?"

Marla nodded and got up as well. "We'll be back in a little bit," she said.

We'd chatted amiably with Mrs. M, but with her, chit chat meant getting right to the point. She is direct and wastes no time (except maybe with dogs). "Okay, what's it all about? You didn't just come here to pick up the dogs, and introduce me to Marla, as nice as she seems. I wonder if she and Ted would make a good couple? That boy needs to settle down." Mrs. Minniefield's eyes became dreamy for a moment.

"Stop being a *yenta*, just for a minute, and we'll tell you about our case," I said smiling. We told her all about Marilyn Beaufort, really Bean, and her dear non-existent Stanley.

"What do you think her game is?" Zellie asked.

Mrs. Minniefield looked pensive. "Obviously, it has something to do with the two of you," she said slowly. "Otherwise, she really wouldn't have hired you. No offense intended, guys, but you're not exactly household names in the detective business, and your office has a statue of a giant cow in front of it. She wanted to keep you busy on a useless quest for some reason. I would try to figure out her ulterior motive."

At that moment, three dogs, all clamoring for attention, ran into the living room, followed by a laughing Ted and Marla. Well, at least two of the dogs were clamoring. Fideaux, with great dignity, strode into the room as if he was the lord of the manor.

"What's with that dog?" I asked. "Why can't he be a dumb, attention seeking, troublemaking canine like Lazlow, or a moderately intelligent, butt sniffing, garbage invading dog like Larry?"

Naturally, no one answered my question and Fideaux actually stopped in front of me, looked around, sniffed the air and turned his head away. I resisted the urge to further criticize. After all, he meant a lot to Mrs. M.

I turned to Mrs. M. "We'll keep you posted. Thanks again for your help."

I held the door for Zellie and we went outside.

"Hey, Arnie. Marla and I are going to walk the dogs. See you later."

I looked at Zellie and shrugged. "Just you and me, kid," I said in my best Bogart imitation.

CHAPTER SEVEN

"Arnie, we've sort of become emotional crutches for each other," Zellie said. "Since you had your latest episode with Jennifer and I divorced Dan, we've both generally avoided going out on dates and having real relationships with others. At the same time, we're denying that the two of us are in a relationship. Something has to give here, and I think we both need to get out a little - go on a date or two, and try to see if we're comfortable with just being best friends and business partners."

"Zellie," I started, "I know to some degree we are using each other as crutches. Best friends do that, don't they? And as you've said, we've both experienced fairly recent personal disappointments."

"Disappointments doesn't even begin to describe it, but we both need something more than we're allowing each other to experience right now," she answered.

"Should we just declare that we're in a relationship? Would that, do it?" I asked.

"I love you, you know that," she responded. "I'm not suggesting that we stop being best friends, or that we shouldn't keep the business going, such as it is. I must wonder a little, why you seem resistant to us beginning to date again, if we want to maintain our agreement not to mess things up by being a couple. To answer your question, simply declaring us in a relationship is *not* enough. We both have to want it enough to make a commitment, and I'm not sure we're ready for that."

"I will say this, Zellie: I love you, always have, and always will. And I'll try to do as you suggest, if only to see if it helps us to understand what we're both avoiding here. I will admit that I'm afraid that emotionally committing to others has the potential to cause the very cracks in our friendship that we both fear, and that we won't be there for each other to help pick up the pieces."

"I don't want to live in fear, Arnie, either of a commitment to you, or involvement with others. Why don't we see how things go for a while? At a minimum, we can both eliminate some sexual frustration, without the emotional baggage." Zellie raised an eyebrow suggestively.

"Well, amen to that, at least," I chuckled. "I'm basically in a constant state of arousal being around you all the time."

Zellie laughed as well. "Me too."

***

Mrs. Minniefield sat thinking for a long time after the others left. "Fideaux," she said finally, "this Marilyn Beaufort thing could be a real problem for Arnie and Zellie."

Fideaux looked up at her when she spoke. He almost nodded, she thought. He's a very odd dog.

"I better make a few calls about this. It's okay for Arnie and Zellie to mess around with this detective business, and do their little commitment-avoidance tango, but their case could be dangerous, and they don't know it.

***

Ted and Marla strolled along with the dogs.

"Thanks for helping me with their walk, Marla. I think Arnie and Zellie needed some time alone, and it's much more pleasant to manage these beasts with such beautiful company."

"Laying it on a little thick, aren't you, Ted?" Marla asked, laughing. "You really don't need to feed me a line. I was happy to come along."

Ted smiled. "Okay, I get the message. Just relax and be myself, eh? But maybe this *is* who I am, did you consider that?"

"Oh, I think it's *exactly* who you are," Marla replied, "but I'm used to that - I'm an attorney."

"Zellie didn't mention that," Ted said. "Am I in danger of being sued?"

"Not for hitting on me, that's for sure," Marla said. "Last time I checked, just being interested in a woman was not actionable. Zellie didn't tell me what you do, either, Ted. Do you care to share that with me, seeing as I'm on a dog-walking date with you?"

Ted looked a little uncomfortable. "Oh, this and that," he finally said.

"I'm sorry, Ted, are you unemployed? There's no shame in that, you know. The economy is terrible right now," Marla said quickly.

Ted stopped, and looked at her. "Actually, I'm sort of an entrepreneur and inventor. My legal name is Ted, Incorporated. And it's at this point that nice girls like you tend to run away."

"Run away, from a name and untold story like that? Not on your life," Marla said. "I told you that I'm an attorney, and yet I have no clue how to begin asking you questions about your reasons for incorporating yourself. But I'll figure out a way," she added.

"You want to cross-examine me, Counsellor?" Ted asked. "Then join me for dinner tonight, and I'm all yours."

Marla seemed to study him a long moment, then broke into a grin.

"I'm looking forward to it, Mr. Incorporated." She jotted something on a slip of paper and handed it to him. "Call me with the details. I'll see you tonight."

CHAPTER EIGHT

At eight the next morning, I was speaking to Ted on the phone.

"My date with Tanya went well. I think. We went out to dinner at Steak N' Brew, had a very comfortable conversation there, then took in a movie. Tanya is absolutely beautiful, with her long dark hair and those big brown eyes. And she's smart, too. She teaches French at the community college in Lincroft. She's not as pretty or smart as Zellie, not that I'm comparing, mind you. I might have spoken too much about Zellie, come to think of it, but she's my best friend and business partner, what should Tanya expect?"

"You're an idiot, do you know that?" Ted exploded in disgust. "What woman in her right mind wants to hear about another woman in your life? She is *never* going to believe that Zellie is just a friend, not the way you two act around each other. The least you can do is not talk about her to your date. Lie if you have to, but don't talk about Zellie to Tanya."

I sighed. My friend was right and I probably owed Tanya an apology. "This is going to be harder than I thought. I bet Zellie handled it much better on her date with Dave."

***

"Oh God, it was just awful," Zellie said at that very moment to Marla. What have I done? Dave's a nice guy, and he's good looking and intelligent. But all I could think of was Arnie. I know I talked about

26

him to Dave, too. You know how guys react to that. I just didn't think this would be so hard," she went on. "And I'll bet Arnie's date with Tanya went really well."

Marla chuckled. "Relax, Zellie. It probably wasn't as bad as you think. These things just take time. Your next date will probably go much better."

"If there *is* another date," Zellie moaned. Did she even want one?

***

We both arrived at the office promptly at 8:30 am as pre-arranged. "Two coffees with the usual fixings, Eddie."

"Coming right up, Arnie. I'll bring them over to your office," he said with a chuckle.

We sat down facing each other. By silent agreement, we avoided talking about our dates. I think we both knew we'd get *around* to talking about them, because we more or less told each other everything, anyway.

"What do you think about Mrs. Minniefield's theory?" I asked.

"That this is about us somehow? I don't know. She's pretty sharp and we know her mind works in interesting ways," Zellie said. "I think we should stick to the original plan and try to find Marilyn. She really is our only clue, whatever the truth is here."

I nodded. "The only connection to her that we really know is the Stone Parrot," I said. "We should go down there today and talk to Greasy Sid again. In person, this time. Maybe he knows how to locate her, or at least has an old address. Much as we both hate to consider it, we should probably talk to Jack Buckles, too. Outside of us, he's the only one who allegedly talked to Marilyn. It might be interesting to see if they actually met and he sent her over to us. I suppose it's a long shot, but he might even be involved somehow."

"Why don't you have a go at Greasy Sid, and I'll talk to Jack Buckles," Zellie suggested. "I know I'll have to deal with a little leering and coarse talk, but I don't think he's dangerous, at least not in broad daylight, and you two have that history."

Zellie referred to the fact that Jack and I were in many of the same classes in high school, and had some difficulty getting along, to put it mildly. "Anyway, I'm much more likely to get something out of him than you are. We both know he's a sucker for a pretty face." She posed comically, and I smiled.

"Well you are certainly sexy enough to get his attention, Zellie, but be careful, and don't let him get behind you, or you know he'll grab your ass."

"Oh, I can fend him off easily enough. I'll tell him I have a communicable disease, or something. We'll meet back here around noon, or better yet, at AB to get some lunch."

"Okay, see you then. Good luck."

***

I was a little nervous about Zellie meeting with Jack Buckles, but she could handle herself. I needed to think about an approach to get information out of Greasy Sid, who I hadn't really seen since high school. I decided on the direct approach, and walked out to my car, which went through its customary wheezing and coughing before it started.

I headed out to Keansburg and the Stone Parrot. My car stopped dead in its tracks on only two occasions, and not in an intersection this time, so I arrived there safely. One obstacle down, I thought. One to go.

Of course, the Stone Parrot was closed at 9:00 am, but I knew Greasy Sid would be there anyway. Some people said he lived there. Others said he not only lived there, he was *born* there. As no one ever saw him outside the place, it was generally assumed he slept there. I walked around the building to the back entrance. The door was wide open, which was strange enough, but even stranger was the complete chaos inside. There were loose papers, broken bottles, and streams of liquids everywhere.

"Sid, are you here?" I called. No answer. "Is anyone here?" Silence.

This is not good, I thought, in what turned out to be the understatement of the year. Against my better judgment, I slowly ventured inside, looking around for anything that might explain the disaster I'd encountered from the open doorway.

CHAPTER NINE

"It was terrible, Zellie. The worst thing I've ever seen. And the cops yelled at me for being an idiot. Which I was, of course, but they didn't need to be such jerks about it."

Zellie picked me up at the police station after I gave my statement. The cops had insisted that I go downtown with them, and I had yet to return to Keansburg to get my car.

"I'm lucky they didn't accuse me of killing him."

"Who would want to kill Greasy Sid?" Zellie wondered aloud.

"A little sympathy, here, Zellie. Can't you see I'm distraught?"

Zellie reached over and patted my arm. "Oh, you'll be okay, Arnie, I know you. But can you think of a reason?"

"I've been wondering that myself," I said, somewhat mollified. "And is there a connection to our case?"

"Exactly my concern," Zellie said. "What have we gotten ourselves into? We just wanted to have a nice little 'find stuff' business, and next thing you know, we have a murder on our hands."

"And that's another thing," I said. "Apparently, you need a license to be a private investigator in this state. And basically, every state in the country, as it turns out. The cops actually laughed at me. Wanted to know if I never watched TV. I must confess it was a nice change of pace from them yelling at me."

"So, are we out of business?"

"Of course not," I said. "As far as I know, there's no law against private citizens trying to track down someone to give her the report she paid for."

"And we get our PI licenses in the meantime, don't we?"

"Of course, we do. If Jack Buckles can get one, how hard can it be? Which reminds me, Zellie. How did your interview with him go?"

"Well, he was surprisingly nice, at least at first. He thought I was there to apply for a job. And he said a few snarky things about you."

"He's a jerk," I said. "Always has been."

"Well I just ignored the comments. I thought I could get more information out of him if I didn't start fighting with him right from the start."

"So, did you?" I asked.

Zellie thought for a moment. "Well, yes and no. After some prodding, he told me that he never met Marilyn Beaufort. And he said he certainly didn't recommend her to us. And he said, he couldn't have, because he didn't even know the A to Z Agency existed."

"You didn't find out *anything*?" I asked, a little disappointed.

"I didn't say that," she replied quickly. "Jack Buckles was lying to me, I'm sure of it. And that itself is an important clue."

"It sure, is," I agreed. "But how do you know he was lying?"

Zellie smirked. "I appealed to his baser instincts. What was the characteristic you noticed most about Marilyn?"

"I don't really remember," I mumbled.

"Oh please. Give me a break. Even I noticed those big boobs under the semi-sheer blouse she was wearing. You practically drooled over them."

"Okay, I admit it," I said sheepishly.

"Well, Jack noticed them, too. I could tell. I never mentioned that part of her anatomy at all. I'm much too dainty and reserved for that," Zellie added in a Southern-belle-voice.

"Yeah, sure you are Zellie. You forget I've known you all your life. Dainty and reserved are not your strong points," I retorted.

She laughed. "Jack Buckles slipped up, Arnie. I described Marilyn generally, but without those two very large details. His response was that he never met Marilyn. When I pressed him on it, he said that he wouldn't have forgotten bazongas like that."

I thought about that and stared out the window. We were just passing Audacious Bagel and I asked Zellie if she wanted to get some lunch before we picked up my car.

"Sure, let's get lunch, but skip AB, and go somewhere quieter, so you can tell me all about finding Greasy Sid's body."

"How about D'Agostino's?" I asked. "Salvatore will give us a nice quiet booth in the back and leave us alone."

"Sounds good," Zellie said. "I'm starving, and D'Agostino's' pasta makes my mouth water."

***

"Arnie, Zellie, dear. It's been too long," Salvatore D'Agostino said in a warm greeting. Over his shoulder, he called, "A nice quiet spot in the back for the lovebirds, Mama."

"You never stop trying, do you Salvatore?" I asked with a smile.

"I'm an incurable romantic, Arnie, you know that. And the two of you have been together since you were both knee high."

Zellie looked up at me and smiled.

"When in Rome..." she said to me. And she put her arm around me and we followed Mama to our booth. Of course, Mama insisted we sit down next to each other rather than across the table.

"It's more intimate this way, darlings, and you can talk more quietly," she whispered.

I looked at Zellie. "I'm sorry, maybe this wasn't such a good idea to come here in view of yesterday's talk about sort of extricating ourselves from this codependent thing we have going."

"It's okay, Arnie. I don't mind. I'm enjoying it. Salvatore and Mama are so sweet, and so sincere, it's infectious." At that, she leaned over, her lips lightly brushing my ear, giving me shivers.

"Besides," she whispered, "we really can talk more quietly this way." Not giving me time to respond, she added, "Now tell me all about finding the body."

It took me a few seconds to recover from the bolt of electricity Zellie had delivered. And she clearly knew my reaction and enjoyed it immensely. But taking her cue, I didn't comment on it.

"It was really terrible, Zellie. There was blood everywhere, and Sid was lying in the middle of it. I really shouldn't have gone in at all, but you know when you see a door wide open, you tend to walk in. And that's what I did. At first I just stood there in the doorway and looked at the chaos inside. I called out for Sid, and when there was no answer, I asked whether anyone was there. Still no answer. So, I just decided to look around. And that's when I found him."

"Did you touch anything?" Zellie asked.

"Well, not the body. With my medical training, you would think I would at least check his pulse or something, but I sort of froze." I said ruefully. "But my real mistake was to use the phone on the wall to call the police instead of just using my cell phone. I don't really know why. And I may have stepped in some of the blood on the way over to wall."

"That would tick them off, that's for sure," Zellie said. "But they had to understand the situation. Anyone could have done the same thing."

"I think they understand that, Zellie, or they probably would have kept me at the station longer. I don't think I'm a suspect, or anything like that. I think they just think I'm an idiot."

"But you're a well-meaning idiot," Zellie replied.

"Thanks. I think," I said, feeling more like my old self.

"If the situation changes, and they start to look at you like you're a suspect, don't forget that Marla is one of the best criminal defense lawyers around."

"Yeah, I thought of her, but I don't think it will come to that."

"What do you think we should do next?" Zellie asked.

"You mean about the case?" I replied, somewhat mischievously.

She smiled. "Yes, about the case. Do we keep looking for Marilyn, or did the cops warn you off?"

"Oh, they warned me off, all right, but I don't think that should stop us. Don't you want to get to the bottom of this?"

"Yes, I do." Zellie said firmly. "I most certainly do."

CHAPTER TEN

"I think I'm driving Arnie crazy," Zellie said to Marla later that day. "First I tell him we should start to date again and try to see if we can connect to others romantically, then I practically give him a hard-on in a restaurant."

"Those things aren't necessarily inconsistent," Marla replied. "No harm in showing him what he's missing. Did he tell you about his date?"

"No, and I didn't tell him about mine, either. I think he would have told me, but I distracted him."

Marla looked thoughtfully at her friend. "What do you really want, Zellie?" Marla asked quietly.

"I think I just don't know," Zellie wailed. "Arnie and I get such constant pressure from everyone to become a couple, that sometimes I wonder if we're resisting just to prove to everyone what good friends we are."

"I don't think so, Zellie," Marla said. "If I had to guess, I'd say that you both have recently had emotional letdowns, and you're relying on each other for the support you've always given each other, and you're scared to death that you might lose that support by changing the nature of your relationship. Give it time, my friend. It will work out."

Zellie looked at her with wide eyes. "Marla, are you sure you're a lawyer?"

Marla laughed. "Well they don't call us counselors for nothing. I know what you went through with Dan," Marla continued. "But what's Arnie's story?"

Zellie sighed. "It's a long and very personal one. I'll give you a bit of an outline, but the details are up to Arnie to disclose or not as he sees fit. He hasn't even told *me* everything.

"It started when Arnie was in medical school about twenty years ago. We had sort of lost touch with each other during that time. I mean, we were in contact periodically, but it was different. We had our own lives to pursue, and we basically went our separate ways, as childhood friends do." Zellie paused, and took a sip of water.

"After college, Arnie went to medical school in Massachusetts, and I started at the public relations firm in New York - you might have heard of them - Millicent & Wells. We did a lot of P.R. for musicians.

"Anyway, Arnie had completed two years of medical school, when he met Jennifer. She was a Bohemian sort, with those long, flowing, colorful skirts and granny glasses. You know the type. Well she caught Arnie's eye one day and he just lost his mind. Went head over heels for her. Understand, he was a lot younger then, and much more easily swayed than he is now. Arnie has a good head on his shoulders now, but he was much more impulsive then. When Jennifer suggested he put off school and travel the country with her, Arnie jumped. To this day, I don't know whether he just hated medical school and was looking for a way out, or whether he just was that smitten by her charms. I don't think he even fully knows that answer. But he left medical school abruptly - right in the middle of an exam, actually. He just got up and left. As far as I know, they toured the country for a while, followed the Grateful Dead part of the time, and other times just bummed around. Ultimately, they parted ways.

"After that, Arnie came home to Middletown, and had to explain to his parents why he left medical school. He looked to me for support, which of course I was happy to give. Ultimately, he went to work at a securities firm in the city, and we commuted on the train together."

"But that was twenty years ago," Marla said. "What happened last year?"

"There's more," Zellie said tiredly. "Jennifer showed up again."

"Omigod," Marla said. "Was she still a hippie?"

"No, she wasn't. She was every bit the sophisticate, with expensive clothes and jewelry, and Arnie was like a little puppy around her. It's almost like she had some sort of Svengali-like hold over him."

"Probably more like a lost first love magically reappearing," Marla said. "It would have a strong effect on anyone."

"Well it did on him, Marla. And she used it to con him out of most of his savings, and then left town."

Marla looked shocked. "Arnie's lost love conned him? He's not exactly the gullible sort."

"Well that's what I call it," Zellie said. "He doesn't really want to see it that way. He calls it a bad investment. These things happen, *et cetera, et cetera*. But he knows better, and it was very traumatic for him."

CHAPTER ELEVEN

"I have an idea on how to approach finding Marilyn," I said.

We were sitting in our office at the Moo Mart, sipping some French roast coffee Eddie had brought us. Zellie lifted one brow in response.

"Remember those big, ornate cowboy boots she was wearing?"

"Who could forget them?"

"Those things couldn't have just been purchased anywhere."

"You know, you're right. And I know just where to start."

"Where?"

"At Brazen Saddles, in Eatontown."

"The fancy new horsey-set store? You're a genius!"

Zellie smiled. "Not really. I was dying to see what it was like, so I peeked in there a couple of weeks ago. Anyway, you came up with the idea. I just filled in the name of the store."

"What's the place like?" I asked. "I'm sort of curious, too."

"It's a little on the bizarre side. Filled with fashionable clothes, but interspersed with fancy equestrian regalia - you know, saddles, riding hats, crops, and more down-to-earth stuff like cowboy hats, big glitzy belt buckles..."

"And cowboy boots," I filled in.

"And cowboy boots," Zellie agreed.

"I'll go there today and ask a few questions."

"We'll both go there," she said, putting down her cup on the table.

"Does it really call for both of us?"

"Yes, it does," she said firmly. "The last time I left you alone, you found a body. And besides, you'd look silly going in there alone."

Well, when she's right, she's right. I shrugged. "Okay, okay, we'll go together."

"One other thing, Arnie," she said. "We need to be careful. The cops aren't going to be happy with us continuing to search for Marilyn. They're probably looking, too, considering you told them that Marilyn worked for Sid at one time."

"I thought of that," Arnie said. "But the lead investigator on the case is Mike Mullen. Remember him?"

Zellie blushed. "I can't say that I do," she said. Then she smiled. Zellie had dated Mike for almost a year in high school. "He's a good guy," she said. "I always liked him. He ended up marrying Helen Terwilliger, didn't he?"

"Yes, but they split up a few years ago, I heard. Don't know the reason. No kids involved, I don't think."

"Mike will be serious about the case," Zellie warned.

"I know he will. And he should be. But he won't be a jerk, and won't do us any harm, if we mostly stay out of his way."

***

Zellie drove her dependable Honda. My car was just too unreliable–a topic we discussed on the way.

"You should get a new car," she said. "You can't keep going on like this, with it breaking down all the time."

"I know. But I just can't part with her."

"You act like that car is something more than a rickety pile of nuts and bolts."

"She is not a rickety pile of nuts and bolts. Matilda is an environment, a quiet port in a storm, um, a ...."

"An *environment* that doesn't get you where you're going," Zellie said dryly. "Face it Arnie, that car lets you down all the time, sometimes in dangerous situations. Remember the day it died in the intersection? You could easily have been killed. You were a sitting duck. And when you *do* get a new car, maybe you shouldn't name it. It will make it easier to let go of it when the time comes."

I pouted silently, while Zellie drove. I wasn't ready to get a new car, even though truthfully, I could afford one. My buyout from the securities firm was substantial, and thankfully occurred *after* Jennifer had taken me to the cleaners.

Looking over at Zellie, I thought about how often she had been there for me. She was such a wonderful friend.

"Lost in thought there, Tiger? I didn't mean anything. Keep the car. Just be careful, okay?"

Startled, I sat upright. "Oh, it's okay. I know you just care about my welfare. And, I'm sure I'm just being silly about the whole thing. I'll go shopping for a new car soon. I promise. Maybe you'll help me pick one out?"

"Car shopping might be the most oppressive thing there is to do on this earth," she replied, "but because I suggested it, I'll help. We're here," she added, pulling off the highway and into one of New Jersey's famous and prevalent strip malls, colloquially referred to as "shopping centers."

While Zellie looked for a parking place, I examined the facade of the store. Brazen Saddles was displayed prominently on the front, with an image of a horse leaping over a fence. A well-dressed woman, with short-cropped blonde hair was entering the store, followed by a tall, sandy-haired man wearing cowboy boots and a ten-gallon hat. Interesting patronage, I thought.

Zellie parked and turned to look at me. "Any ideas on an approach?" she asked.

"I think we'll just be direct and see what happens," I said.

"Okay, you take the lead, and I'll follow."

We got out of the car and walked to the entrance. I was wearing my usual khakis and button-down shirt and loafers. Zellie wore ordinary jeans and a V-neck sweater and sneakers.

"We're probably seriously underdressed for this place," Zellie warned.

"It sells cowboy boots and saddles," I said. "How fancy could it be?"

"Just wait and see," she said. "But they might not care."

We walked to the front door, entered, and I immediately knew what she meant. The store was walled in what appeared to be pure mahogany, including the ceiling. It was dimly lit by scores of hanging amber lights. Along one side of the store was an array of very high fashion clothes which could have come straight from Paris, for all I knew.

In a weird juxtaposition, throughout the fancy clothing racks, were interspersed little inlets of equestrian regalia - riding hats, fancy English saddles, riding crops, boots and things like that. Men's clothes and women's clothes shared the same shelves. It was as if the store designer had no sense of the type of departmentalization we've all come to expect. Maybe even stranger was the other side of the store itself.

That wall was replete with extremely casual clothes - everything from work shirts and boots to cowboy-themed apparel, including ornate cowboy boots of the type that Marilyn had worn. Looking at both sides of the store created a sort of schizophrenia. Zellie and I stood in the entryway for a few seconds, just taking it all in.

An attractive brunette wearing an expensive silk blouse, colorful flowery short skirt and shoes with three inch heels, approached, and gave us a once over. If she disapproved of our attire, she didn't let us see it. Her face bore a guileless smile.

"My name is Gloria. May I help you with anything?"

"We're new to this place," I offered. "Maybe you could tell us a little about it."

She smiled brightly. "That's what I'm here for," she said. "Follow along, and I'll give you a bit of a tour of the place. As you can see," she continued, "we don't follow ordinary conventions in organization of the store contents. That's why our management offers customer specialists like me to help first-timers like you, find an approach that suits you."

We were walking down the gold-carpeted center aisle of the huge front room. Gloria stopped and pointed to the equestrian side.

"As you can see, we do not separate men's and women's clothes. The idea is for couples to shop together and maybe find outfits that complement each other." Gloria looked at us appraisingly.

"I'm guessing the two of you have been a couple for a long time, and you're looking to better coordinate your outfits." Without waiting for an answer, she said "you've come to the right place. Brazen Saddles caters to couples."

I started to say something, but Zellie's brief eye movement cautioned me to stay silent. It's amazing, I thought. The two of us can communicate without saying a word. I snapped back to attention.

"As you can see," Gloria continued, "there are various displays containing the finest equestrian accessories available anywhere." She looked from one to the other. "Do you two ride?"

When I hesitated, Zellie quickly jumped in.

"I rode much more when I was younger. Arnie prefers the business side of things."

Gloria looked at me with renewed interest. She thinks I might own some thoroughbreds, I thought, which is exactly what Zellie intended to convey to her without actually saying so. Time for me to speak.

"Gloria, can you tell us what is on the other side of the store?"

She smiled.

"The strong cowboy type, I see. Let's go look."

We walked across the center aisle to the racks of casual attire.

"You'll see that the layout here is very similar to the other side. Men and women sharing racks together, with the same little coves of saddles, riding gear, cowboy hats and boots and other less formal clothes."

"Do people ever mix and match between the two sides?" I asked.

Gloria laughed. "Almost everyone who comes in here does that. I've seen people matching Paris originals with work boots. Mr. Desmond - he's the owner and visionary behind this place - has created a style all his own here."

"You don't seem to have combined multiple styles, Gloria," Zellie said.

"I'm not much of a trend-setter myself, "Gloria said sadly. "Mr. Desmond has told me I'm too conservative, and should take some chances with my wardrobe. Hopefully it won't affect my job," she whispered. "I really like it here."

"I think you look terrific the way you are, Gloria," I said gallantly.

Gloria's smile returned. "I'm pretty good at helping people pick things out they really like. And you don't have to mix and match, if you don't want to," she added quickly.

Zellie piped up. "I love these cowboy boots," she said. "Can you tell me a little about them?"

"A very popular choice. And they're lovely, aren't they? They're made from the finest leather, and are hand-tooled by very skilled Pawnee craftsmen. The designs are sewn by hand. As you can see, the ornamentation is very intricate. Each pair of boots is unique. And they are only available here," she added proudly. "Mr. Desmond has an exclusive arrangement with the leather workers who create them."

"They are certainly special," Zellie said.

I nodded my agreement. "They certainly are." I said.

"Is there a particular pair you're interested in?" Gloria asked.

"Well, my friend Marilyn bought this type of boots at your store," Zellie said, "and I don't want mine to look anything like hers. So, I just don't know."

"Can you describe her boots?" Gloria asked.

"I guess I can try, but is there any way you can check your records to see what she bought?"

"Oh no. Mr. Desmond takes client confidentiality very seriously. I wouldn't dare share personal information."

"It's not really personal information. It's just the type of cowboy boots she bought so we don't look alike at the next big formal event."

"Why don't you just ask her?"

Zellie leaned in conspiratorially. "I just couldn't do that. I just couldn't. Would you ask a friend before a formal ball what dress she was wearing so you could get something similar? I don't think so. Ordinarily I wouldn't even consider wearing the same style of dress as her, but these boots are so darling, and unique."

"I'm really sorry, ma'am, but I could lose my job if I shared that information with you."

Zellie looked over at me. "Honey," she said. "They're only $2,500.00. I can just pick ones I like, and before I wear them, look at Marilyn's boots again. If they're too similar, we haven't really wasted much money if I never wear them."

"I suppose so, sweetheart, but it seems a shame to do that and have to come back and get another pair before you've even worn them...."

"Maybe a little peek at the file wouldn't hurt," Gloria said. "Mr. Desmond wants his clients to be happy. I'd just be ensuring that. Now what was your friend's last name?"

"Beaufort," Zellie said. "But she may have used her maiden name, Bean."

"And thank you, Gloria," I added.

"Let's wait a minute until the coast is clear at the computer terminal," Gloria said in a whisper. "I don't need anyone seeing me do this." In a louder voice, she said, "So tell me what your friend looks like. Maybe I was the one that helped her."

"Well she's kind of a buxom platinum blonde with shoulder-length hair, fairly straight," Zellie said.

"Tell her the truth, Zellie," I said. "She goes out of her way to highlight her breasts, often wearing semi-sheer blouses with no bra."

"I don't think I have ever assisted her," Gloria said. "I probably would have remembered that." She smiled at me.

Out of the corner of my eye I noticed that a young man with a short haircut, and neatly dressed with a shirt and tie had perked up when I described Marilyn's bosoms. But he continued without stopping, and went into a side door towards the back of the store. I mentally made a note to talk to him after we got all the information we needed from Gloria. It might be simply a young man's reaction to a description of semi-naked breasts, or it might be a sign of recognition.

And truth be told, I wasn't real comfortable putting Gloria's job at risk in order for Zellie and me to play detective, when we already pretty much knew Marilyn had bought her boots here.

Maybe I don't have the unscrupulous nature required to do this job. Maybe this stuff is for the Jack Buckles' of this world. And I was just the teeniest bit bothered that Zellie was better at deception than I had ever thought.

As if reading my mind, Zellie turned to me. "Arnie, can we talk privately a moment? Don't do anything yet, Gloria, thanks." We stepped aside.

"I can't do this," Zellie whispered.

"I was thinking the same thing. We can't lie to this nice woman about maybe buying these overpriced boots and put her job at risk in the process."

Zellie breathed a sigh of relief. "I went overboard with the rich couple *schtick* before I knew I was doing it, but I don't want us to be that kind of people. We'll find out the information a different way."

"Agreed," I said. We returned to Gloria, who looked puzzled.

"Gloria, we can't lie to you. We're actually private detectives looking into the disappearance of Marilyn Beaufort, nee Bean."

"Private detectives? Do you have some sort of identification? Let me see your license."

"Does everyone but us know you need a license to be a private detective?" I asked, looking at Zellie.

"Apparently so," she said.

"Don't the two of you ever watch television?" Gloria asked in amazement.

Zellie and I looked at each other.

"I guess not enough," we said at the same time.

"You know that even if I was considering getting information for you, I won't now, right?"

"We completely understand," I said.

"Then why did you stop me?"

"Neither of us wanted you to get in trouble and lose your job." Zellie said.

"And you decided to be private detectives for what reason?" Gloria asked us. "Private eyes– at least the ones on TV–are generally pretty unsavory. You two couldn't even carry through a lie to someone like me, who didn't even suspect a problem. You're not even licensed, and don't want to lie." She shook her pretty head. "What in the world will you do when someone challenges you?"

"I thought we would give a disclaimer like… 'You should give us information because we are completely unlicensed and totally unauthorized by any legal authority to make any inquiries of any kind in the course of an investigation.'" I said.

Gloria burst out laughing. "Private-eyes with a conscience. That's a first."

But it worked. Gloria told us to wait for her, and she went to the computer, printed something out and handed it to us.

"Here you go," she said. "Name, address, e-mail, and phone number. And type of boots she purchased, not that you really care about that."

"Why the change of heart?" Zellie asked.

"With your approach, you guys need all the help you can get. Also, your honesty is a refreshing change of pace from what I usually see in here. Now leave, before you get me in trouble, and I do lose my job."

"We're out of here, don't worry," I said, "and thank you, Gloria."

"Yes, thank you." Zellie added.

***

As soon as we left the store, I pulled Zellie close and kissed her right on the mouth, with an ever-so-brief bit of action, if you know what I mean.

"What was that for?" she asked, when we disengaged. "And don't misunderstand me, it was very nice."

"For not letting us lose our souls," I replied. "Let's get out of here."

Zellie smiled at me. "You wouldn't have let it happen either, would you?" With that she took me by the hand and we returned to the car. As we walked, we heard a voice behind us.

"Wait, wait," the voice said. It belonged to the young man I had spied in the store.

"I heard you talking to Gloria about a woman with blonde hair and ...," he looked at Zellie shyly, barely concealed... breasts," he managed finally. "I've seen them…I mean her," he said.

"Where?" I asked.

"In the store. Yesterday. It was Gloria's day off," he added.

"Had you seen her before?" Zellie asked.

"Yes. One other time, a few weeks ago. I remember she bought some cowboy boots. She is kind of hard to forget," he said, with an embarrassed smile, looking again at Zellie.

"Oh, don't worry about that," Zellie said. "Boys will be boys, and she certainly intends for you to look at her. But do you have any information about her?"

"That depends. Why do you want to know?" he asked, with a suddenly sly look on his face.

I sighed. "He wants money, in exchange for information, Zellie. Okay. I'll give you twenty bucks if you tell us something we don't know already."

"Make it fifty."

"I'll give you somewhere between twenty and fifty depending on the quality of your information. Now give."

"Okay, okay, you can't blame a guy for trying to make a buck. I don't get paid all that well. I'm not even a customer satisfaction representative. They get the real money."

"Let's hear it," I said. "What do you have?"

"I followed her out to her car. Not for the reason you think," he said. "I thought a rich lady like that might give me a tip if I offered to help. I got nothing," he added with disgust in his voice. Then he smiled. "But I got a close look at her. At least I got that much for my trouble."

"That information is not worth even twenty bucks," I said, disappointment apparent in my voice. "We already know that much."

"Do you know the make and model of her car? And where she was heading when she left here? How much is that worth?"

"That's better," I said. "You may be able to reach the full amount if it doesn't seem like nonsense to us."

"It was a brand-new Mercedes convertible," he said. "With vanity plates that said 'Fncy Cwgrl.' I'll bet that car cost a fortune," he said. "And she was heading to New York City. There was a New York City slicker-type map open on the passenger seat. I was admiring the car," he said as if in justification for snooping. "Can I have my fifty bucks now?"

"Did you notice anything else?" I pressed.

"I really didn't. My mind was sort of occupied," he said. "My money, please sir, I need to get back inside."

I paid him the full fifty bucks and gave him one of our A to Z Agency cards with a cell number on it. Leaving the Moo Mart phone number would just be too embarrassing if anyone called.

"Call me if you see her again, or think of anything else. We'll make it worth your while."

"Wow, private detectives. Okay, I'll call if I see her again. Bye."

"Well that's interesting," Zellie said when he left. "Fancy Cowgirl? New York? What do you make of that?"

"I don't know," I admitted. "Just another piece to the ever more complicated puzzle of Marilyn Beaufort."

"Well, we have a phone number, address and e-mail, as well as the make of her car and a vanity license plate. That's more than we had before."

"I'll bet the address and phone number are bogus," I said.

"Why do you think that?"

"Marilyn has proven to be a kind of sneaky character, hasn't she? Why would she give her actual address and phone number to a retail store?"

"Well, the name is the same. She used Beaufort this time." Zellie said. "And if her license is really Fancy Cowgirl, that sounds like a connection to Brazen Saddles, doesn't it? That's the look they're selling."

"Yes, it is," I said. "We should probably look into the background of this Desmond fellow. There might be a connection that would be useful. Maybe Ted can help us with that."

"He is the computer *maven*," she agreed. "He can do one of those bizarre search merges he patented through Ted, Inc."

"Yes, that's what I'm thinking. He can use the one that merges regular search engines with public databases and information sources we don't even want to think about."

"I wonder what the New York destination means?" I mused aloud. "It's really not much to go on. It's a big city. She could be going there for any reason. This is central New Jersey. New York is forty miles away. People go there all the time."

"I know," Zellie replied. "But I'll bet there's a reason we need to figure out."

CHAPTER TWELVE

"I understand, Hiram. No, I won't breathe a word of it to him. But I'm glad he's not a target of the investigation." She listened a moment and smiled.

"Yes, always a pleasure to talk to you. We can catch up another time. And thank you, Hiram. Give my regards to Elizabeth. Tell her I may call her next week to have lunch."

Mrs. Minniefield hung up the phone and frowned. Mortal Securities, Inc. was the securities firm that Arnie had not only worked for, but was a junior partner in, and it was under investigation by the Feds. Her old friend, Hiram Towers, was very high up in the Department of Justice, and he'd given her a heads-up about it when she called. Of course, the information hadn't been incidentally volunteered–she'd had to remind him of the many times her assistance had been invaluable to him before he grudgingly provided the information.

"I know how you feel about him, Mabel," he had said warningly, "but telling him about this will only cause problems, both for him and any prosecution that results from this investigation. He's not a target here, Mabel. Of that I can assure you."

She'd of course taken some solace from Hiram's reassurance. But there's real cause for concern, she thought. I'll keep my promise to Hiram and not tell Arnie about the investigation. It won't, however, stop me from taking any action necessary to protect him. There will be no compromise on that.

***

"So, how's the investigation going?" Ted asked. The four of us were sitting at Audacious Bagel, waiting to order lunch.

"I'm glad you asked, Ted," I said. "Along those lines, we have a favor to ask of you."

"We do," Zellie agreed.

"It will require your particular brand of specialized and devious assistance," I added.

"I am intrigued," Ted said. "What do you have in mind?"

"A simple, yet thorough background check on someone."

"You're asking me to use the Searchalyzer? Without any restraints? I am in awe of your boldness."

Ted turned to Marla. "I created a software program that combines ordinary on-line searches, public database collection, and mining of assorted other somewhat less-available data into a global search program that I call the Searchalyzer. All perfectly legal," he added. "Mostly. In some countries. Maybe not this one. But probably so, I think."

Marla rolled her eyes, but said nothing.

"Uh, oh." Ted said. "Are you two trying to completely torpedo my chances of hitting on this lovely woman?" He exchanged a quick smile with Marla. "Who's the lucky subject?"

"Two, actually," I said.

Zellie turned to look at me. "Two?"

"It occurs to me that we never employed Ted's somewhat unorthodox methods to look into Marilyn's background, either."

"True. It may give us new leads."

"The first person is Marilyn Beaufort or Bean, whatever she is calling herself. We sadly have little information about her, but we do have a vanity license plate: 'FNCY CWGRL'. That new information is why I think we're ready to have you do a search on her. The other person is Rene Desmond, the owner and mastermind behind a store in Eatontown, called Brazen Saddles."

"I will begin the search this very afternoon. It will run overnight, and I should have something for you tomorrow, late morning."

At that moment, Delilah came up to our table and asked for our order.

"May I suggest the lasagna bagel for you, Arnie? I just know that you'll enjoy something as delicious as that."

"Okay, Delilah. You've never suggested anything that I didn't end up enjoying. I'll have that. Thanks."

Ted ordered his usual hamburger-infused bagel, and Marla and Zellie split a lox and bagel and cream cheese-infusion.

"She's hot for you, Arnie," Ted said.

"Oh, we're just kidding around. Delilah is a nice person just doing her job–selling specialty bagels."

"If you say so."

"I do," I mumbled, feeling quite indignant about his observation.

Over lunch, we told Ted and Marla about our Brazen Saddles visit and what we'd learned. They both laughed at our unusual method of obtaining information from Gloria.

"I don't think the two of you are prepared to deal with the seedy underbelly of your chosen line of work," Ted said. "It's an unbelievably crooked, nasty, and frankly dangerous profession."

"Are you sure this is what you guys want to do?" Marla asked. "Maybe the two of you could somehow combine Arnie's securities background with Zellie's public relations skills and do something else. Just a thought," Marla said quickly, noticing us both setting our jaws in a rough approximation of steely resolve.

"We're not going to run away from this just because it's hard and our approach is unconventional," I said.

"Or that we're unlicensed and have no skills," Zellie added. We all laughed at that. "But seriously, we have made some progress here, and really would like to see it through."

"Well you can certainly count on me to help," Ted said.

"Me too," Marla added. "You know we just want what's best for you."

"We know," I said. "But if we ultimately decide to do something else, it won't be securities trading or public relations. We've both had our fill of those jobs."

"Amen to that," Zellie echoed.

My phone rang. I looked at the caller ID. "It's the state police. My long-anticipated interview with Mike Mullen, I bet." I answered and listened for a moment.

"Sure, two o'clock is fine with me. I'll be there. Thanks." I hung up. "It's as I thought. I was invited, nicely I might add, to meet with Trooper Mullen this afternoon."

"Do you want me there with you? I'm relatively free this afternoon," Marla asked.

"I don't think it's necessary. No one has given me the slightest indication that I'm under suspicion, or in any way involved in this but for my dumb luck in finding the body. I think Mike just wants to hear it from me directly. My initial interview, you'll recall, was with local cops. If I think the questioning is going in a different direction, I'll call you. And thanks, Marla."

"I agree that if you were a suspect, the manner in which you were invited to speak with them would be different," Marla said. "Tell the truth, and don't hold anything back because of some television idea of client confidentiality. They will have no patience for that, and they're within their rights to ask. Among other reasons, you're not even licensed, and as such, any confidentiality that existed, and frankly there is none anyway, doesn't apply to you. And one more thing. You called Trooper Mullen, Mike. Do you know him?"

"We went to school with him" Zellie said.

"Well, my experience with him, is that he's smart, tough and thoroughly honest. Don't let personal feelings make you think he's a pushover."

"I'm just going to tell him the truth," I said. "I have no intention of making his job difficult. He's investigating a murder. That's serious business, and I know it."

"Okay, just putting my lawyer hat on. And friend hat, too," she added.

"I know, Marla. Thank you."

"Do you want company?" Zellie asked me.

"No, that's okay. You won't be allowed in anyway. I'll just give my statement and meet you back at my place in an hour or so. But thanks."

Zellie looked at me without her customary smile, then nodded. "Okay, if you're sure. Marla and I will be here for a while. Call if you need either of us."

***

"He kissed me today," Zellie said when the men had left the restaurant. She and Marla had remained at the table.

"Whoa. Tell me about it. Was it a *real* kiss, or a kind of lame, we're-just-friends-you-could-be-my-sister-type kiss?"

"Oh, it was a real one. A doozy, if you want to know the truth."

"Tell me more," Marla begged. "Leave no detail unspoken."

Zellie told her the events leading up to the kiss. "He pulled me real close. I could feel his heart beating, or maybe it was mine, I don't know. But it was real intimate. And he planted one right on my lips. It was really gentle - he has the softest lips - but incredibly passionate, with just the slightest bit of tongue grazing my lips."

"How do you feel about it?"

"Well, I know it was a spontaneous action on his part. But it felt right. It was warm and safe, but incredibly sexy and bold. I do love him, you know."

"I know you do, Zellie. And he loves you, too."

"I know he does. But we're still working things out. And we need time to find ourselves. Neither of us wants to screw anything up, so maybe we're playing it too safely. We don't want to just be rebound partners, either. It hasn't been that long since our two messy breakups."

"It's been more than a year, Zellie," Marla said gently. "At some point people need to throw caution to the wind, and take a chance. Whether that's right for you and Arnie is of course up to the two of you. But I'd hate to see two soul mates avoid what could be a wonderful life together out of fear."

"I know, Marla. But you should understand that one of the few things that saved us after our breakups was our unyielding, uncomplicated, strong friendship."

CHAPTER THIRTEEN

Mike extended a hand. "Nice to see you again, Arnie. I truly hate it to be under these circumstances, but it can't be avoided. I really appreciate you coming over on short notice."

"Of course. Investigating a murder takes precedence over anything else I might be doing. What can I do to help?"

"I just want to go over the circumstances leading to your discovery of Mr. Martin's body."

"Mr. Martin? Oh, of course. We all knew him as Greasy Sid. So, Martin was his last name?"

"Yes, Sidney Martin. Aged 83. Married to Abigail Martin. Owner and very long-time manager, cook, bartender and anything else that was required, of the Stone Parrot Pub in Keansburg. Could you start from the beginning, please? How did you come to visit the Stone Parrot that day?"

"As I explained to the police officers, I wanted to ask Sid some questions about our client. I suppose you heard that Zellie and I opened a detective agency, but forgot that you need to be licensed. If you could get the laughter out now, I'd appreciate it."

Mike smiled. "I'm not going to laugh at you Arnie. But I'm a little curious why a securities trader and a public relations expert decided to open a detective agency. That's kind of a seedy profession, isn't it? And how is Zellie? She's one of the good people in this world."

"She's fine, Mike. I'll tell her you asked about her."

"Yes, please do. Let's get back to the background, if we could."

I told Mike about Marilyn's visit, including her dress, demeanor, and her apparently bogus desire for us to locate her long lost ex-husband Stanley. I also told him that Sid had said that Marilyn (or at least someone named Marilyn) had worked for him as a bouncer, and that she used to weigh 300 pounds. I explained our reasoning in continuing to try to locate Marilyn – to give her the report she had paid for, including our intention to charge her for time spent locating her, and Mike chuckled at that.

"Very mercenary of you, Arnie," he said. "But certainly warranted under the circumstances," he quickly added.

"We just figured that if she was going to waste our time, she should pay for it."

I gave Mike the rest of what we knew, which was not much as it turned out. I told him about our trip to Brazen Saddles, and what we found out there, leaving out the details on how we obtained the information.

"Look, Arnie..." Mike began, "I probably shouldn't tell you this, but I think I will anyway – maybe to protect you and Zellie. It's too early to tell for certain, but Sid's death was probably a mob hit."

I looked at him in amazement. "Greasy Sid? A mobster? He was the fatherly figure who always looked older than dirt, and more or less always had a kind word for all the kids. He was as much a good influence on us all as a bar owner could be while serving alcohol to under-aged teenagers."

"Arnie, Sid's older brother is Nicholas "Fat Nicky" Martinson. He's the head of the South Jersey mob. Or at least the former boss. He's probably in his eighties now. Look, I don't really think at this point that this Marilyn character of yours is particularly related to what looks to be a family dispute. But this is not something you and Zellie should be messing around with. There is a certain reluctance on the part of mobsters to kill policemen, and we all carry guns in any event. But the two of you don't really have those protections." He stopped for a moment. "Well, you're not a cop, anyway, and can I assume that you don't carry your weapon?"

I shook my head. Mike was referring to my fairly accomplished marksmanship skills. I had in fact won many awards as an amateur competitor in high school and college. I still practiced at the range pretty regularly, but no, I emphatically did not carry a gun for any other purpose.

"And Zellie doesn't carry a gun, either," he continued. "Also, you don't really even have a client at this point. For your own good, leave this one alone. Please."

"I appreciate what you're telling me, Mike."

"Arnie, it's been a long time, but I know you. You'll smile and act like you're agreeing, but you never really say you are. And then you go ahead and do what you want anyway. Zellie is exactly like that, too, and truth be told I kind of liked that about her. But this one's for keeps, Arnie. Please leave it alone. There will be other cases."

Mike smiled, "And maybe you'll be licensed by then. Heck, I may send you cases myself if they don't look like police matters. Lord knows we need decent people in that business. Not like our good friend Jack Buckles, eh, Arnie?"

"No, we're nothing like him, that's for sure."

"Arnie, are you and Zellie a couple now?"

"Well…not exactly." I stammered. And what's with the stutter? I wondered. Competition alert! Competition alert! Go into defensive mode!

Mike smiled. "You two have been "not exactly" for a long time, haven't you?"

"Zellie and I have been best friends since we were kids, Mike. That hasn't changed a bit."

"So, it's strictly platonic, like it was in high school? That's good to know." Mike didn't wait for an answer. "Because, I find myself single again." Mike continued somewhat ruefully. "Helen and I broke up."

"I heard about that. I'm sorry, Mike." Uh oh. . ..

"Oh, it's okay. It has been over for some time. We just made it official. Anyway, thanks again for coming in Arnie." Mike transformed back into professional law enforcement officer. "We'll let you know if we require any further statement from you."

We shook hands and I left, feeling vaguely upset by the whole conversation.

I drove back home and Matilda mercifully behaved herself. No sudden stalls or coughing fits either to the State Police barracks or home. Probably all that talk about a new car made Matilda behave. But the "Matilda Effect" had worked. I was just a little calmer after getting into the car.

"Don't worry, Matilda. I'm not about to part with you," I said. Then I let out a chuckle. Mike had described me accurately. I had told Zellie we could look for a new car. I never said I'd buy one. Agreeable, but mostly unyielding.

Zellie was playing with Lazlow when I got home. Basically, that means throwing the ball for him, and then more or less chasing it yourself, because he's far too lazy to actually chase after it. He just kind of looks at you, gives you this "why are you bothering me" put-upon look, slowly rises to his feet, and more or less strolls in the direction of the ball. At that point-and I swear this is true-he points to it so that one of us actually picks it up. We engage in this little game, because it *is* fun. Really.

I told Zellie about giving my statement, and our discussion. I did tell her that Mike had said hello. But I didn't share the part about our relationship discussion. I'm not going to interfere with any relationship Zellie might have. But I'm damn sure not going to help one along, either.

"You don't want to give up the investigation, do you?" she asked.

"No, I don't think so. I appreciate Mike trying to protect us. But he sort of had to say that as a cop, didn't he?"

"Probably so. And didn't you tell me he said that he doubts that Marilyn is related to his murder investigation?"

"Well, he did qualify it by saying 'at this point' and 'particularly related,' but that was the gist, yes."

"But he didn't specifically order us not to stay involved, did he?" Zellie pressed.

"No. He didn't order us. He asked. And probably a lot more nicely than the jerks who took me downtown would have. And he did point out the potential danger."

"But we don't want to interfere with his murder investigation. We just want to find Marilyn. I think we're making some progress."

"I'm on board, Zellie. I just thought I should tell you what Mike said about the potential danger."

"I understand. We'll just have to try to stay out of trouble."

I laughed at that. "Easier said than done."

"I'm glad we settled that. So, what's next?" she asked.

"Mike won't like this much, but I think we visit Sid's widow."

"Isn't that perilously close to Mike's murder investigation?"

"Maybe. But we'll only ask her whether she knew Marilyn. And any information she may have about her. That's it."

"Okay. We can go right now. I already took Lazlow for a walk.

"I think we should call ahead and see if she's willing to see us. She's in mourning, you know. And really, I haven't seen her since high school. Have you?"

"No, I haven't seen her, either. But maybe we can just say we want to pay our respects, and if it doesn't seem too forward, ask a few questions about Marilyn."

"There are some real unpleasant things about this business, you know that?"

"Agreed. Have to take the bad with the good," I mumbled.

I fished out my phone. "Hello, Mrs. Martin? My name is Arnie Fischer. My friend Zellie Morgan and I knew Sid from our days going to the Stone Parrot. We'd like to stop by and pay our respects either this afternoon or tomorrow morning. Is either time okay with you? We don't want to impose. You have other visitors there today? Okay. We'll be over shortly. Thank you, Mrs. Martin. Okay, I'll call you Abigail. We'll see you soon."

"This is sort of their version of sitting Shiva," I said to Zellie, comparing it to the Jewish custom of having visitors drop by bearing various kinds of food when someone in the family has passed away.

"Should we get a fruit basket, or something?" Zellie asked.

"I think maybe a coffee cake or some pastries would be nice," I said. "We can stop at Spectacularly Sweet on the way over there."

"Okay. I'll drive. You may not have had an incident with your car yet today, but we don't want to push our luck."

"Fine with me. I'll just get Lazlow some fresh water and we can go."

We walked out to Zellie's car and got in. "To the bakery, Madame driver. And step on it."

"Don't you want to sit in the back, Miss Daisy?" Zellie laughed.

"No. I think not. Today, I join the little people, up front."

"Then let's go. Stepping on it as directed, sir."

We rode in companionable silence. Some people are uncomfortable with silence. Zellie and I know each other so well that we can keep quiet sometimes without one of us feeling the need to speak just to engage in chit chat. We are good at communicating without words, too, but sometimes we both just want to quietly enjoy each other's company—or think things over independently.

I didn't know what Zellie was thinking about, but I felt a little confused and slightly uncomfortable about my conversation with Mike. And, the fact that I didn't tell Zellie about it was unsettling, too. I tell Zellie everything.

What do I want? Are Zellie and I looking at each other differently because of our recent failed relationships? Are we afraid of losing each other by becoming more to each other? And if so, are we cowards by not just taking a chance?

I glanced ever-so-slightly in her direction. She's so beautiful. And *so* smart. She's my best friend. What on earth could go wrong for us? But what would we do if we lost each other? A life-long friendship, gone because we had to mess with a good thing.

Zellie interrupted my reverie. "There's a lot going on over there, Arnie. I don't mind us being quiet, but I don't see how you could be any noisier with your thoughts."

My laugh was short, nervous. "I think Mike is interested in calling you, Zellie. For a date." I blurted out. "And I think I didn't tell you because I see him as a threat."

"Let me pull over and we can talk," She said, putting on her turn signal.

She pulled into a strip mall, and parked. "Okay, out with it."

"You want to hear about what Mike said?"

"No, you dope. I want you to tell me why you feel competitive with a guy I went out with more than thirty years ago, in high school. While you were going steady with Laura, I might add."

"I don't know. Things have been different between us in the last year or so. We've turned to each other for affection and support and we've been there for each other. We've even had rebound sex. I know we've discussed dating other people again, in order to get things back to normal, but I'm not sure I'm ready to leave the comfort zone we've established with each other."

Zellie looked at me and smiled. "I'm going through the same things, Arnie. And I'm not particularly ready to commit to other people again, either, even if it may be better for us to explore that. I do know that we will never lose each other, no matter what we do. We've been best friends for more than fifty years. I will say this: There is no rush here, and no crime in us taking the time to sort things out. And by the way – it was *great* rebound sex."

I smiled at her. "Yes, it was. It truly was. Thank you, Zellie. I love you."

"I love you, too Arnie."

"Okay, driver, on to the bakery."

We picked up a box of pastries and drove over to Keansburg. Mrs. Martin greeted us warmly at the door.

"Arnie, Zellie, it's nice of you to come by. I haven't seen you in many years. Sid would have liked to know that two of his kids, as he called all of you, remembered him so many years later. And thank you for the pastries. They look delicious." She leaned in conspiratorially. "I'm going to set these aside to eat later, myself. If I put them out, these vultures will scarf them right up." She gestured at a group of people milling about in her living room.

"We're so sorry about Sid…" I began.

"Yes, a terrible thing to happen," Zellie added.

"Thank you, dears. It really is quite a shock. But I'm trying to stay composed. For the guests, you know."

"We'll get out of your way quickly, then," I said. "We don't want to impose."

"Nonsense. You two are a delight to see. It's Sid's family over there that I would dearly like to see leave quickly. But they won't. They did everything they could to ruin Sid's life, and they'll hang on forever like the bloodsuckers they are."

Zellie and I shifted on our feet uncomfortably.

"But please don't listen to an old lady and her complaints. Can I get you a soda, or something stronger? Perhaps a finger sandwich? From Stalwarts?"

Stalwarts was a local caterer with a terrific reputation.

"Maybe we'll help ourselves in a little bit, Mrs. Martin. Don't trouble yourself."

"Please call me Abigail. All of you used to say yes ma'am and no ma'am to me, while you called Sidney by his first name." She smiled. *"Greasy."*

We looked at her in amazement.

"You're surprised, aren't you? Sid loved that nickname. It made him feel like he wasn't just some old fart who ran a bar. He was part of it. And if you don't mind, I don't need an adjective in front of my name. Abigail would be just fine."

"Abigail, it is," we said in unison.

Abigail looked at us closely. "Are the two of you married?"

"No, we're not married. We are very, very good friends." I smiled at Zellie and she smiled back.

Abigail looked at us for a moment. "You look good together," she said. "My Sidney and I were married for more than fifty years. We had our ups and downs over the years, but we never stopped loving each other. It's what made the last couple of years so hard."

"What do you mean? Did something happen in the last couple of years that changed things?" Zellie asked.

Abigail gave her a shrewd look. "You're nice kids. And you kindly bit on an old lady's hanging statement, one that almost begged you to ask about it. Sweet of you. But are you sure you want to hear my laments?"

"Only if you want to tell us," I said.

"I think I need to tell someone, so you're elected. Thank you. Let's go onto the porch to get a little privacy."

We all moved outside. If anyone else in the living room noticed, they didn't evidence it.

"Sit down, dears. Sidney wasn't necessarily what he appeared to be," she began. "His brother Nicholas Martinson is a crime boss – you may have heard of the Martinson crime family - and he never stopped pressuring Sidney to join him. My Sidney never wanted to, and as far as I know, he resisted his brother's entreaties for many years. He even legally changed his name to Martin. But Nick never gave up. You see, the Stone Parrot was a perfect legitimate business for money laundering, and Nick wanted it badly."

"So badly he would kill his brother?" I couldn't help asking.

"No, I don't think Nick did it," she said. "I suppose one of his associates might have. But let me continue."

"Nick upped the pressure in the last few years. The bar was not as busy, and the expenses piled up. Sidney was in danger of losing the bar – not to Nick – but to his creditors. I told Sidney that we didn't need the bar, that we could live just fine on Social Security and our savings. But the bar meant everything to him…"

"So, he borrowed money from his brother," Zellie filled in.

"Yes," she said sadly. "He did. Without telling me. And his bastard of a brother finally got his claws into Sidney, and the Stone Parrot. But I swear, Sidney was never part of the Martinson crime family. He was just a guy who owed them money. He never engaged in any criminal activity. And the police are saying he was a crime family member. That's just not true."

"Did he allow the Stone Parrot to be a conduit for laundering money?" I asked gently.

"Probably. But he never would have told me that, so I couldn't say for sure. It was probably the price he had to pay to get the loan."

"I'm sorry, Abigail. This must have been very hard for you," I said.

"At least I got to tell someone," she said. "Thank you."

"May we ask you something, Abigail?" Zellie asked.

"What is it?"

"Just a person we knew at one time. Have you ever heard of Marilyn Beaufort, or Bean? We think she used to work at the Stone Parrot."

"A lot of people worked there, but the name is not familiar to me."

"She is a buxom blonde, who may have worked as a cocktail waitress, and may have worked as a bouncer when she was much heavier," I said.

"I don't recall anyone like that, although Sidney had many blonde waitresses over the years. I don't remember any female bouncers, though."

"Okay, thank you. We were just curious."

On our drive home, I asked Zellie to pull over and park in the same place we had talked before.

"Listen, Zellie. About what we said before. I don't think our fear of commitment should stop us from going out on dates. If Mike calls you, and you want to go, please don't turn him down because you're afraid I might be upset. He's a good guy, and you might enjoy his company – and anything more you two want to do. It's okay with me. Really," I said.

"This isn't giving permission – you don't need that – it's just an expression of how I feel. I think you're right about us getting back into the game, so to speak. If we end up having real committed relationships again, that's fine, we're living in the present, not the past. It's not going to hurt our friendship – it hasn't for fifty years. That's one commitment about which we've never wavered. And if we find that nothing out there compares to us being together in all ways – I'm pretty sure that would work out just fine for us. In the meantime, we can enjoy the company of members of the opposite sex, without necessarily having to think they might be marriage material and without rushing into anything between us that we aren't ready for."

"Arnie," she said. "I'm okay with us going out again. I suggested it after all. We've avoided it because we were both burned in our most recent ventures into the wonderful world of romance, and don't want to repeat our mistakes. All we're talking about is getting out there a little. I don't see this as a trial separation, by the way. We've always had a wonderful friendship at the same time we were dating other people. Our talk of getting together is a recent phenomenon, more or less thrust upon us by a convergence of events. A nice phenomenon, to be sure, but definitely a new one." Zellie smiled warmly at me. "At the end of the day, Arnie, we'll be together in one way or another. That much is certain."

She drove me home. "I have a few things to do now, Arnie. I'll meet you at the office in the morning."

I kissed her gently on the lips. "Okay, I'll see you tomorrow."

I waved goodbye to Zellie and walked to the door to my house. Funny, I didn't remember leaving any lights on. Probably Lazlow trying to gaslight me, I thought, with a smile.

I fished out my key and inserted it into the lock and turned it left as I always do. No pressure. *It was already open.*

I opened the door and went inside. Jennifer. Sitting calmly on my sofa. The picture of serenity.

And completely, utterly, stark naked.

CHAPTER FOURTEEN

"Hi, Arnie. Miss me?"

I hesitated for only a half second. "You have a hell of a nerve showing your face…and everything else…around here after what you did to me."

She ignored me. "You know, if you really wanted to keep me out, you might have thought to change the locks. Imagine my delight that my key still worked."

"I'll remember to do that tomorrow," I said dryly. "What do you want? Haven't you already bled me dry?"

"Now, now, Arnie. You know it wasn't me who took your money. It was a bad investment, that's all. And is that the way to talk to a former lover?" She stood up. "Do you like what you see?"

The truth was, I did like what I saw. Jennifer just exudes sexuality. She's five-eight, has shoulder length, very thick, dark-brown hair, and deep, dark, sapphire-blue eyes. Her bosom is ample, but not too large, and those pert breasts stand up firmly and proudly on her chest. Her perfectly toned abs and curvy butt are equally magnificent, and those legs, my goodness, those legs – firm and almost muscular, yet sleek and delicate. Jennifer had the whole physical package and she knew it. She stood before me without a flicker of self-consciousness or inhibition.

"Yes, Jennifer, you're totally hot," I finally said. "But I'm still not interested. Now cut to the chase. What do you want?"

"Maybe I just want to rekindle our longstanding romance," she said.

"Sure, you do. And maybe I'm the same kid who left medical school to follow you around the country, or the gullible adult who welcomed you back into my life only to be stripped of my retirement savings."

"That's putting things a little harshly, Arnie. For one thing, I didn't lure you away from medical school. You wanted to leave long before I even got there."

She was right about that, damn her. I didn't respond.

"For another thing, I told you. I was as surprised as you when that investment went sour. I no more stole from you than the New York Stock Exchange steals from anyone whose stocks lose their value. Anyway, you're the expert securities trader, not me. If anything, I should be mad at you, not the other way around. But I hold no grudges, Arnie. You've always been the best thing in my life. I'm back, and don't want to screw it up this time."

I sighed. "You're not going to make this easy, are you? Fine. Put some clothes on, Jennifer, and get out of my house. As much as I'm enjoying the view, I don't want to give you the impression that I give a shit about anything you say."

If I'd hurt her feelings, it didn't show. Almost without a blink, she shrugged. "All right, Arnie. We'll play it your way. I'll leave. But I'm not going away. This time, I have no intention of running off. Oh, and Arnie...," she paused for dramatic effect. "Tell Zellie I'm looking forward to seeing her again."

I wondered what she meant by that, but I wasn't going to let it show. "Sure, sure, Jennifer, I'll bet she's dying to see you, too. Now get out of here."

Jennifer pulled a white cotton one-piece dress over her head – without bothering to don her underwear - and smiled at me lasciviously. "Okay, I'm out of here. For now. See you again soon, Arnie."

She picked up her purse, dropped her underthings into it, and headed for the door, kissing me on my neck as she passed by. I hated myself for it, but the kiss gave me goose bumps. Jennifer *still* had an effect on me.

To say that Jennifer's visit had unnerved me was possibly the understatement of the century. I sat for a long time in my living room, going over the whole brief episode in my head. I was proud of myself that I had sent her away without succumbing to Jennifer's considerable sex appeal.

In all honesty, however, I had to admit that it was considerably harder to do than I would have imagined. We had a history. And, we had a mutual sexual attraction that I couldn't just ignore.

Of course, romanticizing our past relationship is what got me into trouble the last time she showed up, I thought bitterly. She's not going to do it to me again. But to be honest with myself, I had to recognize that there was a part of me – a very horny part of me – that wanted very much to partake of what she had offered. I needed to keep that under control if she made good on her promise to stick around.

A larger concern for me was her comment about looking forward to seeing Zellie, again. She knew that Zellie hated her guts, and would do anything to protect me. And, vice versa. I had little doubt that Jennifer had a specific and non-benevolent reason for her comment. Zellie needed to be warned.

***

"Omigod, omigod, omigod. I'll be right over," Zellie cried into the phone when I told her about my surprise visitor.

"Zellie, it's okay. I just wanted to. . .."

But she was gone. What must have been two seconds later, I heard a knock on the door and she burst in and embraced me.

"Are you okay, Arnie? Should I call Ted and Marla? Do we need to do, like, an intervention or something?" She looked around suspiciously. "Is she still here?"

"Zellie, she's gone. I'm fine. And how did you get here so fast? I know we're in the same neighborhood and everything, but it should have taken you at least ten minutes to walk."

"I drove. Fast. Very fast, okay? I was worried."

"Well thank you for your concern. But really, I'm okay."

"What did she say? What did she do? What did *you* do? How long was she here? Were you happy to see her?"

I laughed. "Those are a lot of questions. And said almost in a single syllable. Very impressive. You may want to take a deep breath." I sobered at her expression. "Seriously, she denies that she ripped me off – insists that it was a bad investment and not her fault. She inferred that since I was the securities trader, I should have prevented it. She went on about I'm the best thing that ever happened to her and she plans on staying around awhile. She was here only about ten minutes before I threw her out. She was stark naked, sitting pretty much where you're sitting now."

Zellie jumped up as if hit by a cattle prod. "Eww, ick. I need a shower."

Under different circumstances, her reaction would have made me laugh myself silly, but I was worried. "She also said to tell you that she's looking forward to seeing you again. Any idea what she meant by that?"

She shook her head. "Probably just looking to cause trouble. She never liked me, you know. Maybe she's referring to the pretty heated argument we got into after your so-called investment went sour and now she's looking for payback. I did go so far as to threaten her with bodily harm if she showed her face around here again. I know I shouldn't have said that, but I was pretty mad at the time."

I smiled. "It's okay, Zellie."

"So, she just left after you threw her out?"

"Pretty much. Or at least, I think so. I didn't go outside to make sure she left." I closed my eyes. "She said she wasn't going away. . .."

"Arnie…" Zellie started. "Do you still have feelings for her?"

"You know, I don't think so. Although, I will admit to being a little affected by her sexual energy, and please don't make me spell it out."

"Well, we' have to take care of that right now." Zellie said

"Really, Zellie?" I said with a wink. "After our heart to heart discussion today? I thought we were putting that in abeyance for the time being."

"No, I didn't mean…, er, well okay, I guess, it would be fun, but…Arnie! This is so confusing."

I burst out laughing. "It's okay, Zellie. But I'm curious as to what you had in mind."

"Before your little fun at my expense, I was going to suggest that you call one of those nice, but very slutty women you used to date before 'She' returned the first time."

"Hey, they weren't slutty," I objected.

"Oh please. Of course, they were, and are. Exactly what the doctor ordered. Now what were their names? Tanya… or Tammy, I think."

"I went out with Tanya this week. She's the French teacher. I think I ruined that one by talking about you too much. But I will call Tammy, the aerobics instructor."

"The one with the big….?"

"Yes, her. She's very nice. I'll give her a call."

"The perfect choice."

***

I stumbled into the Moo Mart at a little after nine. Zellie was already there, sipping her mocha latte.

"Good morning!" she said brightly.

"Gdmrng," I managed in reply.

"Long night?" She giggled. "Eddie, get my friend here an extra, extra, large coffee, please. How was your date with Tammy?"

I took a big swig of the coffee Eddie brought. "She's nice. I had a really good time. I relaxed for a change. It was pleasant. And she was okay with the last-minute call. Said she wasn't busy, and was happy to hear from me."

"I'm glad, Arnie. I really am. Maybe a little jealous, but happy it went well."

"I must admit that I'd be sort of disappointed if you didn't care at all. But it's nothing serious with Tammy – she's a lot of fun and a truly nice person, but she's not looking for a commitment any more than I am at this point."

"I won't ask for details…although I'm dying to know."

"And I don't kiss and tell," I said with a smile.

"Oh fine, be that way. Appropriately discrete and all. It's an outrage." She laughed. "So, should we talk about the case, about Jennifer, about the weather, sports? What?"

"I think we should go over what Abigail Martin told us. We never really analyzed it."

Zellie nodded at me. "It was a little unusual, wasn't it?"

"Yes. She didn't seem that distraught about Sid, although she told us she was just keeping her composure for the sake of the relatives. I guess that's possible," I said doubtfully. "And the timing was weird. At a wake, with a bunch of mobsters sitting in the living room, while we talked about them on the porch."

"And why tell us the story?"

"That's the $64,000 question, isn't it?" I said.

"It seems like we've been here before. Don't we also wonder why Marilyn chose to tell us that cock and bull story about Stanley and working at the Stone Parrot? And Jack Buckles, who hates us, just happening to refer a potential client to us?"

"And Gloria, just giving us information at great risk to her job."

"And the kid in the parking lot of Brazen Saddles just appearing and wanting to give us information," I added.

"At a price, though."

I shook my head slowly. "But if you remember, I was the first one to raise the issue of money. I just assumed that's what he was after. He may very well have given us the information without paying him, and like a dolt, I played right into his hands." I sipped my coffee. Being played the fool wasn't a happy experience for me. "We're being led around by the nose, aren't we? But why?"

"Maybe Ted will have some information. That, at least, will be legitimate."

"Let's hope so. And I think we can also trust what Mike Mullen told me. We have no reason not to believe him."

Zellie sipped her coffee, thinking about something before she replied. "No. But you can be sure he's not giving you the full story."

"No. He certainly isn't."

"So, what should we do until Ted gives us his report?"

"I think we should think about what we actually know, as opposed to what we've been told."

"Doesn't that leave very little? We've learned most things through talking to people."

"Not everything," I reminded her. "For example, we did meet with Marilyn. She's real, although certainly not who she said she is. And I think we can safely say that she obtained those boots from Brazen Saddles. I don't know anywhere else that carries them."

"And if we are being fed information, whether or not it's true, there is some connection with Brazen Saddles, or why bother to tell us anything?"

"That's what I mean, exactly. There's obviously a connection to the Stone Parrot as well. We need to start considering what we're *not* being told, and looking beneath the information we *are* being given."

"Do you think everyone is lying to us?"

"I don't know that we need to go that far. But we probably should take everything said with a large measure of skepticism, that's for sure."

"Okay, so what do we know for certain?"

"We know that Marilyn exists, whoever she is."

"And we know that she asked us to find her lost husband, Stanley."

"Right. And we know what she was wearing that day. And that she's worn similar outfits before, too."

"Yes. The 'Brazen Saddles' look all the way down to the cowboy boots."

"We know there is some connection to the Stone Parrot. For one, because Marilyn made a point of mentioning it, as did Abigail Martin, but also because I was unlucky enough to find Sid dead there."

"Was that by luck or design?" Zellie asked pointedly.

"Good point. We don't know."

"No, we don't. But we do know that Sid was related to a mobster."

"Do we know that, or were we just told that?"

"I think we know there's a mob connection of some sort. Mike told you that, and Abigail made a point of telling us as well. But the real proof was in that group assembled in Abigail's living room. They had mob written all over them, if that's possible."

"They sure did," I agreed.

"Arnie, I hate to ask this, sensitive a topic as it is, but is it possible that Jennifer is related to this somehow?"

"Hard to see how. Why do you ask, other than her less-than-stellar financial dealings?"

"Why did she come back now, as opposed to a month ago, or a month from now. It's an odd coincidence, that's all."

"Good point. Another thing we don't know, I guess. But I'm not about to call her and ask."

"I'm guessing we haven't seen the last of her, so you may get that opportunity whether you like it or not."

I sighed. "You're probably right."

"Well enough of this for now. We'll know more when Ted tells us the results of his overnight search. If we can pry him away from whatever he's working on."

"Some new invention having to do with shoelaces, or something, he said. I never know what he's talking about. While we're waiting for him, we might as well check out the information Gloria gave us, for what it's worth. I'm guessing it's all bogus."

"You'd be guessing correctly. I already checked it out this morning. The address doesn't exist, the phone number is for the Sisters of Charity, and the e-mail address just bounces. Return to sender."

"So, we have the Sisters of Charity dead to rights?"

"That's about all we have. And I'm not thinking the charges will stand up. We're back to waiting for Ted."

"That's my cue."

Ted slid in next to Zellie on the couch, then waved to Eddie, who moved to fix a coffee for him. "I have in my hand the report you asked me to run. The price is one cup of coffee."

Eddie handed him the cup and waited. "Ah, very good, thanks Eddie."

"Okay, here's the rundown. Marilyn Beaufort, Marilyn Bean, doesn't matter – neither person exists. FNCY CWGRL license plate – *does* exist. Issued to one Madeline Desmond, the beautiful and talented spouse of Rene Desmond, the owner and genius behind Brazen Saddles. Rene Desmond – looks like you were right to ask me to run him as well. He is both exactly as he seems–a successful specialty boutique owner and trendsetter and–drumroll please–connected to the mob.

"Looks like Brazen Saddles is a legitimate business set up by the South Jersey mob to launder money. Nominally part of Fat Nicky Martinson's organization, but also separate, and arguably in competition with him. Brazen Saddles was probably financed through drug or other illicit funds. Desmond is also up to his ears in all sorts of shady dealings from housing swindles – you've heard of the scams – low income housing created just for the purpose of getting Federal money then torching or demolishing the houses and leaving poor people out in the cold – that kind of thing – to insider trading and other financial rip-offs. He's a real peach, Rene Desmond. Somehow he has eluded prosecution."

"I'm not going to ask how you found all this out, Ted, but tell me – how do you know Marilyn doesn't exist?"

"No one is that totally off the grid, Arnie. No one. My search algorithms are the best. If she existed, there'd be traces. There are no traces."

"Well, we met someone," Zellie said.

"Of course, you did. Just someone who has no past of any kind."

"There's only one type of person I can think of with no past," I said.

"Exactly. Witness protection."

"But that doesn't make any sense, either. Why would someone in the witness protection program expose themselves like that?"

Zellie giggled. "Expose themselves, Arnie? She was pretty scantily clad, I grant you that. But she was fully clothed. Sort of. But seriously, there is nothing about this thing that makes any sense."

"I wonder if *our* Marilyn is really Madeline Desmond?" I mused.

"Nope. Don't think so. Here's her picture." Ted held up a magazine photo. "Tall and thin. Very little bosom. Dark brown hair. Definitely not Marilyn."

I held up my hand to ask for quiet. "That's my phone." I looked at the caller ID. "It's Mrs. Minniefield. Let me see what's up."

"Hi, Mrs. M. Is everything okay?" I looked at Zellie and Ted as I listened.

"Sure, Zellie and I can come over now. Anything in particular?"

"No, I understand. We can talk when we get there. Is it okay to bring Lazlow?"

"Great, I'll call Betsy and tell her not to bother walking him today. I'm sure she would appreciate having one less dog to worry about."

I ended the call and looked over at Ted. "She asked for Zellie and me. And you know Mrs. Minniefield. She is very precise in what she requests."

"It's no problem, Arnie, I take no offense. I want to get back to my lab anyway."

"Thanks Ted. If you want, we can swing by your place on our way, pick up Larry and bring him along, too. I'm sure Mrs. Minniefield won't mind. It will give Fideaux both of his henchmen to plan ways to torment us all."

"Sounds good. Let's go," Ted said, getting to his feet.

I called Betsy, and she sounded relieved when I told her. "That's great, Arnie. Two of my walkers are out sick today and I have to cover for them. And I always like to take care of Lazlow personally. And this takes care of Larry, too. Perfect. I'll just pick them both up at Mrs. Minniefield's house later in the afternoon, and bring them both home."

"Okay, I'll tell Mrs. Minniefield to expect you then."

Zellie and I followed Ted home and collected Larry, then went to my house. "Wait a minute, I'll get Lazlow and come right out."

I unlocked the door and dashed into the house.

"Oh, no!"

CHAPTER FIFTEEN

I went outside and motioned Zellie to come in.

"Look at this."

Zellie stopped short when she saw the mess.

"Whoa! What happened here?"

"Looks like someone was conducting a thorough, but unbelievably messy search. But I can't imagine what they were searching for. I only keep a few emergency bucks in a drawer, and I don't have any jewelry or valuable possessions. I have old tax returns and mostly non-sensitive old work records in my file cabinet...which clearly has been rifled through," I said, looking at it.

"Is anything missing?" Zellie asked.

"I can't see anything offhand. The cash is still here in the top drawer – all $100 or so of it ...wait a second...my old personnel folder isn't here, and I'm sure it was before. I've been meaning to put that in my safe deposit box with the rest of the stuff, but haven't gotten around to it."

"You put personnel records in a safe deposit box?"

"I put lots of stuff in there, but mostly financial records, the house deed, and personal items I want secured. And by the looks of things here, that was probably a good idea."

"Geez, I better get one myself. But I wonder what they were looking for?"

"Beats me. But I'd better call the police and report it."

I called it in, and was assured someone would arrive shortly. Then I called Mrs. Minniefield and told her what happened. I promised we'd be by after the police finished.

"I tell you, Zellie, that woman is sometimes downright spooky."

"She is definitely not ordinary," Zellie agreed, "but what is it this time?"

"It's almost like she expected this to happen. She acted utterly unsurprised. Concerned, yes. But surprised, no."

"Well maybe she'll explain when we get there. If we ever get there. Where are the police?"

"They said within the hour. It hasn't been that long. At least they asked whether it was an emergency– I told them it wasn't."

"I'll let Larry out, so that he doesn't go in the car," Zellie said as she headed outside.

I looked at Lazlow. "Some watchdog you are. I'll bet you helped the intruders toss the place. This is the second time in two days that you've let intruders just walk in and do anything they want to…." I trailed off, and put my hand on my temple. The second time. I still hadn't changed the locks on the place. The door was closed, and the lock didn't look forced. I wonder if….

Zellie led Larry into the house, and he promptly collapsed next to Lazlow. The dogs barely exchanged a greeting, but their tails were wagging.

"He emptied about a gallon of pee on your front yard. I'm glad I went to get him."

"Me too. I don't need another mess to clean up."

"I'll help you, Arnie. But we should probably wait for the police to examine the place. Preservation of evidence and all."

And that would have been a good idea, if the Middletown Police had sent over competent officers. Which they didn't. I opened the door to Officers Heckle and Jeckle, the very same cops who had brought me downtown after Sid's death and given me such a hard time.

"Hello, Mr. Fischer. What trouble are you in this time?"

"Who's the babe?" The other one gestured in Zellie's direction.

"The babe, as you put it, is Ms. Morgan, officer," Zellie huffed.

"Just being friendly. No need to take offense."

Discretion being the better part of valor (and punching him in the nose not being an option), I ignored the exchange. "Officer Madison, Officer Dunston. Thank you for coming. As you can see, my home has been ransacked."

"Not much of a housekeeper, are you, Fischer?" Dunston laughed at his own little joke.

Once again, I ignored him, and filled them both in on the details as far as I knew them. I didn't want to, mostly because I knew what their reaction would be, but I pointed out that the lock hadn't been forced. And when they asked who had access, I told them that only trusted friends had access. I told them about Jennifer's visit yesterday, without the lascivious details, of course. Predictably, as soon as I told them about Jennifer's visit, Officer Madison made a big show of closing his little notebook, into which he was probably doodling anyway. "Lovers quarrel," he'd pronounced. "We're done here."

"Aren't you going to dust for prints, or anything?" Zellie asked.

"No need for that here. Lover boy here needs to avoid pissing off his girlfriends, that's all." He looked at her. "You better watch out, too."

Both cops laughed, and then departed.

"Well that was a waste. I said in disgust. "Those guys aren't qualified to find an orange at a fruit stand."

"And they're nasty, too," Zellie added. "But do you think it could have been Jennifer? She is the only untrustworthy one we know who has a key."

"I don't think so," I said slowly. "Remember, she had a lot longer to search the place yesterday, because we were out most of the day. I didn't think to check to see if anything was missing."

"Well, from what you told me, it would have been hard for her to conceal anything, anyway," Zellie said dryly.

"That's true, but I didn't look in her pocketbook. She could have put something in there. And anyway, this is not her style. She's more the subtle, sneaky sort. This is in-your-face-I-don't-care-if-you-know-about-it."

"No question about that. As Officers Mutt and Jeff apparently did not care if the crime scene remained intact, we might as well clean up the mess."

"Okay. Thanks for the help, Zellie."

"You'd do the same for me, but I hope you don't have to."

We looked at each other. "Uh oh. We better skedaddle over to your place, pronto. I can get to this later. It's not going anywhere."

"We might as well take Larry and Lazlow with us. We can go to Mrs. Minniefield's house after we survey whatever damage was done to my place. I mean, it's not like we're going to call the cops again."

"Okay, but let's reserve judgment about calling the cops until after we see what the story is," I said grimly.

Zellie's house is at the opposite end of the same street as mine. It's a cute ranch-style home that her parents painted yellow when they lived there prior to moving to Florida. Zellie had taken the place over and put her own mark on it, but had left the yellow color. "I like it," she'd always said. "It's bright and cheerful and reminds me of sunshine."

Today we had anything but the sun in mind as we approached with trepidation.

"It looks okay from the outside, at least," she ventured.

"Mine did too, remember? Let's take a look."

We went inside. The place was perfect. Totally pristine with no dishes in the sink, the living room freshly vacuumed, and a pleasant Spring-like odor, smelling vaguely like flowers, permeated the house.

"Whoa," I said. "Your intruders cleaned your house for you."

Zellie laughed. "I must admit, it doesn't always look like this. But I was up early and used my nervous energy to clean."

"It doesn't look like you had any unwelcome visitors, thankfully."

"No, it doesn't… uh oh, wait a second."

"What is it?"

Zellie held up a single sheet of paper. "Look at this."

I looked. It contained a few handwritten lines:

Dear Zellie,

I am back in town and I'm determined to win Arnie back. We are meant for each other and you know it's true. There is no other reason why you would try to prevent me from seeing him other than your desire to have him all to yourself. But you know that's not possible. Our true love cannot be denied. Your friendship with Arnie is undeniable, however, and I have no wish to force Arnie to choose between his friend and his lover. I care about him too much for that.

Let's try to bury the hatchet, Zellie. Meet me at Rosario's tomorrow at noon. I know we can achieve at least an uneasy peace. If you are not there, I guess I'll have to approach this in a different way.

Sincerely, Jennifer.

I ground my teeth. It was unmistakably Jennifer's handwriting.

Zellie looked a bit stunned. And truthfully, I was too. This was incredibly disturbing. I put my arm around her.

"Are you okay?" I asked.

"No, I don't think so. I need to sit down. This is crazy. She invades my home and leaves a letter like this? Were you aware of the depth of her feelings?"

"No," I said firmly. "I certainly was not. And it only goes one way, I assure you. I'm over her. Period."

"Well it doesn't look like she's over you."

"I'm not so sure about that."

"What do you mean? Just look at the letter."

"Doesn't this strike you as a little odd, knowing Jennifer? I mean, has she ever behaved like this?"

"Now that you mention it, no, it doesn't seem like her at all. She's all about being carefree and completely unattached to anything stable and conventional."

"Right. It's almost a studied detachment. And this is more in the nature of 'lovelorn schoolgirl.'"

"Which is the opposite of the Jennifer we know. But what is she after?" Zellie asked.

"I don't know. But we can assume it's about money in some way. She's incredibly mercenary. Not like the Bohemian girl she once was," I said, almost wistfully, but caught myself. "Although she hasn't been like that in almost twenty years."

By the look in her eyes, Zellie didn't miss my brief nostalgia trip, but graciously didn't mention it. "But where do I fit in? Why write to me like that? It's not like I'm rich and can pay her to go away."

"She has some purpose in mind. And she wanted to make a point about her ability to enter your house even without a key. I think you should get better locks. I'm getting a locksmith over to my house today, and I'll have him come over here, too. We should do at least that much. She also wanted to get into your head. And into my head, for that matter. She would assume that you'd show me the letter, even if we didn't discover it together. And the statement at the end is most assuredly a threat."

"Do you think I *should* go to Rosario's tomorrow? Although having lunch with a crazy person is not on my preferred list of things to do, I'm willing. At least we will be in a public place."

"I don't think you should go. While you might learn more about her true motivation, I don't think that would be worth the aggravation she'll put you through. And it will be giving in to a threat, which is not generally the best approach."

"I'm not so sure, Arnie. We're supposed to be investigators. What kind of private eye shies away from a difficult interview? Especially one that falls into our laps."

"Let's think about it for a little while, okay?"

"Okay. And maybe Mrs. Minniefield has an opinion about it."

CHAPTER SIXTEEN

"I think you should go, Zellie," Mrs. Minniefield said when we told her about the strange invitation.

We sat in her living room while the dogs were outside playing, or plotting–whatever their little doggy brains could come up with.

"But you should put this in your pocketbook before you go." She held up something that resembled a small paperclip, then smiled. "It's a bug, dear."

One of Ted's inventions, by the look of it, I thought. Ted was partial to miniaturizing electronics in the form of office supplies. I didn't know that he made such things for Mrs. M. Interesting.

"Arnie, you should listen in and rush to the rescue, so to speak, if it gets too far out of hand," she continued. "But the potential for information here is too good to pass up."

I wondered about this a little. But I'd long since given up trying to understand Mrs. Minniefield's motivation for doing the things she did. If she wanted us to do something, there was a very good reason. Just not one she'd probably ever tell us.

Zellie probably felt the same way. Or, she wanted a confrontation with Jennifer, it was hard to say.

"Okay, then it's settled," Zellie concluded.

I nodded my grudging agreement. "Okay, I'm outvoted."

Without any further preamble, Mrs. Minniefield said, "Arnie, what do you know about Thomas W. Carter?"

"Tom?" I asked in confusion. "We worked together at Mort," I used the shorthand way we referred to Mortal Securities (*Stocks and Bonds Have a Lifespan*), "until I left last year. As far as I know, he's still there."

"I need you to tell me the exact terms of your buyout from Mort, and I can't tell you why," Mrs. Minniefield said. She looked at Zellie. "Is there any reason Zellie shouldn't hear this?"

"Of course not. She pretty much knows it anyway– I don't keep secrets from her."

"Good. Then tell us please."

"I will, but what's this all about?"

"Arnie, please trust me. I can't tell you any more than that."

"You've never given me a reason not to trust you. Okay. I have a written agreement. It's in my safe deposit box, by the way."

I looked at Zellie, and her eyes showed she got my point.

"I was a member of the firm, one of the twelve partners. Tom was one too, if that matters. He probably still is." Mrs. Minniefield nodded. "So anyway, for a lot of reasons, I was through. I needed a break. My problem with Jennifer was certainly part of it, but not the whole thing. I negotiated a settlement that gave me about two million dollars, plus complete lifetime access to Mort's trading algorithms. As a practical matter, that's probably worth more than the cash I received. All this occurred after I lost that money in Jennifer's scheme, and I assume she knows nothing about it."

"Oh, she knows about your dealings with Mort, all right," Mrs. Minniefield said. "That's why she's back. And as desirable as you are," she looked at me kindly, "and you truly are," she added, "Jennifer's letter to Zellie is complete and utter hogwash."

Zellie, God bless her, because I was unaccountably upset, jumped in at that moment. "We assumed as much as soon as we saw it. We were just trying to figure out what to do." She turned to look at me and pressed her hand on my arm, and I managed a smile.

"Arnie, Zellie, you both need to take this seriously. Jennifer is not the person you knew long ago. She is very dangerous, and presents a threat to you both. Nostalgia is fine, Arnie, unless it fogs your vision of the present."

"I know, Mrs. Minniefield. And I am over her. But we go back a long way. It's hard to look at the whole thing coldly. But I'm trying."

"Good. Because you can't let your emotions control your behavior. Now let the dogs in. I want to see my little sweethearts."

We looked at her. Amazing. She could be cold and calculating one second and warm and fuzzy the next. She's an interesting woman. One we'll never fully understand, I'm sure.

"Is it okay if we leave Lazlow and Larry here until Betsy can pick them up later?" I asked Mrs. Minniefield.

"Of course. You know they have an open invitation to stay here. I enjoy their company."

When I got off the phone with Becky, Mrs. Minniefield seemed to know how I was feeling.

"It will be okay, Arnie. It's necessary, I assure you."

"I trust you, Mrs. M, but that trust doesn't come without some concerns."

"That is as it should be. But life is *not* without its turmoil."

"Maybe. But I don't want Zellie to have to endure the pain of my problems."

"Do I get to say anything?" Zellie demanded. "I'm standing right here, you know."

"I'm sorry, Zellie," I said. "Of course, you have a right to be heard on this."

"Thank you. If Mrs. Minniefield thinks it's important, she wouldn't have suggested as strongly as she did that I go. I think it's pretty clear that she doesn't think it will be a pleasant experience for me."

"I don't think either one of you will like it much, actually," Mrs. Minniefield said. "But I do have reasons for encouraging you, and given the public location of the meeting, the danger seems minimal. It's of course up to you in the end whether you go or not."

"Okay, okay," I said.

We bid Mrs. Minniefield and the dogs goodbye and left her house.

***

We strolled down the street quietly. I spoke first.

"I don't want you to go to the luncheon with Jennifer, Zellie."

"I know you don't. I don't really want to go, either."

"Then why tell Mrs. Minniefield–"

"Because, I *am* going," Zellie interrupted.

"If you don't want to, and I don't want you to, *why* are you going?"

"Because if Mrs. Minniefield says it's important, even though she knows we won't like it, there's a good reason. How often has she told us to do something that could be painful?"

"Never," I admitted.

"Exactly. She's always had our best interests at heart. Always. If she thinks I should go, I should go."

"I don't want you to endure any unpleasantness, Zellie. It's my problem, really."

"Since when are we not involved in each other's problems? We've been involved in each other's lives, both the good parts and the bad parts, for fifty years. And besides, judging by the tone of her letter, she's made this my problem."

We kept walking.

"She's going to try to get inside your head, Zellie," I warned. "And she's pretty good at it."

"I'll have to be prepared for that. Although we don't really know what she's after."

"Mrs. Minniefield thinks it's more of my money."

"You know, I get the feeling she suspects it's more than that. But I'll be damned if I know what."

"Honestly, it would be helpful if she just told us, wouldn't it?"

"She has some reason for not telling us. We just have to trust her."

We walked until I stopped and turned to her.

"Zellie, did I have anything to do with your breakup with Dan?"

Zellie turned to face me. And we stood there for a moment, holding each other by the forearms, our eyes locked.

"No, you had nothing to do with it. Dan was just not the person I thought he was when we got married. You know he was cheating on me almost from the moment we were married, maybe even before, for all I know. And he took off with his secretary and the entire proceeds of our joint checking account. Why would you think you had anything to do with that? You know better."

"I don't know. Look at us. We're holding hands, walking around the block we grew up on together. Truth be told, we've done this since we were five. We've had this easy, comfortable relationship with each other our whole lives. I just wondered if that made it difficult for the people we've had relationships with."

"I think everyone's known that we're close friends. I don't think it has had any effect on our relationships. Do you? Do you think Jennifer had a hard time with it?"

"No, I really don't. And I don't think Dan did, either. I'm trying to picture if you and I were married, and you were holding hands all the time with Ted…but I just can't picture you holding hands with Ted."

We both laughed. It was good to laugh with Zellie. And neither of us mentioned whether we could picture us married.

"Arnie, Dan was just a weasel. He would have been a weasel whether you were my friend or not. And Jennifer is just too smug and self-confident to have been affected by it either."

"Yeah, you're right about that. On both counts. Although to be sure, I never thought Dan was good enough for you."

"And I never thought Jennifer was good enough for you."

"Dan never liked me."

"Jennifer never liked me, either."

"They weren't good enough for us, were they?"

"Nope."

I took Zellie by the hand and we practically ran back to Mrs. Minniefield's house, where Zellie's car was parked.

"What now, partner?" Zellie asked.

"Lost in all this is Mrs. Minniefield's strange question about Tom Carter and my buyout."

"Yes. What was that all about?"

"I don't know. I wish Mrs. Minniefield wasn't so damned inscrutable."

"She has her reasons. We know that."

"Yes, but I don't think we can just let it go."

"Is it related to our continuing quest for the elusive Marilyn? Or do we just abandon that?"

"Good question. With all the Jennifer, Tom Carter, and Mort talk, we let our paid job languish."

"Might as well leave the Jennifer talk alone until tomorrow morning. We can plan strategy on the luncheon then."

"Yes. I suppose we should leave Tom Carter and Mort alone for the time being as well."

"Okay. But what should we do next about finding Marilyn?"

"Well, our last lead was Ted's information about Rene Desmond. Maybe we should go back to Brazen Saddles."

"It does seem to be at the center of all this, doesn't it?"

"It sure does. And I'd love to meet the great man in person."

"Talk to a mobster? Is that a good idea?"

"We won't be talking to a mobster, we'll be talking to a fashion visionary. There's a difference."

"If you say so."

"Now we just need to devise a plan to get in to see him."

"How about our Ma and Pa thoroughbred owner *schtick* again?"

"Nah, he'd see through that in a second. We might have fooled Gloria, but Desmond won't be so gullible."

"And he might have heard the story of the two dopey private eyes who visited the store last time."

"True. And he wouldn't talk to private eyes or bogus horse owners anyway. So, we need a different approach."

"How about we just go as ourselves?"

"I thought we just said he wouldn't talk to private eyes."

"No, I don't mean that. What are we best at? At being Arnie and Zellie, right? So, we go as Arnie and Zellie, private citizens shopping at Brazen Saddles."

"And how do we get in to see Desmond? He isn't going to just invite two ordinary customers in to see him, is he?"

"Do I have to think of everything? I came up with the private citizen's idea, didn't I? You come up with a reason for Desmond to see us."

She smiled prettily at me.

"Okay. Then I will. I'll show you." But I was smiling, too.

"I look forward to your brilliance, she said. "There's my car."

"Okay, let's go."

We got in and Zellie headed out towards Eatontown. As we were driving, I told her a little about Tom Carter.

"He was a good guy, as far as I knew. He did keep to himself mostly, but we pretty much all did that."

"Did you notice anything about him that could pique Mrs. Minniefield's curiosity?"

"No, not as far as I can recall. Turn right at the light. Now turn left here. It's a shortcut. He was married, and had two kids I think. As I told Mrs. M, he was a partner, just like me, but I really didn't know him well."

"He's still at Mort?"

"As far as I know, he is. I was the only one that left, and as you know, it was for personal reasons. The company was doing pretty well, at least on a balance sheet and cash flow basis. I didn't really handle the accounting, though. I was on the trading end of things. Come to think of it, Tom was a CPA by training, and one of the partners in charge of overseeing the accounting department."

"Maybe he knows something about your buyout. That interested Mrs. Minniefield, too."

"Maybe. But it was straightforward, and my share was calculated by an independent accounting firm. I can't see why it was so important to her. Another Minniefield mystery, I guess."

"Indeed. Maybe we should consult the A to Z Agency to unravel it."

"I understand that they don't come cheap. Finding unlicensed private detectives is harder than you'd think, so they cost more. Can we afford them?"

"Only time will tell. Okay, we're here. What's your brilliant plan?"

"Watch and learn."

"Oh dear. We're in for it now."

We walked to the now-familiar entrance and went in, stopping again in the entryway and surveying the schizophrenic racks of clothes and equestrian paraphernalia.

"It really is impressive, in a weird way, isn't it?" I whispered to Zellie.

"Yes. And weird doesn't even begin to describe it."

A tall blonde woman wearing an obviously expensive, long, flowing dress and classic Brazen Saddles cowboy boots approached us.

"My name is Linda. May I help you?"

Zellie nudged me to speak first. I had to think fast to come up with an approach that I'd led Zellie to believe I already had. I opted for simplicity.

"Yes, thank you," I said.

"What would you like me to show you? Would you like European chic or casual cowboy? Or our preference, a combination of both."

"We just love the Brazen Saddles look," I said. "Who designed it?"

"Our founder and owner, Mr. Desmond, is the visionary and designer behind this entire enterprise," she replied proudly.

"Would it be possible for us to meet the great man?"

She smiled faintly.

"Oh, I'm afraid that's not possible. Mr. Desmond is a very busy man, and while I'm sure he'd appreciate your interest, he is simply not available to meet with his customers."

"That's disappointing," I said. "We would have liked to meet him."

"I will convey a message to his executive secretary that customers had expressed interest in complimenting his work personally."

"Thank you. Have you ever met him yourself?"

She paused.

"Actually, no. As I said, he is a very busy man. I do communicate with his senior staff, though," she said somewhat defensively.

"We didn't mean anything by it," Zellie piped up. "We were just curious about him, that's all."

Linda looked somewhat mollified.

"Of course. Now can I show you anything in particular?"

I started to say something, but stopped when a woman with dark, shoulder length hair, wearing a white silk blouse, short skirt and heels, walked up and whispered something in Linda's ear, and quickly departed. Linda looked a little startled at what she had just been told, and studied us for a moment. Uh oh, I thought. This is probably not good. I glanced at Zellie, who looked a little uncomfortable as well.

"I've been told to escort the two of you to the executive offices upstairs. It seems you will get the opportunity to meet Mr. Desmond after all."

Of course, this was ostensibly what we wanted, and we should have been pleased with it, but I had this sense of foreboding. Maybe it wasn't such a good idea after all. I could feel Zellie's consternation as well. Have to just make the best of it, though.

"Great, lead the way," I said, trying my best to sound upbeat.

We followed Linda to the back of the store, to a locked door, into which she inserted a key card. The door opened to an elevator with yet another key card access. Once in the elevator, she pushed a button marked "Executive Offices" and up we went. The elevator opened to a beautifully appointed reception area, with the now-familiar mahogany walls and ceiling, and fresh (very expensive) flower arrangements flanking a desk at which a flat-out gorgeous receptionist sat. She was the very picture of voluptuous, had blonde hair and blue eyes and was wearing a runway model type original dress, and a diamond pendant around her neck, which hung just above a hint of her ample cleavage. She also sported teardrop diamond earrings. The jewelry was clearly genuine, and must have cost a fortune.

"This is where I leave you," Linda said.

"Okay, thank you," I said, my eyes only briefly leaving the scene in front of me.

Zellie gave me a clandestine elbow, which basically said "put your eyes back in their sockets, this is serious" but before I could say anything, the receptionist addressed us.

"Please sit down. Mr. Desmond will see you shortly."

We sat down on a very comfortable leather couch that faced the reception desk and said nothing. A few minutes later, the door behind the reception desk opened and a very pretty woman with short red hair came out. She was conservatively dressed in a grey business suit and sensible heels. Interesting that there is absolutely no sign of the Brazen Saddles "look" in the executive offices, I thought. Also, curious that there are very few men working here, and that all the women were beautiful. Mr. Desmond likes having pretty women around. Who doesn't? But interesting nonetheless.

The woman interrupted my reverie by smiling and telling us to follow her through the door, which I noticed, also had a key card lock on it. Lots of security here. We followed the woman into a suite of inner offices, and down a long hallway to a corner office. The door was closed. She knocked on the door.

"Your guests are here, Mr. Desmond," she said.

A quiet voice emerged from inside the office. "Send them in, please, Ms. Banks. And you may be excused. Thank you."

We tentatively opened the door and entered the office. And it didn't look anything like an office, which I suppose is to be expected from someone who created Brazen Saddles. It more or less looked like someone's living room, complete with logs burning in the fireplace. Unlike the strong, masculine mahogany with its ubiquitous presence throughout the store, and even in the reception area, this room had been painted in a soft shade of yellow, with a classic modern décor. There was a sectional sofa in the center of the room sitting kitty-corner to two comfortable looking easy chairs covered in a faint, floral upholstery. Mr. Desmond had occupied one of the chairs when we entered. He had since risen to greet us.

He was not what I had pictured, and I looked at him with interest. He was of medium height, with a mop of brown hair that looked uncombed, but probably had been carefully arranged that way by a team of professional stylists. He wore the pants to a light-colored linen suit, and stood before us in shirtsleeves. His suit coat was hung on a coat rack in the corner of the room. He wore what looked like slippers on his feet, as if he was in his own living room. A thin, gold chain was draped around his neck. Frankly, he looked nothing like the classic depiction of a mobster.

"Mr. Fischer, Ms. Morgan. I am Rene Desmond. Welcome to my inner sanctum."

"Thank you…" I managed to stutter. "But how…?"

He laughed.

"Of course, I know who you are. Your previous visit did not go unnoticed. I try to keep apprised of everything that goes on here. Just good business practice, you understand. I had you checked out almost immediately after your encounter with one of my sales representatives – Glenda I think her name was."

We didn't correct him. Despite his outwardly friendly manner, there was something about him that suggested that contradicting him was a bad idea. And there was the matter of Gloria to consider. Maybe he really didn't remember who had given us the information, and she didn't get fired. Or worse, I thought somewhat guiltily. But of course, he knew. He knew a great deal, it seemed.

"Then I take it you know we are looking for a woman who calls herself Marilyn Beaufort."

"I know that's who you say you're looking for. And you were given the name, address, phone number and e-mail address we have in our sales records for this person, I believe. Also, the type of cowboy boots she bought. Information that I require be kept confidential, for the obvious purpose of preserving my customers' personal information. A common courtesy and good business practice that I assume you would also desire were you actual customers. So, I ask you again. Why are you here?"

There was an almost imperceptibly harder edge in his voice this time, although he sought to portray an easygoing, casual attitude. I better just tell him the truth, I thought. He'd know if I was lying anyway.

"The information turned out to be incorrect," I said.

He laughed. "A customer lied to us about her personal information? Customers do that all the time. Frankly, between us, I'm amazed that people tell almost anyone the correct information in the first place. But as I'm sure you can agree, we have no control over that. We simply ask for the information to enhance our marketing efforts. The information gives us an audience that is already interested in our products. It is very useful information to increase sales. But it depends on customers voluntarily providing the information."

"We had hoped you might know her as a regular customer, or could provide some further insight unavailable to your staff."

"Look. I wouldn't tell you a single word about any of my customers, even if I knew anything. But I will tell you this – I looked at the information that was provided to you, and I personally interviewed the sales representative that gave you the information."

I internally shivered at that statement for some reason, but I don't really know why.

"I can assure you that I have absolutely no familiarity with or knowledge about the person described. As far as I can tell, she was just one of thousands of customers that came here and bought something."

Zellie finally spoke up, pretty bravely, I thought. "Are you familiar with a Mercedes with the license plates FNCY CWGRL?"

Desmond turned to look at her, and paused a moment.

"Not that it's any of your business, Ms. Morgan," he said somewhat icily, "but as she's somewhat of a public figure in Monmouth County society, I suppose there's no harm in telling you. That's my wife's car. But now I have a question – why do you ask?"

I jumped in at that point. Because he had not mentioned our other source, I saw no reason to identify him either. "We thought so, but weren't sure. We're trying to rule out any car that isn't that of Marilyn Beaufort, which we can certainly do now. Thank you."

Desmond looked at me for a moment with those dark, piercing eyes. He didn't believe me any more than I would.

"Pleased to be of service," he said, "but we're done now." He raised his hand, and almost like a remote control, the door opened, and the redhead appeared again.

"Please escort my guests out," Ms. Banks. "And I trust that our business is concluded, Mr. Fischer and Ms. Morgan? I do not expect to see you again."

"Thank you for your help, Mr. Desmond," I said. "I hope we weren't too much of a bother. We know you're busy."

"Not at all, Mr. Fischer. It was charming to meet both of you."

Ms. Banks escorted us out of the office suite, and out to the reception area. She then pushed the elevator button, and waited with us silently until the doors opened, and until we entered and the doors closed.

As we went down in the elevator, I told Zellie with my eyes that we should stay silent, and she nodded. When we reached the bottom floor, the doors opened, and another pretty woman met us. If we expected our new escort to leave us at that point, we were mistaken.

"I'm to escort you to the exit," she said, without any apparent emotion at all.

And to the exit we went. Once outside, I took Zellie by the hand and we walked quietly to the car.

CHAPTER SEVENTEEN

"That was spooky," Zellie said once we were in the car, with the doors shut. "Let's get out of here."

"Agreed. The faster, the better."

As Zellie drove, we rehashed the visit.

"Did you get the feeling that he was sizing us up?" Zellie asked.

"Oh, definitely. He wanted to meet us in person, and we made it easy for him to do so."

"We didn't really get any information that we didn't already have."

"Well, we got to size him up, too, at least. And we know he was telling us the truth about one thing – he confirmed what we already knew – that the car was registered to Mrs. Desmond. And he knew we already had the information, or he wouldn't have given it to us."

"He's a scary guy. Outwardly, he looks almost boyish, although he's probably in his fifties. But he has an unmistakable inflexibility about him, and he gives the impression that he's working hard to control a volcanic temper that could explode at any time."

"Yes, he certainly is tightly wound, that was apparent, in spite of his attempts to display a casual attitude."

"And isn't it a little weird that there were no men around? Wouldn't you kind of expect a mobster to have all kinds of bodyguards?"

"He had a lot of security, though, didn't he? And I bet those women are good bodyguards. He seems to like creating misimpressions. The women are probably retired special forces, or something," I postulated.

"It wouldn't surprise me."

I glanced at my watch. "It's almost five o'clock. What a day!"

"Any plans tonight?"

"No, thank goodness. I'm beat."

"Me too. This investigating business is exhausting."

"And we really haven't particularly found anything. Let's recap. We were retained by a woman we can't identify, and haven't ever seen again. We were supposed to find her lost husband Stanley. We haven't found anyone at all, much less a Stanley. What we've found is a dead bartender and a weird clothing store."

"And all kinds of references to the mob."

"Right. And Mrs. Minniefield making all sorts of strange comments and asking odd questions without any explanation."

"And add to that, 'Her' reappearance."

"Yes. And about that, Zellie…"

"I know. We need to talk about tomorrow. I'd be lying if I said I wasn't nervous about it."

"You know my view on this. I don't think you should go."

"I know, Arnie. But for some reason, Mrs. Minniefield thinks I should. Any idea why?"

"No," I admitted. "Usually, I'm pretty sure she'd oppose something that had no apparent benefit to us, especially something that has a high probability of unpleasantness."

"I know. How many times in the past has she tried to protect us?"

"I couldn't even begin to count."

"Exactly. So, it's safe to assume that she thinks she's protecting us this time, too."

"I guess. But why was Jennifer so intent on getting you to go to lunch with her? I mean, she broke into your house just to give you an invitation that she could have mailed. Or simply called you on the phone."

"She was clearly sending a message. Presumably, to point out my vulnerability."

"But if she's after my money, as Mrs. Minniefield seems to think, why would the lack of security on *your* house be relevant?"

"I don't know. But I guess to gain an advantage somehow. I mean, don't you want the other side of a negotiation to be as insecure as possible? I know I'm reaching for straws here, because I can't even conceive of what the negotiation would be."

"You might have hit on it, though, Zellie. Jennifer knows we're close. Your opinion obviously matters to me, and she would be aware of that. But there's another thing. She probably searched your house."

"We didn't see any signs of that."

"No, we didn't. And I didn't really see any signs of a search after she visited me. But I think *both* our places were searched."

"For what possible reason? I guess she could have searched your house for money, but she didn't even take your spending money. The real money would be elsewhere. But my house? What's there to find?"

"I think Jennifer searched my house for the same reason as the people after her searched my house. But for the life of me, I couldn't say why. As for your house, I think Jennifer was probably looking for any information she could use. Thoroughness, I suppose."

"Bottom line, we don't know. And I'm getting a little tired of working hard only to figure out I don't know anything. This is very frustrating."

"It is," I agreed. "But I suppose we'll get answers at some point."

"Let's hope so."

"I'm not exactly ready to give up on finding Marilyn. Are you?"

"No, but I'm not sure I know what our next step is."

"I know. It seems like we're at a dead end. We've explored every avenue available, based upon the very limited information we were given."

"Let's see – we looked into the Stone Parrot, and oh Lord, look what that got us."

"Nothing but aggravation, but no apparent connection to Marilyn."

"Still, I wonder how that investigation is going."

"Yeah, me too, but I don't think we should be investigating that, much. Mike is thinking it's a mob hit."

"Okay, that's out for us, at least for now. What about Mrs. Minniefield's reference to Tom Carter?"

"Yup, another cryptic question. Just what we needed. I can't see how that's connected to Marilyn, either."

Zellie shrugged. "Frankly, I don't see how that's connected to anything at all."

"I wonder…," I said slowly, "remember that guy at Brazen Saddles?"

"The one who took you for fifty bucks?"

"Yeah, that one. And I wasn't taken. It was a gratuity of a sort."

"Sure, it was," Zellie replied, "a tip to get bogus information."

"You know, it might not have been bogus information. If any information was bogus, it was the information Gloria gave us. There really is a FNCY CWGRL license plate."

"Yes, but it belongs to Mrs. Desmond, not Marilyn. He probably just saw it in the parking lot and used the information to make a few bucks."

"I know, but that doesn't mean Marilyn didn't walk to that car when the guy was following her. I don't think he ever said she got in it and drove off, did he?"

"I don't think so…I think he just said there was a map of New York City on the front seat."

"Which there may well have been."

"But what use is that to us? Even if he was giving us accurate information as he saw it, the information is useless."

"I suppose so, but what about the New York City reference?"

"Even that's useless. First, based on the theory that the information is accurate, all we have is that Marilyn went to Mrs. Desmond's car to mislead our informant. So, there's a New York City map on the seat. That presumably belongs to Mrs. Desmond as well."

"And even if a New York City map is somehow relevant, it's a big city, and we have no other facts."

"So, we're back to square one."

"Yup. That's about the size of it. We'll have to decide on a next step, but it can wait until after the big luncheon tomorrow. In the meantime, I'm starving, and Chow Chow Ming's is a half mile up the road. How about we pick up some takeout and head back to my place?"

***

Chow Chow Ming's was a Chinese restaurant owned and operated by a short, curly haired man named Joseph Mingowski. The Chow Chow reference was to his dog, Mutton, or Mutt for short. Mutt was a mix of a Chow Chow and a bunch of other things. He had the reddish hair and blue tongue of a Chow, and probably had some sheepdog in him, hence the Mutton and Mutt references. He was incredibly furry and playful, and his omnipresence at the restaurant doubtless violated a dozen Health Code provisions. But the customers loved him, and Joe probably couldn't part with him each morning, anyway.

"Hi Joe," I said, leaning down to pet Mutton.

"Hi Arnie. Hi Zellie. What'll you have?"

"Let's get some chicken lo mein," said Zellie's muffled voice coming from a face buried in Mutton's fur. "And sesame beef. Joe, I just love hugging Mutton. He's so soft."

"Chicken lo mein, sesame beef and one furry dog to go," laughed Joe.

I grinned. "We'll get some chicken fried rice, too, thanks."

"It'll be about twenty minutes."

"Ok, thanks. I don't think Zellie will be done with Mutt by then, but we can hope."

"She can have him, for all I care," Joe said with a smile. "That dog's eating up all of the profits."

"I know what you mean. Lazlow is costing me a fortune, too. But look at all the barfing in my slippers I get for the money. Can't do without that, now can I?"

He nodded. "Mutton likes to chew. He chews on those rawhide things, you know what I mean, the ones that shatter and spread scum all over the carpet?"

"Oh yeah. I know. Lazlow eats them, too."

"Well, with Mutton, those are preferable to the alternative."

"What's the alternative, I hesitate to ask?"

"If he doesn't have rawhide to chew on, he'll chew on anything. Shoes, slippers, clothing, the odd sofa and chair, the bottom of the refrigerator…"

"He chews on the bottom of the refrigerator?"

"Yeah, I'm pretty sure he thinks there's food in there. Did I mention how much he eats?"

I shook my head. "Still, without him, you'd have to change the name of the restaurant."

"I know. But sometimes I wonder–cost of a new sign and menus, versus a two-hundred-pound bag of kibble and new shoes. But then, of course, I come to my senses. I love the big guy. What can I say?"

"Yup, gotta love 'em," I replied.

"And egg rolls, don't forget the egg rolls," Zellie said from her spot on the floor.

"And egg rolls," Joe said. "Coming right up."

We played with Mutton while we waited for our food. He is a great dog, after all. And Joe wouldn't part with him for anything. Something about dogs–we love them, but we love to complain about them, too.

"This is nice," I finally said. "Just playing with the dog, and not thinking about all the nonsense."

"Yes, it is," Zellie said, "why don't we clear our minds tonight, watch a movie or a ballgame or something, play with Lazlow. I don't know, play checkers or something and get our minds off this for a while. I think it would be good for us."

"Okay. It's a deal. Starting now, no discussion of the case until tomorrow morning at 8:00 a.m. We're officially off duty."

"Good."

Joe brought us our food and we paid him and left.

As we walked back to Zellie's car, I started to say something, and she held up her hand.

"This had better be about the Knicks, the latest action movie, or a book you just read."

"Is that what we used to talk about before we did this?"

"Pretty much. But we also talked about work, and the people we were dating."

"We did, didn't we?"

"Yes, we did. And we didn't worry about it all as much as we do now."

We got into the car and settled the bags of food. I looked at her. "Is it the new business that's made us so serious?"

Zellie laughed. "I don't think so. If anything, it's been a good distraction. I think our experiences with Jennifer and Dan are what have us all turned around."

"Yeah, probably so. But hey, the two of them would make a great couple, wouldn't they? Jennifer and Dan. A match made in Hell. And by the way, you just violated the agreement."

"I did, didn't I?" Zellie said with a grin. "What's the punishment for such naughty behavior?"

"I'll have to think of something," I said with a wink.

I love watching Zellie smile and laugh. It's been less common since her breakup with Dan, but lately, it's come back a bit, and it never ceases to warm my heart. Somehow, her laugh is both boisterous and ladylike – hard to describe, but always delightful.

"I'll bet you will, Arnie," she said.

We went to my place. It was preferable, Zellie said, because she didn't want her house smelling like Chinese food for the next week.

"So, it's preferable to have *my* house smelling like Chinese food?" I asked.

"Well, it's preferable to me." Again, she laughed and lit up my heart.

We spent the evening together, laughing and joking like we had always done. We enjoyed each other's company, taking the time to remember what our friendship was built on. No value judgments, no questioning of motives, just that deep, unbreakable bond born of many years of mutual support, understanding, and friendship.

We wrapped up the evening around midnight. "You can stay here tonight," I said. "On the couch," I added.

"Thanks Arnie–and it's not like I haven't slept there before–but we have a big day tomorrow. I should probably get a good night's rest."

"It was really fun tonight, Zellie."

She picked up her purse and turned toward the door. "Yes, it was. We used to do this all the time. We really should get back to just having fun."

I gave her a hug. And held her just a little longer than a friend . . ..

CHAPTER EIGHTEEN

I had slept, but not as well as usual. I didn't know what Jennifer was up to and I didn't like Zellie being in the line of fire. At around eight, I called Zellie to see how her night had been.

"I've been up since about seven o'clock. I slept great until then, and then started worrying about today's lunch."

"Me, too. But I think it will be fine."

"Sure, it will, but I don't think either of us is going to like it much."

I agreed.

Her voice shifted and I could picture her raising her chin and pasting on a smile. "Let's meet at the office at ten. I still have to figure out what to wear, anyway. Rosario's is pretty fancy."

"Okay, ten o'clock. See you there."

I hung up, and decided to go for a run, since I had time before I had to leave to meet Zellie. As I turned, I felt a tap on my shoulder, and I spun around.

"Hi Arnie. Miss me?"

Jennifer. In my house. Again. At 8 am. Thankfully, wearing clothes this time.

"What the…?"

"I thought you were going to get the locks changed. Change your mind, sweetheart?"

"Jennifer," I said wearily, "Please leave. Don't come back. I told you I didn't want to see you."

"That's not the message I'm getting. Since you aren't stopping Zellie from meeting me for lunch, I assume you're at least curious."

"How do you know Zellie is meeting you for lunch? And even so, what makes you think I could stop her if she wanted to do so?"

"Oh, she'll show up. And I also think you could stop her if you just asked. And I *know* you're still attracted to me. No denying that."

"Stop it, Jennifer. You don't know anything."

"You're practically ogling me now. Your words say one thing, but you can't hide your physical reactions."

I fought the urge to grab her arms and forcibly remove her from my house. Instead, I swallowed and lowered my voice. "Just stop it. Of course, you're very attractive. It's your mind I can't stand."

"Oh, that hurts, Arnie. That really hurts. But this isn't about my mind. You're still upset over that bad investment you blame on me. I intend to make that right, you know."

"It wasn't a bad investment. It was a swindle, plain and simple."

"That's just spin, Arnie, and I think you know that."

"I know no such thing, but I don't intend to argue with you about it anymore. I'm just done with you, period. Now get out!"

"Regardless of your view of it, I told you I intend to make it right. I will get you back every cent you lost."

"Sure, you will, Jennifer. Probably in another rip-off scheme. Out you go."

"You won't be involved at all, Arnie. I'm going to get you your money back. I promise."

"I don't care about the money. I don't want you in my life. So, have your lunch and play your little charade with Zellie, then go away forever. I'll get a restraining order if necessary."

With that, I pushed her out the door and shut it with the deadbolt. I picked up the phone to call the locksmith, and an alarm company. I also called Zellie, explained in three sentences about Jennifer's latest visit and warned her to leave her door dead-bolted.

She sighed. "Was she naked again?"

"No, thankfully clothed this time. I made the calls I should have made yesterday to a locksmith and a home security firm. We're both set up for appointments later this afternoon."

"What did she say this time?"

"She's certain you'll show up for your luncheon, and she insisted that she is going to get me my money back."

"Yeah, I'm sure that's going to happen. But Arnie, how does she know I'm going to meet her for lunch?"

"She just knows. I don't know how, and she didn't say."

"Arnie…are you still attracted to her?"

"I don't know, Zellie. Physically, I suppose so. I'm a guy. We like to look at pretty women. And she's certainly pretty, and we have a history. But that doesn't mean I want to be involved with her because I don't. In fact, I told her that irrespective of her physical beauty, I can't stand her mind."

"Ouch."

"Yes, she said that hurt. But it didn't seem to faze her. I told her to get out, and pushed her out the door. All the time, she was promising that she'd get me my money back."

"Maybe I shouldn't go to lunch with her, after all."

"I haven't wanted you to all along. Mrs. Minniefield wants you to go. Jennifer can say anything she wants, but it isn't going to affect the reality she has to live with – that she just isn't very appealing as a person, and that I don't want anything to do with her."

"You need to be careful, Arnie. I know you are strong-minded, and you might not want to hear this, but men in general do lots of things out of character around pretty women. And you had a relationship with this one."

"I know, Zellie. And I don't mind you saying so. I really don't want to be hoodwinked again."

"You won't be. Now let me finish getting dressed."

"Are you naked?"

Zellie laughed. "See? I told you. And wouldn't you like to know?"

I chuckled too. "Yes, I would. But I'll just use my imagination. See you at ten."

She was still laughing when she hung up the phone.

***

I was sitting on a sofa, sipping my coffee, when Zellie walked in.

All the men in the Moo Mart practically dropped their coffee cups, put on their glasses, and bugged out their eyes as they turned to gawk at her. Well, maybe it wasn't that dramatic, but Zellie looked fantastic. I mean, eye-popping spectacular.

She had on full make-up, and her brownish-blonde hair was shoulder length, with a single braided set of strands hanging down near her left ear. She wore a black silk dress, with a hint of cleavage, above which hung a single strand of pink pearls, with matching pink pearl drop earrings. The hem of her dress exposed her pretty knees, and maybe the tiniest bit of thigh, all clad in sheer silk stockings. She wore three-inch black strappy heels.

"Well, what do you think?" she asked me, twirling slowly before me.

"Hang on. I need to put my tongue back in my mouth in order to speak. My goodness, Zellie. You look great! Sexy and sophisticated. Unbelievably hot, to tell you the truth."

Zellie smiled. "Hot. I can live with that. Will I fit in at Rosario's?"

"It's perfect. Really. You look wonderful. In fact, too good for the likes of this place. Sorry, Eddie."

"No offense taken, Arnie. I agree."

"Let's get out of here," I said, getting to my feet. "You have two hours before lunch, and we should talk somewhere private before you go."

"Let's go back to my house," Zellie said. "We probably should have met there in the first place."

I followed Zellie to her house, my car stalling only twice, and neither time in the middle of an intersection. My luck was holding. I arrived a few minutes after her, knocked briefly and pushed on the door. Locked. With a deadbolt. I knocked again, and Zellie opened the door.

"Glad to see you're locking up,"

"I'm not taking any chances until we get new locks and a security system in here."

"Good idea."

We walked through an archway into Zellie's comfortable living room, and sat down on the main couch together. Zellie kicked off her shoes.

"I didn't really want to get dressed up this early, but I decided to give you a preview."

"I'm glad you did. You look fabulous. We don't dress up much anymore, do we?"

"No, we don't really have occasion to. We got dressed up to commute to the city to work, but we haven't done that in quite a while."

"I generally prefer the casual look anyway, but it's nice to do it for a change of pace."

"Yes, it is. I guess we have Jennifer to thank for that."

"Well, I wouldn't go that far…"

"We're putting off talking about it, Arnie. Any suggestions on an approach for today?"

"I think you should just be your skeptical self. I mean, I've told her I don't believe anything she says, and to get lost, but you can speak to her without the baggage I carry."

"So, I should just tell her to get lost? Kind of defeats Mrs. Minniefield's reason for meeting with her. Aren't I supposed to find out what she's up to?"

"Oh, I think you can do both at the same time. But I don't want to tell you what to say. You have your own mind - one I like very much, by the way - and I'm sure you will figure out what to say."

"I hope so. I wish we weren't so much in the dark as to Mrs. Minniefield's reasoning."

"I know. She can be very frustrating. But she usually gives us the information we need, just not an iota more. We have to assume that this is sufficient information for whatever her agenda is."

"I guess."

"I would just caution you to not be surprised at anything she says. She's really good at head games, and has shown she's willing to say almost anything to support things as fact that are simply not true."

"Do you think she's delusional?"

"You know, I get the strong feeling that she's not. I hesitate to say this about someone I guess I once loved, but I think she's just very cold and calculating, with a specific reason for everything she says. Just a feeling, though."

"I trust your gut on this," Zellie said. "And I'll try to take whatever surprises she springs with a grain of salt. But, I need to ask you this. Because you know I'd never stand in the way of any relationship you have or want…"

"I'm sure I'm over her. We go back a long way, and I don't want to discredit that, but that was a different time and place, and we're totally different people now. She's taken a very bad path, and I have no desire to follow her. I don't think she even remembers the person she used to be, or could recognize how she's changed. Please help me to continue to remember that. Your opinion matters to me, and I never want you to stop offering it. That's not standing in the way of anything–that's being my best friend."

"Okay, Arnie. But I had to ask."

"I know. And thanks."

"You can offer opinions to me, too, you know," she said.

"I know."

"Like, don't eat that, it's rancid. Or don't date Dan, he's a butthead."

"I'll keep those things in mind, Zellie."

"Okay, good."

We sat a couple of moments in silence. Until I'd said the words a few minutes ago, I'd still wondered if I was over Jennifer. But now I knew the truth.

"Now, just a few things to remember," I started. "I'll be listening to the paperclip microphone in your purse. If you want help, we should have a code word. How about earlobe, like my earlobe hurts, or something like that which won't be part of your conversation."

"Okay, earlobe it is."

"If you say that, I'll come running."

"Where will you be?"

"I can't take the chance on being spotted, so I'll be parked towards the other end of the parking lot. Rosario's is in a strip mall, like every other business in Monmouth County, and there's a grocery store at the end. I'll be in front of that."

***

I left Zellie at 11:15 a.m. and drove home to let Lazlow out.

After letting him frolic briefly, I patted him on the head and left him sleeping on his bed when I went outside to my car. Which wouldn't start. Again. Maybe I should take Zellie's advice and get a new car. Maybe something sporty, like a Volvo. Okay, not a Volvo, a Mustang, yeah, that's it, a Mustang. I got back in the car, tried it once again, and it started right up. Freaky. Almost as if she knew she might be replaced.

I drove to the large parking lot that served both the Food Emporium and several smaller stores and businesses, including Rosario's, and parked where agreed, keeping as far away as I could from the area in front of Rosario's. I looked at my watch. 11:50 am. Good, I'm on time, with only a brief Matilda-delay. I switched on the receiver to the paperclip mike and almost immediately heard Zellie speaking to me.

"Arnie? Can you hear me?"

"Loud and clear. I'm in place."

"Okay, good. I'm just around the corner. I'll be there in a few minutes. I didn't want to test the mike once I got to Rosario's, in case I run into Jennifer in the parking lot."

"Good thinking."

"Okay, signing off. The next time you hear me, I'll be at Rosario's."

"All right. But leave the mike on anyway. No sense turning it off now."

The next voice I heard was Jennifer.

CHAPTER NINETEEN

"Zellie darling, it's so nice to see you again."

"Hello, Jennifer." Zellie's voice was considerably colder.

"Whoa, frosty. I see I'll have my work cut out for me."

I heard another voice, mingled with others. Then Jennifer again. "Yes, two for lunch. We have a noon reservation under the name Marquette."

"Very good ma'am. Right this way."

***

Zellie and Jennifer followed the host to a table next to a window overlooking a small garden, complete with tiny waterfall, in the back of the restaurant. Amazing, Zellie thought. In the middle of a New Jersey strip mall, a waterfall. The table was covered with a white tablecloth and white cloth napkins, and flowers in the center. They sat down.

"The waiter will be with you in a moment."

"Thank you," Zellie said, and studied Jennifer briefly.

She looked the same as the last time she'd come around. She's quite beautiful, Zellie thought. And the all-white ensemble was very tasteful, but sexy at the same time, with the array of small black buttons running down the front of her chemise providing mystery, and the only color contrast other than her black four-inch heels. Very expensive Ferragamo heels.

Interesting that she's wearing white and I'm wearing black. Zellie hoped that didn't mean that she was wearing the black hat here, so to speak.

"I meant it, Zellie." Jennifer broke Zellie's brief reverie. "It is really good to see you."

Zellie allowed herself a faint smile which seemed a better option than a snarl or a sneer. "Jennifer, I must admit, I'm confused. It's not like we were ever particularly friendly. We were acquaintances because of your relationship with Arnie. And we parted on ugly terms. Why would you be happy to see me?"

Jennifer leaned forward, her look one that could be described as earnest. "You were one of the few women I knew in Middletown. I always considered you a friend. I still do. And that whole thing with Arnie's bad investment is the only thing that prevented us from becoming close friends."

Zellie had been prepared for a confrontation. Not this. She paused for a moment and chose her words carefully.

"Jennifer, I don't know what you're after here, but you should know that I disagree strongly with your characterization of your financial dealings with Arnie. As I said, our acquaintance was solely based upon my support for my best friend, whom I think you swindled."

Jennifer looked completely unfazed by this.

"I understand, Zellie. Arnie's your best friend. You can't believe he could have made an investment mistake like that, as smart as he is. But it's the truth. But that's one of the reasons I want you to be my friend. You're honest and loyal. I like to think I'm the same kind of person. But I recognize that the bad investment has caused friction between Arnie and me, and between us as well. I aim to change all that. As I told Arnie, I'm going to make sure he gets his money back."

"You'll excuse me for being skeptical, Jennifer, but I don't see how you're going to do that, and if it was just a bad investment as you say, I don't know why you'd feel compelled to make amends."

"Oh, I'm not making amends. I didn't do anything wrong. I love Arnie, though, and but for this issue, we'd be together right this moment. He loves me, too, you know."

Zellie sighed.

"Jennifer, that's between you and Arnie. Even if that's true, which I frankly don't believe, I don't play any part in Arnie's relationships. He's free to do as he pleases. Why are you telling me this?"

"Oh, you play a pivotal role in Arnie's relationships and you know it. He's your best friend, and really there's an emotional connection between the two of you that's hard to explain. You're almost lovers, but not exactly. Hmm...," she paused for effect. She placed a beautifully manicured fingertip at the tip of her chin.

"Are you fucking him? No, probably not. You two would never let that get in the way of your beloved friendship. Doesn't matter. Bottom line, your opinion matters to Arnie, so it's important to me."

Zellie wanted to slap that mouth. Would Mrs. Minniefield understand? Zellie thought not. She swallowed, put a smile on her face and placed her folded hands on the table in front of her.

"What do you want from me, Jennifer?"

"Just to be my friend, Zellie. Just to be my friend. How are things going for you? Let's catch up."

Now, this was a game Zellie could play. "I'm fine, Jennifer, just fine."

"Please, Zellie. Help me out here. I'm just asking you about how things are going, it's not an inquisition. It's friendly chatting. I understand you and Arnie have started a private investigation firm. How's business?"

"I don't want to discuss that with you, Jennifer."

"Oh, sure you do. It's very interesting, and I'd think you would like to talk about your first client – Marilyn Beaufort."

Zellie felt her jaw drop. And, she noted the gleam in Jennifer's eyes. "But how? What do you know?"

"Oh, I know a lot of things, Zellie. When I aim for something, I do my research. I plan it out carefully and I always get what I want."

"A bad investment, right? With all that research you do?" Zellie's laugh was brittle. "I'm about done with this, Jennifer. What do you really want here? What's the real goal?"

"I told you. I want Arnie. I've loved him for over twenty years. I thought we had rekindled that love affair last year, but that bad investment just got in the way. But I'll win him back. That's for sure. He can't stop thinking about me. I know that."

"And how do you know that, Jennifer?"

"Oh, a woman just knows. For example, did Arnie tell you that I showed up in his house totally naked? Of course, he did. He tells you everything. But did he tell you that he stood there practically drooling? That when I kissed him on the way out the door, he positively shivered? Did he spell that out for you, Zellie?"

"I'm getting tired of this, Jennifer. And I'm not the faintest bit hungry at this point. I don't know why I agreed to see you in the first place."

"Yes, why did you? A person you supposedly hate breaks into your house, and leaves a note. And you just show up? Why Zellie? I'd really like to know."

If she'd thought for a second that Jennifer had changed for the better, that notion was wiped away. For Mrs. Minniefield, she'd carry on. "I just wanted to hear what you had to say for yourself. But, I guess I've heard enough."

Jennifer's eyes narrowed, her voice dropped to a hiss. "I think you wanted to meddle in Arnie's affairs, that's what I think. I think you wanted to see if you could scare me away like you tried to do last time. But it won't work, Zellie. It just won't. Arnie thinks about me all the time. I know you suggested that he go on a date with that aerobics instructor- Tawny or Tammy whatever her name was. Trying to distract Arnie from me, weren't you, Zellie? But it didn't work, I'll tell you that. Who do you think Arnie was thinking about while he was in the throes of passion with her? Do you think he was thinking about her? No, he was thinking about the naked body he'd just seen that day — mine. He was thinking about me, Zellie, all the time. Your attempt at distraction didn't work, and never will."

She wondered if Arnie would come bursting through the door to save her and she tugged on her earlobe. But she was stronger than this. And she knew she was better than Jennifer. She straightened her back and looked her adversary in the eye.

"I give up, Jennifer. I am certainly not going to have this conversation with you. But I'm interested in finding out who you are, so I've decided to take you up on your offer to chit-chat."

Jennifer was silent a long moment as though thrown off stride. "Oh, okay, Zellie. I get passionate sometimes, I'm sorry. It's just so important to me."

"Yes, well that's between Arnie and you, as I said. So, where are you living? Have you moved back to Middletown?"

"I haven't moved back yet. I'm hoping to rekindle things with Arnie. Maybe even move in with him at some point. I know I have work to do to win him back. I *know* that Zellie."

Zellie tried to keep her voice nonchalant. "So where are you staying in the meantime?"

"Um, at the Holiday Inn on Route 35, at least for a few days until I decide on more permanent housing."

Just the slightest hesitation. She was making that up, Zellie thought, and wondered why. *Keep her talking, keep asking questions, so you don't have to answer any.*

"Are you working?" Zellie asked.

"No, not at the moment. I'm going to start looking for a job next week. Rekindling my relationship with Arnie is my job for now. That and executing my plan to get him his money back." Before Zellie could ask another question, she quickly continued.

"You and Arnie are quite busy on the detective front, aren't you? Have you found Marilyn? And that poor man. Sid, I think? Have the police found the killer yet? Are you two looking for the killer? That sounds dangerous. I don't want you two to get hurt."

"That's a lot of questions, Jennifer, but I think I'd better not talk about business, I'm sure you understand."

"Sure, Zellie. I understand." Jennifer agreed, although with poor grace.

"What kind of work do you do?" Zellie asked. Other than swindle smitten men, she thought.

"Oh, this and that. I do like the fashion business, though."

"Well your outfit is beautiful, Jennifer, you have good taste."

"I love yours, too. I bet Dan loved that outfit on you. Too bad about your breakup."

Zellie laughed. "He's a louse. I'm glad he's gone."

"But he seemed so sweet and was terribly handsome, wasn't he?"

Bitch. "I won't waste my breath talking about him, with you or anyone else."

"I'm just making conversation, Zellie. Didn't mean to press on a sore spot."

Sure, you didn't, Zellie thought.

The food mercifully arrived at that point, and they ate for a little while in silence, though for Zellie it was more a matter of not choking on the food or throwing it in Jennifer's smug face.

"I'd forgotten how good the food was here," Jennifer said.

Zellie was thankful for the change in tone. And topic.

"Yes, it is. What did you order? I've already forgotten."

"I ordered the grilled salmon. Want a taste?"

Zellie cringed inside. The day she'd eat from the same plate as Jennifer, the world would freeze over.

"Oh, no thanks, Jennifer."

"What did you order?"

"I ordered a salad Nicoise. It's delicious. I'd offer you a taste, Jennifer, but I think I have the beginnings of a cold. Don't want to spread the germs."

"No, of course not. Thank you. I'm sorry, Zellie."

Alarm bells rang in Zellie's head. "What are you apologizing for, Jennifer?

"Oh, this is not an apology. I'm sorry about what happened to you."

"Jennifer, please get to the point, *if* there is one."

"Well, I'm totally innocent. I didn't do anything to encourage him, I assure you."

"Who? What?" Zellie snapped.

"Dan made a pass at me. More than once, actually. But I turned him down each time, I promise you."

"Well, he was a louse. I told you that already."

"I'm sorry you have such bad taste in men, Zellie. Maybe that's why I want to get back with Arnie. He's good and decent. I deserve someone like that."

I will not rip her face off. I will not storm out like a juvenile. I will not slap her silly face. She thought of the little paperclip and smiled. "Well, I certainly agree that Arnie is good and decent. Whether you *deserve* someone good and decent is between you and your conscience."

Jennifer feigned injury and not convincingly. "Pretty harsh, isn't that? A girl is entitled to hope for a good man in her life."

Zellie was saved by the waiter's return. "Any dessert or coffee?"

"No, I don't think so," Zellie said. "Two girls who have to watch their figures. Just the check please. Thank you."

When the check arrived, Jennifer picked it up. "I invited you, Zellie. I'll get this," Jennifer said.

"No, that's okay. Let's just split it down the middle."

"As you wish. Let's see, your share is $38.00, including a good tip for our darling waiter."

They left the money on the table, and walked toward the door.

"Thanks for meeting me, Zellie. I enjoyed our lunch together. Let's do it again sometime."

Zellie turned and looked the other woman in the eyes. "I don't think so, and please stay out of my home. If you have messages for Arnie, don't leave them with me."

Jennifer unsuccessfully tried to look contrite. "I won't. I promise. And could you put in a good word for me with Arnie? I'd be so, so appreciative."

"Jennifer, I told you, your relationship with Arnie is between the two of you. I have nothing to do with it."

"Yes, you do, Zellie. Yes, you do."

***

For the last forty minutes, I had battled the urge to show up at their table, throw a glass of water in Jennifer's face and escort Zellie out of there. But she'd hung in like a trooper. When the women had parted ways, she'd let me know she was in her car and I was relieved that she seemed okay–for the most part.

I called her as soon as I heard her car door shut.

"Zellie, I'm here. Do you want me to get in the car with you? We can come back to get my car later."

"Yyyess. I think so. I'm so upset I don't know whether to cry or throw up my thirty-eight-dollar lunch. Please get over here."

"Okay, stay where you are. Jennifer's car just left. I watched for it. I'll be there in a second."

I got in Zellie's car a few moments later. "You did great, Zellie. It was nearly impossible not to haul you out of there, but you were magnificent."

Zellie burst into tears. "She's crazy, Arnie. Completely nuts. And I'm scared of her. I wish I'd never met her, and I wish Mrs. Minniefield had never asked me to do that."

"Me too, Zellie. On all counts, I agree with you. Remember, I was listening. I was hoping you'd pull the plug, but you certainly toughed it out."

"I felt like I had to, Arnie. But I'm not doing it again. How are you going to deal with her?" she said as she found a tissue in her purse.

I felt like my heart was breaking. "I don't know. But I'll figure it out. You shouldn't be involved in this at all. It's my problem." I leaned over and gave her the kind of awkward hug you give while sitting in a car. "Let's switch places. I'll drive."

Zellie readily agreed, and I started to put the car in reverse to exit the parking lot, when she stopped me.

"It's both our problem," she said firmly, the tear tracks drying on her face. "I said I'd never do that again. I meant lunch with Jennifer. I never said I'd abandon you. We'll figure this out together. Now take me home, please. I need a shower and clean clothes."

Okay, I admit it. I leaned over and kissed Zellie right then and there, and right on the lips, with considerable passion. Then I drove us home.

We made it home uneventfully. It was Zellie's reliable Honda, of course, that got us there. I was beginning to wonder if it was seriously time to get a new car. Matilda was just too unreliable, and truth be told, her 'environment' wasn't so great anymore, either. The heat was sparse and the air conditioning was just plain anemic. Car shopping was a horrible task, but it might be a good distraction for Zellie and me. Yes, both of us. She'd promised to go with me, after all. We didn't have to buy, right? Just look a little–no harm in that.

As soon as we arrived at Zellie's place, I collapsed on her sofa.

"I have to change out of these clothes, Arnie. I'll just be a few minutes. Of course, I'm sure you'll be sleeping by the time I get back, but I have evil ways of waking people up."

I didn't really want to find out what she meant, so I sat up, and placed a call.

"It's done, Mrs. Minniefield. And a very difficult experience, I should add."

"Is Zellie okay? I worried about her, and you too, all morning."

"She was pretty distraught at first, but she seems to be coming around now."

"Please come over and tell me all about it."

"Can it wait until tomorrow morning, Mrs. M? We're both exhausted, and we still have the locksmith and alarm company coming to both our places later this afternoon."

"It can wait, Arnie. And I'm glad you're enhancing security at both your places. It's a good idea."

"We've had enough invasions of our privacy already, that's for sure. Maybe this will help."

"I'm sure it will, Arnie. Get some rest tonight. Both of you. And tell Zellie I'm sorry she had to endure that."

"I will, Mrs. M, but you should tell her yourself tomorrow, okay?

***

Zellie walked out of the bedroom, dressed in her customary jeans and a sweatshirt. The sweatshirt said Princeton on it. There was no longer any evidence of her earlier tears. And honestly, she looked prettier in casual clothes and less makeup than she had in formal dress.

"You know, Zellie, you look great even without those fancy clothes and makeup. And much more comfortable. But Princeton? Why Princeton?"

"Thanks Arnie - for the compliment - not the snarky Princeton comment." She held her nose up in a caricature of a snob. "It so happens that I once dated an Ivy League graduate, and I myself applied to Cornell and Columbia before I ultimately matriculated at Rutgers. A matter of economy, you understand, my boy. But I am certainly Ivy League material."

I laughed. "Yes, you are, woman. You most certainly are. I told Mrs. M that we'd stop over tomorrow morning. I think she wanted us to come today, but I told her we were exhausted. She was worried about us, and you in particular."

"Well, I'm sorry, too. And I'm a little ticked off at her. I still don't see the point in all that."

"I don't really, either," I admitted. "But maybe she'll explain more tomorrow. In the meantime, we have a locksmith and the alarm company people coming later this afternoon. Are you up for it?"

"Omigod, yes. I don't think we should put it off any longer."

"No, I don't either. They are coming here first, then to my place." I looked at my watch. "They'll be here in about an hour. Feel up to a debriefing?"

"I guess so. I suppose I'm about as ready as I'll ever be. And thanks for getting in the car and driving me home, Arnie. We can get your car later."

"It'll be safe there overnight. We can get it after we go to Mrs. Minniefield's tomorrow morning. And before we go car shopping," I added.

"We're going car shopping tomorrow, Arnie? I never thought you'd actually do it."

"It's time, Zellie. I know I keep putting it off, but I need to have reliable transportation. I would have hated to leave you all alone at your lunch with Jennifer just because my car wouldn't start. Not that I did anything there – you handled it all by yourself – but I wanted to be there in case you needed me."

Zellie gripped my arm. "I did need you there, Arnie. I felt a lot safer knowing you were listening. And I needed you after the luncheon as well." Zellie released her grip on my arm. "So, what kind of car do you want?"

"Well, I don't really know. We can talk about that over breakfast tomorrow, if that's okay with you."

"Sure."

"Great, then it's settled. Now about today, what are your impressions other than Jennifer is crazy? I could hear, but of course, I couldn't see her reactions to anything."

"Well, she certainly projects a self-confident demeanor. No doubt about it. But there's something roiling inside her that's hard to define. I mean, it's not like she's about to explode, or anything like that, and I wouldn't call it nervousness. I don't know, it's something I can't put my finger on. Maybe some inner conflict going on, or something akin to conflict, but not precisely that."

"Was she uncomfortable with what she was saying? I mean, the 'desperately in love with Arnie' thing was more than a little over the top, wasn't it?"

"I don't know, Arnie. She just sounded crazy to me. Not that it's crazy to be in love with you," she quickly added. "But there was an element of desperation to it that was extremely unsettling."

"Was it contrived? And if so, what was the purpose of it?"

"Both good questions. And I have no answer for either one."

"I couldn't tell by just listening."

"That makes two of us. And I was there. I will say this – if the whole thing was contrived, she's a hell of an actress."

"She probably is. I mean, I was taken in by her. Although maybe I was just gullible."

Zellie put her hand on top of mine. "Arnie, you weren't gullible. You were in love. And she took advantage of the trust that comes with that."

"But she can't possibly be thinking I'd be so trusting again, can she? I mean, how dumb does she think I am?"

"Arnie, if she knows you, and she does, she'd know you're not dumb."

"So, what's the point of all this? I just can't figure it out."

"Well, you heard me ask her that at least three different ways. But we'll figure it out. And maybe the new locks and alarm system will keep her from showing up naked in your house."

"Well, gee, does that really have to stop?" I whined.

Zellie punched me in the arm. "Okay, wise guy. Yes, the unannounced nudity has to stop. It's for your own good," she said with a laugh.

I sobered. The luncheon had cost Zellie a lot more than thirty-eight dollars. The conversation was mean and malicious, at least in my mind. It wouldn't make me happy to know it was for nothing.

"So seriously, what did we learn today?" I asked.

"Did we learn anything other than Jennifer wants me to think she is desperately in love with you? And that you are thinking of nothing other than her? And about that, Arnie…"

"I'm not spending my time thinking about her, Zellie, and I don't care what Jennifer says she knows."

"Well, there was one particular comment she made that gave me pause, and I just have to ask…about you and Tammy…" Zellie almost blushed and I let her suffer for a moment.

"Zellie, you know I don't kiss and tell!" I waited for just a second before I added, "But I will say this – I had a nice time with Tammy, and I can assure you that I did not think about Jennifer at any time while I was with her."

"Well, that's a relief. I mean, I'm sorry I had to ask. But I just had to know. Not that I thought…, and I don't want to interfere in your…"

"Zellie, it's okay. Don't worry. I'm over Jennifer, really I am."

Zellie breathed a sigh of relief. "Okay, good. Now don't make me go through that again with you."

I laughed. "Okay, I won't. I promise."

She rewarded me with a smile. "Good, I'm glad we settled that."

"So, guess what kind of car Jennifer was driving," I said.

"Ooh, I forgot about that. You watched her leave. What was she driving?"

"A Mercedes 450 SL convertible, the little bitch. Presumably purchased with my money."

"Whoa, nice wheels. I'm sorry, though, Arnie."

"Yeah, I was kind of hoping she'd be driving a Plymouth or something, but no such luck. But there was another thing that was even more interesting."

"What?"

"She was being followed."

"How do you know?"

"My finely-honed detective skills, of course."

"No, really? How?" Zellie was smiling.

"Once again proving that we unlicensed, inexperienced detectives are superior in all ways to the inferior licensed kind, I observed the second car pull out immediately after she did, and watched it proceed in the same direction."

"Could have been a coincidence."

"Yes, it could have. But something tells me it wasn't. Although I admit, I'm unsure."

"What was the other car?"

"One of those non-descript sedans. I don't know, a black mid-size Ford or Lincoln, or something like that."

"Did you get a license plate number?"

"No, I was too far away. I didn't get one for Jennifer's car, either. I did think it was very clever of you to ask her where she's staying, if only to make sure we keep away from there."

"Thank you. It was my finely-honed detective skills, of course."

"Of course," I agreed with a grin, then glanced at my watch. "The locksmith should be here any minute. I figured that we needed to change the locks immediately, then consider what other security arrangements are necessary. The alarm system folks will be along in about a half hour."

"I'm all in favor of changing the locks, given our respective break-ins. But I don't know about having complicated security arrangements. They can really interfere with your life."

"Well, we should at least consider what's available. Maybe there's something that provides protection, but is relatively unobtrusive."

"Arnie, do you think we're in danger at all? I mean, our privacy has been violated and all that, and believe me I want that to stop. But does Jennifer really pose a threat?"

"You know," I said slowly. "I can't figure out what she's up to, or even who she is now. I do know that this is not the Jennifer I knew many years ago. That Jennifer was warm, carefree and funny. She had a rebellious streak a mile long to be sure, but certainly not in a dangerous or even improper way. This Jennifer seems cold and calculating." I shook my head. "I have to tell you. I'm just not sure what she's capable of at this point. But I want to be sure you're safe."

"Backatcha, buddy. Here's the locksmith now. I'll get the door."

"Have him show you his ID through the peephole, Zellie. He'll be familiar with the procedure. Might as well get used to it."

The locksmith knocked, and without even being asked, held up his ID so we could read it.

"That's him," I said.

We opened the door and admitted Al Barnegut, master locksmith.

"Thanks for coming, Mr. Barnegut."

"Call me Al. I understand that I'm changing locks on two houses."

"Yes, this one and one at the other end of this street."

"Okay. As you requested, I brought the double-deadbolt locks, and the extra heavy duty titanium chains. These are really good locks, by the way."

"That's good. Thanks for coming on short notice," I said.

"No problem. I'll get this installed in a jiffy and we can scoot on down to the other house and do the same."

We watched him work his magic on the front and back doors.

"All done," he proclaimed presently. "Check this out. Much better than these." He showed us the old locks. "These are very old, and frankly, not very secure. You'll feel safer with the new ones."

"Thanks Al. Let's go down to my house and do the same. Just follow the green Honda out front."

"Okay."

We hopped in the car and Al followed us to my house, where he performed the same operation.

"Thanks Al. Just send me the bill. We can split it between us later."

"Okay, Mr. Fischer. Will do." And he left.

"The alarm people are coming here first, and we'll just hear them out, okay?"

"Okay, but you know how these things are. They scare you to death to sell you a system with 24-hour monitoring."

"I know, Zellie. But we can at least listen to what they have to say. We're not required to buy anything."

"Arnie…" Zellie was fidgeting nervously. "I don't really…"

"What's up? Spit it out."

"These systems are pretty expensive. I might not want to spend my money that way."

"Oh, Zellie. I didn't mean to put pressure on you. I'm sorry. I just wanted you to be safe. I didn't really think it through. We don't have to do this. We may not want to anyway."

"Arnie, to be clear, my income is fine. I have the annuity from my old job, and the ADMS. (The Asshole Dan Monetary Settlement). I can pretty much do what I want. I have the paid-off house from my parents. My needs are modest. But I have to make choices sometimes."

"Could I just this once, cover the cost? I know you're militant about never taking anything from me, but maybe just this once?"

"I don't think so. If it makes sense, I'll pay for it myself. But thanks."

"How about the A to Z Agency taking on the cost? It's in the interests of the agency to keep its partners safe, isn't it?"

"It is," Zellie said, laughing. "But you forget, the A to Z Agency is more or less broke."

"Now wait a minute. The A to Z Agency has Marilyn's retainer. And zero overhead other than the cost of coffee at the Moo-Mart, and maybe gas for the cars."

"I'll think about it. We should consult the firm's accountant about it."

"The firm has no accountant."

"Well, we'll consult the accountant if we ever hire one."

"Okay. So, it's settled."

"What's settled?"

"We should get an accountant."

Lucky for us, at that moment, the doorbell rang.

"It's the alarm company."

We went through the same drill, looking at their ID though the peephole, and admitting them.

"Good afternoon, Mr. and Mrs. Fischer. I'm Jeffrey Burke. I'm here from Adam's Security Systems."

"Someone wasn't warm on acronyms that day, were they?" I muttered and Zellie giggled.

It didn't seem like Mr. Burke heard anything, as he pushed ahead. "We can offer you a state of the art security system for your lovely home."

"Mr. Burke…" I started.

"Please call me Jeffrey, Mr. Fischer."

"Um yes, but…"

"You and the missus are worried about intrusiveness, I can see that. But our systems are completely seamless and virtually invisible to the naked eye."

"But how…"

"Microwaves. Yup, just like your oven. But these control your security system. Shall I sign you right up?"

"Jeffrey…"

"Of course, the cost. You and Missus Fischer are worried about the cost. It's almost free. Really, only pennies a day keeps you both safe in your lovely home. I told you how lovely your home is, right?"

"Yes, you did, Jeffrey." I held up my hand and Jeffrey closed his mouth. "Are you for real? I mean, I expected a hard sell, but I've never seen or heard anything like this. You haven't really told us anything."

"Well, it's my first day. I'm a little nervous." He reached toward his briefcase. "Maybe I can convince you with what I have here."

When he turned again to face us, we were staring down the barrel of a gun.

CHAPTER TWENTY

"Into the living room. Quickly." His voice was no longer breathless and naïve sounding. It was harsh and commanding. We walked into the living room. Lazlow was sleeping in the doorway, having not made a move when Jeffrey arrived. We were used to this of course, and gingerly stepped over him. Jeffrey was not so lucky. Intent upon watching us, he didn't see Lazlow, and promptly tripped over Lazlow's prone body, falling on his face and dropping his gun, which I quickly scooped up. Bless his little puppy heart, Lazlow didn't budge an inch, and continued snoring softly.

"Don't move a muscle," I commanded Jeffrey, who was still face down on the carpet.

"I'm getting up. You won't shoot me," he said from the ground.

"Sure, I will. Probably not in the heart, though. I was thinking foot or leg, what do you think, Zellie?"

"Give the gun to me. I'm tired and angry. I'll shoot him in the gonads," she said as smoothly as though delivering the weather report.

"This is very impolite of us. We should ask him," I said. "What do you prefer, Jeffrey? Or do you harbor the illusion that we won't shoot you somewhere?"

Jeffrey mumbled something, but stayed face down on the rug.

"Good boy. Now tell us your real name and why you threatened us."

Jeffrey didn't say anything. I fired a shot just to the right of him and he jumped.

"Look at that, Jeffrey. You must have made me all nervous and jumpy. I just shot a hole in my carpet. If I'd been more accurate, I'd have hit you, and wouldn't have ruined my Berber. Although I guess, with the blood and all, it would have made quite a mess anyway. Silly me. Well, now that it's ruined anyway, what's the difference? Right Zellie?"

"Sure. It's got a hole in it. No need to keep it clean anymore. You'll have to replace it anyway."

"You people are crazy," Jeffrey said from his position on the floor. "Just go ahead and call the cops. I'm not saying anything without my lawyer."

"Cops? Who said anything about cops? What I think we have here is a case of mistaken information, don't we, Zellie?"

"It would seem so."

"You see, Jeffrey, if that is indeed your real name, which I doubt, you pulled a gun on us in my house. Under section 232 of the New Jersey Penal Code, appendix A, I'm entitled to shoot anyone and anything that attacks me in my own home. No questions asked. Well, maybe a few questions, and I'm sure I just made up the statutory reference, but you get the idea. New Jersey is very liberal about defense against home invasions. Deadly force is A-OK here. And I'm not even going to use deadly force. I'm going to just maim you a little. Now once again, what's your name, and why are you threatening us?"

"Okay, okay. You people are nuts. My real name is Bobby Weaver, and I was told to threaten you into giving me the password to your Mork account."

"My Mork account? Robin Williams? Like Mork and Mindy?"

"That's what I was told to ask for. Your Mork account. I don't know anything else."

"Who told you to ask that? And who were you to give the information to?"

"I don't know. Honest. The guy approached me and gave me the assignment. Told me I'd get a thousand dollars for the information. For that kind of money, I'd pull a gun on my mother."

"You probably would, wouldn't you Bobby? How were you supposed to deliver the information to him?"

"We were supposed to meet outside of Rancid tomorrow. He gives me the money and I give him the information. No other contact."

Rancid was a dive bar in Highlands. We continued asking Bobby for information, but we became convinced that he didn't know anything.

"What should we do with him?" Zellie asked.

"Well, we can't just let him go. Why don't we just shoot him and get rid of the body?"

Bobby shivered. "You people are crazy. Why don't you just call the cops like ordinary people?"

"I suppose so. But we should call the State Police, not the locals."

We called Mike and told him what happened. He promised to come over personally and take charge of our prisoner.

"Can you hold on to him for another twenty minutes?" he asked.

"Oh sure. He's been very cooperative."

"I'll bet he has, Arnie. Practicing our marksmanship again, are we? No don't tell me. I'll be right over."

I turned my attention to Zellie. "So, I wonder what happened to the real security guy. And how did Chuckles here know we were waiting for one? How about it, Bobby?"

"I don't know, I swear. Please don't shoot at me anymore. I was just given this ID and told to come over here. I don't know anything else."

"He's probably telling the truth, you know, Arnie."

"I know. But I'll call the company and see what happened to their representative. He may be injured, or something."

When I called them, the company had no record that I'd made an appointment at all.

"Very strange," I said after I'd hung up.

"Is it the same company?" Zellie asked. Maybe you called a different one."

"No, I'm pretty sure I called Adam's. It's the same one we used at the firm," I replied, looking over at Bobby, and using the generic "firm" rather than providing the name that he might overhear. After all, Bobby still thought he was looking for a password for a character in a classic TV series. I saw no reason to clue him in.

***

Mike arrived promptly, as promised. He had another trooper with him.

"Hello Arnie, Zellie. This is Trooper Maria Alsott. She will take custody of your prisoner, while I get the details of what happened."

"Mr. Fischer, Ms. Morgan. I can take that firearm from you as well." She examined it, engaged the safety, and smelled the barrel. "Looks like one shot was fired. Did the suspect discharge the weapon?"

"No, he never got a chance to. He tripped over my dog, fell on his face and dropped the gun. I picked it up."

"Did it discharge when he fell?"

"No, Trooper Alsott. I fired it."

"Can you explain the circumstances?"

"The suspect was getting to his feet and was prepared to threaten us again. I fired one shot into the carpet next to him to demonstrate my seriousness in keeping him at bay on the floor."

"It's lucky you didn't hit him by accident."

Mike cut in at that point. "No luck involved at all, Maria," he said smiling. "Arnie is a former amateur state champion marksman. He can handle an easy shot like that with his eyes closed."

"Well, you've ruined your carpet, Mr. Fischer. And it was a nice one. Okay, Mike, I'll bring the prisoner out to the car and secure him. Mr. Fischer, Ms. Morgan, good day."

"Goodbye Trooper Alsott," we said in unison.

And she departed, with Bobby the Incompetent Criminal in tow. We told Mike what happened.

"You guys are lucky you didn't get hurt," he said. "Do you know why he pulled a gun on you?"

"He said he was told to force me to give him my password to Mork," I offered.

"Mork?"

"Well, I'm pretty sure he meant Mort, short for Mortal Securities, where I worked until about a year ago."

"And I'm sure he gave this information to you voluntarily? The shot to the carpet probably had nothing to do with it, I'm sure."

"I certainly have no intention of suggesting otherwise, Mike. Or saying anything at all about it, if I can avoid it. I want to be completely truthful with you."

"I'm sure you do, Arnie. I'm sure you do. You just might be leaving stuff out. But he's the criminal here, not you, so let's move on. Unless you have a different version Zellie? And by the way, it's good to see you again, although these are not the circumstances I would have chosen to run into you."

"Nice to see you again, too, Mike. And I wouldn't dream of contradicting your impression of the manner in which we obtained the information from the criminal who threatened us," she added sweetly.

"I'm sure you wouldn't, Zellie," Mike said drily. "Okay, then, let's continue. Who did he say told him to get the password from you?"

"He didn't say. And I think he doesn't really know. He just said he was to meet the guy outside Rancid tonight and give him the information."

"Is the password still active, given that you stopped working there a year ago?"

"Yes. It's still active. Continued access was part of my severance package."

"Does it have value to someone else?"

"That's the thing, Mike. I don't think so."

"Why not?"

"Well, by itself, the password wouldn't work. There's sensitive information underneath all those firewalls and security procedures, so it would require a minimum of a two-step verification process. A password, which I can readily change, and, in fact, *do* change every thirty days is only half at a minimum of what would be needed to get into the system."

"What's the other half?"

"A key card, specially encoded to match an ever-changing password. It involves a random number generator built inside the card, and other security procedures that I'd rather not go into."

"Is it possible that whoever wanted the password, has the key card?"

"I doubt it. I certainly don't keep it around unsecured."

"Well, you should check on it. Either the people behind this aren't aware of the need for the key card, or they have it, or, not to scare you, they have a plan for getting it."

"Well this guy was supposed to be from Adam's Security. Zellie and I both had our locks changed today, and we were going to hear a sales pitch for a security system. He turned out to be an impersonator."

"Did you get a chance to call Adam's? It's a good outfit."

"I did call them. And they had no record of the appointment at all."

"Well that's odd. You're sure you called the right company?"

"Zellie asked me the same thing. I certainly thought so. They're the same outfit that Mort uses, and I already had the number. Maybe I made a mistake."

"Well, we'll look into it, Arnie. But there's only so much we can do. This is really a local police issue, but I understand why you called me instead. I'm afraid the town police department is having some problems with getting qualified officers."

"I think you're right. My recent experience was not great. By the way, how is the investigation of Sid's murder going?"

"I can't tell you much, Arnie, but it's kind of on the back burner for me. It looks like an ordinary mob hit, if you can call any murder ordinary. We have a separate task force for mob-related crimes, and I'm only nominally on it as a member of the major crimes unit. I don't think there's been much progress though. Well, I better get back out to Maria. She'll be wondering where I am. We'll be in touch if we need anything more from you." He gestured at Lazlow. "When he wakes up, if that ever happens, let the hero over there know that we appreciate his fine police work."

"We'll do that, Mike. Thank you for coming over. We really appreciate it."

"Yes, thank you, Mike," Zellie added. "It's nice to see you again."

"You too, Zellie. You okay to get home all right? Be glad to drop you off," he said without looking at me.

But Zellie looked at me, then at him. "Yes, I'll be fine, but thank you for asking," she said.

When he closed the door behind him, she swung to face me. "I'm going home and set those nice new locks. Not a single word from you, Arnie Fischer. Do you hear me?"

***

What a zany day! That was some *tour de force* by Jennifer. What did it all mean? She certainly appeared crazy. And absolutely unlike the Jennifer I knew, even the new Jennifer of a year ago. *What's going on?*

Why the need to meet Zellie for lunch? Why the crazy veering from coldblooded to unbelievably hot, to she loves me dearly. Did she? It seemed terribly unlikely. Yet there was an element of yearning in the midst of the overplayed hand.

And what was the attempt to get my Mort password all about? Very bizarre, to say the least. And crude. Certainly, not Jennifer's style. She was much more about psychological pressure, not flat-out physical violence-or attempted violence. Foiled by my super dog over there. I really should spend more time with him.

And the break-ins. Jennifer's break-in of both our houses was much more understandable in a weird way, than the complete upheaval attendant to the second search of my house. Come to think of it, that search was more the style of the hoodlum we'd just met, and whoever hired him, than anything Jennifer would ever do.

What were they after? The password alone was useless, yet they wanted it badly enough to send a thug to threaten us. It was a silly approach in any event. I could have told that idiot *anything*. He would've had no way to verify it.

That was it! He was never supposed to get good information. He was just there to make us nervous. Same thing for the shambles they left my house in-they weren't necessarily looking for anything. Designed to poke and prod to see what we'd do.

And what role did Mrs. Minniefield play in all this? She'd been acting weirder and weirder each time we met. I postulated and pondered, and roiled all evening, then wandered into my bedroom, and tried to sleep.

***

I awoke to the sound of pounding. Still groggy, I wandered to the front door, wondering who the heck was bugging me in the middle of the night. As if I hadn't had enough aggravation for one day. I peered out the peephole. Zellie. Standing there in the bright sunshine. I undid the locks and swung open the door.

"Arnie it's almost nine o'clock! Where have you been? I've been calling you."

Nine o'clock. *Wow*. I must have really been tired. I let her in.

"You're just getting out of bed? I've been up for hours. You didn't answer the phone so I finally just came over. And we forgot to exchange the new keys, so I couldn't get in. I've been out here for at least fifteen minutes."

"I don't remember hearing the phone, Zellie. Sorry to worry you. I guess I was just exhausted. I stayed up too late ruminating about everything that's happened."

"No harm done. Go shower and get dressed. I'll have coffee ready for you when you're finished."

"Thanks, Zellie. And the new keys are on the counter. Take the spare."

"I will. And I'll put mine right here so I don't forget. Now go. You look like hell."

"Gee, thanks for the support. And I suppose you looked like a bunch of fresh flowers this morning when you got up?"

"Yes, I did. A beautiful bouquet of daisies, if you must know."

"Daisies. Sure. In your dreams."

She threw a dish towel at me. "I am simply shocked by your expression of disbelief. Now go already." But she was smiling.

I heard her puttering in the kitchen as I shed my clothes and jumped in the shower. "Daisies," I muttered under my breath.

But daisies described her pretty well, I thought, while the water streamed on my head. Uncomplicated, but beautiful all the same. Sunny and smiling, just like the Zellie I'd known for my whole life. It was good to see the happy Zellie, with that easy laugh, peeking through the veil of darkness that had descended over her in the last year. Over me, too, if I was honest. We'd been through a lot in the last year. Maybe not the kind of hardship that many suffer in this world, but difficult to be sure.

I finished my shower, dressed and headed out to the kitchen. Zellie was on the phone.

"Hold on a sec, Marla, here he is now." She held her hand over the mouthpiece as she turned toward me.

"Marla is free for breakfast at Audacious Bagel. Do you want to join her, or should we go right to Mrs. Minniefield's after we pick up your car?"

"I think we have time for some breakfast before we go, but I'd like to drink my coffee for a few minutes before we leave, seeing as how you fixed it. And we can call Ted–see if he's available."

She relayed a time to rendezvous, then listened for a moment. "Okay, see you then."

"As you heard, we'll meet her at ten and you can get in your Delilah flirtation fix."

It was my turn to throw a towel at her. "Delilah's just being nice, and trying to sell bagels. They probably get a bonus or something if they sell the complicated types of bagels."

"Oh, she's hoping for a bonus, all right," she laughed.

"Let's sit for a few minutes while I drink my coffee. It was a long day yesterday, and I'm really tired. I still need to wake up."

"Well, I admittedly drank about fourteen cups this morning myself before I came over here, so I won't begrudge you a little caffeine."

"Why would a fresh bouquet of daisies need coffee?"

Zellie turned her nose upward in mock indignation. "Even the most beautiful buttercup needs a little watering from time to time."

I finished my coffee as she called Ted. After ending the call, she turned to me. "He's up for it." She rolled her eyes. "Just for me, he'll make an appearance."

"Yeah, I'm sure Marla has nothing to do with it."

"Not a thing, I'm sure."

"Ted's developing quite an interest in Marla. He's not usually so attentive to the women he dates."

She looked thoughtful for a moment. "I know. I wonder what's different this time?"

"I wouldn't even hazard a guess. Not that Marla isn't nice and all," I quickly added, "but she deals with criminals on a daily basis. It's a tough business, and Marla is certainly up to handling them. She's nothing like Ted's usual dates."

"She'd say that they're *not* criminals. They're innocent unless proven guilty, that everyone is entitled to representation, and that she's vindicated many innocent people. I've certainly never seen her job affect her. She's good at keeping her business life separate from her personal life. And maybe Ted is enjoying a strong personality for a change."

"I haven't seen it affect her, either," I admitted. "And really, it's good to see Ted get out of the lab sometimes. They certainly look good as a couple."

"They really do. It's ten to ten. Finish up your coffee, and let's go."

I took a final gulp, Zellie grabbed my extra key and I pocketed hers, and we departed.

Once in the car, we headed toward Route 35.

"We better pick up your car after breakfast," she said as she drove. "We're late as it is."

"That's fine. We don't need two cars at AB. That parking lot is getting more and more crowded."

"The place is getting very popular."

"It really is. Fortunately, we're practically charter members of the place. They'll usually find a spot for us."

"Yes, and for some reason, it's always in Delilah's section."

"For some reason. Very peculiar."

But I smiled when I said it. It was entirely possible that a gratuity of sorts had passed between me and the hostess some weeks ago. Not that I'd admit that, of course.

"Yes, very…suspicious, actually," Zellie said with a chuckle. "It's almost like it's been pre-arranged. But of course, that's impossible, isn't it Arnie?"

"I would think so."

Zellie didn't press the issue. But she knew me like a book, didn't she? I smiled to myself ruefully. But that's not so bad, is it, to have someone know you that well? The hostess showed us to our table, which miracle of miracles, was in Delilah's section.

"Your usual table is acceptable, I trust?"

"It's great. Thanks, Tina. Ted and Marla are joining us. I'm actually surprised they're not here yet. Could you please show them over here when they arrive?"

"Sure, no problem."

Delilah approached our table. She was wearing a bright yellow t-shirt that had "Audacious Bagel" emblazoned in sequins across her ample chest, and a hat that said "The Bagel – A Cook's Canvas" across the front.

"Hi Delilah," we both said. "Ted and Marla will be here in a few minutes, so we'll order when they get here."

"Okay," she said brightly. "And when you do, I have something special to suggest to you, Arnie. I'm telling you right now, you'll be very happy if you sample what I have to offer."

"I'm sure I will, Delilah."

Zellie gave me a meaningful look as Delilah walked away. But before I could respond to the unspoken snarky comment, Ted and Marla arrived.

"Look who I ran into in the parking lot," Ted said.

Everyone exchanged greetings and the new pair dropped into their seats.

And as if awaiting her cue, Delilah appeared at our table, silent and ready like a bagel ninja.

"What'll it be?" she asked with a bright smile for us all.

Ted ordered a hamburger infusion, Zellie asked for a bagel with goat cheese, and Marla ordered a falafel bagel. As for me, I accepted Delilah's suggestion of an enchilada infusion.

"It's extra spicy, Arnie. I think you're someone who'd really get into extra spicy if you tried it."

I agreed, although somewhat reluctantly this time. It was hard enough viewing a bagel in a new way, but using it as the wrapping for an enchilada seemed beyond even Audacious Bagel's considerable *chutzpah*. But what the heck – nothing ventured, nothing gained.

And, it was actually good. I mean, it wasn't an enchilada, but it tasted a lot like one. It probably wouldn't replace tortillas in Mexico, or anywhere else, for that matter. But that's the beauty of Audacious Bagel. It isn't trying to replace or imitate anything. It's unique. And incredibly popular.

We brought Ted and Marla up to date on the long and arduous events of the previous day. Ted laughed at my firing the shot into my carpet, just inches from the thug's head.

"I'll bet that stopped him short, Arnie."

"It did. He flopped back down pretty fast."

"Have you been practicing?"

"Not really. I mean, I go to the firing range from time to time and certainly not on a regular basis. But I was three feet away - it wasn't a hard shot to make."

Marla had listened to our story with rapt attention.

"Did he say who sent him?"

"No, but maybe Mike will get something out of him. Personally, I don't think he knows much. He's supposed to meet the guy who hired him tonight at Rancid, and I assume Mike will set a trap."

"I'm sure you'd like to find out who sent him, that's for sure."

"Yes. We're getting tired of not knowing what's going on."

"So, what was the purpose of Jennifer wanting to go to lunch with you?" Marla asked Zellie.

"I still don't know. She kept talking about wanting to get back together with Arnie, but I just don't think that was her real purpose. I mean, she said that, over and over, but it was almost like she was playing a part. Just a hunch. I've never seen her act like that, although my previous contact with her was pretty minimal."

"It was definitely unlike her, that's for sure," I agreed.

"Did she tell you anything else?" Marla asked.

"I don't know. What do you mean?"

"Well, like what's she doing now, where's she living, that kind of thing?"

"She said she was living temporarily at that Holiday Inn up the road, and that she was interested in fashion, but was focusing on getting Arnie back right now."

"Nothing else?"

"I don't know, Marla, I don't think so. Does it make any difference?"

Marla looked thoughtful. "You never know." Then she softened her tone. "I'm sorry, Zellie. Must be the lawyer in me. Didn't mean to cross-examine you."

"It's okay, Marla. We're trying to figure it all out, too."

"You're welcome to cross-examine me, Marla," Ted said with a little-boy grin.

"I might just do that, Edward."

I almost spit out my coffee. "Edward? You haven't let anyone but your parents call you that in years."

He shrugged. "It's way more sophisticated for a man of my station, than *Ted*."

We all laughed at that, and mocked Ted mercilessly about his "station." Then Zellie nudged me.

Mrs. Minniefield was waiting.

CHAPTER TWENTY-ONE

When we got in her car, Zellie laughed until she had to hold her sides. "Edward? Boy, he's really fallen for Marla, hasn't he?" she finally said through her gasps for air.

I smiled. "It sure looks that way. Well, good for him. Settling down would be great for the old boy."

"I can't see Marla hanging out in his basement, though."

"No, he may have to come upstairs from time to time."

"No harm in that. I mean, it's not like he's a mole or something."

"No, but he really does love it down there. It's his creative space. We all should have something like that, really."

Zellie looked doubtful. "Well, sure, but it can be above ground, can't it?"

"Of course. Anyway, there's my car. I'll drop it off at home, and meet you at Mrs. Minniefield's. I can walk over."

"You want me to wait to see if it starts up?"

"Nah, it should be okay. I'll call you if it's a problem."

"Okay, see you in a few."

I unlocked the door and put the key in the ignition. It started right up, and purred like a kitten. Well, maybe not, but I liked the characterization. Actually, it made quite a racket, but I was used to that. I wasn't entirely sure that I *wanted* a new car.

Matilda had served me well, and really, didn't let me down. Much. Only occasionally. At *really* inconvenient times. But she was certainly comfortable, in a Spartan sort of way. I sighed. Okay, maybe it was time to get a new car after all.

I put the car in drive and off we went, Matilda and me. A carefree soul and his trusty vehicle. Which stalled almost immediately. I started it up again, and once again it purred like a…well you get the idea. We went along like that for a while, stopping and starting until finally she just gave out and wouldn't start up again.

Fortunately, I was off Route 35 by then, so I didn't have to deal with the speeding traffic. I was close to the Moo-Mart, so I called Eddie, who came out and helped me push Matilda into their parking lot.

"Finally gave out, huh?" he said gently when we'd gotten her into a space.

"I'm not convinced of that yet. She probably can still be saved."

"You're not serious, are you Arnie? The car's ancient, and lasted longer than most cars its age. How many miles you have on this thing?"

"About 275,000."

"Isn't that enough? Time to get a new car, Arnie. And if you're a little short, I could maybe lend you a few bucks to get a nice used one. I have a cousin that sells used cars. He's pretty honest."

"That's really nice of you, and thank you, but I'm in good shape financially. I can get a new car. I just really liked this one."

"I know how you feel. We do tend to get attached to our rides. But things change, right? I mean, you won't run your business out of the Moo Mart forever, either, right?"

I grudgingly admitted he had a very good point, then called Zellie and told her what happened. She had just arrived at Mrs. Minniefield's and said she'd turn around and come back.

When Zellie arrived at the Moo-Mart, I was talking quietly with Eddie. He had a wife and three little kids, and didn't make much money as the Moo Mart manager. Despite basically scraping by economically, he was happy and appreciative of what he had.

And that's the guy who offered to lend me money to get a used car, when he thought I might be a little down and out. It really made me think about things. I don't know if I'd been acting depressed lately, but I did realize that it was high time to start appreciating what I have.

And that appreciation had to begin with the person walking through the door right now. She was showing signs of coming out of her funk, and I needed do the same. Having a bad relationship wasn't the end of the world, after all. No matter our historic mistakes, Zellie and I had each other, and we had a whole world of people out there who weren't the jerks we had ended up with.

"Hi guys," she said with her breezy smile. "Arnie, are you ready to go? Mrs. Minniefield is pretty anxious."

"Sure," I said. I turned to Eddie. "Thanks for everything, Eddie. Are you sure I can't pay you for your time?"

"Don't you dare! You'd do the same for me. And the two of you are my best tenants, maintaining your office here and all," he added with a grin.

***

We walked out to the car and I gave Zellie a quick hug. "Thanks for coming to get me. She started right up. Couldn't keep her going, though," I admitted with a sigh.

"It's fine, Arnie. It wasn't really that far. I assume you're ready to look for a new car now?"

"I'm ready. I probably should have listened to you earlier. But I really love that car."

"I know you do," she said soothingly. "But maybe there's a new car out there to love, and I promise I'll help you find her."

"Pretty good planning, I guess. We intended to look this afternoon, anyway."

"That was the plan," she agreed. "We can start after we see Mrs. Minniefield."

As Zellie drove, I told her about Eddie helping me, and then offering to lend me money to get a used car.

"Isn't that something? Here he has way less than I do, with five mouths to feed, and yet he's unbelievably generous."

"He's a good guy," Zellie agreed. "We need more like him in the world."

"I'd love to figure out a way to help him out without him knowing about it."

"Be careful about that," she warned. "He's a very proud man."

"I know, but maybe there's a way to help without giving him charity that he doesn't want." I'd give it some serious consideration.

***

Mrs. M opened the door and gave me a hug.

"I'm sorry about your car, Arnie. I know what it's like to be attached to a car. I treasure my 1957 Studebaker, as you know."

"Thanks, Mrs. M. But maybe it's just time for me to get a new car anyway. It's not the end of the world."

"Very brave of you," she said, with just the hint of a sardonic smile. "Now, I understand you two had an eventful day. Tell me all about it. And leave no detail unspoken," she added as we sat down in the living room.

We took turns telling her about our day. Zellie told her about her lunch with Jennifer, and left almost nothing out as far as I could tell. She charged right through Jennifer's sexual references, and included the occasional salty language without batting an eyelash. She paused for just a hint of a moment when talking about Jennifer's revelation about being propositioned by Dan. Mrs. Minniefield raised an eyebrow at her recounting Jennifer's statement that she had turned Dan down.

Mrs. M had remained silent throughout Zellie's report, but interrupted to ask whether Jennifer had told her about any other of Dan's indiscretions, to which Zellie replied, with some surprise at the question, that she hadn't. While she didn't speak, Mrs. Minniefield also expressed interest in Jennifer knowing that we'd started an investigation business, that Marilyn Beaufort was our first client, and that I'd gone out with Tammy. She nodded when she heard that. Zellie finished her narrative and Mrs. M. finally spoke again.

"What was your overall impression, Zellie?"

"Arnie and I talked about that. My first impression when I was there was that she was absolutely nuts."

"And when you left?" Mrs. Minniefield pressed.

"She acted so out of character. I mean, I only knew her for a short time when she returned a year ago –when she and Arnie began seeing each other. But she didn't act like this. The Jennifer I knew was cool and calm, not prone to histrionics of any sort. She always seemed totally in control." She looked at Arnie for a moment. "Actually, it kind of bugged me."

I smiled at her. "Your warmth of mind and spirit, and my obvious affection for you, probably bugged her, too."

Mrs. Minniefield smiled for a mere millisecond, and then resumed her businesslike demeanor. "So, you felt like she was acting?"

"I don't really know. If so, she's a great actress."

"She probably is, but that doesn't necessarily mean it was a total act."

"I think you might have put your finger on it. It was only partly an act."

"But what part?" I asked.

"Hard to say," Zellie said. "You were listening, Arnie. What did you think?"

Mrs. Minniefield inclined her head. "Yes, you know Jennifer better than Zellie. I'm very interested in your impressions."

"I had the same reaction. A lot of what she said was total crap. But it was designed to create a few distinct impressions. She wanted to convince Zellie that she wanted to get back together with me. She wanted to provoke Zellie, but only a little, because she stopped short of a full-scale assault. And she wanted to let Zellie know that she was watching us. Finally, she wanted to get as much information as she could about our activities. If she set out to do those three things, I think she would view the luncheon as a qualified success. It was certainly unsettling to listen to, and Zellie was quite shaken up after it was over.

"But the overall performance, if you want to call it that, was uneven. Some parts of it seemed almost sincere. Not the desire to get back together with me," I quickly added. "Don't worry, I don't think that. But the prodding about my close relationship with Zellie. That rang true. Do you think so, Zellie?"

She nodded. "Yes. That part was both wistful and angry, wasn't it?"

I nodded.

"Did you check out whether Jennifer is really staying at the Holiday Inn? I sincerely doubt it," said Mrs. M.

Zellie and I looked at each other. I shook my head. "No, we never checked. I don't think we saw the reason for it, other than maybe to stay away from there."

"You should check," Mrs. M. said firmly. "Jennifer's activities are very important to you, if you want to avoid getting hurt."

When I told her about Jennifer driving a Mercedes convertible and that I thought she was being followed, Mrs. Minniefield nodded knowingly.

"Yes, that makes sense," she said, almost to herself. Without explaining, she continued. "It's a shame you couldn't get her license plate number. It would be interesting to see who it's registered to, and the address. When you see her again...."

She paused to consider the consternation in our faces. "I'm sorry. But you *will* see her again. When you do, try to get the plate number. You might also want to get the plate number of whoever is following her, but I suspect that they will have taken pains to make their plate untraceable."

"Mrs. Minniefield," I said with some exasperation. "Do you know what's going on?"

"I have a few theories," she said. "But all I can say for sure is that whatever Jennifer wants is not going to be in either of your interests. I'm glad you changed the locks on your houses. But I think a security system might be a good addition. Unfortunately, that didn't go very well. Tell me about that," she commanded.

So, we told her about the security company imposter, how he pulled a gun on us, and how Lazlow disarmed him.

"I always expect big things from him," Mrs. Minniefield said fondly. "He's a special dog, that's for sure."

"Oh, he's special, all right," I said gruffly. But Zellie and Mrs. M both knew how much I loved Lazlow, and pretty much ignored me.

Mrs. Minniefield listened to how I'd fired the one shot, and how we kept the intruder on the floor until Mike had arrived.

"He was more dangerous than he seemed, Arnie. If Lazlow hadn't tripped him, there's no telling what he would have done. I think he only seemed inept because of the circumstances."

"But what was the point in trying to get my password? It's useless without the key card that goes into the slot on the computer before you even put in the password. And they wouldn't have that. It's in my safe deposit box. The only other way it possibly could be used is with full access to Mort's servers – but that's only on-site at Mort, and virtually impossible to get to. There's two-step verification with my account. That would take about six different access bypasses to get into. And the only people able to accomplish that wouldn't need my access card or password at all. They'd already have their own."

"Even people at Mort couldn't get into my account. They could get into the general Mort systems, but not the individual cloud accounts of partners, or even former partners. And even assuming they had access internally at Mort, and my keycard, or some kind of duplicate, which I don't think they do, I could just change my password remotely by the time they were able to use it."

"Think about what you just said, Arnie. If they had your password, and separate access at Mort, you'd just change your password before they could use it."

I thought about it, and became very distressed. Zellie had figured it out, too, because she looked as upset as me.

"He was going to kill us, wasn't he?"

"Either that, or incapacitate you in some way. But either way, it wouldn't have been good. You two need to be careful. It may seem unlikely that there is that separate access within Mort, but I wouldn't assume that whoever is after your access codes doesn't know that it's just one part of the verification needed to access the system."

"Maybe Mike will catch them tonight. I think he was planning to spring a trap at Rancid to catch anyone who shows up."

"That would certainly be the best outcome. But somehow, I think it will be more complicated than that."

I had the same feeling. And it wasn't a good feeling. Almost a premonition. But I kept my mouth shut.

"I don't know why Adam's Security had no record of my call. I mean, it's not like I'm completely unknown to them, given that they provided the security for Mort."

"I think you should assume that Adam's has been compromised in some way, Arnie. I will give you a name to call to get the two of you set up with good security. But please try to stay away from places without a lot of people around until this gets sorted out."

"Mrs. M, it's not like we were on a secluded beach. We were in my house – ironically enough - trying to arrange additional security."

"I know, Arnie. I don't mean to be melodramatic. I just want the two of you to be safe. We'll get you set up properly."

"In the meantime, Arnie and I are going car shopping this afternoon," Zellie said firmly. "We're going to get him a new car. Preferably one with air conditioning that works."

"That's a good idea. May I suggest you start with the Mercedes dealership on Route 35?"

"Why would I want a Mercedes?" I asked.

"Doesn't Little Bobby Dalton work there?"

"I think so, why?"

"You might want to ask him about his recent Mercedes sales."

Zellie and I looked at each other. Wow. "We might do just that," I said.

We left Mrs. Minniefield's house and walked to Zellie's car. By force of habit I reached for her hand, and she took it, maybe clasping it a little more firmly than usual. She was shaking a little, and I stopped to look at her.

"I'm scared, Arnie. It looks like we had a very close call, and Mrs. Minniefield is being dead serious. We might have treated the episode with the gun a little too lightly."

I pulled Zellie to me, and hugged her tightly. "I'm a little scared, too. But it'll be okay, Zellie. Mike will probably catch the guy behind this tonight. In the meantime, we'll stay away from that whole mess, and just look for cars today. It might not be anyone's idea of fun, but it should keep us out of trouble."

Zellie held on for a few more moments, then gradually let go.

"Okay," she said slowly. "But let's get some lunch first. All this being terrified has made me hungry."

I looked at her and smiled. "The stomach triumphs over fear once again."

"Let's go to D'Agostino's. It's quiet, but I think we're immune from danger there, aren't we? And it always gives them a thrill to see us together."

If I was a little surprised that Zellie suggested a romantic setting, I didn't let on. Frankly, it was okay with me.

"Okay. D'Agostino's it is."

***

Predictably, Salvatore and Mama D'Agostino greeted us with open arms.

"Look Papa, it's our favorite little lovebirds, here again so soon. Let me show you to your regular table in the back, she said loudly, emphasizing the "regular." It's very private and very intimate. You sit here, Zellie dear, and yes, right there Arnie. Right next to her. Oh, you look so wonderful together. I almost want to take a picture."

Zellie moved slightly so that she was snuggled against my side. I felt her warm body pressing against me, and it felt right. Zellie spoke first.

"Something about this place just makes you feel romantic."

"It does always seem to have that effect."

"Maybe it's just the danger, but I just want to enjoy a little closeness right now. Is that okay, Arnie?"

"It's more than okay, Zellie. Why don't we just call this place the 'romantic zone?' Anytime we're here, we can have a romantic meal together, and not worry about screwing up our friendship. It seems to work out that way anyway."

"Works for me." She held up her water glass. "To romance," she said, and we clinked glasses. Then I leaned over and kissed her, much to the delight of Mama, who was approaching with the menus.

"Oh Papa, look over here. Young love, isn't it beautiful?"

We disengaged quickly, and somewhat primly, smoothed out our clothes. Then we ordered our lunches, and chattered away like two old friends.

Or lovebirds, take your pick.

CHAPTER TWENTY-TWO

"Where do you want to go first, Arnie?"

"I guess we should get the Mercedes dealership over with first, but I don't see me driving one."

"Maybe Little Bobby Dalton will change your mind. He's a car salesman, after all."

"Hopefully he'll give us some information without requiring me to buy a car."

"Little" Bobby Dalton stood six-feet-seven-inches tall, with a slightly balding head of white hair that resembled the snow cap on Mount Everest. He'd been called Little Bobby his whole life, because he was named after his dad, Big Bobby, who founded the Mercedes dealership that we were now entering.

An earnest young salesman appeared almost magically before us, introduced himself as Tim, and offered to help us choose the "drive of a lifetime."

"Thank you, Tim. Maybe in a few minutes. Is Mr. Dalton here?"

"Little Bobby? Sure, he's always here. Who should I tell him is asking for him?"

"Tell him it's Arnie Fischer and Zellie Morgan."

Tim left us, and we tentatively peered at the cars in the showroom while we waited.

"That 450 SL is a beauty, isn't it, Arnie?"

But before I could answer, Little Bobby appeared. "Are the two of you looking to buy a Mercedes?"

"I'm in the market for a new car, Bobby. Mine died today. But we're also hoping you can help us with some information."

"I can certainly offer you the first thing, and I'll try like the dickens to help you with the second. What's it all about?"

"Can we go somewhere a little more private?"

"Sure, right this way to the nerve center of this place. Since Dad passed on, I've invested in a lot of technological improvements, some serious automation. Get it? *Auto*-mation?"

We allowed as how we understood and dutifully chuckled.

I offered him my hand and we shook. "I'm sorry about your dad, Bobby. Does his passing make you Big Bobby now?"

"Nah, I'm Little Bobby. And I like it that way. Here, come on in and sit down. It's nice to have some visitors. Especially old school friends. Now what can I do for you? And don't forget, you agreed to buy the most expensive car in the showroom in exchange for any help I give you. Aw, just kidding. What do you need?"

"I don't know how you'll feel about this, Little Bobby, but what we really need is, um, I'm not quite sure how to put this…"

"Just spit it out already, Arnie. Maybe I can help you guys."

"Okay, here goes. We want information on some of the people who probably bought cars from you."

"You want to look at my customer lists? At the confidential information that is the very lifeblood of my business? If people knew that information was being given out, they'd never trust me. Probably wouldn't ever buy a car from me again. Is that really what you want?"

Zellie and I looked at each other for a moment. "Yes," I said.

"Oh, okay. No problem. But let's do this the way they do it on television. I'll say I can't possibly give out that information, it's private, confidential, and I'd get in big trouble with the boss if I let you see it. And then you say, 'it's really important, couldn't we have just a little peek?' And I'll say, 'I'm sorry, it's simply not possible.' And you'll say, 'Please, just this once, it's really for a good reason.' And I'll start to break down a little, and say, 'Well…I can't give you the information, but coincidentally, I'm about to walk down to the showroom floor, and it will take me at least fifteen minutes during which time my computer terminal will be completely unattended, with my password already entered, but I won't tell you that the sales information including purchaser information is in a folder marked "Auto Sales," with subfolders by year.'

"Then I'll just coincidentally leave you alone in my office and wander amiably downstairs. Let's do it like that, okay?"

"Um, okay," I managed. "Sure, Little Bobby, that would be fine."

"Back in a bit. Make yourselves comfortable while I'm gone."

"Thanks."

Bobby looked back at us and smiled as he left, and I swear he was whistling "Secret Agent Man" as he departed. Zellie and I didn't waste time. We quickly opened the file Bobby had referenced and scrolled through Bobby's sales for the year. Nothing stood out at first, although there were names of some prominent people as customers. A Mercedes dealership would bring the rich and famous, I guess. But no Jennifer Marquette was listed.

"I guess she bought it somewhere else," Zellie said. "So, no address or other personal information, what a bummer."

"Yes, that's unfortunate. Mrs. Minniefield thought it was important. I guess we struck out."

"I don't see any purchase by Marilyn Beaufort or Bean, or whatever her name is, and I don't even see Mrs. Desmond's car. Wait a minute, forget that. There's a corporate sub-folder here, and look at the second listing."

"Brazen Saddles."

"Looks like he bought his wife her car with the corporate credit card."

"Yes, and Brazen Saddles, or Desmond, whichever, actually bought four cars. Nice perks for the employees. I'll bet that redhead in his inner office is driving one of them. And maybe Mrs. Desmond doesn't know about it."

"Who knows? But the listing is just that of Brazen Saddles, and we already have that information, so we're at a dead end again. Oh well, it was worth a try."

We played out Little Bobby's charade by quickly moving to the other side of his desk when we heard him returning, and both sat primly in his customer chairs.

"I hope I wasn't too long, guys. I had to attend to some things on the floor. A manager's work is never done, you know. Now what can I do to put you behind the wheel of that 450 SL you were admiring?"

"Well, I'm not really sure that a Mercedes is for me, Little Bobby."

"If you took one for a test drive, you wouldn't say that. All leather seats, five speed standard transmission with movements so smooth you just think about changing gears, and they change. Unbelievable array of electronic controls for just about everything. True *auto*-mation and a surround-sound stereo system that makes you think you're in Carnegie Hall."

"Um, I like it quiet when I drive. It lets me think."

"It probably has an off switch, Arnie," Zellie said.

Little Bobbie jumped on that. "An off switch? All you have to do is imagine it quiet and that baby will obey your silent command. You should really take it for a drive."

"Well, you do need a car, Arnie." Zellie was enjoying letting me fend off a sales pitch.

"You couldn't get a better one anywhere, Arnie. I promise you that." He looked out the window to the parking lot below. "I'll give you a great deal on a trade-in for that clunker of yours."

I bristled at the characterization, but he seemed blissfully oblivious.

"It's a '68 Chevy Impala, am I right?"

"It's a 1966, but yes, it's an Impala."

"Do I know my cars, or what? Anyway, I like the light blue. Very classy."

I decided to cut off any further discussion by referring back to the Mercedes.

"That thing probably costs $100,000. Although there were no price stickers on the cars in the showroom."

Little Bobby laughed. "Well you know what they say, Arnie, if you have to ask the price, you probably can't afford it. Just kidding," he added.

"The one on the floor has a manufacturer's suggested retail price of $128,000.00. But I'll give you a real good price if you're interested, Arnie, and I'm really not pressuring you – honest, it's really okay with me if you leave here without buying – I'm just a salesman through and through."

"Why don't I just sleep on it, Little Bobby, would that be okay?"

"Sure, Arnie. But I'll tell you, as a salesman, people rarely come back. Always better to close the deal before they leave. But we're old friends, and I'm going to let you just walk out that door."

"Thanks, Little Bobby. We really appreciate your help."

"What help? I tried to sell you a car, and it just didn't work out. Happens. And that's my story. Can't let the boss think anything else, can I?"

"Aren't you the boss?" Zellie just had to ask.

Little Bobby chuckled. "A mere technicality, Zellie. Enjoy the rest of your day. And think about that car, Arnie. I mean it, you'd love it."

He looked at Zellie for a moment. "You too, Zellie. I can just see it, twin convertibles. Hmm… a double sale, doesn't get better than that."

We left Little Bobby happily whistling and reflecting on his imaginary double sale of hundred-thousand-dollar cars.

"Nice looking cars," I said to Zellie as we left, "but that's a lot of money for transportation."

"Seems crazy to me. Should we look for cars you actually want to buy?"

"That was the plan. We could use a break from the craziness of the last few days and that wasn't exactly it."

"Yes. Little Bobby was great, though, wasn't he?"

"He's a good guy. Active imagination. He's always been like that – totally decent, head in the clouds. Interesting choice of professions."

"Probably not his choice. Someone needed to take over from Big Bobby."

At that moment, my phone rang. I looked at it, saw that it was Mrs. Minniefield, and answered. I listened for a few minutes and hung up. Zellie eyed me closely.

"Mrs. Minniefield has arranged for security professionals to visit us in twenty minutes."

"That's fast. Even for her."

"Yes, it is. She must really be concerned. I think our car shopping trip has been canceled, before it even started."

"You can always just call Little Bobby and get a Mercedes," Zellie said with a grin.

"Yeah, sure, both of us. Twin Mercedes convertibles, that's the ticket."

"Oh, that's just so dreamy," Zellie said, and burst out laughing.

"So, Mrs. M went to pains to describe who would be meeting us, insisted we check identification through the peephole, and not open the door to anyone other than Lawrence Baskin and Dominick D'Angelo. She described them in very detailed terms, and said they would be required to verbally state a passcode."

"Very cloak and dagger, but probably reasonable precautions given what happened on our last foray into security land. Okay, let's go."

We arrived at my house and went inside. I let Zellie know that Mrs. Minniefield had told them to come here first, and they arrived shortly after we did. As instructed, I viewed their credentials through the peephole. They helpfully stood back from the door so I could look them over and see if they matched Mrs. M's description.

But I didn't open the door until the taller of the two announced through the door that they were there for the "poles of the alphabet." Those were the magic words. I opened the door and let them in.

The tall one spoke first. "Good afternoon, Mr. Fischer. Ms. Morgan. My name is Lawrence Baskin, and this is Dominick

D'Angelo. We're here to assess the security situation, and to provide immediate solutions. I trust Mrs. Minniefield briefed you?"

We looked them over more closely, now that they were inside. They both were over six-feet-tall and muscular. Baskin was a little taller, but D'Angelo appeared more formidable, if that was possible. They both wore dark suits, were clean shaven and had neat haircuts. If they were wearing dark sunglasses, they would have looked like Feds. For all I knew, they could be ex-FBI, or special forces, or something. But they were all business, that's for sure.

"Mrs. Minniefield gave me only a cursory briefing, but I assume that you intend to improve the security around here and at Ms. Morgan's home?" I asked.

"Exactly. And we'd like to get to it right away. If that works for you, of course, sir," Baskin added, almost as an afterthought.

He's taking orders from someone other than us here, I thought. Mrs. Minniefield probably directed them in her most imperious way. She's worried about us. Well it was okay with me. I had tried to do the same thing, after all, but that had turned into a disaster. Mrs. M was taking no chances this time.

"Okay, Mr. Baskin. What do you need from us?"

"Nothing at the moment. If you would be kind enough to stand aside, we'll conduct a routine preliminary sweep of the place for hidden microphones."

"Bugs? Here?"

"We have been advised that you have had more than one break-in in the last week, and that certain information may have been obtained without your knowledge. We would do it as a matter of routine anyway, but under the circumstances, it is a particularly prudent step."

The two of them then began slowly, but systematically walking around the house with an electronics gadget. While one held a protruding wand, the other read the dial. They were thorough, that was for sure. They continued walking until a loud beeping sound interrupted their silent search in the living room.

"Looks like we have one, Larry." He tipped my television back an inch or so, and exposed a tiny black object no larger than a staple. As we looked, it suddenly fizzled for a nanosecond and was gone.

"Sophisticated little bugger. Designed to vaporize, if exposed to light once it's set."

"Who put it there?" Zellie spoke up. "Can you tell?"

"Unfortunately, this kind of technology is way too available. Almost anyone could have placed it, and at any time. But I'd hazard a guess that it occurred at the same time as one of your break-ins. But that's just a guess. Have any other people had access for enough time to put this here?"

"No. The only people who have been here by invitation are totally trustworthy."

A continued search revealed no further bugs.

"Okay, looks like you're clean now. Let's get to work on securing the place."

Baskin explained what they had in mind. It included securing the front and back doors with extra deadbolt locks and wiring an alarm system on the doors and windows, as well as installing strategically placed pressure bumps and "panic" buttons. And the whole thing was monitored twenty-four hours a day with immediate response guaranteed.

"What if I have to go to the bathroom in the middle of the night? I don't want to turn off the alarm system every time."

"You don't have to. All you need to do is hold up two fingers like this." He spread them apart in a "V" signifying victory or peace, I wasn't sure. I supposed going to the bathroom was a little of both.

"That tells the system to turn off the pressure bumps until you do it again. If you don't do it again within twenty minutes, it will turn on again automatically."

I started to ask if I was supposed to hold up one finger if I just had to pee, but thought better of saying it when I looked at Baskin's serious countenance. It was not the time to joke. Instead, I asked when the installation would take place. As if I had a choice, I thought, thinking of Mrs. Minniefield.

"Right now, if you give the go-ahead."

"I should probably ask what this is going to cost."

"It's already taken care of, Mr. Fischer."

"What do you mean, it's taken care of?"

"You should speak to Mrs. Minniefield about that, sir. My orders are to install this system, with your consent of course, at no charge to you, either now, or in the future."

"Okay, wait a second, while I call her."

I called Mrs. M, and before I could say anything, she told me that Baskin and D'Angelo were absolutely trustworthy, that they owed her for something she had done for them, that she wouldn't tell me what because it was confidential, and that I shouldn't look a gift horse in the mouth. As was usually the case in dealing with Mrs. Minniefield, I grudgingly agreed.

"Okay, go ahead, gentlemen. Thank you."

The two of them worked quickly and efficiently, and completed their work speedily. After demonstrating how the system operated, I was handed two sets of keys, and proceeded to give one to Zellie, along with the new alarm code.

Then we proceeded to Zellie's house and went through the same procedure. Thankfully, there were no bugs in Zellie's house, but we didn't have time to figure out why. When they had completed their work, Zellie gave me the extra set of keys and her alarm code, and our homes were officially secured.

We thanked Baskin and D'Angelo. They both simply shrugged, and said goodbye. We sat in the kitchen after they left and talked about what had happened.

"Who bugged your house, Arnie? And why yours and not mine?"

"Let's think about this logically. Jennifer broke into both of our houses. The really messy and destructive people broke into my house, but not yours, at least that we know of. But I think we can safely assume that. Your house wasn't turned upside down like mine."

Zellie frowned. "But all that means is that Jennifer could have decided to only bug your house, because that is the most likely spot for her to gather information. Or it could mean that she didn't bug either house, and the other people not only searched, but bugged only your house for the same reason – it was the best source for the information they wanted. Either way, we still don't know anything."

"Let's look at it differently. What information are they after? And what do you think they found out already?"

"They really couldn't have found out much, because we don't know much. But I will say that Jennifer knew an awful lot about what we were doing, like the name of our client, the nature of our investigation, and the fact that you went out with Tammy."

"True, she knew more than either of us told her, which was nothing," I said. "But that information could have been derived by just overhearing it, or from another source."

"Desmond knew we were at Brazen Saddles when we went there a second time."

"Same thing, though. He could have seen us through cameras in the ceiling of the place. You know they're up there."

"Yes. They're well concealed, but definitely there," Zellie conceded.

"He did seem to know a lot more, but was pretty good at keeping his mouth shut."

"Comes with the territory, I guess."

"So, what are they trying to find out by listening to us?" I asked in frustration. "Our investigation seems irrelevant to all this intrigue. It's a simple lost and found case, really. Lady loses husband, A to Z finds him, case solved."

"With a murder along the way."

"There is that," I agreed. "Kind of complicates things."

"And a scheming ex-girlfriend. And Mrs. Minniefield acting very peculiar, even for her."

"Yeah, I do wonder what that's all about."

"And what on earth could she have done for the Men in Black to get them to install an expensive security system with twenty-four-hour monitoring?"

"Don't know. And you can be sure she'll never tell us."

"Well, at least it means we can put off getting an accountant." We both laughed "What do you want to do now? It's too late to resume our car shopping, but you need transportation."

"Maybe I'll rent a car tomorrow. It'll give me something to drive until I buy a new one."

"That'll work."

"In the meantime, we should probably think about dinner."

Zellie smiled wickedly. "I'd suggest D'Agostino's again, if I wasn't so exhausted."

I smiled at her. "I really enjoyed our time in the "Zone," and going there again would certainly put Mama in a swoon. But I must admit, I'm wiped out, too."

"How about I fix us soup and sandwiches, we scarf them down, and I drop you off at home to watch a ballgame or something, and get a good night's sleep in your newly secured home?"

"Perfect."

By silent agreement, we didn't talk any more about the "Zone," or relationships. Bottom line, we needed each other as friends more than we needed each other as lovers. On some level, I think we both wanted to try the lover thing anyway, albeit in an incredibly plodding and incremental way. But now we have the "Zone." I think that's a good thing.

***

I went inside, locked the door and set the alarm. I had to admit, I felt a little safer now that the security system was installed. Per our temporary agreement, she called me once she was safely inside her house as well and admitted she felt better about the locks and all, too.

I took the opportunity to tell her my plan for tomorrow. As all our recent troubles seemed to swirl around my old job, I had decided that I was going to New York to visit Mort.

Zellie sighed, then said, "I'm not sure that's a good idea, Arnie. It's probably safer and smarter to just leave your access card in the safe deposit box and stay the heck away from Mort."

"I'm tired of just reacting to the craziness. I think it's time to go on the offensive."

"Well, you may be right," she said. "Maybe there's a scintilla of sense in that. But I'm going with you."

"It doesn't make any sense for both of us to go. It's my old workplace, not yours."

"So, I'll wait outside. The last time I let you do something by yourself, you discovered a dead body."

"You're probably right, Zellie. If you'd been along, Sid would probably still be alive," I joked half-heartedly. It was my turn to sigh. "Really, it's just a simple trip to New York, one we've both made zillions of times. I'll be okay by myself."

"Okay, maybe you can handle this on your own. But no dead bodies, agreed?"

"Word of honor. I'd appreciate a ride to the train station, though. I still haven't rented a car–or taken any steps to get Matilda fixed."

"You're getting her fixed? I thought you were buying a new car."

"I'm thinking both. I hate to give up on her, but I do need reliable transportation."

"Okay. I'm not going to argue with you about it. Should I pick you up at 6:30 am, our usual commuting time?"

"No, I want to go to the bank first, and they don't open until nine. We can sleep in."

We bid each other goodnight and I wandered into the bathroom, holding up two spread fingers. (Yes, I remembered). Then I got into bed and stared at the ceiling for a long time before I fell asleep.

CHAPTER TWENTY-THREE

I was up by seven am, and turned the house alarm system to "awake and present" to eliminate the need for holding up two fingers all the time. That setting turned off the pressure bumps, but left the doors and windows alarmed.

Zellie picked me up at 8:45 so we could swing around to the bank before circling back to the train station. I set the alarm and walked out to where she was waiting. I was wearing a dark suit, and red tie, fully in professional securities trader mode.

"Are you still sure you want to do this?" She asked anxiously as soon as I got into the car. "I mean, your access card is safely squirreled away. Why mess with that?"

"From what Mrs. Minniefield said, I'm not sure my access card is what they're after. Anyway, I'll be among lots of people the entire time. First on the train, then the subway, then at Mort. I'm sure I'll be safe, and I'll be careful. I think we need to try to figure out what's going on, and the place to do that seems to be Mort. So off to Mort I go."

"Did you call Mrs. Minniefield to tell her what you have in mind?"

"Nope. Maybe I'll call her when I get there."

"She won't like that."

"Probably not. But I'm a little tired of being kept in the dark about everything. Time to find out things on my own."

"Well, obviously, your mind is made up. Just be careful, okay?"

"Yes, ma'am."

We pulled up in front of the bank and I went in while Zellie waited outside. It didn't take me long to collect what I needed. Zellie left me at the train station where I caught the 9:25 North Jersey Coast Line train to New York.

I commandeered two seats in the half-full compartment, and handed the conductor my ticket when he approached. Then I settled down, a little restlessly, for the fifty-five-minute trip, which was uneventful.

Upon reaching Penn Station, I walked to the subway and took the N train uptown to Mort's headquarters at Fifty-Third and Avenue of the Americas. The setting in the lobby was unchanged. The floors and the lower part of the walls looked like gray marble, although I wasn't entirely sure of their exact composition. It looked opulent, though, which I assumed was the point.

A security desk sat in front, manned by a uniformed guard. I didn't recognize him, but the personnel often changed even when I had worked there. I flashed my badge, and signed my name to the register, noting the time in: 11:17 am. Then I walked to the elevator and proceeded to the twenty-third floor, which is where the extremely active part of Mort resided. The company occupied two whole floors in the building. The twenty-fourth floor was occupied by the executive offices. I had started on the twenty-third floor and eventually worked my way upstairs, so to speak.

I exited the elevator and walked through glass doors bearing the words "Mortal Securities" etched in gold script. Very classy. I was greeted by a loud exclamation.

"Arnie! Great to see you! Wait a minute. Let me look at you. You look terrific! Retirement suits you fine. You don't miss us at all, you dog."

I smiled with pleasure at seeing my old friend. "Oh, I miss you all right, Laura. Why do you think I'm here?"

Laura Wild had been the receptionist, secretary, administrative assistant-person who actually ran things (even though management thought they did) since forever. Certainly, long before I joined the firm.

She was about sixty years' young, with bleached-blonde hair and more energy than a twenty-year-old. We had formed a close bond early in my tenure and I had tremendous respect for her. Right now, she was looking at me in that shrewd way of hers.

"You're not here to see me, Arnie. Or to visit for old times' sake. What do you need?"

"Can we talk somewhere privately?"

Laura made a motion with her hand to someone sitting at a desk nearby. The person promptly jumped to her feet and walked over. "Mary, take over for me here, please."

"Yes, ma'am."

We walked to a conference room, sat down, and I told Laura that someone was trying to get their hands on my Mort password for some reason I couldn't ascertain.

"I don't know, Laura," I continued. The most they could get from my account is a proprietary tool for program trading. Valuable to me in conjunction with Mort's activities, but hardly usable for just anyone."

Laura looked thoughtful. "You know, things have been a little odd around here lately."

"What do you mean?"

"Well, Charles has not really been his usual teddy bear self, and some of the other partners are spooked by something. They're just not acting like themselves."

"Charles" was Charles Hastings, III, Mortal Securities' founder and chairman.

"What partners have been acting strangely?"

"I wouldn't call it strange, exactly. More like uncomfortable. Particularly Tom Carter. But he's not the only one. Lenny DiCaprio and Marty Coral as well."

"Anything in particular that you noticed?"

"Cheerfulness, or rather the absence of it, certainly. A little bit of paranoia, probably. Jittery, definitely."

"Okay if I wander around a little before I go upstairs?"

"You know that's not permitted, Arnie," she said sternly. Then she smiled. "So, go right ahead."

I gave her a quick kiss on the cheek and we walked back. From Laura's desk, I could see literally hundreds of cubicles, with people staring at computer terminals in each one. It was truly an incredible sight, but very depressing, to tell the truth.

I wandered through the aisles, greeting a number of the workers by name, asking them about their families, and generally exchanging pleasantries. A couple of the workers made a show of covering up their terminals when I walked past, as if they housed state secrets. Other cubicles were unoccupied, although their monitors were powered up and access cards remained in the card readers adjacent to the terminals. People in meetings or going to the bathroom, I decided.

Not very good security procedures, though. I thought about making a few keystrokes and leaving them with a snarky message like "SECURITY BREACH" as their screensaver, but thought better of it. I didn't work there anymore, and it was none of my business. Anyway, I'd been a terrible violator of security protocols, as were most of the partners. We'd left our computers unattended upstairs on a regular basis. We all could have used some of the security training we imposed on the other workers. All that security consciousness of the past couple of days had made me a convert, that's for sure.

I looked at my watch. Almost twelve-thirty. Had to get upstairs for my meeting with Charles. I waved goodbye to Laura, and went upstairs to the executive suite. The elevator opened to the familiar Gwendolyn ("the Curmudgeon") Pilkin. She sat imperiously at a large mahogany desk, with richly paneled walls behind her. The desk was flanked by huge bouquets of fresh flowers on both sides. The carpet was thick, lush and expensive. The furniture in the waiting room probably cost more than the wages they paid the minions in steerage below.

I should know, I thought. I was one of the few to occupy the executive suite after serving time on the twenty-third floor. Oddly enough, Charles also served time there, reasoning that he couldn't run things without knowing how they worked. It was one of the reasons I liked him. And he was a great leader in his time. But he was getting older, and more and more out of touch. He had become the Chairman in name only, with his long-time deputy, Dick Burns serving as the CEO and *de facto* Chairman. Charles' "retirement in place" was one of the main reasons I left Mort, albeit on excellent terms. It wasn't that I disliked Dick. To the contrary, he was quite personable and a decent manager. But, it just wasn't the same place anymore.

"Hi Mudge!" I said with a smile. I might be the only one who could get away with calling her that.

"Well if it isn't the guy who just couldn't take the heat anymore. Here to crash under the pressure again, are we?" Gwen smiled when she said it. "Arnie, nice to see you. Charles is acting like he's being visited by the President. Go on in."

"Good to see you, too Gwen. I so miss the snarky commentary."

"Me too. Nobody around here has any sense of humor. We miss you."

I leaned over and gave her a kiss on the cheek, then pushed open the heavy door to her left and entered.

The layout behind the heavy door was simple, but elegant. Essentially it consisted of a single hallway encircling the reception area like a giant rectangle, with offices dotting one wall as you walked the hall. As it occupied the entire floor, the offices faced outside, and had windows with varying views of the city, depending upon the side of the building they were on. When I worked there, I had a lovely view of the Chrysler Building. All the offices were spacious and expensively decorated. These were the places of business of the top officials of Mort. As a partner, I had occupied one of them, but as the Chairman, Charles had the very best corner office with a view of Central Park.

And it was to that office I was headed at the moment. I had called Charles at the last minute from the train, hoping to get a few minutes with him today, and to my surprise and gratification, he had expressed pleasure at the proposal.

His secretary and administrative assistant, Betty Williams, sat at a desk in front of the door to the office and I greeted her warmly. Betty was about seventy-years-old, had been with Charles for probably thirty years and was extremely loyal to, and protective of, him. If they weren't both happily married, I would have thought they'd make a great couple.

"Hi Betty. Nice to see you. You look great."

"You too, Arnie. To tell you the truth, things have changed here since you left. So, I'm not entirely sure I feel as good as you say I look."

I studied her for a moment. "Well, there are some signs of fretting in that beautiful face. What's up?"

She lowered her voice. "You know, I might not have thought so at the time, but I think you did the right thing leaving when you did."

"How so?"

"It's just that the family atmosphere that used to exist, and I think we all thrived upon, has been replaced by a pretty mercenary approach. And Charles is not himself. He seems inordinately obsessed with money. Oh, I know the whole point of this place is to make money, Arnie, don't look at me like that. It's just I think Charles has more of a worried demeanor, than a positive outlook."

"Wasn't Charles ready to slow down, Betty? He's almost eighty, after all. Maybe he's looking to get out."

"Seventy-seven, but who's counting. And yes, he is ready to slow down, but he just can't let go."

"Dick has been his deputy for years, though. And wasn't he Charles' handpicked successor?"

"Yes, and he isn't really a bad person, or a bad manager. But he doesn't have Charles' charisma, or vision."

"Few people do, Betty."

"I know, but Dick is not really a strong leader, and you know we have some strong personalities here. I don't know, Arnie, it just isn't much fun anymore."

At that moment, the inner office door opened, and Charles Hastings, III, all six-feet-two-inches and three-hundred-pounds of him, emerged. He was wearing an expensive dark business suit with all the buttons fastened, and was bursting out of it like an enormous armchair with protruding stuffing. He was an imposing figure, even in his seventies, and he fairly filled the room with both his physical presence and his larger than life personality.

"Arnie, my boy," he boomed. "Stop flirting with my secretary and come on in. I want to talk to you." He winked at Betty who gave him an indulgent smile. Then he put his arm around me and escorted me inside, depositing me on the leather sofa in the seating area adjacent to his desk. He dropped into his favorite leather recliner, and leaned forward earnestly.

"I hope you're not here because you want to resume your old job," he said without preamble.

"No, I'm not, Charles," I said, a little taken aback by the intensity with which he made the statement. "I'm still happy with my choice. And, I hope there aren't any hard feelings," I added quickly. "I always assumed our parting was amicable."

"Oh, of course, Arnie, of course. Very much so. I told you I respected your need to move on, and I meant it. I still do. Let me explain. I meant that you wouldn't be happy with your old job, but you might consider coming back if there was a new challenge for you."

"What do you mean, Charles? I didn't come here seeking any job at all."

"Your call was a little cryptic, and I assumed you were going to be in the City anyway, and just wanted to stop by and say hello to your old family." He paused and looked at me for a moment with those intelligent eyes. "But I also assumed that there was something else on your mind, and I hoped it wasn't a desire to come back and resume your old duties. And I want to hear about it. But first, I want you to think about whether you'd be interested in running this place after I retire at the end of the year."

I looked at him dumbfounded. And he seemed pleased with his bombshell, sitting back in his chair and waiting for my response.

"Charles, that's crazy," I finally said. "And I don't know where to begin. First of all, you love this place, why are you retiring at the end of the year? And Dick Burns is your hand-picked successor – you've been grooming him for years and he's clearly management material. I'm not a manager. I don't have that skill set. And I don't even work here. I left, remember? I could go on and on with this, but I won't."

"Interesting," was all Charles said in response.

"That's it? *Interesting?* What's going on?"

"Interesting that in all your histrionics and questions, all of your characterizations of the craziness of it all, you never said no."

"Then I'll say it now. No. No. No."

"Too late, Arnie. It had to be in your initial response. So, you'll think about it? Talk it over with that pretty blonde girlfriend of yours?"

"Charles, you're infuriating, do you know that?"

"Arnie, I didn't get to where I am by taking no for an answer. Especially not a belated no."

I looked at him and laughed. "You're pulling my leg, aren't you, Charles?"

"Actually no. I'm deadly serious. Things are not being well-managed here. The family atmosphere is gone. You know I've sort of been sidelined, right?"

"Yes."

"Initially, it was mostly by choice. I'm not as young as I used to be, Arnie. I don't really want to put in eighty-hour-weeks anymore. I want to travel with Phyllis, visit with my grandkids. But I care about this place. Some would say I can't let go, and they're partly right. The truth is that I don't feel like I can leave the company in its current form. I didn't make the right choice of a successor, Arnie. Don't get me wrong, Dick is a good man. And he's increased profits. But he's taken the family attitude we had and flushed it down the toilet, always trading it for that last extra dollar in every transaction.

"I'm the firm's largest shareholder, and thus supposedly the largest beneficiary of the firm making more money, but I don't want it this way. The sense of honor, of the honest, but tough-to-get-buck, that's what the firm was built on, and it's mostly gone. I'm a realist. I know it's partly the times, but it's also the nature of the current leadership. And I want it to change before I leave." Then his tone hardened. "I'd do anything to save this company, Arnie. Anything. If that means Dick has to go, he has to go."

I wasn't really that surprised at Charles' grimness. He was a tough guy, and he didn't get to where he was by being a milquetoast.

"Surely there are others who are qualified to run the place. I'm not in the securities business anymore. I have a private detective business now."

"Arnie, listen to me. You have a lot of fine qualities – you're honest as the day is long, you're kind and generous, and people like you. You're qualified, that's for certain. And what was the first thing you did today? You walked around the floor."

I looked at him in amazement.

"Of course, I know about that, Arnie. I try to keep informed, as you would. You wouldn't just stay up here and hope things are going well. This detective thing might be a lark right now, but is it really what you want to be doing?"

I thought about that. And I really didn't know the answer. I certainly wasn't sure I wanted to be a detective, and I was surely much better at this than I was as an investigator. But we all have to try new things sometimes, and I got to do the detecting with Zellie, which made all the difference in the world. If I was being one-hundred-percent honest, I'd say that it was the *only* thing that mattered. I'd probably be a pastry chef if Zellie did it with me. I didn't tell Charles that, of course. I just demurred, saying only that I was flattered, etc. etc., and hoped he'd look around a little more to find someone truly qualified.

"I stand by my statement that you're the most qualified, Arnie, but I respect your right to think about it for a while."

I started to say something in response to the thinking about it part, like I'd made up my mind already, but he held up a hand.

"I know, Arnie. I heard you. But the offer is open if you change your mind. Now I promised to hear you out on the true point of your most welcome visit."

I explained that someone was looking to get their hands on my Mort passcode, but kept most of the details to myself. I wasn't sure why, exactly. I trusted Charles, but something was amiss at Mort, and I thought it best to keep my own counsel.

"I'm not sure what that would do for them, Arnie, especially without your access card. But even with full access to your account, what could they get their hands on? You only left a few thousand dollars in your account here. Certainly, not enough to make it worthwhile to threaten you. And the only other thing is access to the trading algorithms, but even that is probably only valuable to you, or to someone who works here and presumably has access already. Even our competitors have their own trading algorithms, and probably aren't interested in ours in any event. Maybe a rogue operator? But they'd generally have to be big operators to even use our programmed trading systems. So, I'm at a loss. I'm sorry, Arnie, I'm not much help."

"No, you've been a big help, Charles. You basically confirmed my speculation on it. Doesn't answer the question, but ensures I wasn't missing something. I think while I'm here, I'll access the system to check my account anyway. Maybe something will turn up."

"Might as well use your old office, Arnie. It's empty right now, and you know the way."

"Thanks, Charles." I bid him goodbye, thanked Betty on the way out, and headed down the hall to my old digs. Once there, I picked up the phone and called Mrs. Minniefield and told her where I was. Her response was curt.

"What phone are you using, Arnie?"

"The phone on my old desk."

"Call me back on your cell."

I complied and she answered on the first ring. "That might not have been a good idea, Arnie, but as long as you're there, you *should* examine your account. But don't let anyone look over your shoulder. No one."

"Understood." I knew better than to question her when she was like this.

"And Arnie, *using your cell phone only…*," she emphasized, "call Ted and ask him for specific instructions on how to check for hidden files and how to disable them. He'll know how to do that."

She didn't elaborate, and I didn't ask.

"Will do, Mrs. M."

"You might want to talk to Tom Carter just to see how he's doing. But don't tell him anything about your activities, just exchange pleasantries, and assess his state of mind. And Arnie…be careful. Please call me when you've left the building."

"Okay."

We hung up and I called Ted, who was predictably in his lab. I told him what Mrs. Minniefield had said and he told me precisely what to do before I even accessed the system, and what to do after I'd accessed the system. Ted never asked why I wanted the information, or any details. He just fired off the instructions without comment, and I thanked him and disconnected. Then I went to work.

I kept my access card in my pocket while I booted up the computer, and entered the generic Mort password to open the Windows operating system. I then hit the start menu and typed the sequence of letters and numbers Ted gave me into the command line that opened. For what I was about to do, I had no need to enter my protected individual account. The configuration I typed reminded me of those old MS-DOS commands we used to have to type to do anything with a computer. Now we never had to do that anymore, and even the mere double clicking on an icon was replaced by a single click, and finally, voice commands. We were getting lazier and lazier, and soon almost no one would have a clue about things like operating systems. Computers were pretty much as easy to operate as toasters now.

But people like Ted still knew how they worked, and the insidious things that could be placed on them to track movements, identify personal habits and preferences, and generally learn a lot about the people accessing them. And lo and behold, a complete file list was being generated before my eyes. It was long, and included the names of many programs I recognized, and many more that I didn't. Ted had told me that the information would be mostly opaque, so I was prepared for it. We could analyze all the items on the list later, and I printed it out for that purpose.

I was looking for certain specific programs, though, and after a while, I spotted one of them. The other one didn't appear, but Ted had told me that I should expect only one of the programs to be installed, as two would be overkill and completely unnecessary.

He had described them as keystroke programs, which tracked every single entry typed. I double-checked the list to be sure, and even that took a fair amount of time, because of its length.

I didn't have the luxury of time to ponder why the computer of a former partner of the firm, in an office that was now vacant, would have a keystroke program installed on it. Who could be using it now, anyway? And was it there when I still occupied that office? If so, and if I'd known about it, I would have raised hell, and tracked down the architect of the snooping. I wasn't able to do that now, anyway, so I didn't belabor it. I could think about that later.

Following Ted's instructions, I disabled the executable file, taking care not to delete anything else. Then I focused on the directory containing the program. It had a single folder in it, which contained a single file. I double clicked on the file and got a message saying it couldn't be opened without proper authorization. Okay, time to insert my access card and enter my passcode, which Ted had assured me it was safe to do once I'd disabled the keystroke program.

I inserted my key card into the card reader and accessed my individual account. Then I went back to the file and tried to open it again. Still no luck. Someone had locked it down in a manner even *my* security level couldn't access. I supposed it was possible that my security clearance had been downgraded because I no longer worked there, even though my agreement with the firm included continuing unfettered access to the system. I guess I couldn't blame them for limiting me to the securities trading access that was specifically part of my agreement.

Unfortunately, that gave me no information to look at easily, and no good way to copy it for later analysis. I rued my lack of foresight in not bringing an external flash drive to copy it to, as attaching it to an e-mail from the computer was akin to blaring a horn and saying, "Look what I just did."

The good news was that Ted had told me how to set up the computer so that it could be accessed externally with minimal evidence that it had been done.

I followed his instructions, then checked my individual cloud account. As expected, it overtly reflected no access or activity for almost a year. I hadn't personally accessed my account, and it was good to see that no one else had either, at least as far as I could tell. The last access was the day I left, which corresponded to my recollection. These accounts are not like general computer accounts in an office that are accessible by someone with IT Administrator access.

Because of the strict rules imposed by the securities laws and the SEC, having an IT person have access raised serious insider trading potential. My individual activity was saved on my personal cloud account, theoretically at least, accessible only by me. The files did not reside on the computer's hard drive. The SEC required the individuals trading securities to be totally accountable for any information that got out, so giving general access was frowned upon. I really was the only one with access to my account, and it looked like it had stayed that way.

I did a rudimentary check of my transactions within the year prior to my departure, and saw nothing amiss. That was good. I performed the same function looking for hidden files as I had before, just within my account, and it once again generated a long list, but no evidence of a separate tracking program within my account. Once again, I printed the list for later analysis, but was less worried about this one. I exited my account and shut down the computer, put my access card and printouts in my inside pocket and walked down the hall to see if Tom Carter had a few minutes to chat.

A woman I had never met sat at the desk in front of Tom's closed inner office.

"May I help you?" she asked politely when I approached.

"I'd like to speak with Tom, if he has a few minutes. I'm Arnie Fischer."

"I will check, sir."

At least she didn't ask if I had an appointment. I was obviously someone she thought she needed to pay attention to, as I was wandering freely in an area not generally open to the public. If we had meetings with clients, we rarely conducted them in our private office suites, preferring instead to meet in the many conference rooms sprinkled throughout a secured hallway on one side of the office, to which there was a separate entrance. The office suites were limited to the partners. Access was generally strictly controlled, and as a result, people in this part of the office rarely questioned anyone's presence, even if they didn't immediately recognize them. Tom's assistant returned and gave me the go-ahead to enter.

"He said he has a few minutes for you, Mr. Fischer. You may go right in." She gestured to the heavy door.

"Thank you, Ms…? I looked at her questioningly.

"Fremont, sir. Alice Fremont. I'm Mr. Carter's secretary, sir," she added somewhat bashfully. I smiled at her.

"He's a lucky man, Alice. Thank you for your help."

She gave me a look that seemed to say "no one ever speaks to me at all other than to bark at me." She gave a timid smile back.

I went into Tom's office wondering what the heck happened to the generally friendly place where I once worked.

Tom was sitting at his desk making a show of reading an important paper, and was only reluctantly rising to his feet to tear himself away to greet me. I wondered what the playacting was all about.

"Arnie, nice to see you," he said unconvincingly.

"You too, Tom. I was here checking my accounts and thought I'd drop by and say hello."

A brief, but unmistakable hint of a smile crossed his countenance when I said that. I was sure of it, as I watched his face carefully. If I hadn't been, I probably would have missed it. He was pleased about it, no question.

But he said nothing, and I followed his lead, exchanging vacuous pleasantries with him. The ladies were right. Something was way off around Mortal Securities.

CHAPTER TWENTY-FOUR

Zellie dropped Arnie at the train station and returned home. Her first instinct was to take care of those vexing little chores that she never seemed to get around to, but she didn't feel like it.

Arnie's looking into the "why are they trying to rob me" thing, so why not do a little independent investigating?

That settled, she went into her old bedroom–which had been converted into a home office–and turned on the computer.

The topic of the day…is the New Jersey mob, she thought. We don't really know much about it, but they seem the most likely candidates to be harassing Arnie. And the first place we all go now to find stuff out is Google, of course. Once upon a time we went to the public library, and Middletown still had a great one. Maybe that would be next. But first, she typed in "New Jersey mob" to see what she would find.

Presto–2,300,000 hits–some with New Jersey in the name, some with mob, some with flash mob, rock stars being mobbed, Mobius strips, whatever they were, Mary Ann Mobley, (she sort of remembered that name…) okay, mobsters here we go. *No, we don't*–Al Capone is not what she had in mind. Maybe she needed a librarian after all.

Remembering Greasy Sid's brother, she typed in Nicholas "Fat Nicky" Martinson, and bingo, only forty-thousand hits, mostly about…lo and behold, the New Jersey mob, of which he was the undisputed kingpin. Well, maybe a little disputed. Fat Nicky was getting old, and that doesn't bode well for mobsters – plenty of people ready to kill you and take your place.

Zellie read about Fat Nicky with interest, his upbringing in a particularly tough part of the Bronx, the family's move to New Jersey, his start as an "alleged hitman," (alleged, although there didn't seem to be any question about it, but journalists are careful about these things – protecting the potential innocence of a mobster – after all he might not have done *all* of those killings) and moving up the ranks more or less by killing everyone in his way. Zellie shuddered. *Dangerous guy, and not one we want to cross, or even cross paths with.*

Something's off here, Zellie thought. If Nicholas Martinson wanted us dead, we'd be dead. The efforts to get information from us had been clumsy, at best, although that self-vaporizing listening device was very sophisticated. The gunman notwithstanding, these were not the actions of Fat Nicky and his crowd. From what she read, they didn't mess around. They had taken over multiple formerly-legitimate businesses, such as sanitation, construction, trucking, cement and gravel, import-export and multiple retail establishments in southern New Jersey, mostly through terror, with a few killings thrown in to keep people honest. Keep them honest, isn't that ironic?

No, our thugs were not these people. But who are they? She read a few more articles, and one particularly caught her eye. It was a longer piece, from the magazine section, and it was by a psychiatrist, who attempted to explain the psychology of the criminal. But what struck Zellie was the way criminals – in this shrink's view – started young, with shoplifting and small time theft, then robbing little old ladies, then engaging in more and more violent crimes until they impressed a more seasoned criminal and got trained as an apprentice for bigger crimes such as murder.

Zellie thought about that, and decided that she and Arnie were dealing with very bad people who had not yet hit the big time. *So why are they interested in us?* And if they aren't part of the South Jersey mob, what is the connection with Greasy Sid, who was clearly killed by the mob? Or is there any connection? Hard to believe it was just a coincidence.

And what about Jennifer's reappearance? That made no sense as a coincidence, either. For all her bad qualities, and they were considerable, it was hard to see Jennifer as a murderer. A thief, a con-woman, yes, but a murderer? But people do things all the time that no one expects. Like the classic mass murderer viewed from the vantage point of the next-door neighbor:

"He seemed like such a nice boy, helped me with the groceries, and shoveled the walk for me in the winter. In a million years, I wouldn't have expected this. I can't believe he's the one."

It still could have been an unrelated mob hit. Mike Mullen seemed to think so, and it certainly had all the earmarks of one. Zellie pondered this for a while, and finally gave up trying to figure it out. Not enough information. She'd just have to keep looking. Seemingly unrelated or not, they were involved somehow.

Of course, the real question, in fact the one they were hired to find the answer to, was who and where is Marilyn Beaufort? Well actually, that wasn't what they were hired to do. It was what they hired *themselves* to do, but that was a mere technicality. Neither Marilyn nor her supposed long-lost husband, Stanley, existed, ergo, she and Arnie needed to find Marilyn to give her their report. And truthfully, they were exactly nowhere on figuring that out.

Zellie gave that some thought. What did Marilyn want? Obviously not to find Stanley. So, what was the purpose of hiring them and then disappearing from the face of the earth?

Then it dawned on her. Only one logical answer existed to that question. And it made sense, even if the ultimate goal remained unclear.

And it definitely involved her and Arnie.

CHAPTER TWENTY-FIVE

My conversation with Tom was stilted at best, and after a few minutes, Tom looked at his watch pointedly. I took that as my cue to leave.

"Nice to see you, Tom, but I have to run."

"You too, Arnie. Good to see you."

I walked out to the outer office where Alice Fremont sat, and said my goodbyes.

I thought about stopping by to visit the other two people Laura said were acting strangely, Lenny DiCaprio and Marty Coral. I knew both, of course, but not well. They'd both arrived only a year or so before I left Mort, and we hadn't connected except in the most cursory of ways.

The partners I was most friendly with, except for Charles, of course, had left even before I did. That probably played a part in my decision to leave. The culture was changing, even then. I decided visiting DiCaprio and Coral wouldn't accomplish much, as I had no real baseline to which to compare their current behavior. I had already gotten the flavor of the place, and it wasn't pretty.

Charles was grasping at straws, here. He had to know what I had learned downstairs about the poor morale, and presumably tried to lure me back in a last-ditch effort to salvage his vision of the company as family.

While it might be theoretically possible, it seemed very unlikely to me. You can't go home again. No question, something was very wrong about Mort, and it would take more than a well-meaning founder and his protégé to fix it.

I resolved right then and there that I'd paid Mort my last visit. Ever. I took the elevator back down to the twenty-third floor, stopped to kiss Laura goodbye, and headed out.

I signed out at 2:48 p.m., and exhaled in relief once I was out of the building. I hadn't realized that I was holding my breath. Apparently, I'd been fortunate to get out when I did a year ago.

Then I remembered that Mrs. Minniefield had asked me to call. I had turned off my phone after concluding my conversations with Ted and Mrs. M, and when I turned it back on, I saw that I had a message. Zellie. She said it wasn't urgent, so I called Mrs. Minniefield first.

***

Zellie looked at the clock. 1:30 p.m. She'd try to reach Arnie. She called his cell, but the call went right into voice mail. She left a brief message telling him her call wasn't urgent, but to call her when he got a chance. Then she headed out to meet Marla at AB for their pre-arranged two o'clock coffee break. She could continue her research later.

They sat down at one of Delilah's tables. Delilah wore her hair in a pony-tail, which protruded through her red Audacious Bagel baseball cap. The cap said "It's Infusion Time" on the front. She wore a bright yellow Audacious Bagel T-shirt that said, "A Bagel A" on the front. She had tied the bottom of the shirt up into a knot, baring her stomach, and obscuring what presumably was the word "Day."

"Hi, Zellie," she said brightly. She nodded at Marla, who she apparently didn't know or remember.

"You're dying to ask whether Arnie is joining us, aren't you, Delilah?"

Delilah was so naturally effervescent and confident, it didn't occur to her to blush. "Well sure, Zellie. Is he?"

"Not today, I'm afraid, but I'm sure he'll be back soon."

"Well that's good. I do try to keep him wanting more, you know."

"I know, Delilah. I know," Zellie said, struggling not to burst into laughter.

Zellie and Marla ordered coffee, and Delilah bounced away. The back of her shirt read, "Solves Everything."

"So where *is* Arnie today?"

"He went to Mortal Securities to check things out. He thought going to the source might give us some leads on who is stalking us."

"Kind of follow the money, huh?"

"I guess so."

"Did he find anything out?"

"Don't know. I haven't heard from him. I tried to call him, but got voice mail. He'll call me when he gets a chance."

"I'm sure he will, you being his sweetheart and all." Marla smiled broadly at her words.

"Oh, stop it, Marla. We're best friends. Maybe that will turn into something else at some point, but no need to rush anything."

"I'm just teasing, Zellie. You know that."

"Speaking of which, how is the budding romance between you and Ted?"

"I like Ted. I really do. I don't know if it's serious or not, but we get along well, that's for sure."

"Ted's a good guy. He can be a little peculiar at times, but he's incredibly smart and a loyal friend. Pretty good-looking too."

"I might have noticed that last part," Marla said, smiling. "The other stuff, too, of course."

"Of course."

"What did he do before he became this retired mad-inventor type?"

"You'll have to ask him that. I have no idea."

"Really? None?"

"Arnie probably does. It was some sort of government work. That's all I know. And I'm not even sure I *know* that."

"He hasn't told me, but we've only been on a couple of dates."

"He seems to really like you, Marla. And Ted is not generally known for commitment, or for dating strong women like you. You must have cast some sort of spell on him."

"No witchcraft, I promise. Just plain old-fashioned feminine wiles, I assure you." She laughed, and Zellie laughed, too.

"Can I get in on the joke?"

Zellie and Marla abruptly looked up to see who was talking. *Jennifer*. Standing next to their table. When neither one of them answered, Jennifer ignored their stunned looks and pulled up a chair.

"Why yes, I'd be happy to join you. Thank you for offering," she said with a wave of her hand.

Marla recovered first. "I didn't hear an invitation."

"Well, it wasn't verbal, but you know you both want to hear what I have to say."

"I don't think so," Zellie said. "I heard plenty at our luncheon."

"Yes, wasn't that a hoot, Zellie?"

"Many adjectives come to mind, but that isn't one of them."

Jennifer never missed a beat. "Let me get right to the point. I'm in trouble Zellie, and I need Arnie's help."

"Ask him, then. I'd seriously like you to stay away from me."

Jennifer sighed heavily. "I thought we went through this at our luncheon. You're very important to Arnie, and as such, very influential. And besides, there's no one home at his house. I thought he might be here, but you're here instead. No substitute for my lover boy, of course, but potentially helpful nonetheless."

Zellie couldn't resist. "Why didn't you just wait stark naked in his living room, Jennifer?"

"I would have. And Arnie would have loved it, of course. But it seems that he finally got around to changing the locks and putting in a security system. And good for him. You can't be too careful, you know. You too, Zellie, protecting yourself was a very good idea. Arnie's, I assume?"

Zellie picked up her coffee, but didn't bother to answer.

"Please leave," Marla said. "Can't you see that she doesn't want to listen to you anymore?"

Jennifer eyed Marla thoughtfully. "Aah, Marla Perez, the famed criminal attorney. May I have your card? I might need legal assistance, and having you on retainer would give me a feeling of security."

Marla stood firm. "Get lost. Now."

"Please leave, Jennifer," Zellie added.

She shrugged and got to her feet. "Okay, I'm out of here. But tell Arnie he'll be hearing from me."

Marla watched until Jennifer was through the door and out of sight, then turned back to Zellie. "Whoa. That's some tiger you guys have by the tail, Zellie."

"I'm not sure who has whom by the tail, but yes, that's quintessential Jennifer. I think she's completely crazy."

Marla shook her head. "I don't know…there's a certain amount of affectation in that performance. Something not quite right. In my line of work, I meet a lot of people who are consummate actors. And they're *all* innocent," she added wryly.

"I'm sure they are," Zellie said with a shiver. "I don't know how you do it. It would get to me."

"Oh, it gets to me sometimes. But I swallow the bile and ignore it. Only way to do the job is to assume everyone's innocent."

"But don't you *know* some of them are guilty?"

"Not up to me to pass judgment. That's for a judge and jury. Presumed innocent unless proven guilty, and all. Everyone is entitled to legal representation, no matter how heinous they appear to be."

Zellie thought it interesting that Marla said innocent *unless* proven guilty. Most would say innocent *until* proven guilty. A true criminal attorney. She didn't comment on this to Marla, though.

Marla checked her watch. "I have to run. Appointment with a client at 3:15. Have to pay the bills, you know."

CHAPTER TWENTY-SIX

Arnie called Mrs. Minniefield as promised. He briefed her on his examination of his Mort account and told her about Tom's initial reaction to hearing about it. He assured her he'd disabled the keystroke program and followed Ted's instructions to the letter so it was working again when he left.

"Well done, Arnie. We'll just have watch what happens next, and see who attempts to access your computer. They won't get into your account, of course, but by accessing their own keystroke program we can track any further use of the computer."

"Poetic justice," I said.

"Indeed."

I briefed Mrs. Minniefield about Charles' offer.

"You didn't accept, did you Arnie?"

"No of course not. I rejected it immediately, but he took my declination as a promise to think about it. Typical Charles."

"I hope you're not actually thinking about it. At least not right now."

"No. I'm not thinking about it. Although a part of me is flattered and thinks I could do a good job."

"Of course, you could do a good job. Charles isn't an idiot. But now is not the time. Take my word for it."

"I will, Mrs. Minniefield, don't worry. I've already vowed never to go back. Something is very wrong there. It just isn't the same place."

"I think that's a good choice, Arnie."

"You know, Mrs. M, one of these days you're going to have to explain to me what's going on."

"I know, Arnie. But now is not the time for that. And frankly, what I know is extremely limited."

After Mrs. Minniefield ended our call, I called Zellie. She was just getting into her car after coffee with Marla–and as it turned out–Jennifer.

"Whoa!" I nearly shouted. "Again?" For some reason, Jennifer's latest appearance took me by surprise. I had no idea why. At this point, she could appear at any moment. I looked around to see if she had magically materialized next to me.

"Are you okay? What did she want this time?" I asked as I continued to look around.

"Yes, I'm okay. She said she's in trouble and needs your help."

"About what? And why ask you and not me?"

"Both good questions." She laughed. "And you need to stop asking questions in pairs."

"I'm glad to hear you have a sense of humor about it."

"Not really. I was furious, to be honest with you. I'm as nervous as you sound about it. But in answer to your questions, she didn't tell us what the trouble was. Apparently, she was looking for you and found me, instead."

"What did she say?"

"She went into that same *schtick* about how I'm important to you, so I'm important to her. Also, more to the point, she tried to get into our houses again, and was stymied by the new security systems. She came right out and said it."

"Well, that's good at least."

"Agreed. Anyway, we asked her to leave, and she did. But I'm sure we haven't heard the last of her."

"You know, mentioning the security system reminds me of something."

"You forgot that Betsy wouldn't be able to get in to walk Lazlow, and that you probably wouldn't get home in time to let him out."

"You remembered. I completely forgot."

"To be honest, I didn't exactly remember. Betsy called me when she couldn't get in, and I just popped over in the morning to let her take him. She was going to drop him off at Mrs. Minniefield's house after their walk."

"Thanks, Zellie."

"Just being a good neighbor, sir. Happy to oblige," she said in an exaggerated Southern drawl.

I laughed. "That you are. You surely are."

"What train are you getting on?"

I looked at my watch. "If I hoof it, I can make the 4:10. Arrives at 5:08."

"I remember. It wasn't all that long ago, you know. That was the train we took if we could sneak out early."

"That's the one."

"I'll pick you up."

"I can grab a cab, if you have something to do."

"No trouble at all. Besides, I want to tell you about my research today, and we can talk when you get back."

"Okay, good. Thanks. See you in an hour or so."

I made it to Penn Station in time to board the intended departing train. I found a seat, gave my ticket to the conductor when he came by, and sat back to relax. It had been a hectic, and emotional few hours, and I felt very tired. I found myself nodding off when I was jarred awake by the buzzing of my phone.

"Important. Meet me at Mrs. M's at 5:30. Bring Z," the text said.

I texted Ted back that we'd be there. I thought of calling him and asking for a little explanation for the abrupt message, but I had learned that when Ted was terse, he could be just as inscrutable as Mrs. Minniefield.

And that was interesting, too, if I thought about it. Sometimes the two of them looked like they've worked together. But, I can't really see it. They're both loners, or so it seems.

I wondered what today's message was about, but I'd guess it had something to do with today's computer intrigue. I'd find out soon enough. I sat back and closed my eyes, and before long I was awakened by the announcement of various central Jersey towns: Perth Amboy, Matawan, Middletown.

I got off the train and walked over to where Zellie was waiting - with all of the other commuters' spouses. I smiled at the thought, and gave the 'missus' a perfunctory kiss on the cheek before getting in the car.

"Hi honey! Good to be home. Thanks for picking me up."

Zellie rewarded me with a punch on my arm. "Watch it, buster." But she laughed. "It *was* a little weird waiting with the New Jersey Desperate Housewives. Did you get a text from Ted?"

"Yup. Sounds important."

"I know. Cryptic to say the least. Did he tell you what it's all about?"

"Nope. But I'd guess it has something to do with some hacking we did on my old computer today."

"Sounds like you had an eventful day."

"It was interesting, to be sure. And you, too. What did you find out?"

"I have some information, some conclusions, and one big giant honking theory. And I want to do more research tomorrow."

"Can you tell me about it while you drive?"

"Sure, but I want to hear about what happened at Mort."

"From Ted's message, I think we're all going to hear about my day at Mort. And I think I'm going to hear new things I didn't know while I was there. So, let's hear your stuff first."

And she told me all about "Fat Nicky" Martinson and the South Jersey mob, and pointed out how the actions taken against us didn't sound like them. "It wasn't the mob searching your house, or getting that thug to threaten us with a gun."

"No, it wasn't," I agreed.

"So, if not them, whom? First question."

"Marilyn had no intention for us to find Stanley, right?"

"No. He doesn't even exist. She doesn't either, for that matter."

"Right on both counts. So, second question: Why hire us in the first place?"

"Okay, so we have two big questions– that we still don't know the answers to."

Zellie pulled up in front of Mrs. Minniefield's house and parked. Then she turned to look at me.

"What if we're being manipulated just to stir things up, by looking into the obvious clues Marilyn left us. What if the point of our investigation is to just muddle around, sticking our noses in things, never really finding out anything, but providing valuable information to whoever is watching us?"

"Well we're really good at that 'muddling' thing. And the not-finding-anything-out part. We're aces at that. But I have to admit, your theory is the only thing that makes sense here. *If* anything makes sense at all. I mean, no one hires anyone to find something or someone they know doesn't exist. Much less create a false identity to do it. But it begs the question – who the heck is 'Marilyn' and why is she using us?"

"Yes, same question we started the case with. Who and where is she? That's why I want to do some more research. And I think the courthouse is the place to go next. I want to look through some of the case dockets. I'm thinking I may get lucky and find something interesting – maybe a lawsuit, or criminal case involving our motley cast of characters."

"Sounds good, Zellie. I'm glad one of us is thinking about our actual case, and not just all the distractions that seem to be arising."

"You know, Arnie, I've been thinking about that. I wonder if they're more than distractions. Maybe they're related. Maybe there's a correlation here to something bigger, that we don't understand yet."

"Could be. Let's talk about it after we're done here. We better get inside. I get the feeling this is important."

Ted and Mrs. Minniefield were sitting in the living room, chatting quietly, when we walked in. They greeted us, and Mrs. M motioned for us to sit down.

"Lazlow is outside with Fideaux and Larry," she said. "And Ted has some interesting things to report."

Ted cleared his throat. "Interesting is an understatement. But I still don't know much."

We looked at him and waited. Ted usually took a little while to get going when he had something serious to say. And we could tell by looking at the two of them that he was not kidding around.

"I have completed my analysis of the first of the two lists of files from Mort," he stated.

I involuntarily reached for my pocket, where I had placed both lists earlier. They were still there. Ted looked at me and smiled.

"I took the liberty of printing the first list myself. I couldn't print the second list, because I need data from your access card to enter your personal account. Although I'm guessing that with time, I could access that as well even without the card. But it would take time, and it's not necessary. After all, you have the list and your card right here."

"What did you find, Ted?"

"Nothing from the list itself. As we already determined, someone installed a keystroke program on your computer."

"The one we disabled, and then reactivated."

"Yes."

"Was there another file to worry about?"

"No."

"I don't follow, Ted. If we know already that there is a keystroke program on my computer, and there was no other suspicious file, why the urgent meeting?"

"Someone accessed your computer right after you left Mort."

"Tom Carter?"

"Charles Hastings, III."

I was dumbfounded. "Charles? That can't be right."

"Well, I certainly wasn't there to see him do it, but it was <u>his</u> first-level access number. It matched the employee list I retrieved."

I didn't want to know how he "retrieved" it, but I didn't doubt he was right. I'd known him too long for that.

"Maybe someone stole his number," I said hopefully.

"It's certainly possible. Did he know you were going to be using your computer?"

"Yes, in fact he suggested it," I admitted. "But what could possibly be his motivation? It's his company. Or at least he owns most of it."

"I don't know what his motivation is, but if it's his company, he has the most to lose if it goes belly-up."

"But it's not in danger of that," I said slowly, "or do you know something I don't?"

Mrs. Minniefield chose that moment to weigh in. "Mort is being investigated by the Justice Department for possible criminal violations of the securities laws."

I stared at her. I was stunned into a long silence. I finally found my voice. "How…how do you know that?"

But I knew better than to ask. Mrs. Minniefield always knew things like that, but never, ever, told us how she knew. This time apparently was different. She sighed heavily.

"I have a friend in the government that owes me a few favors. He told me a few days ago about the investigation. He didn't want to tell me, but I pressed the issue, and he relented. But he specifically asked me not to tell you, because of the chance that anything you did thereafter could affect a prosecution. In other words, if you knew, you'd likely react to people in Mort differently, and maybe tip them off inadvertently."

"Is Arnie being investigated?" Zellie asked softly.

"No. My friend assured me of that. But Tom Carter is somehow mixed up in it. I don't have any other names, or much in the way of other details. And I didn't know of Charles Hastings' possible involvement until Ted told me."

"If he asked you not to tell me, why disclose it now?"

"I have several reasons. One, I never expected you to visit Mort, and you didn't let me know you were going. Not that you are required to keep me informed, Arnie," she quickly added. "But if I'd known, I probably would have tried to dissuade you. So, I had no reason to think that not knowing about the investigation would affect you. Two, your mentor, whom you trust implicitly, likely installed snooping software on your computer, encouraged you to use it, then tried to retrieve information from you in a most clandestine manner. And three, and this is the big one – he offered you a job taking his place on the proverbial throne. And presumably a throne with a sword of Damocles hanging over it."

"So, what should I do about it?" I asked.

Mrs. Minniefield looked at me incredulously. "Arnie, haven't you been listening? You're to do nothing. Nothing at all. Stay away from Mort. Let the Feds do their thing. Let Ted examine the second list of files, and he can tell us if anything is interesting there to turn over to the government."

"What if Charles contacts me?"

"You already turned him down. Tell him you haven't changed your mind."

"Okay, okay. I get it. Stay away. Don't talk to people at Mort. But you must be curious about it all, too."

"Of course, I'm curious," she said. "But I can wait for the outcome, as long as you're safely out of it."

"I guess I shouldn't execute any trades using the Mort trading algorithm, huh? Not that I have done that in a long time, anyway."

"Arnie, it's the reason I asked about your buyout deal. I was glad to hear that your livelihood does not depend upon anything at Mort. And no, do not trade on that account."

"Mrs. Minniefield, I've been wondering, just out of curiosity–and not that I object in the least," I began awkwardly, and involuntarily reached for Zellie's hand, "but why did you want Zellie present for our discussion about my personal financial situation?"

Mrs. Minniefield looked at Zellie and me for a long moment. "My goodness. The two of you must be the only ones in the world that don't see, with absolute clarity, the sweet and symbiotic life you live together. But you will. You surely will."

She cleared her throat and raised her chin, back to all business. "Now give Ted the list, and let's at least find out whether there's anything we need to turn over to the Feds."

Ted took the papers from my hand. "I'll let you know," he said, rising to his feet. "It shouldn't take long. But I'll need access to my databases back at the lab, so I'm going to get going."

With Zellie's hand still in mine, we stood and bid Mrs. M. and Ted goodbye, retrieved Lazlow from the backyard, and walked out to Zellie's car. With tomorrow's agenda decided, she dropped me and Lazlow off at home, and headed back to her place.

"It's been a long day, Lazlow," I said as I inserted the key in the lock and entered the code once we were inside. Being a spy was sure exhausting. I took off my suit and changed into more casual attire, then threw a frozen dinner into the microwave. I needed to think. About a lot of things. And I was about to do just that, when the phone rang.

The Caller ID announced a restricted number. I don't usually answer them right away, so I listened for the answering machine to pick up.

"Arnie? Pick up. Please! It's Jennifer. I really need to talk to you."

CHAPTER TWENTY-SEVEN

I heard something urgent in her voice. An inflection I'd never heard before. Jennifer was nothing if not calm, collected, and serene in her demeanor. That whole crazy act at the luncheon with Zellie was out of character, but so was this. In a big way. Against my better judgment, I picked up.

"What can I do for you Jennifer? And please, take that as the empty offer I meant."

"Arnie, thank God you picked up. I'm in trouble, and I need your help."

"Jennifer, it's been a long day, and I have little patience for this right now. Can you wait until tomorrow for me to turn down whatever you want me to do, or should I just take care of that right away?"

"Arnie, I know you don't want to help me. I understand that. And you have good reason. But you're a good, decent person, and I need that right now. And we do have a history, you can't have forgotten that."

"That was a long time ago, Jennifer," I said wearily. "Neither of us is the same innocent person we were then."

"Please, Arnie. Please at least hear me out. You want to do it tomorrow, okay, we'll do it then. But please, you have to listen."

"Jennifer, I'd like to care, I really would, but the truth is that I just don't give a crap what you want."

"Arnie, just hear me out, for old times' sake if nothing else. If you don't want to do anything, you can turn me down after hearing my story, no difference. Meet me at the entrance to Holmdel Park at ten am tomorrow. It's quiet there. Bring Zellie if you want."

"Jennifer, I'm making no promises. And if I do come, it will be to the Shop Rite parking lot, not Holmdel Park."

"Okay, the Shop Rite parking lot it is. I'll see you then. And thank you, Arnie."

"I'm not promising I'll show up, Jennifer."

"Understood. But I hope you do."

I thought about calling Zellie and telling her, but decided it could wait. I'd see her at 8:30 anyway. I did wonder what Jennifer wanted, but didn't want to spend any time thinking about it. I wasn't going to show up anyway. And the Mort issues were nagging at me.

Charles? It was bad enough that he was snooping on me. Maybe there was an explanation for that. Maybe this was just his paranoid way of checking up on his potential heir. Although I doubted it. So, what did he want? I was at a total loss.

Maybe Ted would find something in the file list I ran, although it seemed unlikely. But the thing that bothered me even more than the snooping was the possibility that Charles was a crook. I had never heard even a whisper of doubt about his integrity. But I hadn't been there for a year. A lot could happen in that time. And if his empire was crumbling, an empire he built from scratch, I suppose he would do a lot to save it.

And if I was truly honest with myself, I'd acknowledge that a part of me hoped that he was looking to me to save that upright, straight-shooting, profitable family business for him. Well, that's certainly not what he had in mind, I thought bitterly. I would have had no problem believing Tom Carter was capable of dishonesty, but Charles?

Doesn't matter, I guess. Mrs. Minniefield is right. I should leave well enough alone. Let the Feds do their thing. But of course, I knew I couldn't just let it go. I wouldn't visit there again, and wouldn't talk to anyone there, but I might do a little independent digging. No harm in that.

I ate my frozen dinner, watched a little of the Yankees on TV, set the house alarm to the 'sleeping' setting, and went to bed.

***

Zellie picked me up promptly at 8:30, and we headed straight to the office. I informed her that once again, my car shopping and Matilda-repair plans would be on hold. While she drove, I told her about Jennifer's call.

"At least she's consistent," Zellie said. "That's what she told me, too."

"I wonder what she wants."

"You're not thinking of actually going, are you?"

"No. Although there is at least a chance that she may have information that could be useful to us."

"Hard to figure her agenda, although it's probably another attempt to get money."

"Well, we know she likes that. But somehow, her behavior is different this time. I can't figure out why I think that, but the feeling is there."

"I think she's behaving very erratically. She's all over the place – flirtatious, crazy, serious. Hard to know which Jennifer is going to appear next."

"Did she appear nervous when you and Marla saw her at AB?"

"I wouldn't say that. But more serious, more lucid, and less crazy than at lunch."

"She was serious on the phone. No jokes, no flirting, and even a hint of a tremor."

"She's a good actress, we know that."

"I know. Still, I do wonder. And there was zero chance I was going to meet her at Holmdel Park. Too few people around."

"Is there a chance you'll meet her in the Shop Rite parking lot?"

"One-percent chance. And only to find out information, not to agree to do anything. What do you think?"

"I think she's trouble, and have to wonder whether any information you'll get is worth the angst. And let's be honest, Arnie, and please don't be mad at me for this, but there's at least a remote chance she'll get you to agree to do something."

I sighed. She was, of course, right. "I know, Zellie. And I'm not mad. But the circumstances were way different a year ago. I didn't know she was a crook then. I do now." I smiled. "And I'm fortified against her feminine wiles."

"Eating your Wheaties, are you?" Zellie laughed. "All right, we're here. We can continue this discussion over some of Eddie's coffee."

We entered the Moo Mart and greeted Eddie, who brought over two giant cups of coffee. "Arnie, I've got a guy," he said.

Savoring my coffee, I closed my eyes. "Um, that's good, Eddie."

"No, I mean I know a guy who can fix your car. Not good as new—that ship sailed a long time ago. A long, long time ago. But he can fix it up so it runs again, and he can do the work today, if you want."

"I've pretty much decided on a new car, Eddie, but I'd still like Matilda fixed up. I owe it to her. So, thanks."

We made arrangements for it to be towed to Eddie's "guy," then I turned to Zellie.

"The more I think about it, the more I think we should meet Jennifer and find out what she wants. She said to bring you if I wanted, and maybe that's a good idea. You'll keep me from doing something stupid, and serve as another set of ears to assess what's really going on."

"Okay, we'll go together. But I still don't think it's a great idea. However, I must admit to a degree of curiosity. So, we'll find out."

"That's an hour from now," I said, looking at my watch. "In the meantime, we can go rent a car so I have transportation until Matilda is fixed. You don't need to be chauffeuring me around. Although I've kind of enjoyed it," I added with a smile.

"You'd love to have your own chauffeur, wouldn't you?"

"Not just any chauffeur. I insist on a pretty one."

"Let's go get you a car, Romeo. If we don't hurry, I may succumb to your corny charm."

***

I rented a non-descript Chevy Malibu, accepting their offer of a one-class free upgrade. All the better to be discreet in our role as private eyes.

We pulled in to the Shop Rite parking lot off Route 35 right at ten. Jennifer was standing in the back of the lot. We saw no sign of her car. Too bad, I thought. We could at least have obtained her license plate number out of this fiasco. She was being cautious. That in itself was interesting.

"No car?" Zellie whispered.

"I was thinking that myself. She doesn't want us to see it."

"Or she got a ride. And someone else is nearby." She looked around. "I'm glad you picked here instead of Holmdel Park. This is a public place at least."

"That's what I figured. Although I have no reason to believe she's dangerous."

"Doesn't hurt to be careful."

"You called Mrs. Minniefield and told her where we'd be, right?" I asked her.

"Yes, and surprisingly, she didn't consider this a stupid idea."

"Probably happy to have us focus on something other than Mort."

"Maybe, but she said that Jennifer might want to tell us something important, and there was little risk involved, especially if we went together."

"It's all cost/benefit and risk analysis with her, isn't it?"

"She can be pretty calculating, yes, but she always has our best interests at heart."

"That's true," I acknowledged. "Okay, its show time."

We parked nearby, got out and walked toward Jennifer, who waved weakly and greeted us in a clear, no-bullshit voice. It almost looked like a concerted effort to not play-act. Or it was just another act, who knew?

"Hi guys. Thank you for coming. From what you said yesterday, Arnie, I wasn't sure you'd make it."

"I wasn't sure myself, Jennifer. Actually, I was sure I *wouldn't* show up. But I changed my mind."

"Well, I appreciate it. Although after what's happened in the last year, I doubt you care if I'm pleased about it." Jennifer shifted her feet uncomfortably, and continued. "And I don't blame you. I've been a real shit, and I'm in trouble now. Deserved or not, I'm in trouble, and you are in a position to help me if you want to."

"Why should I help you with anything, Jennifer?"

"You probably shouldn't. But you might anyway. You forget, I know you. Maybe not as well as I used to, and certainly not as well as Zellie knows you, but I know you. You like to help people. You probably would have been a good doctor if you'd stuck it out. You have compassion, and more than that, you'd feel guilty if something happened to me and you could have prevented it." She turned to Zellie. "I'm telling the truth, aren't I, Zellie?"

Zellie said nothing. I sighed heavily. "Okay, Jennifer, let's hear it and get it over with already. What's the problem?"

"This is a crappy place to meet, you know that Arnie? Can't we sit down somewhere? At least in the park, there are benches sprinkled throughout."

"Just get on with it, Jennifer," I said, with exasperation in my voice.

"Okay, okay. Here goes. As I told Zellie at lunch, I'm interested in the fashion business. To make a long story short, I got a job with a fledgling young designer and visionary in the fashion field."

"Rene Desmond."

Jennifer didn't look surprised.

"Yes. Rene had this concept, which became Brazen Saddles. You know it, I assume?"

"You know we do, Jennifer, but continue."

"Well, developing a new and very expensive fashion line costs money, as you can imagine, and Rene didn't have enough. He enlisted the assistance of some very unsavory people to help him raise money. I am ashamed to admit that I played a very, very small part in the fundraising, dabbling as I did in somewhat risky investments." She held up her hand to stop Zellie from interjecting.

"I know, Zellie. You have a different view of it. Please just let me keep my little fiction for now, okay?"

Zellie muttered something unintelligible under her breath, but kept mostly silent.

"So," Jennifer continued, "I became a small investor in Brazen Saddles, which is principally owned by Rene and his other investors."

"The South Jersey mob," I said.

"Sadly, yes. Rene is really just a figurehead now, at least on the business side, although the business itself is quite real. He's really a brilliant designer, you know."

"Can you get to the point *please*, Jennifer?"

"Yes, of course. But the background is important. And it directly involves you, Arnie."

"I have nothing to do with Brazen Saddles, Rene Desmond, the New Jersey mob, or even you, Jennifer."

"That last part hurts, Arnie. Of course, you have a connection with me. But I'll let it pass, because I really need your help. And the connection with me is not the only one."

"Jennifer, I'm leaving in one minute. I'm done with the theatrics."

"Okay, I'll get to the point. The New Jersey mob has been laundering money through Brazen Saddles, several other legitimate businesses, and Mortal Securities – yes, Arnie, your old partners. And I understand that you still have an active senior account with them."

I held up my hand. "I'm not here to answer any questions, Jennifer, just to listen. So, keep talking, or we're done."

"Okay, fair enough. You see, I've been told that some of the mob's connections at Mortal Securities have been getting cold feet about their role, and have been gathering evidence to protect themselves in the event they need to–shall we say–turn state's evidence?"

"Jennifer, what could any of that possibly have to do with me? Or you, for that matter?"

"I'll answer the second question first. I may have put myself in a position where I owe the mob money."

Zellie cut in at that point. "Jennifer, you're driving a Mercedes that probably cost over a hundred-thousand dollars. You dress in expensive clothes, and wear expensive jewelry. You don't look like you need money."

Jennifer laughed bitterly.

"For what it's worth, Zellie, the car is a company car, and the clothes are from Brazen Saddles. I don't really own anything myself. I did, however, develop expensive tastes working for Rene, and that is why I'm in trouble. My own fault, I know, but there it is."

"Just what are you asking me to do, Jennifer? I'm not going to give you one penny. I did that already, remember?"

"I'm not looking for money, Arnie. If I can retrieve the file containing the evidence about the mob's activities, I can give it to them in exchange for canceling my debts."

"Or you could give it to the police," I said dryly, "but that option wouldn't occur to you, would it?"

"Arnie, I may not be a saint, but I know which choice is most likely to keep me alive, and the police can't do that."

"Jennifer, even if I was inclined to help you, I don't know where that file is, or even if it exists."

"Oh, it exists. And it's buried somewhere in the computer systems at Mortal Securities."

"How do you know?"

"Let's just say I've been told. And I have no reason to believe that it doesn't. I've already disclosed too much, but I really need your help. You may not be happy with me, Arnie, but you don't want me dead."

"Isn't that a little melodramatic, Jennifer?"

"I don't think so. Look what they did to the guy that owned the bar in Keansburg – Sid Martin – the guy you found dead. He was supposedly Fat Nicky Martinson's brother. If he'd kill his own brother, do you really think he'd have any trouble killing me?"

I shook my head. "Probably not. But you owe money Jennifer, it's hardly something the mob kills over, is it? I don't mean to minimize the problem, but don't they need you alive to pay them back? And isn't it better to try to come up with money than to try to blackmail the mob with some file you think exists?"

"It exists, Arnie, I know it does. And you can find it if you try. You have access, I don't. I still love you, Arnie, and I can't believe you don't still have some feelings for me, too. Please. I'm begging you. Help me. It will cost you nothing, and will save my life. Zellie, talk to him. Make him understand."

"This is between the two of you," Zellie said evenly. "I'm just along for the ride, so to speak."

I shook my head and jammed my hands in the front pockets of my pants. I was furious, but now wasn't the time to let that show.

"I'll think about it. That's all I can offer you. How can I reach you?"

"I'll call you. And thank you."

"Don't thank me. I haven't done anything, and likely won't."

"I think you will."

I shrugged. "Think what you want, Jennifer. I don't see your car. Did you drive here, or get a lift?"

"I drove. My car is parked in front."

"Just how many people have those 'company Mercedes' anyway?" Zellie asked.

"Oh lots. All of the inner circle at Brazen Saddles, and several others, including Rene's wife. Rene has some kind of deal with Bobby's Mercedes. It seems like Brazen Saddles is always buying cars from them, and trading in the old ones for newer models. I'm by no means the only one," she added defensively. "It's not like I'm that important there."

With that, and a slight backward wave of her hand as she left, she simply walked away.

CHAPTER TWENTY-EIGHT

Zellie and I looked at each other, and I shook my head. "Getting her plate number wouldn't tell us anything," I said. "It will just be registered to Brazen Saddles, and we knew that already."

"Should we try to follow her?"

"I don't think so. She'll know we're there–she's seen our car. She'd probably be going back to Brazen Saddles anyway."

"What do you think about all that? You're not actually going to give her a file. If it even exists, that is."

"No, of course not, Zellie. If there is such a file, we'll give it to the police or the FBI."

"Do you think it exists?"

"You know, I think it probably does. This whole thing is so unbelievable, that after yesterday, I think I believe almost anything. She was certainly fishing to see if we'd found it already, which is at least partly the reason she wanted you here, too. Two chances to see if we reacted to the story. And I think we were pretty convincing that we knew nothing about the file."

"Probably because we really don't know anything."

"And that information was significant to her as well. I doubt she really thinks I'd give it to her, so knowing whether we have it already was at least as important to her."

"So, she learned that we don't have the file."

"Probably."

Zellie looked thoughtful. "Did we learn anything?"

"Well, we learned that Jennifer thinks that the mob is using Mort to launder money. We didn't know that before. We thought, based upon what Mrs. Minniefield said, that the investigation was about insider trading, which is a typical kind of inquiry of a securities firm. Mob involvement is an entirely different universe. And I don't know whether we just assumed it was insider trading, or whether Mrs. Minniefield assumed that from what her contact told her, but the dynamic has certainly changed.

"As for the rest of the stuff Jennifer said, I think she was just telling us things we already knew, or she assumed we already knew."

"Yeah, the Mort thing was what jumped out at me, too. Arnie, omigod, it looks like you got out at just the right time."

"It goes to show you, timing is everything," I said wryly. "Although I guess there could have been mob influence while I was there. I just didn't know it."

"Do you think Charles Hastings is a mobster?"

"I just can't believe it. But I also never would have expected him to spy on me, either. I just don't know, Zellie. I'm questioning everything at this point."

"What do you want to do now?"

When all else fails, eat. "How about some breakfast? I could go for some weird permutation of a bagel and innocent and harmless banter with my favorite waitress."

Zellie rolled her eyes, but laughed. "At least there are no unpleasant surprises there," she said. "Okay, let's go. I'm starving. Maybe I'll try an odd concoction, too. And we can plan a course of action at the same time."

We sat down at our usual table and Delilah greeted us warmly. Her shirt was red, white and blue, and festooned with little flag pins. It read in big capital letters, AUDACIOUS BAGEL. At my request, she turned around to show the back of her shirt, which read, "All Bagels Made Entirely in the USA."

"Was there a question about that?" I asked.

"No, but you can be sure that all the goodies I'm offering you are a hundred percent American."

"That's good to know, Delilah, thanks."

"A lot of people in here this morning," Zellie said.

"I know," Delilah said, looking around. "Much busier than usual. I don't know why, but it's okay with me. The more people, the more tips."

"Hey, that's Little Bobby over there," I pointed out.

She smiled. "Yes, he comes in a lot. Probably everyone in Middletown comes here a lot, though."

"You know him?" Zellie asked.

"Not well, but my boyfriend knows him. In fact, he works for him. He's a mechanic at Little Bobby's dealership."

Zellie glanced at me with a little smile. We hadn't known Delilah had a boyfriend. And of course, while I wouldn't ever, ever, acknowledge it, I had kind of enjoyed the apparently totally imaginary thought that she harbored some interest in me. Which, although I had never had any interest in pursuing it, was flattering, to say the least.

Oh well, nothing really lost, and only a little bruised ego, which I could live with. And Zellie was getting a kick out of it, that was for sure.

"How long has he worked there?" she asked.

"Oh, for at least ten years. He worked for Little Bobby's father for years before Big Bobby died. Billy's a great mechanic." She lowered her voice. "He's a lot better mechanic than Little Bobby is as an owner/manager of an automobile dealership."

"What do you mean?"

"Well, Little Bobby is a nice enough guy, but Billy tells me he doesn't seem to have his head in the business. Almost like he's in his own imaginary world all the time."

"We saw some of that when we visited him this week," I acknowledged.

"Big Bobby was all about the car business. He lived it night and day. He enjoyed selling cars, providing service, interacting with the customers. Billy doesn't think Little Bobby even cares if he sells cars or not."

"Maybe he should sell the business, if he doesn't like it."

"Maybe. I think Billy would be happy about that. Anyway, I've talked too much. Have to get back to work, pay the bills. What'll it be, guys? Something unusual, I hope. Push the envelope, aim for the skies."

We both ordered quesadilla bagels and coffee, and Delilah seemed satisfied.

"Don't say it." I said to a smirking Zellie when Delilah left.

"Whatever do you mean, Arnie?" She struck a "picture of innocence" pose. I couldn't help it. I laughed at my own discomfiture, and she laughed too.

"I guess her comments about Little Bobby aren't really surprising, given what we saw with our own eyes when we were there," I said when we calmed down.

"No, his head really did seem in the clouds. And that whole cloak and dagger thing. I thought it was mildly funny at the time, and that he was just kidding around, but maybe there's more to it than that."

"Maybe. I guess he sort of tried to sell you a car, but it was pretty half-assed for a car salesman."

"Doesn't matter to us, I guess. I don't really want a Mercedes, and we got the information we needed from him."

"I guess so."

My phone rang at that moment. I answered it and listened for a few moments.

"Okay, thanks for letting me know. Yes, she's right here. I'll let her know. Yes, we've taken steps to secure both our homes. We will. Okay, bye."

Zellie looked at me inquiringly.

"Mike Mullen," I said in response to her unspoken query. "He wanted to let us know that the sleazebag who pulled a gun on us was just let out on bail, and that we should be careful."

"Oh, that's just great," Zellie moaned. "He could have killed us."

"But he didn't, so it wasn't a capital offense and the court had to let him out on bail."

"That guy is a walking flight risk. Didn't that matter?"

"Apparently not. He had a public defender, but he posted a large bail bond. Mike was a little surprised by that, and I kind of am, too. How did a low-life like him get that kind of money?"

"Obviously, someone else paid the bill."

"Sure, but whom?"

"Whom?"

"I'm pretty sure it's whom."

"Isn't it 'paid *to* whom'? Not paid *by* whom?"

"Really? A grammar lesson, right now?" I shook my head. "Whatever. It's a valid question, though, however it's phrased."

"It is. I wonder *whom* paid the bail?" Zellie giggled.

"I'm just going to ignore that. But this is interesting–Jack Buckles did."

"Buckles? No way he paid it himself. He was just working for someone else."

"I agree. But he'd do anything for a price. I wonder who he's working for."

"Probably not our old mysterious friend, Marilyn. She never hired him, remember?"

"No, supposedly he referred her to us, although he denied that. He had met her, though. How on earth does she fit into all this?"

"I don't know, but I'll bet she's involved somehow. Too much of a coincidence."

My phone rang again. "Geez, when it rains, it pours. I wonder who it is this time." I looked at the caller ID. Ted.

"What's up, amigo?" I asked. I listened for a few moments and disconnected.

"Back to Mrs. Minniefield's. Ted has news."

I took a final sip of my coffee, dropped a few bucks on the table, waved to Delilah, and paid the tab at the cashier's station in front. As we walked out to my rental car, we saw Little Bobby getting into his Mercedes. I waved to him, and he waved back, though reluctantly. A slightly balding, heavyset man I didn't know, got into the car with him, and they sped off. We did the same, and arrived at Mrs. Minniefield's house in short order.

Ted began talking the moment we sat down.

"There's a questionable encrypted file buried in a subfolder in your account at Mort, Arnie. It was incredibly hard to find, and it did not appear on the list we generated when you were there. And," he paused for dramatic effect, "it was in your cloud account, *behind* your login, key card, and passcode. In other words, it couldn't have gotten there unless you put it there, or someone else had access to your account for enough time to put it there."

"I certainly wasn't the one to put an encrypted file there. I put other stuff there, maybe a few letters or other documents, for sure, but not that. What is it?"

"I don't know. I haven't figured that out yet. As I said, it's encrypted, and well done, too. I haven't broken it yet. But I will."

"I'm a little afraid to ask this," Zellie started, "but if only people with access to Arnie's internal Mort account could have put it there, how did you get in to find it? As I recall, you only had a list, and you just said it wasn't on the list."

Ted looked over at Zellie and smiled. "Always the sharp one, aren't you, Zellie? Okay, the keystrokes I had Arnie enter to find the eavesdropping program also gave me a backdoor remote access to files within his account. I thought it would be useful, and it turns out I was right."

I was mildly pissed off at the liberty he had taken, but kind of impressed, too. My response was accordingly muted. "You could have told me, but you know, in hindsight, given Jennifer's request this morning, I think I'm glad you didn't. I had absolutely no way of knowing that actual files were being examined at the same time she was speaking to us."

I looked at Zellie. "What do you think? Same file?"

"I'd bet on it."

"Me too."

"I'm sorry, Arnie. I really should have told you. But we were pressed for time while you were there. I should have told you later, but I just didn't. No excuses. You want me to close the door?"

"Can't we access the system remotely using my access card? That's what I always did in the past."

"You can, but there will be a record of the access in the company servers. No record my way."

"Leave it open then, at least for the time being. But the SEC would not be happy about this."

"We'll close off access just as soon as we figure this whole thing out."

"Shouldn't we just grab the file and never go into the system again?" Zellie asked.

Mrs. Minniefield answered that one. "It seems to be pretty safe right where it is. You have no less than the CEO of Mort unsuccessful in trying to access it."

"If that's what he was trying to do," I said. "We don't really know that."

"It's pretty likely," she said. "And he's not the only one. Tell them, Ted."

"Tom Carter attempted to access your computer only an hour or so after Charles Hastings did. Unsuccessfully, too, I should add."

"So, which one put the keystroke program on my computer?" I demanded impatiently. "You said that there was only one such program on the computer."

"There was only one," Ted said. "I have zero doubt about that."

"One of them must have known that the other put it there. It's the only explanation," Mrs. Minniefield said. "And there may be others that we just don't know anything about. For all we know, it could have been common knowledge in the senior wing at Mort."

"No wonder the company's having problems," I muttered. "Everyone's snooping. No one's working."

"Oh, they're working all right. But apparently not on securities transactions," said Ted.

"Mrs. Minniefield, shouldn't we be turning this file over to your friend in the Department of Justice?" Zellie asked.

"I think it's premature. We don't even know what it is. And our methodology for extracting it leaves something to be desired. It might be better for them to access it themselves directly."

"Sure, and arrest me in the process," I said. "It's in my account, under my password. How do I explain that to a bunch of career bureaucrats?"

"Let's just figure out what it is first. It shouldn't take that long. Okay, Arnie?" she asked.

I thought about it. I wasn't sure who I could trust outside this room, but I knew I could trust everyone in it. I nodded. "Okay."

"Jennifer apparently thinks it's information about the mob," Zellie offered.

"Did she refer to the encrypted file Ted found?"

"Not specifically," I put in. "But she said there was a file with information about the mob that she wanted to trade in exchange for canceling her debt to them. And she specifically referred to my access to my Mort account. It's the same file, all right."

"Any suggestions on what Arnie should do when Jennifer contacts him again, Mrs. Minniefield?" Zellie asked, with the very slightest note of peevishness in her voice.

I might have been the only one who noticed it. Nah, who am I kidding? Mrs. Minniefield noticed everything–but didn't let on.

"It's obviously up to Arnie, but I'd put her off. Tell her you're thinking about it, and whether it's worthwhile to even bother looking for this mysterious file she's talking about. Especially given the apparent mob connection."

"I doubt she'd believe that," I said. "Jennifer isn't stupid, and she does know me, albeit not as well as you three do. She'd figure I'd try to find it, if I didn't have it already, just to satisfy my curiosity. Whether I'd give it to her – that's another question. I'm guessing she'd figure I wouldn't."

Mrs. Minniefield thought about that. "You're probably right, Arnie, but at least it will keep her off balance. She may speculate about a lot of things, but she won't know for sure."

"I suppose. It's worth a try, anyway."

"I don't think it will take me long to crack the encryption," Ted said. "At least I hope not. And then we'll have a better idea of just what we're dealing with and what to do next. I mean, what if it turns out to be some proprietary Mort thing that's totally innocent, but that Jennifer and maybe other people just want to get their hands on it for totally mercenary reasons. That would change your approach, wouldn't it?"

"Yes. But I wouldn't give it to Jennifer in any event."

"But you might not think you had to turn it over to the Justice Department, either."

"True," I agreed, and rose to my feet. "Time to get back to work, then. We have a client to find." I stopped. "That's so sad, isn't it? Our first and only client asks us to find someone, and not only do we not find the missing person, we lose the client, too."

"I'm sure we'll actually find something on the next case," a suddenly cheerful Zellie said. "In the meantime, we should try to finish what we started. Let's go, Arnie."

* * *

"What was that all about, Zellie?" I asked when we were outside the house.

"What do you mean?"

"One second you're practically morose, and the next you're all roses and leaping to action."

"I think we can solve this case, Arnie. The pieces are falling into place. We still have a lot we can do. I was just resisting the whole idea of just stopping short every time we have a lead."

"How have we done that?"

"Think about it, Arnie. Greasy Sid. You find him dead. We interview Abigail Martin, and do nothing else to follow up, because the police are investigating. Supposedly. They haven't found the killer yet, have they?"

"No, but–"

"Brazen Saddles," she interrupted. "We find out a bit of information, and actually follow that up a little bit, but after we meet Rene Desmond, we pretty much stop. We never found Jennifer's connection to either Desmond or Brazen Saddles. She's apparently a shareholder, for crying out loud. How hard would that have been to find out?"

"Not hard," I admitted. "We just never looked."

"No, we didn't. And we should have. And Little Bobby falls all over himself to give us access to his computer. Shouldn't we wonder why? And ask him? We don't really know whether the information we viewed on his computer was complete. We looked at the file he told us to, remember? And we were so darn proud of ourselves getting the information, we never gave a thought to whether it was complete. Or if there were other things to see. If Delilah's boyfriend is to be believed, Little Bobby isn't selling many cars, because he just doesn't care like his daddy did. And Jennifer says that Rene Desmond has some sort of deal with Little Bobby. Maybe we should ask about that."

"Maybe we should. And to continue where you left off, maybe we should ask Jack Buckles what he knows. He denied ever meeting our elusive client, but you knew he was lying. And now we have the information that he bailed out our assailant. He'll be reluctant, but probably will spill something of value. He might be our only connection to Marilyn."

"Absolutely. Arnie. We're not as bad at this as you seem to think. We haven't followed up on some leads, and we've stopped short a lot, but we've made some significant discoveries. We just have to charge ahead. We'll defer to Mrs. M. on waiting to do something about the file, simply because it makes sense to find out what it is before we do anything. But we should go full speed on the investigation."

"Well I'm convinced. Nice pep talk, Zellie."

"It was as much for myself as for you, Arnie. Believe me."

"Okay. Where to?"

"I think to my house to pick up my car. I think we should probably split up for a while and do some separate investigating. We can have a drink of something, and figure out the details."

"Suits me."

***

We split a Diet Coke at Zellie's house, and made plans. I would go see Jack Buckles and then Little Bobby. Zellie would go to the library and then the county courthouse to continue her mob research.

"I think we should know more about what we're dealing with," she explained. "And I was really at my limit on the computer. I need to look at some newspaper accounts and then follow up with some court record research. Maybe I can find a thread to tie things together. I feel like we're really close to figuring out what's going on."

"Okay with me, Zellie. And thanks for not letting me slip into a self-indulgent funk."

"Anytime. But you would have come around anyway. You always do."

I put my hand on top of hers. "Maybe. But thanks anyway."

***

I pulled up and parked in one of the four spaces in front of a one-story edifice aptly named the "Buckles Building." A pretentious name, certainly, and the building looked like a converted garage, which it might well have been.

But he obviously owned it, which is more than I could say about the A to Z Agency. We didn't own anything. I surveyed the outside for a moment. There were no other cars parked in the visitor spaces, but the "Reserved" spaces held two cars – a Ford Taurus of recent vintage by the looks of it, and a truly beautiful Mustang convertible, probably 1965 or 1966, if I wasn't mistaken. And it was in perfect condition. Probably Jack's car. I resisted the urge to take a closer look, and headed to the entrance.

The door opened to a small reception area, with two plastic chairs lining the wall. At the nondescript desk sat a large-bosomed blonde receptionist, who was hard at work – filing her nails and doing something unspeakable with her cuticles. She didn't bother to look up, so completely engrossed in her activity. I watched for a few moments, then I subtly cleared my throat. Nothing.

"Excuse me, miss?" I ventured, and she looked up, with obvious disinterest.

"It's Ms." She looked down at her nails again.

"Um. Okay, Ms.?"

"What? Can't you see I'm busy?"

"I'd like to see Mr. Buckles, please."

She eyed me suspiciously. "Does he owe you money?"

"No. Definitely not."

"Do you have an appointment? He don't see anyone without an appointment."

"No I don't have an appointment, but I'd hoped he'd see me anyway, if he's not too busy."

"Bucky? Busy? That's a laugh. Look around you. See this crappy office? That's how busy he is. He's got maybe one job going on right now. Are you looking to hire him?" She sounded hopeful. "Maybe he can pay me what he owes me. I got bills to pay, and they even threatened to cut off my cable TV. Can you believe those bastards?" She held her thumb and index finger an inch apart.

"I'm this close to blowing this joint. If I don't get paid soon...." She would have continued expounding on her personal travails, but the door behind her opened and Jack Buckles stuck his head out.

"What's the racket going on out here, Belinda? I'm trying to take a nap." He looked over and spotted me.

"Arnie Fischer! Look what the cat dragged in." He laughed at his little joke.

"Hi Jack. Long time, eh?"

"Not long enough."

I studied Jack's sneering countenance for a moment. It was a distinctly unpleasant face, slightly pockmarked, with a pug nose that had clearly been broken at least once, probably more than that. He was mostly bald, with little tufts of jet-black hair, obviously dyed, sticking up above his ears. His eyes were blue, but not a kind blue – a sort of faded azure that might once have been appealing, but now looked mostly vacant.

I hadn't really seen him up close since high school. I had run into him from time to time, of course, as people living in the same community do, but not really for more than a few moments. He had not aged well, and frankly looked like a physical wreck, with a protruding pot-belly that extended for some distance over his belt. He reeked of tobacco, which I could smell from the fifteen or twenty feet that separated us, and he looked and sounded like he had hit the bottle already. I ignored his snide remark.

"If you have a minute, I'd like to talk to you, Jack."

"Why should I talk to you?"

"You never know, Jack. It might be worth your while."

"You offering me money, Arnie?"

Jack suddenly looked interested. Belinda looked real interested. Greed trumps dislike and morals every time, I thought, with both resignation and disgust.

"Maybe. If you have something worthwhile to tell me."

"Well, don't just sit there, Belinda, escort the *gentleman* into my office." Jack emphasized the word gentleman, with exaggerated formality. Belinda shrugged and pointed to the door in which Jack stood.

"It's in there," she said, and went back to filing her nails.

"Hard to find good help these days," Jack said.

"Maybe you should try paying a decent wage," Belinda said, without looking up. "In fact, maybe you should pay the bullshit wages you promised." She looked up and stared daggers at Jack, who scurried hurriedly into his office. I smiled weakly at Belinda, and followed him in.

"Sit down, sit down. I like my paying clients to be comfortable."

"Um, I don't want to hire you, Jack. I just want some information."

"Same thing. You can pay me as a private eye, or pay me for information. You see the constant there, Arnie? Either way, you pay me."

I sighed. "Okay, Jack, we'll do it your way. I have some questions for you. You can decide on a price for the answers. If I think it's worth the money, I'll pay for it."

"Arnie, I think we have the beginnings of a beautiful friendship. I always say that to my clients. Very classy."

Sure, I thought. Comparing a sleazy transaction in a dumpy office in Red Bank, New Jersey to a wartime deal to protect the lives of a lover and her hero husband was very classy. And friends? With this jerk? Be serious. But I had to play along.

"Casablanca, right?"

"Exactly. Now let's get to it. I'm a busy man."

"Did you ever meet someone named Marilyn Beaufort or Bean?"

Jack's mouth curled into a sly smile. "Didn't I go through that with your little girlfriend? The one with the nice ass? Although I must say I'm truly gratified to know that both of you have now come crawling to the professional for help. Out of your league, aren't you? Well, I might be able to help you on some things, for a price, of course, but not that. Never met the broad. I told the hot member of your so-called agency already. Free of charge, I might add. I gave her a hotness discount." He eyed me. "Don't expect the same thing, sport."

"Oh, I won't, Jack, you can depend on that. Okay, I know you met with her, but let's move on anyway."

Jack folded his arms. "Whatever."

"You bailed a guy out of jail yesterday. Why?"

"Assuming for the moment that's true, which I am not for a second agreeing to, why do you care?"

"Let's just say it's personal." Interesting, I thought. He doesn't seem to know that Zellie and I were involved.

"Let's not. Why the interest in some thug I may or may not have bailed out?"

"Jack, I'm not paying you for questions, I'm paying you for answers."

"Haven't seen any green yet."

I sighed, and pulled out my wallet. "How much?"

"Five hundred bucks."

"For one answer? You're crazy. I'll give you twenty."

"A hundred."

"Fifty, and it better be a good answer, or you get nothing."

"Take the fifty, Bucky," a voice from behind the door exclaimed. "I got bills."

"Shut up, Belinda, he yelled at the closed door. "I'm negotiating here." He turned back towards me. "Okay, fifty. Pay up."

I peeled off two twenties and a ten from my wallet, taking care not to let him see how much cash I had. If he saw it, the cost would no doubt magically equal the total amount in my wallet. I held them up for Jack to see.

"Not so fast. Answer the question."

"Okay. I bailed a guy out of jail yesterday because the judge wouldn't let him out without posting bail. There, you have your answer, give me the money."

"I told you it had better be a good answer or you get nothing. That was a wise-ass answer, not worth anything."

"I can't help it if your question was a stupid one. I answered it. You owe me fifty bucks."

I held up my hand. "Okay, Jack. Here's what we're going to do. I'll ask a series of questions, and you give the answers, and we'll agree on a price for the whole story. That makes more sense than I ask a question to lay a foundation for the next one, then ask follow-up questions, *et cetera*. Okay?"

Jack nodded. "Okay. But you still owe me for the first question, and I charge extra for follow-up questions. You know, it might have been easier for you to just hire me at my hourly rate."

"Who did you bail out? Who hired you? Did the person who hired you ask you to do anything else, either before or after? Who gave you the money to bail the guy out of jail? Did you know the guy before you bailed him out? Had you any prior dealings with him? Where did he go after you bailed him out? How much were you paid? And is Marilyn Beaufort involved in this somehow?"

"Whoa. That's a lot of questions." He rubbed his hands together, as if contemplating a scrumptious meal. "And it's going to cost a lot of money to get answers. I mean, you're asking me to violate attorney client confidentiality. I don't know if I can do that at all."

"You're not a lawyer, Jack."

"No, but same thing. I can't just give you the names. I won't get hired again if I do that."

"You're not getting hired now," said a voice from behind the door. "What difference does it make?"

"I'm warning you, Belinda. Shut up."

"Up yours, Bucky."

Jack shrugged. "See what I have to put up with? Okay, business is business. What's it worth to you?"

"I'll give you a hundred bucks. And no bullshit responses, either."

"You drive a hard bargain. Okay." He reached for a file cabinet, made a big show of looking for the right file – if Belinda was right, the whole file cabinet probably only had a couple of files in it – and took out a slender folder with a couple of sheets in it.

"Robert Weaver, Caucasian, aged thirty-six, brown hair, brown eyes. Charged with attempted assault with a deadly weapon. Bailed him out of jail. Certified check made payable to Monmouth County Criminal Court. Retainer fee – I like the sound of that, very professional – five-hundred dollars plus twenty bucks for lunch. Routine matter. Never met the lowlife before, never did business with him before. Job done. Cashed retainer check, ate great lunch. Weaver took off in different direction. Don't know where he went."

"You got five-hundred dollars and still didn't pay me?" Belinda yelled through the door again. "You bastard. I quit."

"Good riddance." He turned to me. "Now I don't have to give her any part of the hundred I just earned. Where's my money?"

"You still owe me the answers to a couple of questions, Jack. Who hired you? Had you done any prior business with the person who hired you? And is Marilyn Beaufort involved in this somehow?"

"Okay, okay. The thing is, I don't really know who hired me. I was given a lot of money to do an easy job, and I did it. I was hired over the phone by a guy I never met. He told me the details. It seemed easy, so I did it. I don't know anything else. And I told you, I don't know any Marilyn Beaufort."

"I think you met her at least once, Jack. Very pretty and personable, blonde hair, big bosom, very revealing outfit. The kind of things you'd remember." For some reason, Jack looked nervous. His eyebrow started to twitch a little.

"Look, I might have met someone like that," he finally said. "I don't know if it's the same person. And she didn't give her name as Marilyn Beaufort. It was something like Denise Dempster." He chuckled. "Double D," that's how I remembered her name. And she wasn't at all personable. That broad was no pushover, I will tell you that. She was a little scary, to tell you the truth."

"What did she want?"

"That's the thing. I don't really know. She asked a lot of questions about what I do, who my clients are, *et cetera*. I thought it was the usual preamble to hiring me for something. I didn't really have anything to tell her. It's been a little slow."

"Did you tell her about the mysterious guy on the phone?"

"No. I don't know if I would have. At least not without seeing some green. But he hadn't called me yet, so I had no information to sell."

"Had you heard from the guy on the phone before?"

Jack looked a little cagey. "You've used up your hundred bucks. I'm saying nothing else."

Try as I might, I couldn't shake him from that, so I shrugged and gave him his hundred bucks. I thought it money well spent, although he didn't really tell me anything of importance, or that I didn't already know. And I had little doubt that he hadn't told me everything.

But truth be told, I was a little surprised that Jack had said anything at all. And I wondered why, after telling me everything else, he had withheld the last piece. He had clearly been hired before by the same person. For what? I kind of believed him that he didn't know the name of the person who hired him. Why tell someone like Buckles that? If you had someone as greedy as Jack Buckles, there was no need to provide a lot of information. He'd do the job anyway. I walked out of the building, and practically ran straight into Belinda, who was angrily pacing just outside the door.

"I'm sorry, Belinda. He wasn't very nice to you."

"He's a prick. But now I'm out of a job, and I need the money."

"I'm sure he'll hire you back, if you want to work there."

"It's not like I have any other options, so I guess I go crawling back, like I always do."

"You've quit before?"

"Let's see. I've been fired six times, and quit, let me think. Three times."

"So, he's hired you back every time?"

"Yeah, but it's a bitch getting paid."

I took out my wallet and peeled off a twenty, and handed it to her.

"Here, at least this is a little something to help."

"What do you want for it?" She eyed me suspiciously. "I'm not that kind of girl."

"No, no, you misunderstand. I don't want anything. Just trying to help someone in need. And just so you know, I just gave Buckles a hundred bucks. You should march back in there and demand your share."

Belinda looked at the twenty, then at me, then leaned forward and kissed me right on the mouth.

"You're a nice guy. I don't see many of those around here. And I'm going to do what you said and march right in there and demand my back pay."

"Good for you. And good luck."

"Thanks, Mister." She paused. "Do you need a receptionist, maybe?"

"I'm afraid not, Belinda. But I'll keep you in mind if I ever do."

"Okay, thanks." She paused again. "I think I saw the envelope with the five-hundred bucks Bucky got that he never gave me any of, the bastard. He could have given me something. All that money, and he still stiffed me, the weasel…."

She would have continued berating Buckles, but I interrupted.

"Did you see a return address?"

"I didn't notice one, and he grabbed it out of my hand before I could open it. Now I know why. But it was postmarked New York, New York. I saw that right away, because we generally only get bills and junk mail. This one was different."

I peeled off another twenty, and gave it to her.

"That's real helpful, Belinda. Thank you."

She looked at it and beamed. "Thanks. I'll let you know if I hear or see anything else."

"You do that, Belinda. Thank you. Now go back and get a piece of that hundred bucks."

She gave me a mock salute and charged back inside. I almost felt pity for Buckles.

Nah, I didn't.

CHAPTER TWENTY-NINE

Zellie had expected to grapple with ancient microfiche machines, and was pleasantly surprised to note that the Middletown Township Public Library had a fully digitized periodical collection. It was a nice, spacious library, too, with comfortable chairs for reading, in addition to ample computer monitors for public internet use and for browsing the newspapers Zellie needed.

She didn't really know what she was looking for, so she decided to simply begin by reviewing as many stories about the South Jersey mob as she could find. And there were a lot of them. Many of the stories prominently featured Fat Nicky Martinson. He was described variously as a mob boss, ruthless mobster, killer, and former hitman-now crime boss. No question, bad guy all around. And his brother Sid was such a nice guy. Same parents, different outcome. Unfortunately, not an entirely unfamiliar situation, Zellie thought, although maybe not to this degree.

She flipped absently through multiple pages of the stories, which began to run together in her mind. Sid and Fat Nicky were both born in the Bronx, but their family moved to Middletown when they were both very young. They had parted ways when they were teenagers, which is when one local newspaper article said Fat Nicky had started his storied criminal career. Sid was charitably described in the article as a respectable local businessman. Zellie figured that it was true, mostly. As respectable as the owner of a bar could be while serving alcohol to underage kids. But certainly, more respectable than his brother, to whom killing was just one of his many fun pastimes.

Zellie continued to peruse the papers, which contained news photographs of various crime scenes, and occasionally, of various crime family members. Fat Nicky received the most coverage, but others occasionally appeared in the photographs. No one was at all familiar to Zellie, including Fat Nicky. Zellie studied his picture, and gave an involuntary shudder. Even in the news photo, Fat Nicky's eyes appeared totally emotionless, and as cold as ice. He resembled Sid, of course, but was shorter and heavier. And those eyes. Oh, my god, those eyes. Sid's eyes were nothing like that. Used to be nothing like that, Zellie corrected herself. Sid was dead, and his eyes were now as cold as his brother's. Irony takes many forms, she mused.

Zellie sat back from staring at the monitor and rested for a moment. This was hard work, and she was having a hard time discerning its purpose. *What am I looking for?* Something to just pop out? She decided that she had a good handle on the origins and nature of Fat Nicky's crime empire, but it provided nothing useful. Maybe she should just give up here, and join Arnie. She wondered how he was doing with Jack Buckles, or that dim-witted receptionist of his. She looked at her watch, and decided that he was probably done with Jack, and on his way to see Little Bobby.

No, she decided. She'd keep at this for a little while longer. Maybe looking at some of the New York mob material would tell her something. There was a New York connection here, somewhere. She pulled up the material on the New York mob and continued reading. The similarities between the activities of the New York mob and the nature of the crimes attributed to the South Jersey mob were striking. Crime is crime, she thought. Evil doesn't adhere to state lines.

But from what she read, it did have clearly defined boundaries. Each crime family had a territory it covered, and there was an unwritten agreement by each not to breach the others' domain. To be sure, there were disputes that arose over the years, depending upon the bosses involved, but there had been relative peace between them for some time. The crime bosses' problems, it seemed, came from within. Zellie read through various accounts of internal strife over the years, essentially underlings challenging the boss for primacy in a kind of Darwinesque survival of the fittest ritual.

Interesting, perhaps, but not really very helpful. She studied the pictures, mostly grainy old newspaper photos with little definition, even as rendered on the high resolution monitor she was viewing. Absolutely no one was familiar, and certainly she'd seen no evidence of Rene Desmond or any of the local people involved in their case.

A group photograph, supposedly depicting members of one of the New York crime families, caught her eye. It was hazy, and contained no identification of the people in the photograph, and bore the cynical caption – "The Real New York City Council?"

Zellie studied the picture closely. It wasn't the group of men gathered around a table that had caught her eye. It was a solitary, hazy figure in the back, looking over the assemblage. Marilyn Beaufort. Even with the poor resolution of the photograph, Zellie was sure of it. It was definitely Marilyn. She was conservatively dressed, with no sign of the provocative outfit she had worn when she hired them. Zellie noted the page so that she could get a print at the front desk, then excitedly scoured the various newspapers looking for any reference to the mysterious woman. No luck.

Finally, she gave up, obtained her print, and walked out to her car to call Arnie.

CHAPTER THIRTY

I was about to call Zellie when my phone rang. It was Eddie's "guy," with the news that he'd fixed Matilda, and would drop the car off at the Moo Mart. He told me that I could just pay Eddie the ridiculously small sum he requested. I inquired about the low price, and he laughed and said that it hadn't been much work, just some tuning up, and that he owed Eddie a favor anyway.

He made a point of saying that it really was "a bunch of favors" that he owed Eddie, that Eddie was a good guy, and that it was fun to work on such a classic car.

I agreed with him that Eddie was a real gentleman and that I probably owed him just as many favors.

"I'll just have to add this to the list," I said. I then called Eddie and thanked him, too, and told him I'd be right over to pick up Matilda.

I called Zellie and got voice mail. Still in the library, I figured, and woe to anyone who let his or her phone ring while under the scrutiny of the librarian. When we were kids, we were pretty much told that making noise in the library would result in certain death...*or worse*, whatever that meant.

As adults, we assumed that the death penalty probably also applied to ringing cell phones, so we always turned them off. I guess it made sense, I mean not the death part, but the silence. Nothing worse than a loud ring, and with today's customized ring tones, the sound could be practically anything. Imagine your quiet reading being interrupted by some idiot's clip from a Nine Inch Nails tune and you get the idea.

Anyway, I left Zellie a message to give me a call when she got a chance, and that I was going to the office to pick up Matilda, after which I intended to head over to Little Bobby's Mercedes dealership. Then I drove over and returned my rental car. As expected, they had no problem dropping me off at the Moo Mart, where I greeted Eddie and retrieved the keys to Matilda.

"She's purring like a little kitty, Arnie," Eddie said as he gave me the keys.

"I'm happy to have her back. I mean, I've been driving a Chevy Malibu, for crying out loud."

"I'm sorry for your pain," Eddie said solemnly. We both paused in respectful silence, then burst into laughter.

"Well, maybe it wasn't *that* bad," I admitted. "Actually, it gave me quite a nice ride. But I'm still happy to have Matilda back."

I got into my car and breathed in Matilda's soothing air. There was something about her that set her apart from other cars, and I basked in the glow. Sort of my own rolling man cave, I suppose. Soothing. Familiar.

I started the engine and it sprang to life. Good news. It hadn't done that in a long while. I still hadn't heard from Zellie, so I headed out to see Little Bobby. I wasn't exactly sure how to approach him, though. The last visit had bordered on the bizarre, and I wasn't really in the mood for playing his games. I decided on the direct approach. Just ask him how many Mercedes' he had sold to Brazen Saddles. I pulled into the parking lot of "Big Bobby & Son Fine Automobiles," and entered the showroom.

A guy in a sports jacket approached, and somewhat lackadaisically inquired whether he could help me. I asked to see Little Bobby and he simply nodded toward the office on the second floor.

"He's up there. He always is. Just go right up."

I climbed the stairs to Little Bobby's office and tentatively knocked on the open door. Little Bobby was looking at something on his computer screen, but he looked up when I knocked.

"Arnie! An unexpected pleasure." He made a show of looking behind me. "No Zellie today?"

"Not today," I said. "I just wanted to ask a few more questions about our case, if it's okay with you."

"Do you want to see more records on the computer that I can't show you, Arnie?" He started to get up. "I have some things to do downstairs, and I'll…"

"No need, Little Bobby," I interrupted. "I just wanted to get a few clarifications."

He looked disappointed, but recovered. "Okay, clarifications. I can probably do those." He held up his hand and pointed his index finger like a gun. "Fire away. I'm ready to do some serious clarifying."

I looked at him dubiously. *Is he for real?* How did the guy run this business? I shrugged.

"How many cars have you sold to Brazen Saddles?"

Little Bobby turned towards his computer monitor. "What did it say when you looked? And I know you looked, didn't you Arnie?"

"Um, yes. I admit that I looked. But I'm not sure all the information was in there. Is that the only place you keep the sales records?"

"I don't think I should be talking to you about this, Arnie. These are confidential sales records. People depend upon our discretion here." His tone was solemn. Then he brightened, and looked slyly from side to side as if checking to see if anyone was listening. "I have to go downstairs for a while," he said loudly. "Please don't touch anything while I'm gone." Then he winked at me and headed out the door.

I just gaped at his back as he departed. *Here we go again.* More games. I went to look at the computer, and began checking the files again. It was the same set of files. Absolutely nothing was different that I could tell. And the corporate folder still showed only four Mercedes' being sold to Brazen Saddles. I began to wonder if Little Bobby had a screw loose, or there were files that he simply wasn't aware of. But how could that be? He's the owner and manager. Surely, he would know about sales.

Unless someone was taking advantage of his penchant for cloak and dagger rituals, and his patently gullible nature. More likely, Jennifer was lying about how many cars Brazen Saddles had purchased. But that was one thing she had sounded sincere about. In any event, I wasn't going to learn anything else here. I sat back down in the visitor's chair and waited for Little Bobby to return.

As I sat there waiting for him, my phone rang. Zellie. I answered and told her where I was.

Zellie told me she knew that I couldn't talk, but excitedly told me what she'd discovered.

I looked behind me to see if Little Bobby was around yet, and seeing no one told Zellie to go ahead. She proceeded to tell me that she'd found a picture of Marilyn with a group of mobsters in New York.

"She's a mobster," she whispered into the phone.

I thought for a moment about the sexy, curvaceous, and almost flirtatious woman we had met, and the almost fearful description Jack had given. I frankly had a hard time reconciling the two images. And now, Zellie was telling me the woman in the fancy boots was a mobster. I was dubious, to say the least. I lowered my voice in case Little Bobby came back sooner than expected.

"I don't know, Zellie. She didn't look like a mobster to me. But it does kind of jive with what Jack told me." I explained how nervous Jack was describing her. "He was scared to death of her, Zellie."

"That doesn't sound like our Marilyn," Zellie acknowledged. "And, the picture surprised me, too, but there was no doubt that it was Marilyn, standing there with some of the most notorious and scary New York crime figures."

"Maybe she's one of their wives, or girlfriends or something. But that doesn't explain anything. Why did she come to see us?"

Zellie speculated that she was after the same thing that everyone else seemed to want – the notorious computer file.

"I suppose so," I said. "Well if so, she should get in line. There are so many people looking for that file, I've lost track."

I heard Little Bobby starting back up the stairs to the office.

"I have to run. Little Bobby is coming back. I'll tell you about it later, but I'm a little worried that he's not in full possession of his faculties."

Zellie told me that she was headed to the courthouse next to see what else she could dig up.

"You've found out plenty already, Zellie. I'll talk to you later."

"How'd it go, Arnie? I almost wished I'd stayed around to see how an actual private eye investigates. I'll bet you feel like Sam Spade."

"Um, sure, Little Bobby. Sam Spade."

"I bet you watch private eyes on TV, don't you? My favorites are Magnum, P.I., the Rockford Files, Mannix, Barnaby Jones – really, I watch all of them – but those are my favorites. And Batman and Robin. Are they private eyes? I guess not, but I love them, too. What are your favorites, Arnie?"

"I really couldn't pick one, Little Bobby." I was beginning to feel uncomfortable, and I rose to my feet. "It's been nice seeing you, but I have to go now."

Little Bobby looked disappointed. "Okay, Arnie, but come back again soon, please."

"Sure, Little Bobby. Sure, I will."

I left Little Bobby in his office, humming the theme to Cannon. I went down the stairs and feigned looking around at the cars in the showroom. I really wanted to engage one of the salesmen in conversation if only to verify that they knew about Little Bobby's slender grip on reality. And I was willing to put up with a sales pitch to accomplish that. I wasn't disappointed.

A salesman came up to me and started to talk about the features of the model I was viewing. To my surprise, however, his sales pitch seemed lackluster. I figured I wasn't dressed like a prospective purchaser of a $100,000 car, so I took on an air of a frequent purchaser of expensive vehicles. It had no effect on him. After a while, you probably get good at identifying the tire kickers, I mused. Well he got me. I wasn't interested, and he wasn't particularly interested in spending the time on someone who wasn't buying.

I tried a different tack. "I've known Little Bobby since high school. He seems a little under the weather. Is he okay?"

"Little Bobby? He's fine as far as I know."

"Okay, just wondering. Thanks for the info about the car. I'm going to think about it. Thanks."

"No problem."

I left the showroom and headed to the parking lot where I'd left Matilda. When I got in, I immediately felt her restorative powers. Okay, maybe not, but it was good to have her back, anyway. I decided to call Ted to see if he'd made any progress on decrypting the file. It seemed like the key to the case, after all.

I called, and he told me the going was slow on the decryption. When I inquired about whether it was beyond his capabilities, he bristled noticeably.

"I said it was slow going. I didn't say it was impossible. But it is pretty sophisticated encryption," he admitted. "I'll get it figured out. Well, my computer and I will get it done," he added. "Individuals generally can't decipher even the simplest privacy protocols. It takes a computer trying millions, even billions of guesses to finally get it, and depending upon the sophistication of the program, a program could theoretically take years to decrypt."

"Years? I don't think we have that much time, Ted."

"It won't take *me* years, Arnie. I promise. I have a few tricks up my sleeve to speed up the process."

"Okay, great," I said dubiously. "Thanks, Ted."

"I'll call you the minute I know something, Arnie."

I hung up, just a little depressed at not knowing more. Maybe Zellie had learned something. I hit speed dial 1 to call her, and laughed to myself. Zellie was most assuredly speed dial 1. There was no one I called more.

But the call went straight to voice mail, which I should have expected. Zellie was in the clerk's office at the courthouse, and court security personnel probably confiscated her phone when she arrived. I supposed I could meet her over there, but rejected that idea immediately. She could handle that on her own. No need for two people to do the same work. Anyway, being after five p.m., they'd be closing the clerk's office soon, and I'd hear from her soon enough.

I decided to head home. I hated waiting, but I had no choice.

CHAPTER THIRTY-ONE

Zellie parked on a side street, a little way away from the courthouse, having circled through the parking lot adjacent to the building and found it packed full of cars.

She walked the short distance on a quiet, tree-lined street and went into the building. Having negotiated her way through security and checking her cell phone with the security personnel, she proceeded directly into the clerk's office, where a large counter and glass (presumably bulletproof) wall separated the public from the clerks working inside. Outside the counter were rows of computer terminals, which were available to the public to search court records. Just what Zellie wanted to do, so she sat down at one and started to work.

Not sure where to begin, Zellie commenced searching various names. She tried Marilyn Beaufort. Nothing. She didn't really expect anything on that, but it was worth a try, she thought. This system is limited to Monmouth County, and the only connection she could find was in New York. There really should be more global coverage, and probably there was somewhere, she thought. Just not here. From experience, Zellie knew that New Jersey court records were a scattered, Byzantine mess. One needed to go to each county to access the records, even though the courts had made progress in digitizing a lot of the information.

She tried Marilyn Bean, and still no hits. And nothing for Rene Desmond, or Jennifer Marquette. Just for the fun of it, she searched

Arnie's name, and was kind of gratified there were no hits for him, either. Her own name yielded her divorce proceeding, but thankfully nothing else. Sid's name yielded several criminal records, all for serving minors at the Stone Parrot. She turned her attention to the known South Jersey mob figures, which was the real reason she'd come in.

Her first search, of Nicholas Martinson, brought up a dozen criminal proceedings, all entitled, The People of the State of New Jersey v. Nicholas Martinson, a/k/a "Fat Nicky" Martinson.

He had been charged with murder, racketeering, assault, extortion, gambling, and numerous other offenses. Interestingly, not anything to do with drugs. Even Fat Nicky had his scruples, however twisted they might be, Zellie thought. His lawyers had obtained dismissals of all twelve cases before trial, which really was a remarkable winning streak for the bad guys.

She looked more carefully at the files, one by one. The same lawyer represented Fat Nicky in each of the first few cases she examined, a fellow by the name of Bruce Merkins. The name was familiar to her from the news stories she had read. He must be one of those old-time mob mouthpieces, who would say or do anything to get their clients out of jail. But he had surely been successful, time after time. The cold court files didn't say so, but from what she had read, the dismissals had likely resulted from witnesses mysteriously changing their stories, or disappearing altogether. Fat Nicky was most assuredly a very evil man, no question about it.

Each file was different, but depressingly the same. Mob boss arrested, charged and ultimately released. The same names over and over again. Until Zellie got to the second to last one, which shocked her to her very core. Zellie stared at the screen.

It can't be. No way.

But it was true. Zellie quickly checked the last file – same thing. She put her head in her hands and choked back a sob. Oh, my god. She couldn't. She wouldn't. This was not just any client, it was the head of the South Jersey crime family, for crying out loud. No matter how good the money was, Marla wouldn't represent that scum, would she?

But she clearly would. It was right there on the screen. Marla Perez, attorney for Nicholas Martinson. And she had obtained dismissals of Fat Nicky's cases just like Bruce Merkins had. And within the last few months, from what the Court records said.

Zellie was shaken at what she had learned. Marla, whom she trusted beyond question, was basically in bed with stone cold killers. Zellie started to boil.

No wonder she's so interested in our activities. She was gathering information to better represent the mob. We were just adverse witnesses to interview. Just another case. And she'd confided in Marla about her feelings for Arnie, too. That's what friends did.

Zellie, you're a dope, she said to herself. She had to call Arnie, immediately. She reached for her phone. Oops. It was checked with the security personnel.

A clerk approached her at that moment. "Miss? You have to leave now. I'm closing for the night. You looked so intent, I didn't want to disturb you, but it's closing time. Everyone has left but me."

Zellie looked around and saw that the clerk's office was now dark.

"Oh, I'm sorry," Zellie sputtered. "I didn't realize. Of course, I'm leaving now. Thanks for your patience." She paused for a moment. "My phone…"

"You can retrieve it from security on your way out. The clerk's office is closed, but security personnel will remain until the last people leave."

"Thank you."

Zellie hurried to the security station and was given her phone back. She left the building, and was surprised to see the parking lot, so full when she had arrived, virtually empty now. She pulled out her phone and called Arnie. Voice mail. Of course. *Just* when she had important news.

Oh well, she'd see him soon anyway, and walked briskly down the quiet street toward her car. It was still light out, but she was nervous anyway. There wasn't another soul in sight, and she'd been reading about mobsters and murder all day.

She heard footsteps behind her, and was glad to see her car up ahead. She didn't dare turn around, but quickened her pace. Almost on cue, the footsteps got louder. Just as she reached her car, a hand reached from behind her and clamped over her mouth, stifling her scream.

CHAPTER THIRTY-TWO

I got home and took Lazlow for a long walk around the neighborhood. He enjoyed it immensely, but to tell you the truth, I felt distracted. I couldn't really get my head around the case, and I hadn't heard from Zellie yet. I looked at my watch. Almost six. I should have heard from her by now.

I was pretty sure the clerk's office in the courthouse closed at five. Or was it five-thirty? Well it was one or the other. I called Zellie again and got voicemail again. I left her another message and disconnected with growing anxiety. I wasn't sure why, exactly. It wasn't like it had been a particularly long time since the clerk's office had closed, but something was giving me the jitters. Zellie and I had known each other so long, we had each developed a kind of sixth sense about each other. I wasn't the only one who noticed it. Zellie had told me she had felt it, too. And that sixth sense was telling me something was wrong. Hopefully just a flat tire or something, and a phone on the fritz.

I waited fifteen minutes more, and called Ted, Marla and Mrs. Minniefield. Neither Ted nor Mrs. Minniefield had not heard from Zellie. I got voice mail for Marla, and left a message telling her to call me. Ted told me that everything was probably fine, and not to worry. Mrs. Minniefield said that it was a little early to be worrying, but to call her again in a half hour if I didn't hear from her. I agreed to do so, then sat down at my kitchen table and pretended to read the newspaper. Really, I just fidgeted uncomfortably. Lazlow came over and looked expectantly at me. I fed him, grateful for the temporary distraction, and just as I put the bowl down, my phone rang.

I pulled it out of my pocket, saw that it was Zellie, and answered, just a bit breathlessly. "Zellie, I am so glad to hear from you. I was a little worried–"

"It's not Zellie," a mechanical voice interrupted.

I sucked in a breath as though all the oxygen had left the room. "Who is this? Where's Zellie? Is she okay? Why are you using her phone? Give it back to her."

"She's fine, Arnie. For now, that is. Her continued well-being depends entirely on you."

"Is she there with you? I want to speak to her."

"All in good time, Arnie. You have something very valuable to me. I want it. Zellie is very important to you. No question, you want her back, alive and unhurt. I'm guessing you value her safety at least as much as I value the item you possess. A simple business transaction. You know what I want – a little computer file. That's all. In exchange for your sweetheart. Sounds like a fair trade to me."

My heart pounded so loud I couldn't hear my own words but they were the truth. "You had better not hurt her," I said with venom in my voice. "You hurt one hair on her head, and I'll track you down and kill you."

"My, my. There's no need for violence. I wouldn't touch her pretty head, or anything else on her…unless you don't come through, Arnie. If you don't, I'll have to nullify our contract. And Zellie–how should I put this? Kapow! Her expiration date passes…. She dies, Arnie. Don't mess this up."

"How do you know I even have the file you're looking for?"

"Don't be cute, Arnie. Zellie's life depends on it. You either have it, or can get your hands on it. If you can't, Zellie will pay."

"How do I know she's safe now?"

"This isn't a TV show, Arnie. You don't know. You'll have to accept my personal assurance that she'll be okay if you deliver the file to me at the place I designate."

"You're personal assurance? I don't even know who you are."

"And I'd like to keep it that way. I'm sure you understand. You'll be hearing from me again on where to bring the file. And no cops. I can't emphasize that enough. No officers of the law. No FBI, no local police, not even a meter maid. No cops. Any cops and Zellie's ticket gets punched. Permanently."

"You put her on the phone, or there's no deal."

"My, how brave you are with Zellie's life. I'll think about it, Arnie. Maybe when I call again. Maybe. And then again, maybe not." And the line went dead. Whoever it was had disconnected.

My mind swirled with all kinds of emotions. Fear, anger, helplessness. And loneliness. Zellie's life was up to me alone. I couldn't just call the cops or the FBI and let them handle it. But I had to involve Mrs. Minniefield and Ted.

Ted had the file after all, and no way was Mrs. Minniefield going to be excluded. I had to tell them, and right away. Should I tell Marla, too? She's Zellie's best girlfriend, after all. No, not a good idea. She'd just worry, and increasing the number of people involved would just put Zellie in jeopardy. In *more* jeopardy, I added to myself. She was in plenty of danger right now.

I picked up the phone and called Ted and told him to meet me at Mrs. Minniefield's house right away, and to bring the file. I told Mrs. M. that we were coming over. Neither one of them asked why. They were like that. They could be all business at the drop of a hat. I was somewhat comforted by the thought of their involvement, and it assuaged my feelings of loneliness. Of course, I was still scared and angry. Nothing I could do about that. I hurried out the door to my car, and sped over to Mrs. Minniefield's house.

Getting into the car did nothing for me. Usually Matilda's familiar environment was a source of stress relief. Not today. I felt a terrible knot in the bottom of my throat and neck that nothing could ease. Zellie was in incredible danger, and she meant everything to me. The thought of anything happening to her was unbearable. We never should have started this stupid A to Z Agency, I thought. We're simply not cut out for this type of work, and all we did was put Zellie in harm's way.

The truth was, I felt guilty too. I'm a securities trader, a desk jockey for heaven's sake. Zellie's a public relations specialist. Just because I know how to use a gun, to shoot at targets that don't shoot back, I fancied myself a gumshoe. Just as a change of pace for both of us, I thought, and Zellie had loved the idea.

It gave us a chance to work together, and wouldn't do any harm. We'd just search for stuff, nothing violent, but if there was any problem, I could just fire a warning shot, or shoot the bad guy in the leg, just to disable him until the cops came. Isn't that how it worked on TV?

But this isn't TV, I thought, as I turned the corner, almost wiping out the power pole. Somehow, our very first case involved the mob. The really bad guys, who weren't going to be stopped just by a warning shot. It would be all my fault if anything happened to Zellie.

***

Arriving at Mrs. Minniefield's house, I screeched to a halt, threw the car into Park, climbed out and dashed through her front door.

I quickly explained the situation to them. Hearing *their* news made me feel worse, if that was possible.

"Tom Carter was found dead at his home this morning, shot in the back of the head, execution style."

"The mob?"

"Most certainly."

"My God, Zellie…"

"Is in grave danger, yes."

"All they want is that file. So, I'm just going to give it to them." I turned to Ted. "You brought it, right?" Ted nodded, and glanced at Mrs. Minniefield.

"What's going on here?" I asked.

"I think you know, Arnie," Mrs. Minniefield said. "There is a chance that turning over the file, which they seem to want desperately, is exactly the wrong thing to do. The only thing that may be keeping Zellie alive is that she is a bargaining chip for the file. Turn it over, no more bargaining chip. We love Zellie, too, you know. We need to consider the ugliest of the possibilities to figure out the best approach to getting her back safe and sound."

"Okay, I get it," I said. "We need to have a strategy for when they call again."

"Exactly," Mrs. Minniefield said quietly. "We all need to calm down and figure out an approach that is best to save Zellie. Period. We're not trying to do anything else, Arnie."

"Agreed."

I was thinking rapidly, and something bothered me, but I couldn't exactly put my finger on it. I knew I wanted more details on Tom Carter, so I asked, "Why do you think the mob killed Tom, Mrs. Minniefield?"

"I don't know for sure. Either to punish him, or to keep him from telling what he knows about the mob's involvement in Mort. Or maybe because he wouldn't give up the file."

Bingo! I knew what was bothering me. The file. It was not unique. It could be copied an infinite number of times. I told Mrs. Minniefield and Ted what I was thinking, and they both nodded. They had figured it out too.

The mob didn't know about the file. Even if they did, it wouldn't have done them any good, because they could never know if it was the only copy. The only people who could make use of the file were people who *didn't care* if there were multiple copies.

Evidence against the mob only mattered to people who could use the information to either blackmail or take down the mob, and that was either competing mobsters or law enforcement–or people who wanted to use law enforcement to get rid of certain mobsters to advance their own interests. Any way you looked at it, the mob wasn't the one who was holding Zellie. Of course, I didn't know if that was a good thing, but it seemed to be somehow.

My thoughts were jarred by the ringing of my phone. I looked down at it. Zellie. Or more specifically, Zellie's phone. It was them again. I looked at Mrs. Minniefield and nodded. In her typical fashion, she jumped into action without hesitation.

"Okay, this is what you do, Arnie. We already checked, so we can't simply track the GPS in Zellie's phone. They've disabled it. And I don't think they will be dumb enough to stay on the line long enough to track it that way, but try anyway –don't overdo it, we don't want to do anything to endanger Zellie any more than she is already. But try to insist on talking to her. Now hurry, answer the phone."

I answered, and was greeted by that awful metallic voice again. "Greetings, Arnie. I trust that you have located the file and are ready to deliver it?"

"I have it, but I need to know Zellie is safe. Otherwise, I take the file to the police because it doesn't matter."

There was a second's delay. "We all have needs, Arnie. Sometimes we don't get what we need. Now listen up. You will bring a flash drive containing the file to the Shop Rite on Route 35, at exactly 10:10 p.m., after the store has closed, and place it, carefully, into the small receptacle for the store's sale flyers in front of the building.

"You will place it at the bottom of the pile, and leave. You will come alone, and if I see anyone there at all, you will never see Zellie again. That, I promise you. No cops, no FBI, not even a Boy Scout. Also, just in case you have ideas of watching to see who picks up the file – it will be someone who knows nothing. He won't know who he is dealing with, or even where it is ultimately going. Don't risk this pretty little lady's life by being stupid. It's simple, Arnie. Deliver the file, and Zellie is set free. I have no desire to hurt her. But I will if you cross me."

"I need to speak with her," I said evenly, battling the urge to scream at this monster.

"And you will, Arnie. After I get the file."

"Please," I begged. "I need to know she's okay."

"Well, since you said please, I'll let her say a few words." The voice was a little muffled, then, "Tell him you're okay, and don't make me regret this, Zellie. Your life depends on it."

The next voice I heard was Zellie's. My knees turned to water and Ted lowered me to a chair. Tears ran down my face and I didn't give a damn. It was like the very best music I had ever heard, combined with an unbelievable sense of dread at the possibility I'd never hear it again.

"I'm okay, Arnie. Jjjjust a llllittle bbbbit ssscared."

"I'll get you back safe, Zellie, don't worry." I said with bravado, but I'd never heard Zellie so scared. She was positively shivering in fear.

There was no answer. She was gone. And so was the caller. He, or she had terminated the connection. I looked at Ted, and he shook his head. No way to track the call. I told them what the caller had said.

"Pretty slick cutting off the possibility of watching to see who picks up the file," Ted said.

I glared at him. "I don't think we need to be complimenting his competencies as a kidnapper, Ted."

"Easy, Arnie," Mrs. Minniefield interjected. "He didn't mean anything by it."

"Oh, I know," I growled, pulling at my hair with both hands. Had I ever been so terrified? So helpless? So utterly frustrated? I took a shaky breath. Then another. I looked at them.

"I'm just upset. We have no guarantee that Zellie will be freed even if I deliver the file, but I wonder…" I trailed off.

I could feel Mrs. Minniefield's eyes on me. I ignored them both for a moment and continued to think. Then I began feel a little better. Just a little. Zellie was still in danger after all, but I was pretty sure I'd figured out who was holding her. I told Mrs. Minniefield and Ted what I was thinking, and they agreed that I was on to something.

"But that still doesn't get her out, Arnie. We need a plan of action."

"Yes, we do," I admitted. But for the first time, I didn't feel so helpless. I turned to Ted.

"Have you figured out what's in that file?"

"I haven't totally decoded it, but I can tell you this – it contains coded details of the South Jersey mob's financial dealings with Mort. I'm not able to tell what the details are, because it's basically a code within a code. But it definitely would be of interest to the Feds. If only we could give it to them," he added ruefully.

"That's the thing, Ted. We can and should give a copy to them," Mrs. Minniefield said. "But given Zellie's immediate peril, it must wait. We don't want her life lost because the Feds act first on the information. If the kidnapper is whom we think, a short delay probably won't affect an eventual prosecution. It's a timing issue, and we and the Feds will just have to deal with whatever consequences arise from that."

We worked out a plan. I would deliver the file, just as the kidnapper had demanded. We figured that nothing would happen to Zellie at least until the kidnapper knew he had the file in hand. It was after he knew he no longer needed Zellie that she would be in the most danger.

We operated on the assumption that she would not be released as promised. Everything we had heard pointed to the fact that Zellie probably knew who had kidnapped her, and her ability to identify her kidnapper did not bode well for her safety. So, we needed to be proactive. Ted put an almost microscopic tracking device on the flash drive containing the file. It looked like a period. I asked him whether it was reliable, given that Zellie's life depended on it. He looked at me incredulously, then assured me that it would work fine.

All we needed to do was monitor the tracking device to see where the kidnapper's fall guy was bringing the file. But we weren't relying on that alone. We thought we knew where he was going, but we couldn't be sure. After dropping off the flash drive, I would proceed to our pre-determined location close to the spot that we thought it would end up, and await a phone call telling me if we had been correct in figuring out where the file was going.

We had to have some patience in following the trail, because we had already been told that even the person picking up the file wouldn't know its ultimate destination. So, if we wanted that information, we'd have to follow it and track each step in its journey. Once it arrived, I would put in a call to the fire department and call in a fire at the premises. We hoped that would provide enough non-police distraction for me to slip in and rescue Zellie in the chaos. It might not have been a great plan, but it was all we had, and I was damned if I was going to trust Zellie's fate to anyone else.

I needed to be prepared to do that, and preparation to me meant not going unarmed. I needed to retrieve my Sig Sauer P2022 from my gun safe at home. Yes, I used it as a target pistol, and it was the perfect firearm for that. But it was also an incredibly precise and effective weapon. I had never shot anyone. But I knew how to handle a firearm, and I knew that I wouldn't hesitate to shoot someone if Zellie's life or safety was at stake.

Ted handed me the flash drive containing the file, with the tracking device affixed. I put it in my pocket and started to leave. Mrs. Minniefield took my arm to stop me momentarily as I headed out.

"Be careful, Arnie, and don't hesitate to call the number I gave you if you find you need help. And bring Zellie back safely. Oh, and one more thing – Ted and I will get the phone number you want and make the call to see if this can be made a little easier."

***

I got in my car and drove quickly back to my house, disengaged the security system and opened the door. I was stopped in my tracks by the feel of a hard object in the small of my back.

I was betting it was the muzzle of a gun.

CHAPTER THIRTY-THREE

"Hands over your head, and keep going, into the house, and no sudden moves," the voice behind me said firmly. "No need for bloodshed."

I raised my hands and went into the house.

"Okay, Arnie, turn around and hand it over."

Jennifer was holding a gun and was smart enough to stand at a distance so there was no way to make a move to disarm her.

"Hand over what?" I asked somewhat lamely, because it was clear she knew what I had in my pocket. But how did she know? I wondered. It wasn't from any of us, and it surely wasn't from a bug at Mrs. Minniefield's house or in my phone—the security guys had made sure of that.

So, it had to be through whoever held Zellie. Either Jennifer was in cahoots with them, or had obtained the information from them without their knowing. Given that the kidnappers had already given me plenty of incentive to turn the file over to them, I assumed Jennifer had been monitoring Zellie's kidnappers' communications, and was somehow in competition with them for the file.

But what to do now? We had a copy of the file, but could the replacement flash drive be tagged again with a tracking device? Did Ted even have another microscopic tracking device? I didn't know, but I did know that it was getting close to the time I was supposed to deliver the file, so I had to decide quickly on a course of action. Zellie's life depended on it.

"No stalling, Arnie. Give me the file. Now! Or I start shooting. And just in case you're the martyr type, and really, I think you are, my first shot will be Lazlow. My second will be at your heart, Arnie. With you dead, I will just take the file. Game over."

I believed her. What had happened to her, I wondered for a fraction of an instant, but there was no time for nostalgic sentimentality. She was a ruthless woman, and I had no choice. I took out the flash drive, and handed it to her, my arm outstretched and leaning toward her.

She took it, and told me to lay face-down on the floor. I complied. There was nothing else I could do, and I couldn't afford to waste any time.

"We could have done this the easy way, Arnie. I tried. Really, I did. My first approach was to get back into your good graces. It didn't work, and I'm truly sorry it had to come to this."

"You know Zellie's in danger, don't you, Jennifer?" I said, turning my face to the side. I could see her feet, but not reach them.

"I know," she said almost tiredly. "And she's a nice person. A much better person than I am. But it can't be helped. I *am* sorry Arnie."

And then she was gone.

I got up off the floor and retrieved my Sig from the gun safe, made sure it was loaded, put an extra clip in my pocket, and high-tailed it out the door.

***

"I need another copy of the file right away," I said breathlessly as soon as burst through Mrs. Minniefield's front door.

"Okay, Arnie," Mrs. Minniefield said. "Calm down. What's going on?"

"It's Jennifer. She was waiting at my house with a gun and took the file. She threatened to kill Lazlow, too. What kind of person is she?"

"A very dangerous one, Arnie. It will be okay, we still have time. Ted, do you have another tracking device with you?"

"Not one small enough to put on a flash drive. That was the only one I brought."

"It's too late for you to retrieve another one from your lab, so we'll have to change the plan."

Mrs. Minniefield sounded calm as always, but I could tell from her eyes that she was terrified for Zellie. Nonetheless, I took a cue from her. We needed to stay clearheaded if we were going to get Zellie back safely.

Zellie had bravely risked providing a clue. It was just a small piece of information, but together with everything else, it had made me sure who was holding her. It was up to us to be as courageous as Zellie.

"What do you have in mind, Mrs. M?" I asked. "I need to get on the road, and fast."

"The whole point of making the drop at the closed Shop Rite is that anyone watching can see if cops are there, too. There's nowhere to hide."

"Yeah, they were being pretty smart, but that doesn't help us," I said.

"It doesn't help us to have cops there, but we may be able to use it to our advantage."

I was getting impatient, and looked at my watch. I really needed to leave within the next five minutes.

"Please get to the point, Mrs. M."

"We can have people watching the entrance and exit from all the way down the road, Arnie. No one will be going in and out to an empty parking lot, except you and whoever picks up the file. They may have outsmarted themselves."

I understood where she was going with this. "So, someone who knows what they are doing, say your security guys, Baskin and D'Angelo, can watch with binoculars from way down the road, not even in the parking lot where they can be seen. Then they can follow whoever exits at a very discrete distance, and abandon the tail and call me as soon as it's clear the person is going where we think. Smart, Mrs. M. Can they be unobtrusive, even down the road?"

"I think they can, or I wouldn't suggest it. Remember, it's Route 35. Not a little neighborhood street. It's a busy road. They won't stand out. The real problem is whether they can follow quickly enough. But it's our only choice at this point, and they're pretty good at what they do."

I didn't even know what they did, but I hoped she was right. "The whole point of our plan is to avoid a frontal assault on a building that we're not sure Zellie is in. We certainly don't want to blow our subtle approach by the kidnappers seeing people other than me."

"It'll be okay, Arnie. I will tell them to abandon the tail if there is any risk of being seen. But that will leave us with your hunch, and nothing more."

"Thanks to Jennifer," I said bitterly. "I wish I'd never met her." And then I took the file Ted proffered, and left, to a chorus of, "Good luck Arnie."

I practically ran to my car. I'm a person who likes to be early, and it was getting late. Truthfully, I had plenty of time, but I was nervous. Who did I think I was, trying to rescue Zellie myself?

This was a job for a professional, and I was surely not that. If anything happened to her because I was an obstinate idiot, I'd never forgive myself. Of course, if anything happened to her because a bunch of overaggressive morons tried to storm the building, I'd never forgive myself, either. After all, this was all my fault.

I liked my odds of a careful, quiet break-in better, but I knew there were risks – to both of us. Momentarily, I romanticized us holding hands and perishing together in a hail of bullets. Omigod, did I really think that? If I could have physically smacked myself at the thought, I would have. How about we hold hands and quietly sneak out of the building? Much better.

It will be okay, I told myself over and over as I drove out of my neighborhood. It's a good plan. And Delilah had provided tremendous help. It all depended on guessing correctly where Zellie was being held. While I was pretty sure who the captor was, I couldn't be certain he was holding her in the place I thought, though he didn't seem to leave that place much. For all I knew, he lived there.

I fingered the flash drive nervously as I wondered what he had in mind. Messing with the mob was a truly bad idea, and it was hard to believe that you could blackmail them and stay alive. They just had too many resources, and were ruthless. Look what they did to Tom Carter – a bullet in the back of his head. And even worse, if that was possible, Fat Nicky killing his own brother. I shuddered, thinking of Sid, lying in that pool of blood, and had brief misgivings about our plan.

Then I thought of Zellie, and my fear both vanished and intensified. Did that make sense? I thought about it, and decided it did. I could be both brave enough to deal with bad people to save Zellie, and afraid for her safety. I passed the turn onto Oak Hill Road that would take me to the Moo-Mart, and kept going straight. I could have gone that way, too, but it was quicker to go past the train station and up to Kings Highway. I turned right and took a quick left. That would take me right to Shop Rite, which I approached with trepidation.

The parking lot was completely empty. At least there aren't any illegal parkers to make the kidnappers think we had called the cops and stationed them there, I thought. Now to make the drop and hope that Baskin and D'Angelo could follow whoever picked it up.

I drove up and parked near the building, and walked up to the bin holding the advertising circulars. Following directions to the letter, I picked up a stack and deposited the flash drive underneath. After replacing the stack, I walked back to my car, and drove away, praying that everything went well. I turned right out of the parking lot, onto Route 35, making a point not to look around lest the kidnappers think I was trying to pull a fast one. Which of course I was, but the plan depended upon them not realizing it.

I was dying to look to see if Baskin and D'Angelo were in position, but resisted the urge. I stared straight ahead as I proceeded on Route 35 to my next destination, just a few miles down the road. And Matilda stalled out.

As cars whizzed past me, I frantically tried to restart her, to no avail. Fortunately, I was on a slight downward incline when she quit and could slowly coast to the breakdown lane. But I was going nowhere, at least not in Matilda. I loudly cursed in frustration, but there wasn't anyone nearby to hear me. Most businesses were closed. And there was no way to flag anyone down – not at the speed those cars were going. Calling for help would do no good, as no one could get there in time.

I considered my options, and chose the only one available. I would run there. It was probably less than three miles, and I could do that in my sleep, just not that quickly. I had to be careful not to tire myself out either. I needed all the energy I could get to rescue Zellie. So, I started running. Fast at first, then slowed to a steady pace. But I knew it was not quick enough. I was about to call Mrs. M to brief her and Ted, when a miracle in the form of a red Mercedes convertible pulled over onto the shoulder just ahead of me.

The driver turned around to look at me. It was Marla.

"Arnie! What on earth are you doing, running on Route 35? Are you crazy? You could be killed," she called through the lowered window.

I ran up to her, somewhat breathlessly. "Marla. Thank God. I'm in a tremendous hurry. I'll explain while you drive."

I got in the car and buckled up. Marla put the car in gear and waited a moment to enter the fast-moving traffic. Finding an opening, she quickly took it, and continued down the road.

"Arnie, what is going on? You look frantic."

"It's Zellie. They have her," I said breathlessly. The combination of physical exertion and nervousness made it difficult to speak.

"Who has Zellie? Arnie, please calm down and tell me what's going on."

"I will, but keep going this direction. It's only a few miles ahead," I managed.

"Okay. I'm doing that. Now tell me what's wrong. Is Zellie hurt?"

I calmed down enough to explain the circumstances quickly, and to tell her where we were going. As I did so, Marla stepped on the gas. Apparently, she had a little bit of a NASCAR driver in her, because we arrived in no time.

I told her to pull a bit ahead and to kill her lights. It gave me a good view of the main entrance. The service entrance where I planned to sneak into the building was on the side, easily accessible from where we were parked. I hoped we weren't too obvious, especially sitting in a red Mercedes. But that might work in our favor, given where we were parked.

"What now?" Marla startled me out of my thoughts and into the reality that I was sitting with someone else. What to do with her? This was emphatically a one-person job, and I told her so.

"Arnie, I don't want to just sit here when Zellie is in danger. I want to help. What's your plan?"

For some reason, I didn't want to tell her the plan. I really don't know why, but I didn't. So, I stalled.

"For the moment, we just watch the entrance. I'm waiting for a call." That seemed to satisfy her, or at least kept her from asking any more questions about the plan.

"Why didn't anyone tell me that Zellie was in danger?"

"We didn't want to worry you." I answered truthfully.

"Arnie, other than you, I'm her best friend."

"I know, Marla. I didn't call her parents in Florida, either. I didn't see how worrying everyone would help Zellie. I figured I could worry enough for all of you."

Marla did not reply, and we watched the entrance silently, while I awaited the call. I started to have doubts about the wisdom of waiting. Maybe I should just sneak in right away. I quickly dismissed the thought. If Zellie wasn't here, I would be wasting valuable time trying to rescue her in the wrong location. That just didn't make sense. I needed to be patient, but the truth was that I was roiling inside.

I felt sick to my stomach, I was so nervous. I stopped myself when I started to have all sorts of horrible imaginings about life without Zellie. It was just too much for my brain to handle, and I needed to have my wits about me. But why hadn't the call come yet? Did Baskin and D'Angelo miss the pickup?

My ruminations were interrupted by a car stopping in front of the building. Marla and I watched to see who got out, and I was not surprised to see who it was. Jennifer. With Rene Desmond.

I was, however, totally confused about her reason for being there. I hadn't expected that. I hadn't had much time to think about Jennifer's strategy once she had possession of the file, but this really didn't make sense. It was more than a little disconcerting. We watched as they entered the building, and Marla started to say something.

I put my finger to my lips signaling her to keep quiet for a moment. I needed to think. And more than anything, I needed to hear from Baskin and D'Angelo that someone had picked up the flash drive. This had thrown a serious monkey wrench into my plans for a silent entry. I also felt a little bad for Marla, but I couldn't help that. I hadn't really told her much other than the fact that someone had kidnapped Zellie, and that I intended to get her out with a carefully laid plan that quite frankly was looking more and more half-assed and lame. And Zellie's life was at stake.

I was completely unprepared for what came next. Another car, a limousine really, pulled up in front of the building. As we watched, a really tough-looking burly man got out of the car and opened the door for the back-seat passengers. And the first one out was our erstwhile client, Marilyn Beaufort, followed closely behind by the criminal-in-chief, Fat Nicky himself. I got a sick feeling in my stomach as my thoughts of a clandestine entry became dimmer and dimmer. But I got an even bigger shock from Marla's involuntary "what the…he's not supposed to leave his compound."

As they went into the building, I turned to Marla in anger, eyes shooting daggers. "You had better explain, and fast, Marla. I have very little time, and absolutely no patience. What do you know about all this?"

Marla sighed deeply. "You're right, Arnie. I need to explain. And I couldn't before because of attorney-client privilege. I shouldn't now, either, but Zellie's life is in danger and I can see that you're about to risk yours trying to save her. You're a good man. And Zellie is truly a wonderful person. If and when you get her out safely, I hope the two of you will stop the nonsense and finally get together."

I waved my hand, signifying that she should move it along.

"I know, I know. Time's running out. Okay." She took a deep breath. "The truth is that I'm one of Fat Nicky's attorneys, and I've been trying to help him with some of his legal troubles."

"Legal troubles? Are you out of your mind? The man is a brutal killer. He should be put in jail for the rest of his life, and then executed. Twice. To make sure."

I was really pissed off at Marla. How could she represent such scum? What kind of person tries to help someone like that? And to think she's my friend! And Zellie's *best* girlfriend. How could we miss what a terrible person Marla had become?

"I know what you're thinking, Arnie, but there are some things you don't understand."

"Oh, I understand plenty. You like money. Fat Nicky has money and is willing to pay it to any shyster lawyer who will keep him out of jail. You are a lawyer. Ergo, a marriage of convenience is born. How's that sound, counselor?"

"It's not like that at all. And I'm not trying to keep him out of jail. And I'm not *any* shyster lawyer. I'm the best. But my feelings are not important right now. I'll explain later when Zellie is safe. Right now, getting her to safety is the most important thing we have to deal with. You can beat me senseless later. But I don't think you will after you hear the whole story."

"Don't bet on that. But you're right about what's important right now." I looked at my watch. Why hadn't I heard from Baskin and D'Angelo? My nervous fidgeting had reached epic proportions.

The sharp ring of the phone jarred us both. I looked at the phone. Baskin. He minced no words.

"File retrieved. Suspect known to you. Jack Buckles. Driving a late model brown Ford Taurus. And heading your way. Suspect that you were correct in determining his destination. Change your phone to vibrate mode. I'll call if destination changes. Baskin out."

"Time for me to go. Stay right here, and don't get into trouble."

"Arnie, I can help. I can distract them while you sneak in and find Zellie. That's what you have in mind, right?"

We had no time to discuss it. But she was right. She was the perfect one to provide a distraction. As Fat Nicky's attorney, she wouldn't be suspected of anything other than looking after his interests. I made a split-second decision and hoped and prayed she was on our side. Either way, she knew what was going on, so if she wasn't sincere, we were screwed whether I agreed to her help or not.

"Okay, I hope you're right. I'm on my way through the service entrance. You walk right in the front door."

I hurried to the side and crossed my fingers that the door would be open as Delilah had promised. I tried the handle. Her boyfriend had come through. I made a mental note to reward them both. *If* we survived.

The service department was dark and empty, but there was a single night-light sized bulb burning. That was good luck, I thought. No need for a flashlight. Then I smiled. Another gift from Delilah. I followed the light to the back of the service department, zigzagging through the group of Mercedes' in various stages of repair. I didn't want to accidentally touch something that would make noise. I tiptoed to a closed door in the back, which I understood opened to a staircase leading to the executive offices and Little Bobby's occasional living quarters. We suspected that Zellie was being held there.

I tried the door, and it too was open, thank goodness. I opened it slowly, and sure enough, there was a staircase, which I began to ascend slowly, and as quietly as possible. The second step had a squeak in it, which of course in my ears was magnified to sound like the roar of a crowd. I was wearing a black windbreaker, which covered up my shoulder holster, in which my Sig rested. I fingered it nervously, but heard no response to the noise.

The next two steps were blessedly silent, but I knew I was not moving quickly enough. Jack Buckles would be here soon, and it wasn't clear what Little Bobby would do once he arrived.

I had a hard time believing that Little Bobby would physically hurt anyone, much less Zellie, but he was clearly not in his right mind. And that was very dangerous.

CHAPTER THIRTY-FOUR

Marla walked right in the front door as if she was an invited guest. She was immediately accosted by two large, very imposing, and very heavily armed behemoths, one of whom was the man who had opened the door for Marilyn and Fat Nicky.

The first man held up his hand, signifying that she should stop.

"We're closed, ma'am. Come back tomorrow."

"I'm Fat Nicky's attorney. I'm here for the meeting. Please step aside."

"You're not on the list. Get lost."

Marla turned to the other man. "Tell him who I am, Lurch," she said, using his nickname.

"She's telling the truth, Hammer. She's Fat Nicky's mouthpiece. And look at her. She can't do any harm. Send her back. If he doesn't want her there, he'll either kill her, or send her packing. Either way, no harm."

"Okay. But I'll escort her back personally."

Lurch shrugged. "Sure. Whatever."

Hammer escorted Marla to the back of the showroom, to a large, glass-enclosed conference room. In the room, she could see Fat Nicky, Marilyn, Jennifer, and Rene Desmond. No one spoke. As far as she could tell, they were just staring at each other. Motioning to her to stay outside, Hammer opened the door and said a few words, after which he waved to Marla to enter. He turned on his heel and left.

Fat Nicky skipped the preliminary niceties. "What are you doing here, Marla?"

Marla chose her words carefully. "I was driving by and saw your limo, Nicky. It wasn't hard to recognize, with the license plate GR8EST HITS. I don't want to say too much around company, Nicky, but I thought you were going to lay low for a little while, while I worked out your legal issues."

Fat Nicky gestured at Marla. "See what I have to deal with? She's like my nanny. Lawyers. You can't live with them, and can't live without them."

The others nodded in silent agreement. He turned back to her.

"This is important business, sweetheart. It couldn't wait. Now run along. I'll fill you in with what I want you to know later."

It was important to keep these people occupied for longer, and she knew it. Pushing it with a guy like Fat Nicky was not a particularly good way to stay alive, though, so she'd have to be careful. She kept her voice even, professional.

"Nicky, that's not really the way it works. You know I'm trying to help you."

"Let's get one thing straight, lady. I tell you how you can help me. You do what I tell you to do."

As a very savvy, experienced criminal lawyer, Marla saw three things very clearly. Number one, she treaded on very thin ice here, and could not underestimate the danger of her position.

Second, there was no way Fat Nicky would show any weakness in front of others, especially these people, who were likely rivals, if not outright enemies.

Third, Fat Nicky was not an idiot. He was a vicious killer, but not stupid. He knew full well that he was risking the death penalty or life in prison by not doing what she advised and staying in his compound. This was more than an ordinary business transaction. This was a really big deal. She was dying to find out what it was, but knew better than to ask. She took the sensible approach instead.

"Of course, I do," she said soothingly. "And I know I'm in the middle of important business here. I don't want to interfere with that. You know us lawyers, always meddling in business with inconvenient legal stuff. That's what you're paying me for. I'll just skedaddle and leave you to continue."

Marla hoped like heck that she had bought Arnie enough time, because her time here was running out fast. But then Fat Nicky surprised her.

"Nah, stick around for a bit, Marla. As long as you're here anyway, I may need your advice, depending upon how this plays out." He paused for a moment, surveying her with those icy eyes. "But you will wait in the limo unless and until I call you."

Marla was escorted out of the room to the front of the building. Lurch opened the car door for her and she bent her head and entered. She looked at her watch. The whole thing had taken less than ten minutes. Had she bought them enough time?

***

If Marla had left the building just a few minutes later, she would have seen Jack Buckles arrive. He pulled his Ford Taurus around to the side of the building, and parked. He went to the service entrance, took out a key and tried it in the lock. It didn't work. When he turned the key, and tried the door, it stayed locked. It took him a minute to figure out that the reason it stayed locked was because it was already open.

"Stupid careless mechanics," he muttered. "Anyone could come in here and steal the place blind."

Following the instructions from the man who had called him, Jack worked his way to the back of the service department to where the door to the staircase was supposed to be located. He found it with little trouble. This time, he just tried the handle, and it was unlocked. Probably never lock this one, he thought. They think the front door is locked, and don't worry about this one.

He was pretty sure it gave access to the whole place. He considered coming back one night to pick himself out a nice Mercedes convertible. He pretended to lean back and drive the luxury car, then remembered what he was doing and opened the door to the staircase beyond.

***

I slowly progressed up the steps, balancing the need for silence with my growing feeling of urgency. I didn't know whether Marla had succeeded in delaying anything, and truthfully, I really didn't know whether she was down there betraying us or providing a distraction. Nothing I could do about it if I'd gambled wrong.

I knew it was possible that very dangerous people waited for me at the top of the stairs. With that depressing thought, I reached the landing, and another door, which I knew opened into Little Bobby's private offices and quarters.

I took a deep breath. This is where it gets dicey, I thought, unconsciously fingering the Sig in my shoulder holster. Well here goes.

I pushed open the door.

CHAPTER THIRTY-FIVE

"What the fuck are we waiting for?"

Fat Nicky was becoming bellicose in the conference room downstairs. Marilyn reached over to settle him down, but he slapped her hand away.

"You're only here because you've been useful in these situations in the past. But I'm in charge here, and I don't wait when there's a sit-down. They wait for me."

Desmond looked at him with contempt. "You're just a has-been, Nicky. And you should mind your manners in front of the ladies. This is a business meeting. If you want to shut it down, just say the word. And you'll be dead before sunrise."

"I'll be dead? I'll kill you with my bare hands. I've exterminated more insects in a week than you have in a lifetime." He paused for a moment and looked at Desmond, and at Jennifer, who was visibly squirming in her chair. Then he laughed.

"You've never killed anyone yourself, have you? You have others do the dirty work." He pointed at Jennifer. "And she didn't know anything about that, did she? Oh, this is priceless."

It would have degenerated into a brutal melee, except for a timely interruption by one of Little Bobby's employees, who looked a lot like the bodyguards for Fat Nicky and Desmond. After briefly knocking on the door, he entered.

"My boss extends his regrets that he is unavoidably delayed for just a few minutes. He knows how valuable your time is, and apologizes for the inconvenience. He asked that I extend you every possible courtesy during what he hopes will be a very brief wait."

"Okay. I want one of those cars out there for the lady," Fat Nicky said, gesturing in the direction of the Mercedes convertibles in the showroom.

If he was expecting resistance, he was in for a surprise. "Certainly, sir. What color would the lady prefer?"

"Say, I like this guy," Fat Nicky said with a laugh. "Okay, I'll wait a few minutes."

Desmond looked like he was about to say something, probably to call Fat Nicky a philistine, but changed his mind and remained silent.

He looked over at Jennifer and shook his head almost imperceptibly. They would wait silently. It was clear that Desmond thought he had the upper hand, and didn't need to engage in a war of words with Fat Nicky. Let the computer file do the talking.

Fat Nicky was finished.

CHAPTER THIRTY-SIX

I cautiously peered through a crack in the door. It looked quiet, almost eerily so, given the group of people I knew were in the building. Fortunately, they appeared to be situated downstairs.

As I opened the door further, I felt a buzz in my pants pocket. The call had better be Baskin and D'Angelo, I thought. I really didn't want to be fielding a call from anyone right this second. I peered at the screen. It was them, all right, with a typically terse text message: "File has arrived. Buckles at service entrance door."

"Crap," I hissed. I'd hoped for a little more time. I fingered my Sig, but I still hoped to avoid using it. My intention was to find Zellie quickly, and spirit her out of the building. If she's even here, I thought with a grimace.

She'd better be, or we're *all* screwed. I quickly put the negative thoughts out of my mind. I needed to hurry up if Buckles was already downstairs. I pushed the door open and looked both ways. The door had opened into an empty hallway. I knew what was to the left. It was the office where we had met with Little Bobby. I knew that office was at the top of a winding staircase that went down to the showroom, and to the conference rooms where the mobsters, including Little Bobby, were probably meeting right this second.

It was hard to see Little Bobby as one of them, I had to admit. But I was sure he was the kidnapper. Everything added up to that. And however much I might not have seen Little Bobby in the past as anything other than a big teddy bear, I knew he was a dangerous criminal who had put Zellie's life on the line. And I knew something else. If it came down to it, I wouldn't hesitate to shoot him.

I turned to the right, and moved quickly and silently down the hall to another door, which I opened as silently as I could. The door squeaked slightly when it opened, and it felt like my heart jumped into my throat. It sounded like an aircraft taking off to my heightened senses. I swallowed nervously.

The door opened to what appeared to be Little Bobby's living quarters. It appeared vacant. I took a moment to survey the layout. Surprise was the only thing going for me right now, and I had to choose my approach carefully. I looked around, quickly, but deliberately. A small kitchen area lay to my right, with a countertop that divided it from a small nook in which a breakfast-sized table sat. Around the nook was an open area with a sofa, two chairs and a huge television. A hallway led to what were probably one or more bedrooms or other rooms.

If Zellie is here, she'll be in one of those rooms. I took a deep breath, and crept down the hallway.

Working meticulously, I tried the first door on the right. I slowly opened it, and looked inside. It was a linen closet. Nothing there but sheets and towels.

I moved down the hall and carefully opened the second door on the right. It was a small room that was being used as a home office, with a desk and computer in the corner, and several file cabinets. It might be interesting to look at the computer and the stuff in the files, but there was no time for that. All I needed to know was that the room was empty.

I closed the door and tried the door across from the little office. It was a bathroom, and no one was inside. I closed that door and looked ahead. Only two rooms left – one more on the left, and one straight ahead. I carefully opened the last door along the hallway. It was a bedroom, with a twin bed, a bureau, and a wingback chair -- in which a tied up and gagged Zellie sat, struggling to loosen the ropes that bound her arms and legs.

"Zellie! You *are* here!" If it was possible to whisper a shout, that's what I did.

Zellie's eyes lit up in a combination of surprise, joy – and aggravation. She was still tied up, after all. I hurried forward to remove her gag and to untie her. As soon as I took her gag off she poured out a stream of consciousness monologue that would have made Finnegan's Wake read like a model of coherence.

But I was pretty sure it was a combination of joy at seeing me, relief at being rescued, anger at being tied up, and inquiry as to the exit strategy. Oh, and also, "Get these fricking ropes off me right now." That was all pretty much said in a single syllable, with absolutely no pause in between words.

"I can't tell you how glad I am to see you safe," I cried.

Her hands and feet were both tied to the chair and to each other, and additional ropes were wrapped around both her and the chair. As I studied how to begin to untie her, Zellie's voice modulated somewhat.

"I mean it's really good to see you. Little Bobby is nuts. He grabbed me on a side street near the courthouse. He used chloroform or something like that."

She looked around as I began untying her feet first. "We've got to get out of here, Arnie."

"I know. The plan was to sneak in here and spirit you out without anyone noticing if possible. So far, so good. But we have a long way to go to safety. Buckles is right behind me."

"Buckles?" she moaned.

"Yeah, he's the guy Little Bobby got to pick up the file we're supposed to trade to get you back. Needless to say, we didn't believe you'd be safe after it was turned over. And he could be here any minute."

I finished untying Zellie's legs, which freed up a rope that led to her wrists. I started in on them.

"Of course, I forgot to bring a knife," I growled.

"You're doing fine, Arnie. But I can tell you brought your gun. Or are you just happy to see me?"

Zellie's (lame) joke was intended to ease the tension, but I could tell she was a nervous wreck. And so was I. We both knew we could be interrupted at any time. The ropes were tightly knotted, and I was working hard to get them loose as I knelt in front of her.

"Are they biting into your skin, Zellie?"

"No, but Little Bobby must have been a Boy Scout. He can really tie a knot. But he took care to not hurt me, I will say that." Then her expression changed to one of fear as she looked at the door.

"Of course, I didn't hurt her, Arnie. We both know she's much too precious for that. But I will not allow my master plan to be foiled. Now stay right there on your knees, and don't even think about reaching for your gun. I want to see both arms stretched out to the side. Now, staying on your knees, with your arms still outstretched, turn around slowly to face me. Slowly, Arnie. I wouldn't want anything to happen to Zellie."

I did what he said and slowly turned around, still on my knees.

He was holding a gun, by the looks of it, an old Colt '45 pistol, with a pearl handle, no less. It figured that Little Bobby would own a gun like that. Filled with history and intrigue, and a staple in the old cowboy movies he watched regularly. Maybe not as accurate as my Sig, but unquestionably deadly. Especially in close quarters.

Zellie's feet were free, but her hands were still mostly tied, although they had been loosened. There was still a rope wound around her midsection, and attached to the chair. I could feel her presence behind me, probably clandestinely testing to see if she could break free when it became necessary.

I knew it was now or never. I'd have one chance at this, and I couldn't screw it up. Little Bobby had gone over the deep end. We had seen it coming, but had both chalked it up to mere eccentricity. Neither of us ever thought he'd turn into a criminal. Even under the present circumstances, I had a hard time seeing him as violent. It was more like a game to him, almost like he was the Joker, or the Riddler, and had captured Batman and Robin as they tried to pursue him in his latest nefarious plot.

"Now, slowly reach into your holster and remove the gun with two fingers, and place it on the floor, barrel facing yourself, and slide it forward."

I complied and waited for just the right moment. I knew he wouldn't be able to resist looking at my Sig. It really is an impressive weapon. As I expected, he reached down to pick it up and I launched myself at his knees, taking him down with a crash. His gun clattered to the other side of the room, and my Sig was underneath me, digging into my stomach. Unfortunately, when I tackled him, Little Bobby fell right on top of me.

I could tell Zellie was struggling at her bonds, trying to get free to help, but she was still tied to the chair. It was going to be up to me to win the wrestling match, against a guy who outweighed me by probably a hundred pounds, and was lying on top of me. And Buckles could be here any minute. Come to think of it, why wasn't he there already?

I didn't know, and didn't have time to worry about it. The shock of his fall had slowed Little Bobby down, but I knew it wouldn't last long. I tried to reach under myself to get my gun, but it wasn't happening. He was too heavy. I couldn't move my body much, but my hands were free.

I grabbed Little Bobby's legs and tried to roll him off me. He was trying to reach his gun, which had fallen just beyond his outstretched arm. While still on top of me, he tried to move closer, but I was holding on to his legs for dear life.

He began to kick, trying to shake loose from my death grip, but this caused him to lose his balance on top of me and he rolled slightly to the side. I seized the moment and rolled him off me, as we both scrambled for the gun that had been under me.

We reached it at the same time, and fought for control. We were lying on the floor as we struggled, but neither of us tried to get up, lest the other win the battle for the gun. So, we stayed on the floor.

Fortunately for me, Little Bobby was not a good wrestler, because I was a crappy one, and greatly outweighed. But it seemed like Little Bobby was unwilling to fight dirty, which was a surprise to me, since he was supposed to be the criminal element. I on the other hand, was perfectly willing to violate every fair fight rule that ever existed.

Like biting Little Bobby's hand while trying to knee him in the groin. I say trying, because I was unsuccessful in the groin thing, but he screamed in agony at his bitten hand. More to the point, he let go of the gun and I pointed it in his general direction as I tried to scramble to my feet.

But Little Bobby wasn't done. He grabbed me by the legs and pulled me back down as I fired a shot wildly over his head.

CHAPTER THIRTY-SEVEN

At the sound, everyone dropped to the ground.

"That sounded like a gunshot!"

"Where'd it come from?"

"Upstairs, I think."

"What's he trying to pull here?"

"That's it, we're out of here."

"No need for that," said an authoritative voice at the door to the conference room. "We will find out what the commotion is, and dispose of it. My apology for this minor distraction." He nodded at a dark suited man at his side. "The dope probably accidentally shot himself while watching a cowboy movie. Take care of it."

"Yes sir." And he was gone. Everyone sat down.

"It's about time you got here," Fat Nicky grumbled. "I don't wait for anyone."

The man regarded him silently for a moment before he spoke.

"I'd think you would want to delay this as long as possible," he said quietly. "It isn't every day that a big-time mob boss like you has everything taken away from him."

If he expected Fat Nicky to squirm, he was mistaken. Fat Nicky just glared back defiantly. "Many men have died trying," the big man said simply.

"I think you know it's different this time, don't you?" Still the pleasant, quiet, but firm tone.

The others watched the scene unfold before them. No one said a word. Desmond just sat stoically. The others looked on, enraptured.

Fat Nicky sneered, an unpleasant look that suited him. "What I think is that you should either show your cards, or take a hike. What do you have?"

"What I have just retrieved from an associate, and what I believe Mr. Desmond has as well, is evidence."

"What are you, a cop? You don't look like a cop. And Desmond sure as hell isn't one. Evidence. I don't give a crap about evidence. No charge has stuck yet. And I got a big-time lawyer sitting in my limo right now who can get me out of anything."

"Oh, this is not going to the cops. And no lawyer can help you with it. Frankly, you'd be better off with the cops. And maybe it should go to them, too, now that you mention it. You'd certainly be arrested, and maybe the charges *would* stick. We could say we just discovered that dirty money came into the business, and we dutifully turned the information over to the authorities. It's good evidence, after all. And it might stop a New York – New Jersey mob war if you were arrested instead of just killed. That way, it would all come out. The part about you ripping off your own boys, shorting them on their cuts, being an informant. Imagine that, Fat Nicky Martinson, a snitch."

"No one will believe I'm a snitch."

"Oh, they'll believe it. What has your lawyer been talking to the Feds for? Making a deal, Nicky, are we?"

"She's getting me outta jail, that's all."

"In exchange for what?" Still the quiet, pleasant voice. His phone squawked at that moment.

"Looks like we have a little ruckus upstairs that requires my attention. Nothing to worry about. Please wait here, everyone."

Fat Nicky rose as if to leave, and Marilyn put a hand on his shoulder.

"We came here to get information," she said. "We don't have it yet. We should wait."

Fat Nicky started to bark at her, then sat back down and nodded. "Might as well see his cards." He looked at Desmond. "And yours." Desmond stayed silent, and Nicky looked at Jennifer.

"Is he a mute?"

Jennifer didn't respond either, and Nicky looked at Marilyn. "They're both mutes," he said with a shrug.

Marilyn gave an almost imperceptible smile, which seemed to satisfy Fat Nicky. He folded his arms to wait.

***

Buckles fingered the flash drive he had retrieved. He didn't really care about its contents. "Confidentiality is my middle name," he said to himself, echoing the pitch he gave to clients. And he wasn't the curious sort. In his line of work, being curious could get you killed. People paid him to do what they told him to do, no more, no less. If he was picking up a file, he picked it up, and that's what he'd done here. He didn't even know who the client was, but given the delivery location, he assumed it was the owner of the place.

Buckles knew of Big Bobby and Little Bobby, of course, but he really didn't care who wanted the flash drive, what was on it, or why they wanted it. He had no details whatsoever, and he liked it that way. All he cared about was being paid, and he had already been given a handsome retainer in cash, anonymously of course. And he would get more upon delivery.

All he had to do was place the flash drive on the top stair, and leave. The final payment would be made the same way the first one had been. Anonymously, and in cash. He liked it that way. And at least in his mind, it was already spent.

He carefully placed the flash drive on the top step as instructed, and headed back down the stairs and out the same way he'd come in. As he neared the exit of the service department, he heard what sounded like a gunshot.

Needing no further encouragement, he hustled out the door, ran to his car, and drove away.

***

Little Bobby froze for a second after the gunshot, and I took advantage of it, aiming in his direction while telling him not to move. He ignored me and lunged in the direction of my legs, which as it happened were now very close to where Zellie sat tied in the chair. Zellie gave him a swift kick right in the face, and he crumpled to the ground.

"Whoa, that was some kick, Zellie! You knocked him completely out."

"All those aerobics. Kick, kick, kick, punch, punch, punch. Now finish untying me while he's still sleeping."

I worked at the bonds securing her hands until they were freed, and unwound the ropes around her midsection. Just as we started to hustle out of there, the door opened again.

Before we could do anything, a man appeared in the doorway, brandishing an automatic weapon that looked way more deadly than Little Bobby's Colt 45. He took in the scene quickly, and noted Little Bobby on the floor.

I started to reach for my gun, but the look in his eye told me I wasn't dealing with someone who lived in the pretend world that Little Bobby inhabited. This guy meant business and he made that clear right away.

"Don't even think about it," he said.

Aiming his weapon at Zellie, and moving with professional efficiency, he pulled out my gun, removed the magazine, and tossed it in the corner. Then he told us to put our hands on top of our heads.

He made a call, spoke a few quiet words and stood calmly, keeping his gun trained at Zellie. Then we all just waited.

***

Desmond started to get impatient and turned to Jennifer. "Go upstairs and find out what's going on." Jennifer nodded and got to her feet.

Fat Nicky tapped Marilyn on the shoulder. "If she's going, you go, too."

Desmond simply shrugged. "As you wish. Let them both go."

They regarded each other warily, but headed out the door. As soon as they left, Desmond started in on Fat Nicky.

"You're a has-been, Nicky. You have no understanding of the modern way of doing things. You're just a vicious killer. I have subtlety. You just bludgeon people to death. When people die in my operation, there are no tracks. None. They just disappear. When I'm running this operation, there will be big changes. And I won't steal from my own people. There's plenty to go around if it's done right. This sit-down is just a formality. You're finished."

Fat Nicky just looked at him. "I may not be as prissy as you, Desmond. I don't sell ladies' underwear. I'm not as refined, no question." He drew out the word "refined," in a voice dripping with contempt.

"But I was running South Jersey when you were still in diapers. Which you probably still are, from the look of you. No little snot like you is going to take a single penny from me. Not one."

Desmond started to slowly clap. "Great bravado. Just great. I'd expect nothing less. But you are finished. And you know it. Both our "friends" in New York and I have you cold. We can do this the easy way or the hard way. Your choice. It's over. And you'll be told that again when he gets back. So, it looks like you killed your own brother for no reason. What was that about, Nicky? Trying to look tough in front of the troops? Holding on to power?"

"Why you piece of shit...I'll fucking kill you."

Nicky leaned over the table and tried to tackle Desmond as several of their respective bodyguards hustled into the room and tried to separate them, all the while pointing their guns at each other.

CHAPTER THIRTY-EIGHT

For the third time, the door opened and a familiar face appeared. Charles.

I gaped at him. "You? You son of a–"

"You should have taken my gracious offer, Arnie. Of course, I don't think you would have liked, shall we say, the darker side of the business. But it would have made things much simpler. And we would have been on the same side, like in the old days. But I have the file, and don't really need anything more from you now. And so, unfortunately, it is going to turn out much more unpleasantly for you. And, of course, for the beautiful and talented Zellie. I believe we've had the pleasure once before."

"It was no pleasure," she said, narrowing her eyes.

"Ah, very spirited. I do enjoy that."

He turned to his accomplice. "As you can see, we have three items to dispose of in the usual fashion."

"Him too?" the man asked, nodding at Little Bobby's unconscious body.

"He's outlived his usefulness. The business more or less runs without him anyway." He turned back toward us.

"For what it's worth, Arnie, I really would have preferred us to work as a team. We made a lot of money together."

I knew I needed to keep him talking as long as possible, because once he left, we were all dead for sure. Just like Greasy Sid and Tom Carter. I shuddered inwardly.

"We did, didn't we, Charles. And I thought we made the money honestly. What happened? Or was Mort always just a front for the mob?"

Charles sighed. "I guess there's no harm in telling you. You won't be able to repeat it. Yes, Mort always had a mob connection, Arnie. And that was me, originally, and some others later. I was detailed to form one of the so-called "legitimate businesses." And as you know, it was wildly successful. And, it was legitimate, too.

"But. in the last year, the money dried up, and I needed infusions of capital that really weren't available through traditional channels. But there was one source of funds. The money was needed to keep the business afloat, and provided a convenient vehicle for laundering family money. What better place than an entity that bought and sold securities at incredible speeds? I wanted to keep it separate from the other businesses, but there was no hope of that. I must say, Arnie, you got out at a very good time, before the SEC investigation–although I don't think that's going anywhere. Did you have inside information about that?"

I shook my head. "No, I knew nothing about it. But I'm glad I left."

Charles' voice turned hard. "You won't be so glad in a few minutes."

He looked over at Zellie, who stared defiantly back at him. "And such beautiful collateral damage. Oh well. But I have no hard feelings that you left us, Arnie. As we say, business is business."

He turned to leave, and almost ran into Jennifer and Marilyn, who both gaped, first at Arnie and Zellie, then at Little Bobby on the floor, then to the man holding the gun. They both turned in unison to Charles for an explanation.

"Just tying up a few loose ends," he said, in that same pleasant voice. "Let's go back downstairs and conclude our business."

At that moment, we all heard sirens outside. "Must be the cops," he said.

Must be the fire trucks, I thought. It's about the right time.

As I listened, I was steadily watching the man with the gun, hoping for an opening. Once everyone left, we were dead for sure.

I saw him briefly turn toward Jennifer and Marilyn and seized the moment, launching myself at his legs. As he crashed into the wall behind him, dropping the gun, pandemonium ensued.

We all lunged for the gun on the floor. All of us except Zellie. As we all fought for the gun, she went for Little Bobby's Colt 45 that was still in the corner. As we all battled on the floor, she fired a shot over our heads. At that, we all looked up.

Because of the jumble, though, Zellie was unable to take a real shot, for fear of hitting me. I seriously doubted she was concerned about hitting anyone else. As Charles grabbed the gun out of my hands, and started to rise, Jennifer, of all people, gave his hand a swift upward kick. The gun came loose, spinning toward Marilyn, who snatched it up, and pointed it at all of us.

"Drop it, Zellie. You may be able to shoot me, but that's a single shot gun, and this one can fire twenty rounds a second. You may be able to shoot me, but you won't be able to save Arnie."

Zellie looked at her, looked at the rest of us, and then dropped the Colt on the floor.

"Good, now all of you in that corner, and on your knees," she said, pointing to the right. "I'm getting out of here. Right now. And I'm bringing the two of you as hostages," she said, pointing to Zellie and me. "I'm not going to jail. Now move it."

We went in front of her as she moved sideways, expertly keeping the gun trained both on us and the others as she moved. It was too risky to run yet, but I bided my time, and I could tell Zellie was alert as well.

Marilyn closed the door on them, and hustled us to the door to the stairway, which we opened, and at her urging, moved quickly down the steps, through the service entrance and out the door. A dark sedan pulled up, and waving the gun, she directed us inside. We had no choice.

She shut the door on us and jumped in the front. We both instinctively tried the door handles. Locked. We just had to see where she was taking us. We heard her tell the driver to move it, and as we left the scene, we saw the flashing lights of fire trucks in front of the building. We heard Marilyn make a call.

"It's fire trucks. It is not law enforcement. Move now. I repeat, move now."

I reached over and held Zellie's hand. It felt so natural, so comfortable. I didn't know what would happen to us, but I knew this was better than staying where we were, if only because it represented a delay in our fates, and gave us another opportunity to escape. And I knew one other thing: I was overjoyed to have Zellie at my side again. As if she could read my thoughts, she squeezed my hand.

The car turned into an underground garage, and parked. We were directed wordlessly toward an elevator, which we all entered.

We rode to the fourth floor. The doors opened to a small reception area, with someone sitting behind plexiglass. On the back wall was a large round seal with a red and white striped emblem against a blue background, and surrounded by gold stars.

More to the point, the gold lettered words "Department of Justice" appeared around the top, with "Federal Bureau of Investigation around the bottom.

We were at the FBI.

CHAPTER THIRTY-NINE

Marilyn turned to us and smiled. "You're safe now. I couldn't risk dropping the mob persona until we were safely inside. Let's go in and I'll explain everything."

The man behind the glass buzzed us in and gave us visitor passes. We followed Marilyn to a conference room, where she told us to sit down and make ourselves comfortable.

"I need to take care of a few things. And I want to bring a few other people in for this discussion." She smiled at us. "Also, I think you two would like a few minutes alone. Can I get you something to drink? A soda, or a cup of coffee?"

We both politely declined, and she left us there, assuring us she'd be back in a few minutes. After a warm embrace, we both began to talk at the same time. Then we laughed and agreed that maybe waiting for a more private venue to catch up was wise.

"But isn't this something? We solved our first case," Zellie said. "We found Marilyn and figured out her story."

"Well, that's certainly one way to look at it," I said, laughing. "Should we offer her the balance of her retainer check, and give her the report she paid for?"

"Somehow, I don't think she wants that. And I think we earned the whole amount, anyway. I mean, I was kidnapped and everything. That had to eat up whatever balance was left."

"I'd certainly say so. Then we're agreed. We keep the money," I said with a relieved grin.

"Agreed."

"Should we send her a bill for work done in excess of the retainer?" I asked. I'd gained some expenses with all this, like needing to replace my living room rug, for instance.

"I think not. We better not press our luck. She did rescue us, after all."

"True."

"Okay, we'll send her an invoice, reflecting payment in full."

When Marilyn returned, we told her what we had decided, and she threw back her head and laughed uproariously. "Actually, you may be receiving far more than that. I'll explain later. But first, I wanted to tell you that as we speak, the FBI is wrapping up a sweep of everyone that was at the Mercedes dealership today.

"Charles Hastings, Fat Nicky Martinson, Rene Desmond, Jennifer Marquette, and all of their associates are in custody. Little Bobby, too. They're all looking at substantial jail time. The operation is a huge success, and largely due to the two of you. And by the way, we called Ted and Mrs. Minniefield. They should be here shortly to collect you."

She smiled again, with a twinkle in her eye. She almost looked like a little kid about to divulge a secret. "Oh, and one more thing. I want you to meet some people. Actually, you already know them. She gestured to the door, where a man and woman stood. We looked at them in astonishment.

"Sid? But I saw you… there was blood everywhere…you're dead." I shook my head to clear it. "But you're not, obviously." We looked at Marilyn for an explanation.

"It really is Sid Martin, and of course you know Mrs. Martin as well. His death was faked. That was Fat Nicky's idea, if you can believe that. He would have killed anyone who fought back against the mob taking over his business, but apparently, he couldn't kill his brother. That's when he retained Marla Perez to try to work out a deal with the U.S. Attorney. But even she didn't know we'd arranged to fake Sid's death. And he will be a prime witness for the government even if Fat Nicky doesn't rat out his organization. The evidence in the file you retrieved almost makes him unnecessary."

"Omigod. Marla. She's still…." I began.

"In Fat Nicky's limo. We know. And she's safe. Already in lawyer mode. She's a good one, too. I'll bet Nicky isn't used to an honest one, though. Against his nature. I'm betting he returns to his old mob mouthpiece. But you never know, I guess."

"So, Marla isn't one of them?" Zellie asked, almost timidly.

"Definitely not."

"Well that's a relief. For a while there I thought–well, I'm just really glad she's not."

"She was pretty helpful distracting them so I could get in clandestinely, too, Zellie. I wasn't sure whether to trust her either, but she really did come through."

"You knew he was alive at the funeral, didn't you Abigail? Arnie and I thought you were holding together pretty well, given the circumstances. And the rest of the people there?"

Sid's wife smiled at her husband, and then at them. "I knew, but they didn't. No one knew, other than Nicky, but it was very much in his interest to keep it quiet, and let everyone think he did it. His willingness to kill anyone, even his own brother, was a powerful deterrent to anyone trying to unseat him, while he worked out a deal with the government."

"We almost didn't tell her, either, to sell it better, but Abigail is a pretty remarkable woman, and we figured she could handle it. And we were right." Marilyn looked at Abigail with obvious respect.

I looked at Marilyn. "Is your name even Marilyn?"

"Yes. But not Beaufort. It's Magnuson."

"Arnie really liked your outfit, Marilyn," Zellie teased.

She laughed. "To tell you the truth, I kind of liked it myself. Beats an FBI windbreaker, anytime. Anyway, Mrs. Minniefield and Ted are here now. I wanted to wait for them to arrive before I give you all the whole story–or at least as much of it as I can share."

Mrs. Minniefield strode into the room, and in an uncharacteristic display of emotion, rushed over to hug Zellie. "You're safe. Thank God. And Arnie, too. You did it. I was so worried about you." Then she straightened up and assumed her all-business demeanor. "Of course, I never had any doubt."

"Of course, she didn't," Ted said, rolling his eyes. "Zellie, Arnie, we're really glad to see you safe and sound." He kissed Zellie's cheek, and shook Arnie's hand robustly. "Really glad."

Then they noticed Sid and Abigail. Mrs. Minniefield was the first to speak. "My goodness, it's Sid Martin, isn't it? And you must be Mrs. Martin."

Abigail nodded.

"Um, we can't help but notice that you're alive, Sid," Ted added. "Not to be indelicate or anything, but aren't you supposed to be dead?"

"To quote Mark Twain, reports of my death have been greatly exaggerated," Sid said.

Marilyn cleared her throat. "Now that everyone's here, I'll try to fill you in on the whole story. It really began with the establishment of a task force to take down the South New Jersey mob. I wasn't really a part of it then. At the time, I was, shall we say, embedded in certain New York organizations, gathering information. I can't really tell you more than that.

Zellie piped up. "The picture. You were in the picture with the New York mob. The real New York City Council headline."

"You saw that, did you? It was a pretty notorious column. Yes, unfortunately, my face appeared in a newspaper photo, which really wasn't supposed to happen, and I kind of faded out of that assignment shortly thereafter. That work is generally best done out of the limelight. But it's only importance to this story is that Fat Nicky saw it, too. It was kind of my entrance pass into his organization. But that came later." She took a drink from a water bottle then continued.

"Anyway, at about the time of the establishment of the task force, and in an unrelated action, the Securities and Exchange Commission commenced an investigation into an outfit called Mortal Securities, or Mort as it's called colloquially. As is often the case, there was no communication between the two Federal agencies, and in fairness, there was no reason to think they could be connected. One involved potential violations of the securities laws by a New York firm, and the other involved violent crime in New Jersey.

"The investigations proceeded separately, with each unit gathering information. At some point, the SEC investigators identified transactions that they couldn't explain, particularly large infusions of cash, the source of which was unclear at best.

"Concerned about potential money laundering at Mort, they referred the matter to the United States Attorney, who opened a criminal investigation. The money laundering angle had mob implications, so it wasn't long before the task force learned of it. There was no apparent link between the two, though, and New York mob activities have rarely, if ever, spilled over into southern New Jersey. So, while it was interesting, it was not considered particularly relevant to the task force. Until..." Marilyn paused and looked inquiringly at the assembled faces.

"A connection to Arnie appeared," Mrs. Minniefield said.

Marilyn nodded. "Exactly. The task force was studying the rise of Rene Desmond for some time. And not for his innovative design sense. He has real talent in that area. No, it was for another area in which he showed tremendous skill – a tendency to leverage his legitimate business activities into all sorts of illegal enterprises. That put him at odds with Fat Nicky Martinson, the unquestioned South Jersey mob boss." Marilyn paused to take another sip of water, and continued with her story.

"When it became apparent to the task force that one of Desmond's deputies was Jennifer Marquette, a tail was put on her to monitor her activities."

Zellie looked over at me, and jumped in. "The dark sedan we saw after my lunch with Jennifer," she said.

"Hmm. Probably, but they shouldn't have been spotted. They're good at what they do. Hopefully Jennifer didn't see them."

"Oh, I doubt it," Zellie said quickly. "And in fairness to them, they were trying not to be spotted by her. They had no way of knowing anyone else was watching."

"In any event," Marilyn continued, "before that time, they followed her right to Arnie's house, which caused them to request a background check on him. Imagine their reaction to them finding out he had been involved in a relationship with Jennifer, was a former partner at Mort, had received a big settlement, and was now an amateur private detective."

She paused to look at Zellie and me with a frown. "Sorry. Amateur was how they described you. I know better," she added kindly.

"Well, it was pretty accurate at that point," I conceded. "You were our first client."

The agent laughed. "Perfect segue to the next series of events, Arnie. There was absolutely nothing in your background to suggest you had any criminal tendencies. And as I understand it, you also have some friends pretty high up in the Department of Justice that believed strongly in your honesty." She looked inquiringly at me, then pointedly at Mrs. Minniefield, but we both remained silent.

"But the coincidences were too much to just ignore," she continued. "The task force thought about just bringing you in for questioning, but frankly thought that they could glean more information by continuing to watch your behavior. Also, to be honest, they thought that you might be able to help in the investigation better if you didn't know what was really transpiring. Your private detective business was the perfect subterfuge for them."

I was fuming. "You're telling me that even though you believed I was honest, you deliberately put us in danger? Zellie was kidnapped, and could have been killed. We both could have been killed. What were you thinking?"

Marilyn held up her hand. "It wasn't my decision, but I fully participated in implementing it, and I understand your anger, Arnie. But in our defense, we didn't think you'd be in danger, and we had no idea Zellie would be kidnapped. As I will explain later, the kidnapping was not even a mob activity, although they certainly took advantage of it. The truth is that we never expected the two of you to be as good as you were at investigating. The danger was created by your own competence. You got results. You broke the entire case, and greatly set back organized crime in both New York and New Jersey. I understand your anger, but from a law enforcement standpoint, the decision was an incredibly successful one. But I'm getting off my timeline.

"The task force needed someone with organized crime experience, who could act a little, and by the way, who could put on a Rene Desmond-inspired slutty outfit. That was me. The idea was to hire you, put a few ideas into your heads, and see what transpired. We really had no idea it would work out so well."

I looked over at Sid. "I know you gave us the idea to talk to Sid, but how did you get me to discover the body? And how did you know I wouldn't figure out that he wasn't dead?"

"We needed to fake Sid's death, because Fat Nicky had reached out through back channels I can't discuss, to help in removing not only him, but taking down the entire South Jersey organization. As I've told you, Nicky didn't want to kill his brother, although there was significant pressure from within his organization to do so, given Sid's attempted obstruction of the use of his business for money laundering and other illegal purposes. Your involvement was mostly a matter of convenience.

"We knew you were going over there, and it wasn't hard to set up. Just create a mess in the bar, which was closed anyway, and spread some animal blood everywhere. Have Sid lying down in the middle, and wait for you to arrive. We guessed you wouldn't get too close, because we knew from our background check that you had dropped out of medical school at least in part because of your aversion to cadavers. But even if you had gotten closer, he would just have "died" in the ambulance on the way to the hospital. It was just an added publicity bonus that he was discovered by a former medical student at the grisly scene.

"You know most of the rest of the story, because it largely involved you, but I'll tell our side of it, and you can fill in the parts we don't already know. From our standpoint, we continued our investigation while monitoring your activities to see if anything valuable turned up. And before long, you gave us a great deal we could use. I pointed you in Sid's direction, which was designed to get you thinking about potential mob involvement. My outfit was designed to point you in the direction of Brazen Saddles, and you figured that part out pretty easily."

"Was the woman we first met at Brazen Saddles one of your people?" I asked out of curiosity.

"No, the information you two got out of her was genuine. It was quite creatively obtained, I must say. That's some investigative technique you showed. Who ever heard of telling a potential witness that they probably shouldn't tell you anything, but you'd really like it if they did?"

"Well that's not exactly what we said, but–"

"It's close enough," Zellie interrupted proudly. "It's our investigative method. And it worked. No arguing with success."

"True enough," Marilyn said.

"And the kid who came up to us later?" I asked.

"He's one of ours," Marilyn admitted. "We'll have to get you your money back for that. But taking it added to his credibility. He was supposed to validate my appearance at Brazen Saddles, and to put New York in your mind."

"That and Hiram calling me," Mrs. Minniefield said quietly, almost to herself.

"Hiram Towers called you? We weren't told that, Mrs. Minniefield. He's a good friend to have. And don't worry, I'll keep that to myself. But may I ask what he told you?"

"He didn't say much, actually. He basically told me that Mort was being investigated by the SEC, and it was not his understanding that Arnie was a target. He thought Arnie should stay clear of Mort while the investigation was underway, and that he couldn't tell me anything more for fear of impacting any potential prosecutions. That was it. I will say this, and no more - after he called, I did a little digging myself, and concluded that Arnie's former partner Tom Carter was a likely target of the investigation, given his position in the company. Hiram never told me that there was a parallel criminal investigation."

Marilyn nodded. "He might not have known at that time, and probably wouldn't have told you anyway."

"Most certainly not," Mrs. Minniefield agreed.

"You know a lot of the rest of the story. Tom Carter was initially part of the money laundering scheme at Mort, then became nervous about his involvement. He knew he was dealing with very dangerous people. Because he was the numbers guy, he was in a unique position to chronicle all the financial transactions at Mort, and he put it all on a computer file, which he kept concealed in his office. When it looked like something bad was going to happen to him, he secreted it in the one available place – Arnie's computer, which was conveniently sitting there not secured while Arnie was in a conference room. We assume that he then deleted all other copies to protect himself. What Tom understood, and almost no one other than Fat Nicky was aware, Mort had become a place for Fat Nicky to stash the funds that he was stealing from his own organization.

"Basically, Tom was playing on both sides of the New York – New Jersey border. He was thus able to blackmail both mob organizations. A very dangerous situation. For reasons known only to him, the file he secreted on Arnie's computer only had the New Jersey transactions on it. Perhaps there was another file, and maybe a forensic analysis will uncover deleted files, at this point we just don't know. We think we have enough on Charles Hastings to put him away for a long time even without it."

"Which organization killed Tom?" I asked.

"It really could have been either one, but we think it was New York."

I glanced over at Ted, who appeared lost in thought. I knew that look. He had the beginnings of an idea, although with him it could be about anything from a new kind of breakfast cereal to a redesign of the ordinary shoe. Anything was possible with him. And he began nodding furiously to himself, and spoke up suddenly.

"All of the transactions are in the *one* file. Tom was pretty smart. I'm guessing that he knew if they found the file, they would be furious, but he might be able to explain the influx of money from Fat Nicky as a win-win for Mort. How could they complain that a company that needed working capital was in fact receiving boatloads of it from a rich person in New Jersey? He could plead ignorance of the actual identity of Fat Nicky. That's probably the last thing he told them, but they didn't believe him and killed him anyway. I've studied that file for hours, and only just a short time ago I broke the encryption. On the surface it looks like an accounting ledger detailing Fat Nicky's transactions with Mort. And it does contain that information, for sure. But the total document makes no sense, as every other line in the spreadsheet is unrelated to the previous one. I'll bet a lasagna-infused bagel that the alternate lines are the Mort transactions."

"We'll check it out," Marilyn said. "And thank you." She looked around the room and nodded to Mrs. Minniefield. "That's some team you have here."

"Everyone was trying to get their hands on the computer file to use it as leverage against Fat Nicky, and tried various methods to get it. Those efforts included Zellie's kidnapping," I pointed out.

She glared at us. "About which we were completely unaware. Trying to handle that by yourselves was pretty dumb."

"Dumber than using innocent people to conduct an investigation into organized crime?" Mrs. Minniefield's tone was pointed, and Marilyn's softened.

"Fair enough. But I told you that we were trying very hard not to put them in danger. And while we're still figuring some things out, we believe that the kidnapping was not originally orchestrated by the mob, although they certainly took advantage of it."

"That was Little Bobby. He's mostly living in a fantasy world," Zellie said.

"Yes. Desmond had purchased a Mercedes there, and realized that the business was a good target for money laundering. It was a high-end dealership, with expensive cars to sell, and whose purchasers often paid cash. Because Desmond discovered that Little Bobby was more interested in television and games than running the business, he slowly took over. He then installed his own people, while keeping Little Bobby ostensibly in charge. But Desmond's goal was to take over Fat Nicky's organization, and he knew he would need significantly more muscle than he had on his own."

"Which led him to New York." I filled it in.

"That's what happened. The New York organization was very interested in extending the organization over the previously hallowed state line, and Desmond was agreeable to being the New Jersey division of the New York mob. He certainly would have tried to split it off later, but first things first. Get a toehold, then separate and expand. He was an entrepreneur, after all. And he had a business plan. New York, through Charles, told Desmond about the file, although he certainly didn't know it contained anything other than information about Fat Nicky. Desmond joined the hunt for the file, with Jennifer as his primary deputy." Marilyn paused a moment, took a breath, and continued.

"In the meantime, a meeting was arranged between Nicky, Desmond, and Charles, and the Mercedes dealership was chosen as the location."

"Did Marla know about it?" I thought I already knew the answer, but wanted to hear Marilyn confirm it.

"I doubt Fat Nicky told her, and she seemed pretty surprised and furious about what happened today. No, I'm sure she didn't know. Remember, Fat Nicky had hired her to try to cut a deal with law enforcement. There was no way that was being discussed at the meeting."

"Well, it was fortunate you were there, Marilyn. Thank you."

"I'm glad Fat Nicky wanted someone to go with him. I think he was comfortable with me in that situation because he knew I was familiar with the New York organization. Anyway, it was fortuitous, because as I said, we didn't know about the kidnapping, or that Zellie was being held there. And by the way, how did you figure out Little Bobby was involved, and that Zellie was being held there?"

"Well, I had an idea about it, but then Zellie told us."

"She told you? How?"

Zellie's laugh was nervous. "I told them I was just a "llll…ittle …bit scared. And truthfully, I *was* a little scared, although I don't think Little Bobby would have hurt me. But I never knew that anyone else was involved."

"Just a "Little Bobby" scared. Quick-witted of you, Zellie. We think Little Bobby was just play-acting. He liked to pretend he was a secret agent, or outlaw, and your visits to him just fueled a plan to kidnap you and then release you safely. Charles just hijacked his plan by telling him what to ask for, and he was only too happy to oblige."

"Arnie, you said you had an idea before you even talked to Zellie. What was it?" Ted asked.

"Well, the kidnapper used the word "kapow" to describe what would happen to Zellie. The only time I've ever heard that word is on the old Batman series. Little Bobby was a huge Batman fan. So, I was a little less worried about Zellie, because I thought the same thing as she did. That Little Bobby would never hurt her. But we were messing with an extremely dangerous situation as it turned out. And it all started with our dumb idea to start a detective agency."

"I don't think it was a dumb idea, Arnie," Zellie replied. "I think we should keep at it."

"It almost got you killed, Zellie. I couldn't live with myself if anything happened to you. And it's not like there won't be dangerous situations in the future. Remember, we started the agency because we thought we'd be good at finding stuff. We didn't intend to try to take down organized crime in New York and New Jersey."

"But that's exactly what you two did, Arnie." Marilyn looked at us appreciatively. "Just my opinion, but I think it would be a huge mistake for you two to close your agency. You're incredibly good at investigating, and your work here was a tremendous success. Look at the good you've done."

"Well, thank you. And we'll talk it over. And I should note that it's not like it was particularly profitable. We spent probably a hundred hours on this, nearly got killed, and made what, $1,000.00, and we didn't even get our expenses reimbursed."

Marilyn started laughing. "We'll make sure you get your expenses, Arnie. Just put in a voucher, and I'll make sure it gets paid. But you're wrong about the lack of profit. There's a little matter of reward money for information leading to the arrest of several organized crime figures. I think that when the dust settles, you and Zellie will receive a considerable amount of money."

"For real?" Zellie asked. "Maybe we can get a real office."

"Why would we do that? The Moo-Mart is well-suited to our needs. Great coffee we don't have to make ourselves. And, we can't leave Eddie, can we?"

"No, we certainly can't," Zellie agreed. "Okay, we'll stay. Forget I said anything."

"I have something to say. And Sidney and I agree," said Abigail Martin.

We all looked over in astonishment. They had been silent pretty much the whole time.

"Sure, Abigail, what is it?" I asked.

"Sidney and I want to see you and Zellie kiss each other. Right here, and right now. And not one of those silly fraternal kisses. A real one. We won't settle for anything less."

There was a murmur of agreement from everyone. So, we kissed - for a long, long, time. It was hot and passionate, and literally made my toes curl. I lost all sense of anyone else in the room, as we remained locked together in the smoldering embrace so long denied by our own stubbornly-held fears.

And what happened after that?

You know I don't kiss and tell.

###

Dear Reader:

Thanks for reading my book! I hope you enjoyed Arnie and Zellie's escapades in Monmouth County, New Jersey. If so, stay tuned for their exciting adventures as the series continues. Arnie, Zellie, Ted, Marla, Delilah, and Mrs. Minniefield all will return, along with many new friends and enemies.

I greatly value feedback from readers, so please send any comments or suggestions for improvement to me at ericsmallbooks@outlook.com.

Online reviews are also very much appreciated, so it would be great if you take a few moments to write a review on Amazon, or any other book review site.

Thank you!

Eric Small

Author Page

Retired after many years of public service, during which he regularly wrote for work, Eric Small began writing fiction. As a longtime reader of cozy mysteries, he found such stories a natural fit for his writing. Brazen Gambit is the first of a planned series featuring the investigations and adventures of Arnie and Zellie in their fledgling detective agency, set in the environs of Middletown, New Jersey, where Eric was born and raised. He now lives in Florida with his wife, to whom he has been married for more than thirty years.

Ordering Information

Brazen Gambit - An Arnie & Zellie Cozy Mystery Series – Book 1 by Eric Small is available at:

Online booksellers and from the author's website:
www.ericsmallbooks.com

Brazen Gambit
ISBN: 978-0-9988592-0-0

Eric Small
P.O. Box 840003
St. Augustine, FL 32080
www.ericsmallbooks.com
ericsmallbooks@outlook.com